GODDESS GIRLS

+ATHENA THE BRAIN+

CREATED BY
JOAN HOLUB &
SUZANNE WILLIAMS
ADAPTED BY **DAVID CAMPITI**

✳

ILLUSTRATED BY **EDUARDO GARCIA**
AT GLASS HOUSE GRAPHICS

Aladdin
New York London Toronto Sydney New Delhi

ALADDIN

An imprint of Simon & Schuster Children's Publishing Division

1230 Avenue of the Americas, New York, New York 10020

First Aladdin edition February 2022

Text copyright © 2022 by Joan Holub and Suzanne Williams

Cover illustration by Manuel Preitano.

Illustrations copyright © 2022 by Glass House Graphics

Art by Eduardo Garcia. Additional art by João Zod, Marcos Cortez, and Noza.

Lettering by Marcos Inoue. Art services by Glass House Graphics.

All rights reserved, including the right of reproduction in whole or in part in any form. ALADDIN and related logo are registered trademarks of Simon & Schuster, Inc. For information about special discounts for bulk purchases, please contact Simon & Schuster Special Sales at 1-866-506-1949 or business@simonandschuster.com. The Simon & Schuster Speakers Bureau can bring authors to your live event. For more information or to book an event contact the Simon & Schuster Speakers Bureau at 1-866-248-3049 or visit our website at www.simonspeakers.com.

The illustrations for this book were rendered digitally.

The text of this book was set in font Anime Ace 2.0 BB at 6 points over 7.5 point leading and SteinAntik at 7 points over 8 point leading.

Manufactured in China 1121 SCP

2 4 6 8 10 9 7 5 3 1

Library of Congress Control Number 2021937751

ISBN 978-1-5344-7387-4 (hc)

ISBN 978-1-5344-7386-7 (pbk)

ISBN 978-1-5344-7388-1 (ebook)

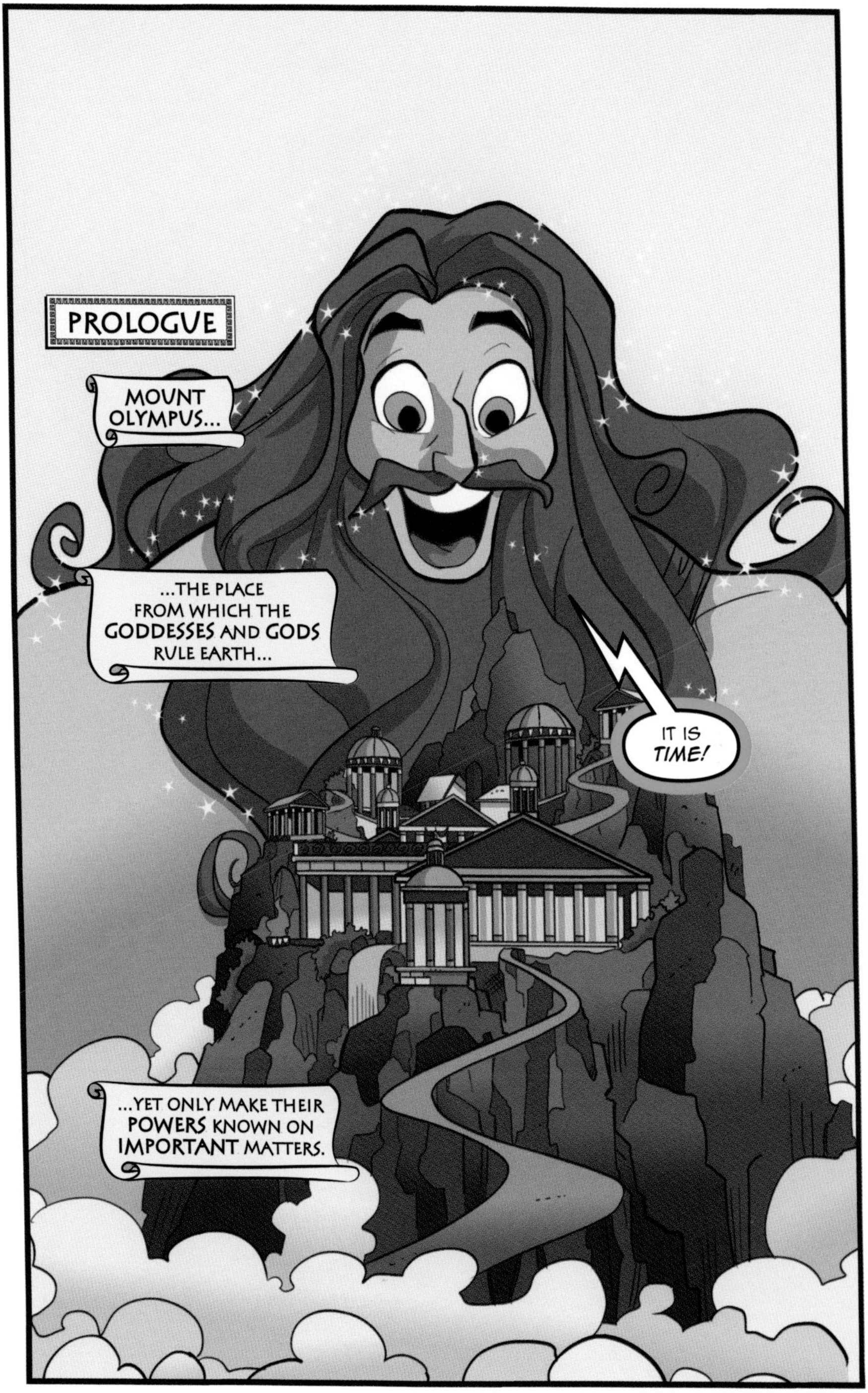
PROLOGUE
MOUNT OLYMPUS...
...THE PLACE FROM WHICH THE GODDESSES AND GODS RULE EARTH...
IT IS TIME!
...YET ONLY MAKE THEIR POWERS KNOWN ON IMPORTANT MATTERS.

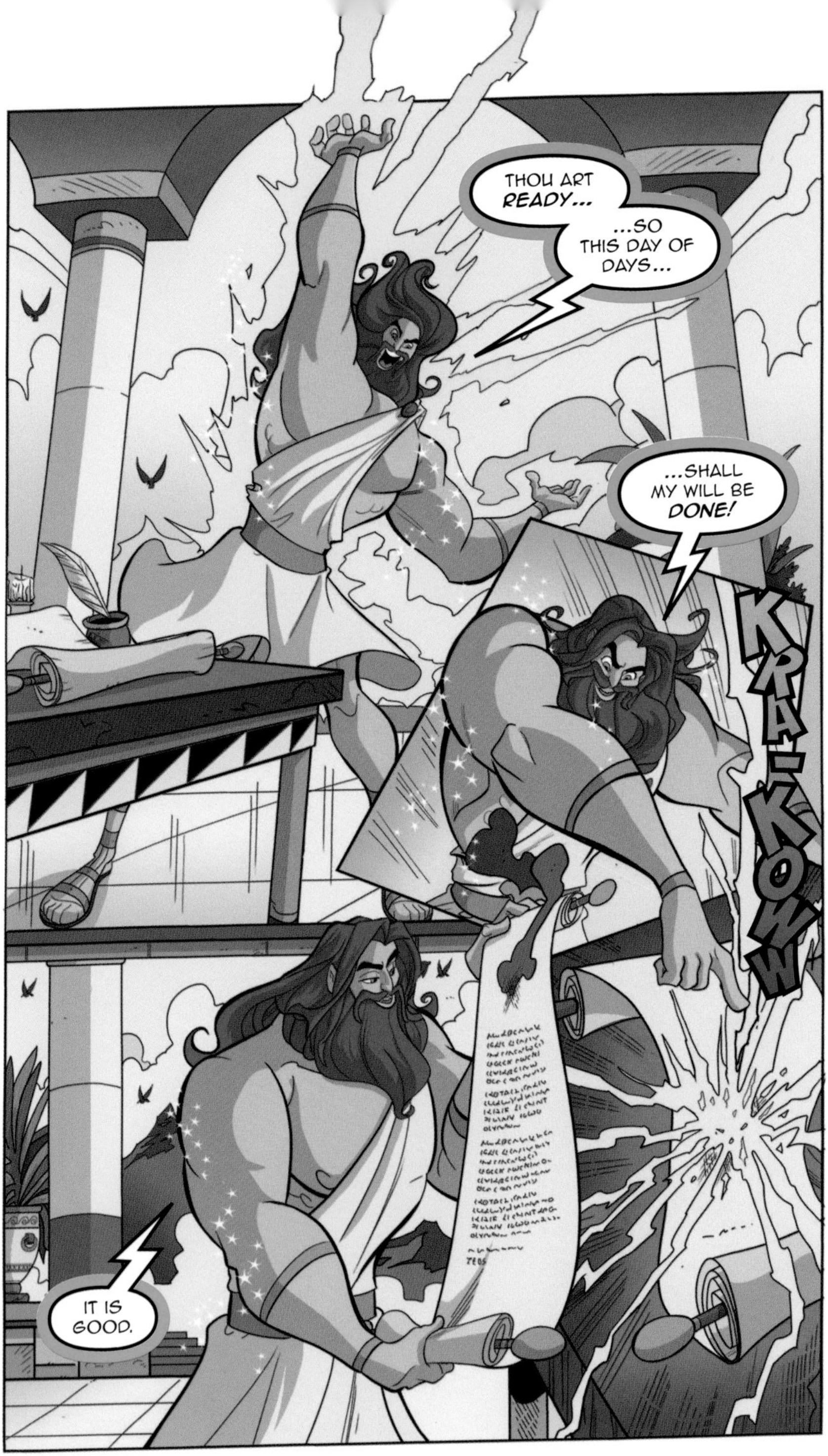
THOU ART READY...
...SO THIS DAY OF DAYS...
...SHALL MY WILL BE DONE!
KRA-KOWW
IT IS GOOD.

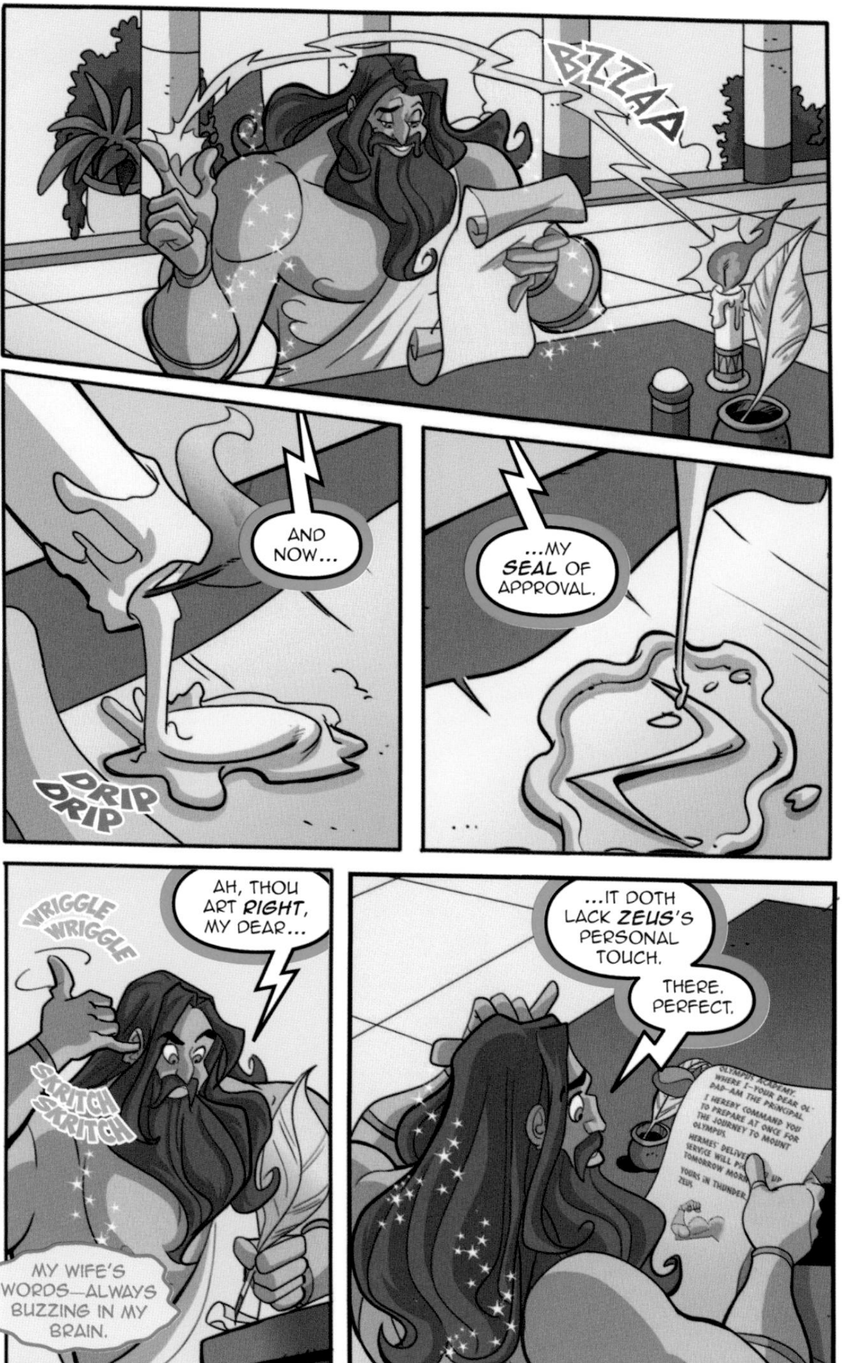
BZZAAP
AND NOW...
...MY SEAL OF APPROVAL.
DRIP DRIP
AH, THOU ART RIGHT, MY DEAR...
WRIGGLE WRIGGLE
SKRITCH SKRITCH
MY WIFE'S WORDS—ALWAYS BUZZING IN MY BRAIN.
...IT DOTH LACK ZEUS'S PERSONAL TOUCH.
THERE. PERFECT.
OLYMPUS ACADEMY,
WHERE I—YOUR DEAR OL'
DAD—AM THE PRINCIPAL.
I HEREBY COMMAND YOU
TO PREPARE AT ONCE FOR
THE JOURNEY TO MOUNT
OLYMPUS.
YOURS IN THUNDER,
ZEUS

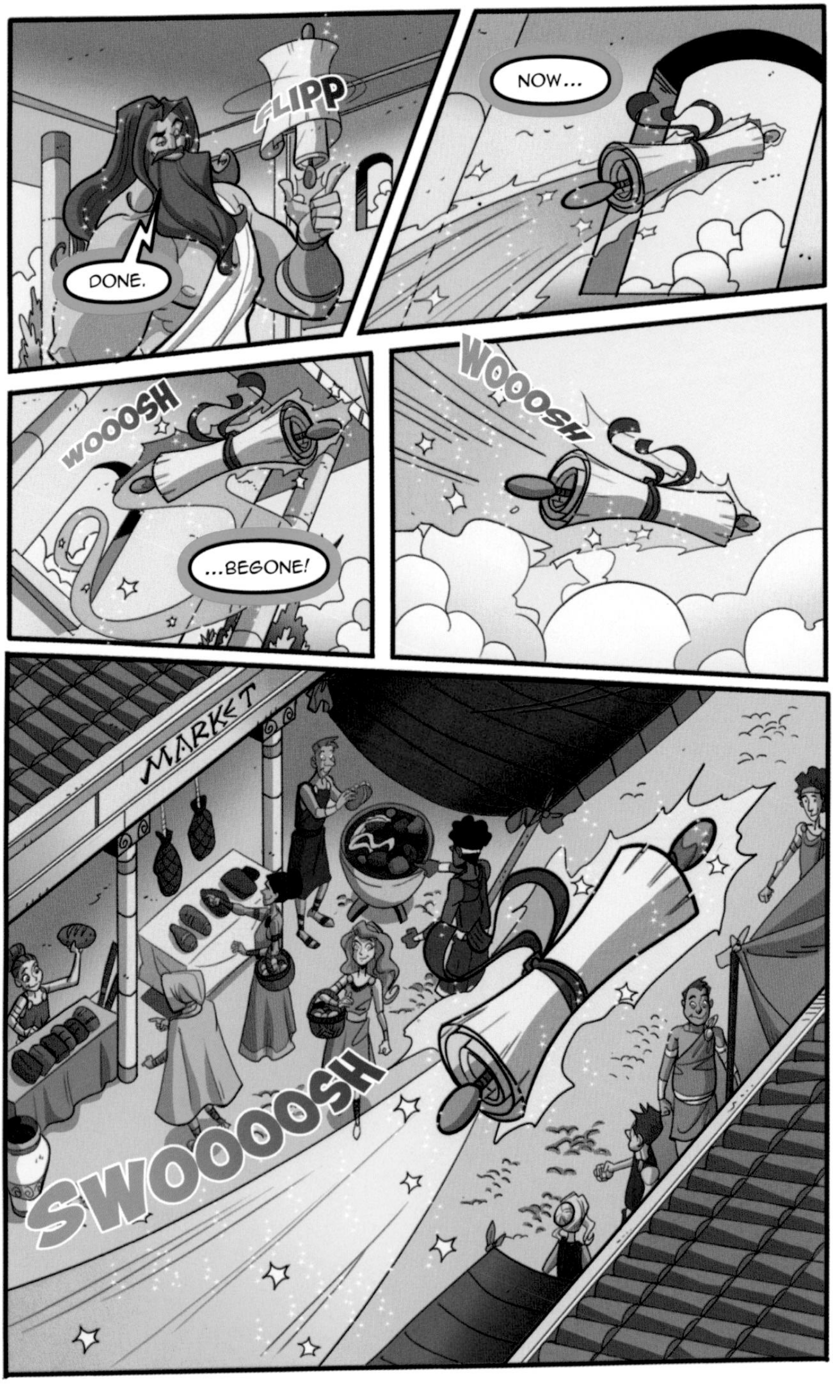
FLIPP
DONE.
NOW...
WOOOSH
...BEGONE!
WOOOSH
MARKET
SWOOOOSH

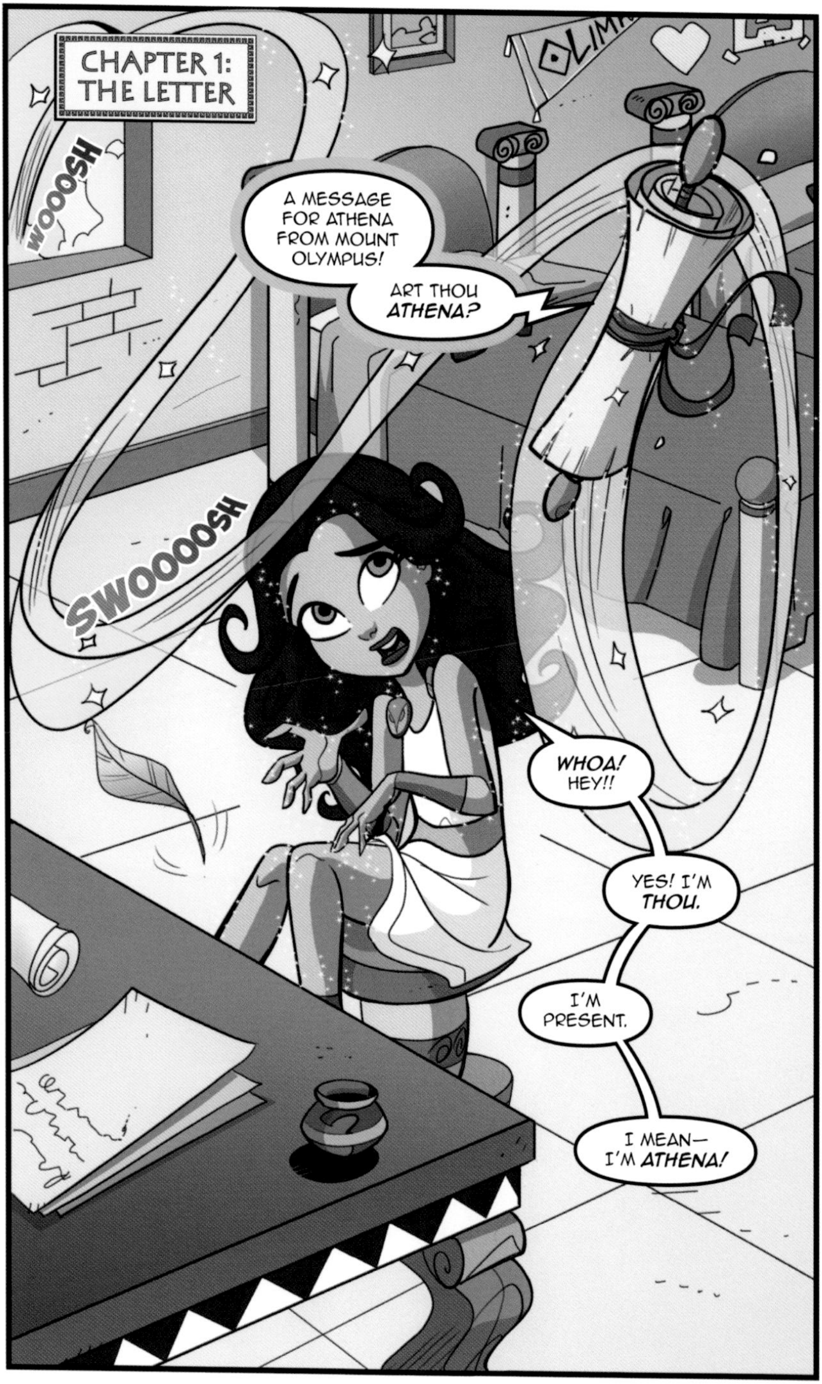
CHAPTER 1: THE LETTER
WOOOSH
A MESSAGE FOR ATHENA FROM MOUNT OLYMPUS!
ART THOU ATHENA?
SWOOOOOSH
WHOA! HEY!!
YES! I'M THOU.
I'M PRESENT.
I MEAN— I'M ATHENA!

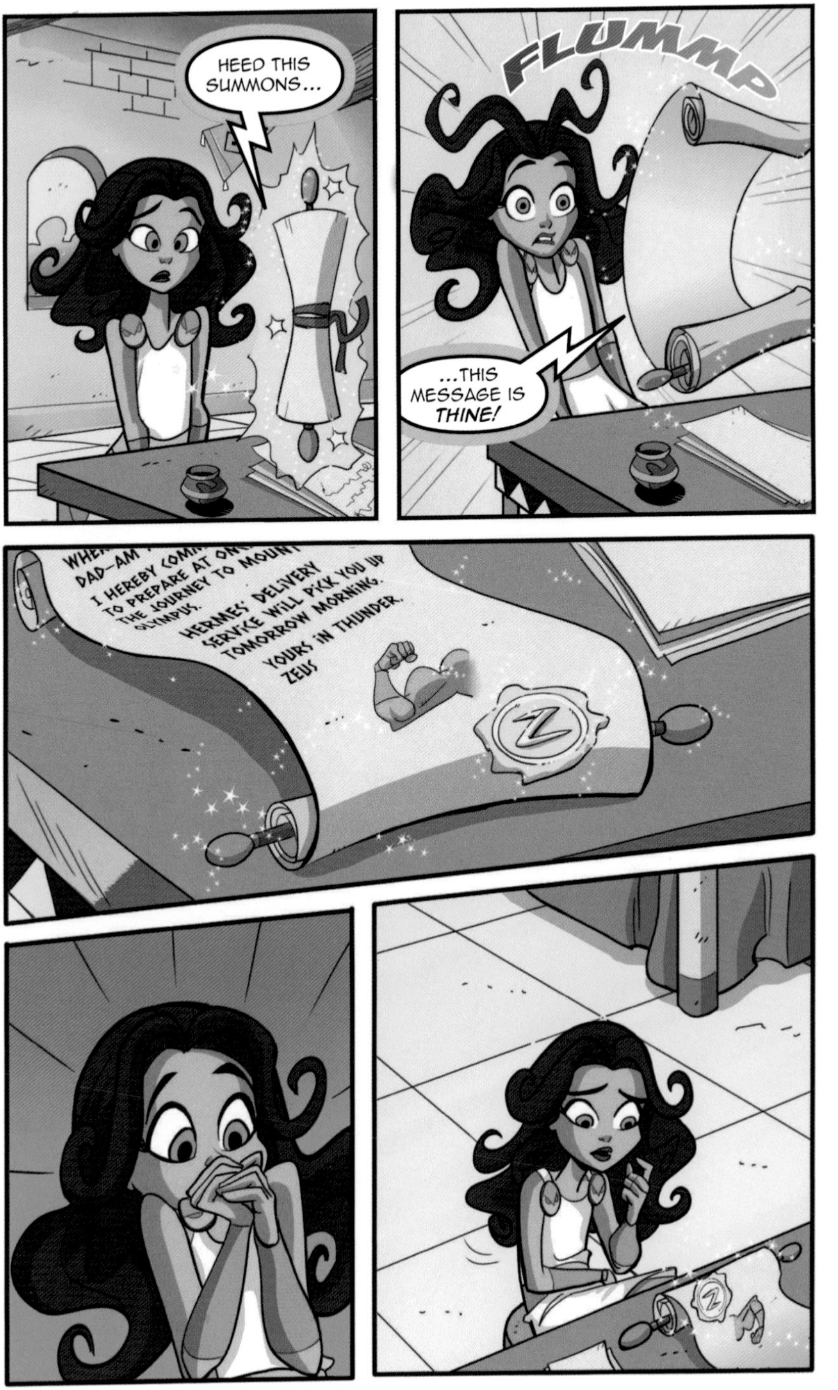
HEED THIS SUMMONS...
FLUMMP
...THIS MESSAGE IS *THINE!*
WHER
DAD-AM
I HEREBY COM
TO PREPARE AT ON
THE JOURNEY TO MOUNT
OLYMPUS.
HERMES' DELIVERY SERVICE WILL PICK YOU UP TOMORROW MORNING.
YOURS IN THUNDER.
ZEUS
Z

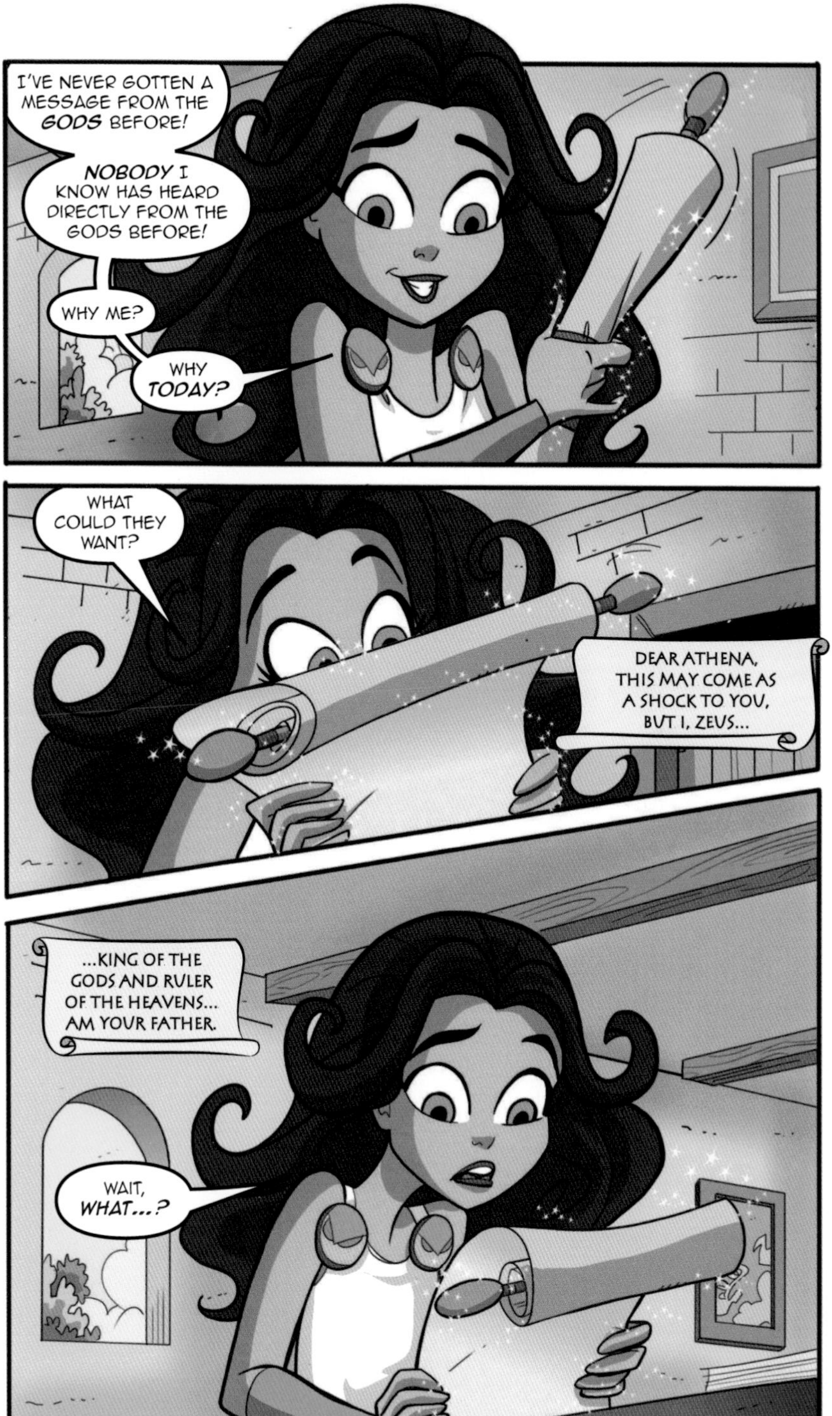
I'VE NEVER GOTTEN A MESSAGE FROM THE GODS BEFORE!
NOBODY I KNOW HAS HEARD DIRECTLY FROM THE GODS BEFORE!
WHY ME?
WHY TODAY?
WHAT COULD THEY WANT?
DEAR ATHENA, THIS MAY COME AS A SHOCK TO YOU, BUT I, ZEUS...
...KING OF THE GODS AND RULER OF THE HEAVENS... AM YOUR FATHER.
WAIT, WHAT...?

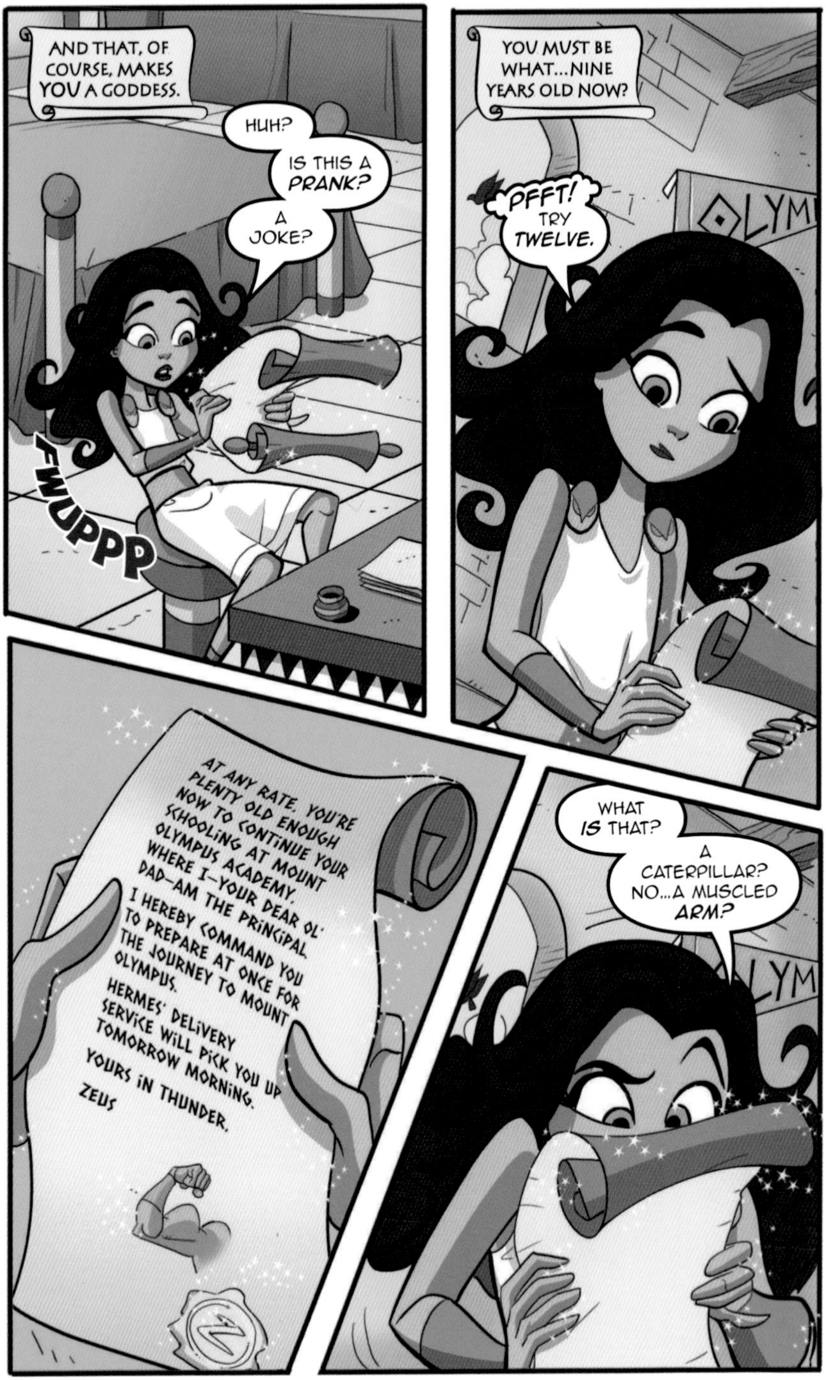
AND THAT, OF COURSE, MAKES YOU A GODDESS.
HUH?
IS THIS A PRANK?
A JOKE?
FWUPPP
YOU MUST BE WHAT... NINE YEARS OLD NOW?
PFFT! TRY TWELVE.
OLYM
AT ANY RATE, YOU'RE PLENTY OLD ENOUGH NOW TO CONTINUE YOUR SCHOOLING AT MOUNT OLYMPUS ACADEMY, WHERE I—YOUR DEAR OL' DAD—AM THE PRINCIPAL.
I HEREBY COMMAND YOU TO PREPARE AT ONCE FOR THE JOURNEY TO MOUNT OLYMPUS.
HERMES' DELIVERY SERVICE WILL PICK YOU UP TOMORROW MORNING.
YOURS IN THUNDER,
ZEUS
WHAT IS THAT?
A CATERPILLAR? NO...A MUSCLED ARM?
OLYM

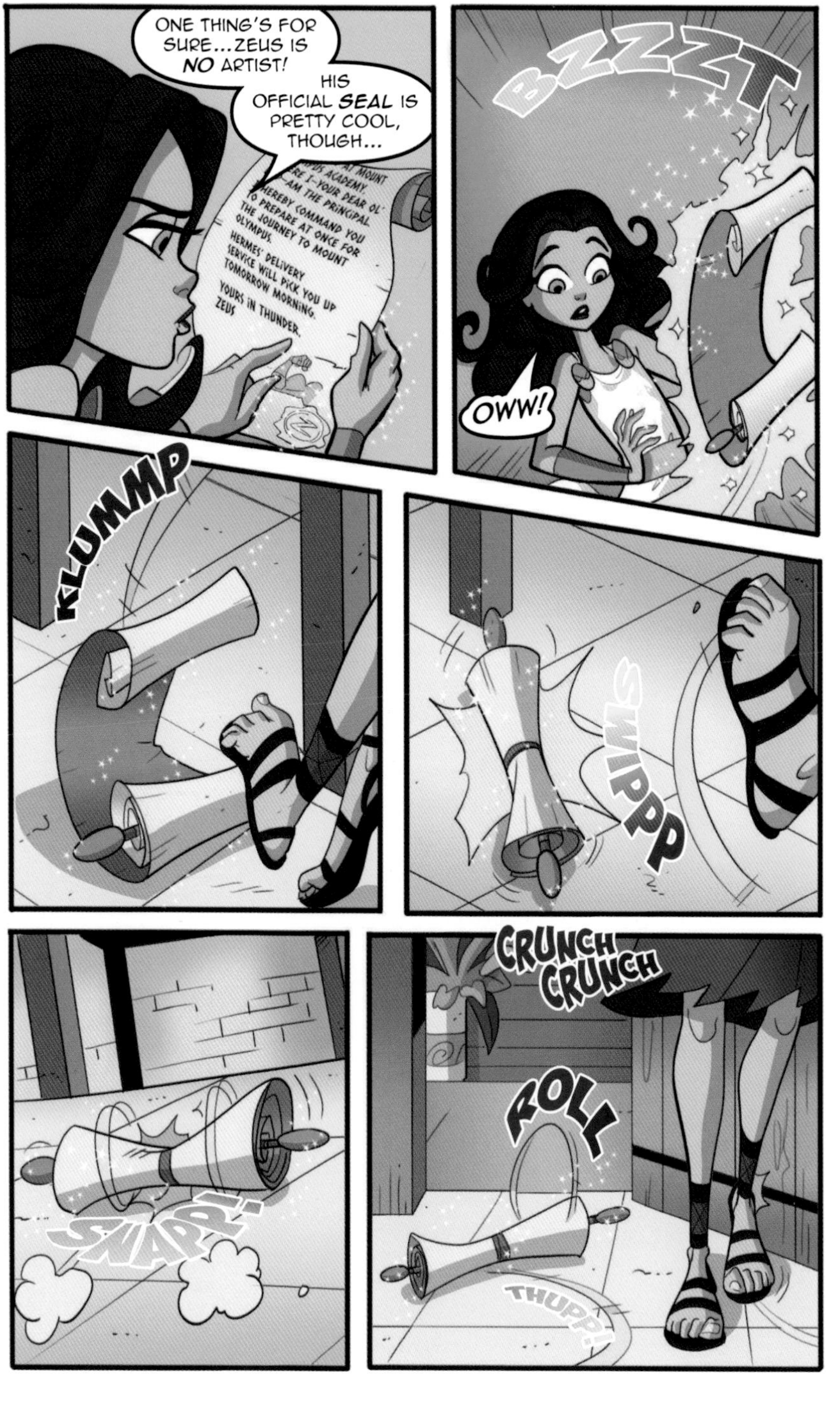
ONE THING'S FOR SURE...ZEUS IS NO ARTIST!
HIS OFFICIAL SEAL IS PRETTY COOL, THOUGH...
THE JOURNEY TO MOUNT OLYMPUS.
HERMES' DELIVERY SERVICE WILL PICK YOU UP TOMORROW MORNING.
YOURS IN THUNDER,
ZEUS
BZZZZT
OWW!
KLUMMP
SWIPPP
SNAP!
CRUNCH CRUNCH
ROLL
THUPP!

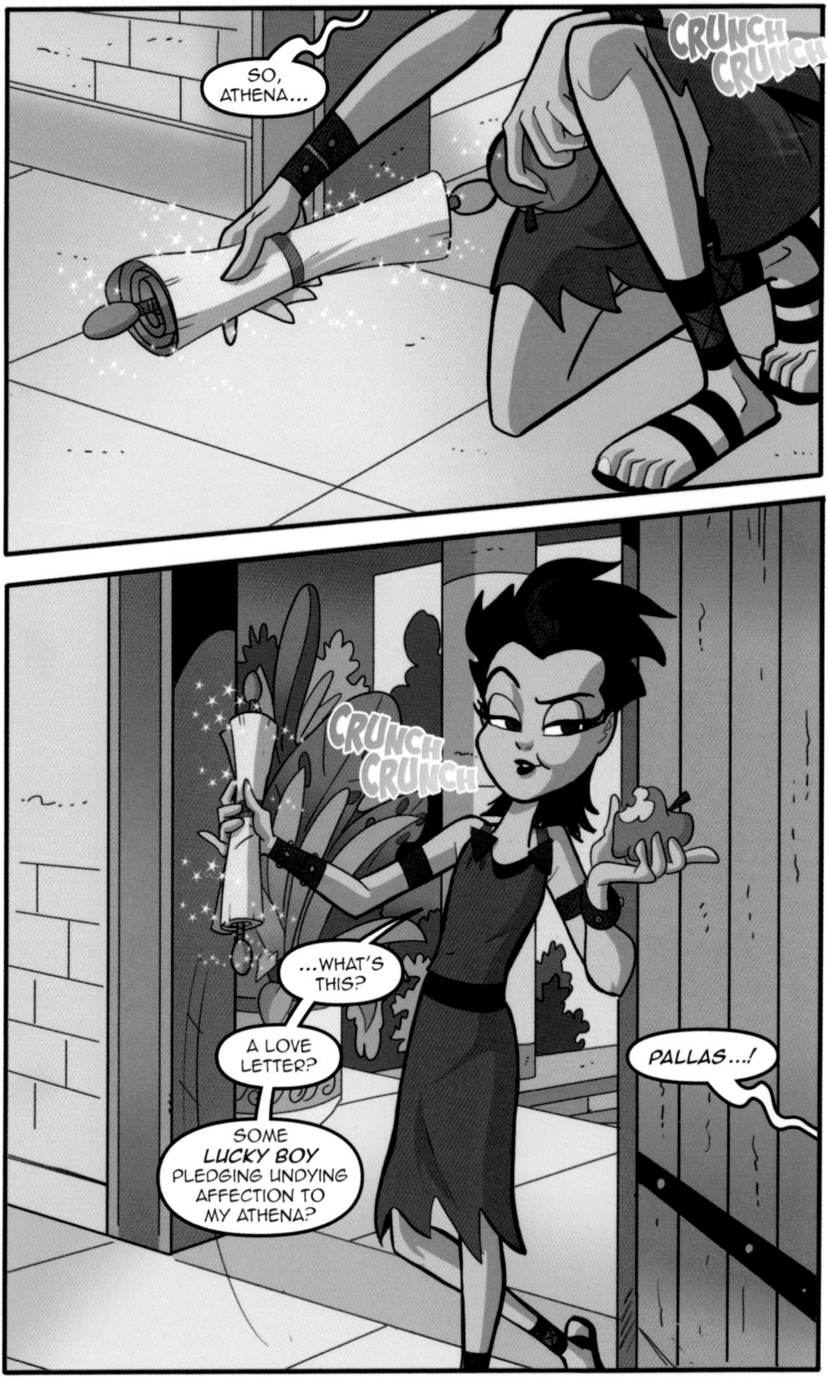
CRUNCH
CRUNCH
SO, ATHENA...
CRUNCH
CRUNCH
...WHAT'S THIS?
A LOVE LETTER?
SOME *LUCKY BOY* PLEDGING UNDYING AFFECTION TO MY ATHENA?
PALLAS...!

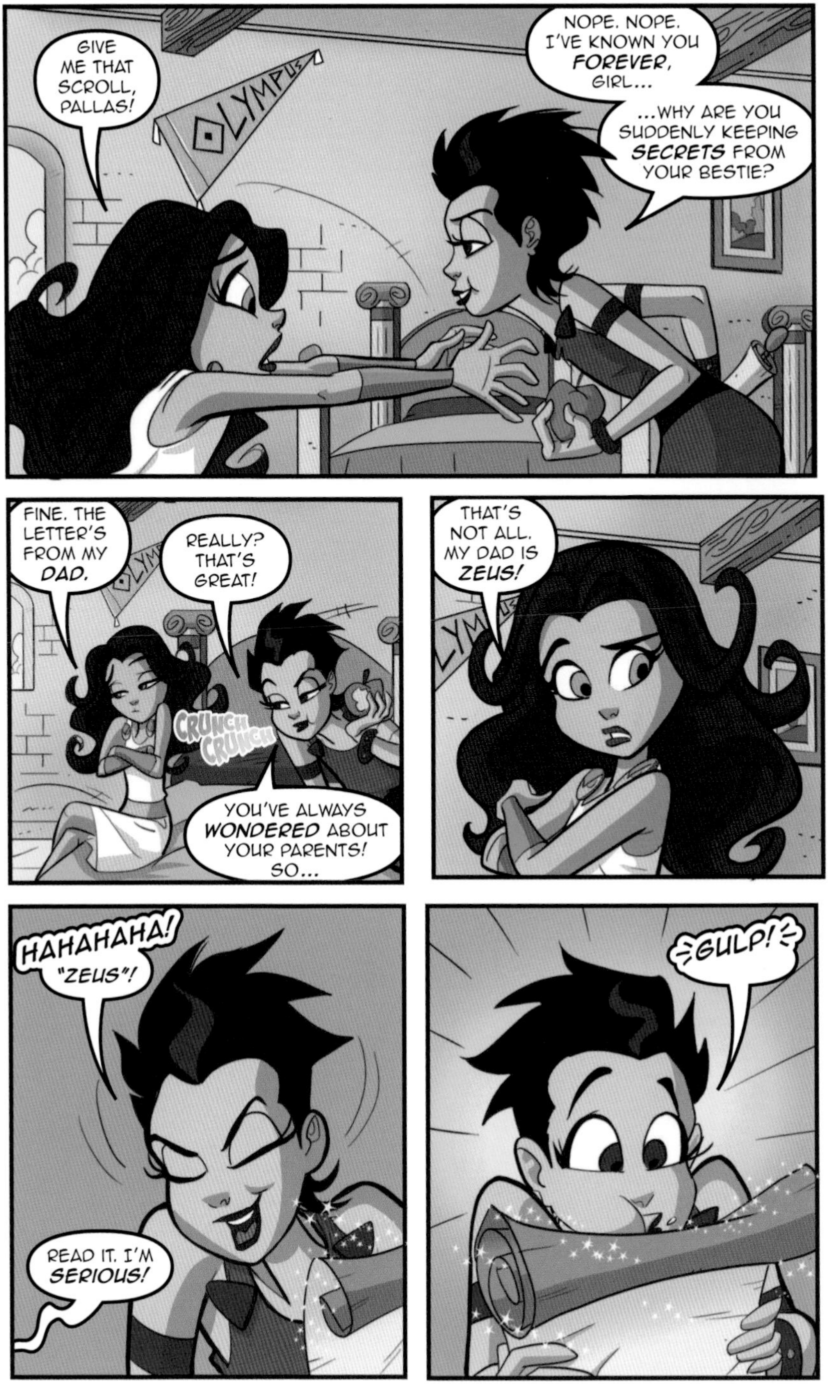
GIVE ME THAT SCROLL, PALLAS!
NOPE. NOPE. I'VE KNOWN YOU FOREVER, GIRL...
...WHY ARE YOU SUDDENLY KEEPING SECRETS FROM YOUR BESTIE?
OLYMPUS
FINE. THE LETTER'S FROM MY DAD.
REALLY? THAT'S GREAT!
CRUNCH CRUNCH
YOU'VE ALWAYS WONDERED ABOUT YOUR PARENTS! SO...
THAT'S NOT ALL. MY DAD IS ZEUS!
HAHAHAHA! "ZEUS"!
READ IT. I'M SERIOUS!
GULP!

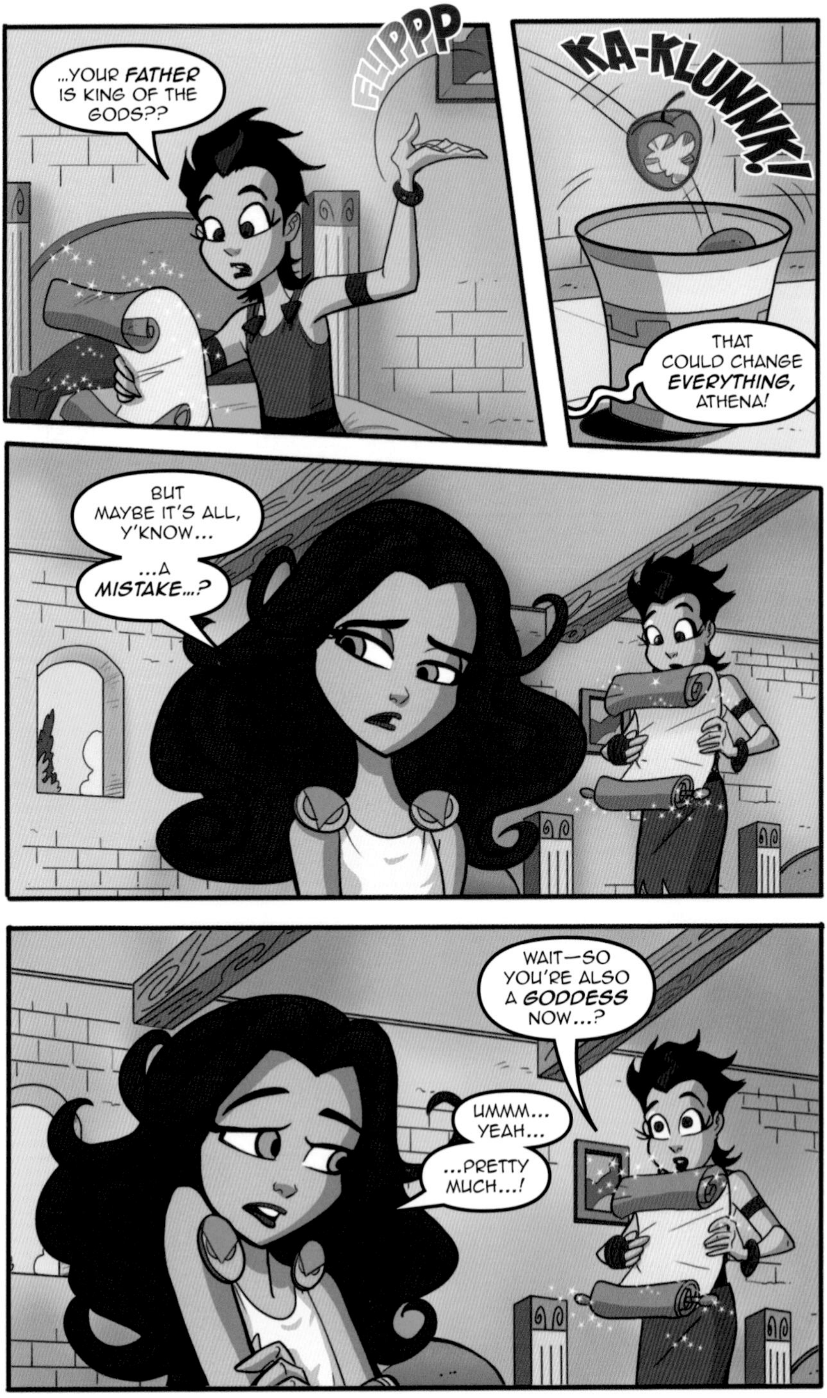
...YOUR FATHER IS KING OF THE GODS??
FLIPPP
KA-KLUNNK!
THAT COULD CHANGE EVERYTHING, ATHENA!
BUT MAYBE IT'S ALL, Y'KNOW...
...A MISTAKE...?
WAIT—SO YOU'RE ALSO A GODDESS NOW...?
UMMM... YEAH...
...PRETTY MUCH...!

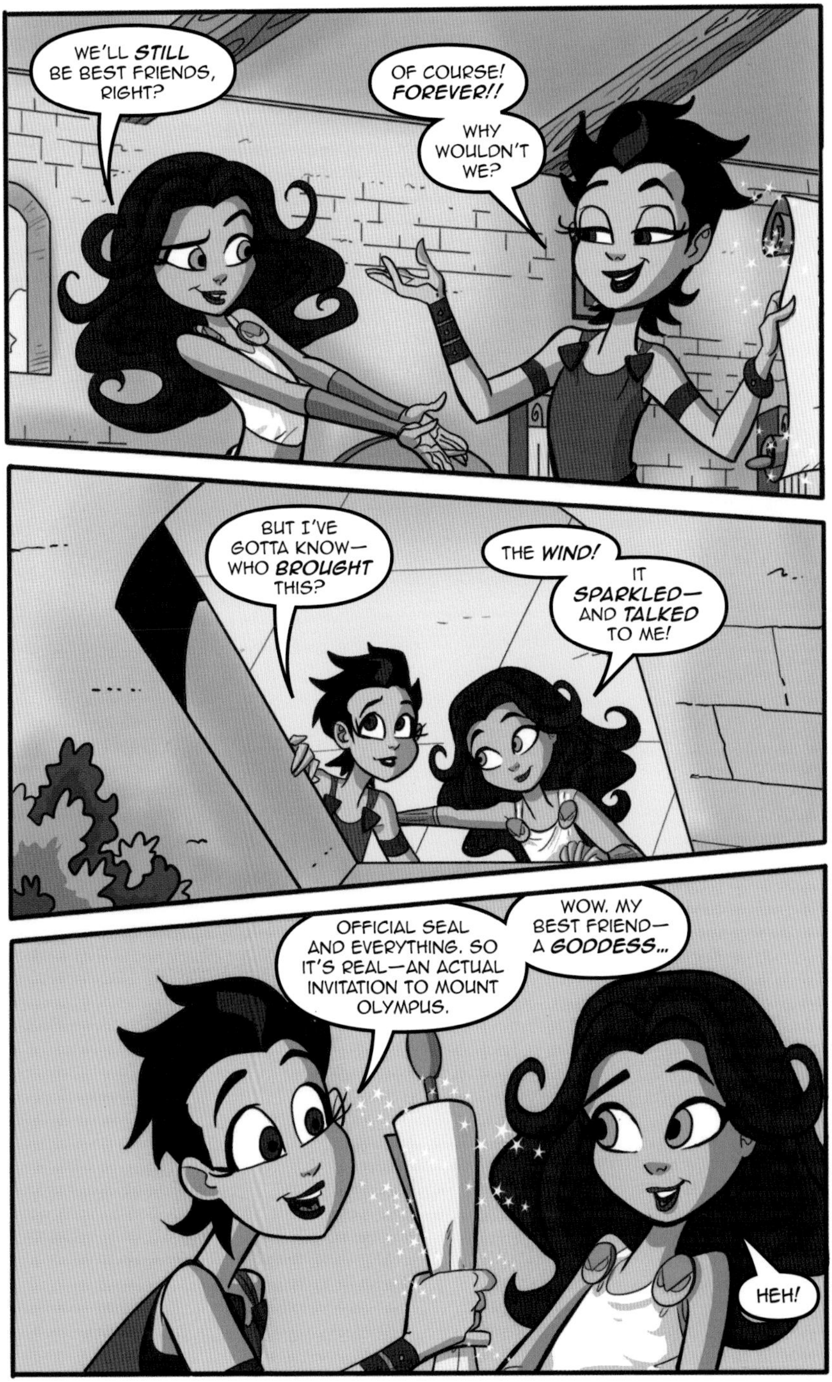
WE'LL STILL BE BEST FRIENDS, RIGHT?
OF COURSE! FOREVER!!
WHY WOULDN'T WE?
BUT I'VE GOTTA KNOW— WHO BROUGHT THIS?
THE WIND!
IT SPARKLED— AND TALKED TO ME!
OFFICIAL SEAL AND EVERYTHING. SO IT'S REAL—AN ACTUAL INVITATION TO MOUNT OLYMPUS.
WOW. MY BEST FRIEND— A GODDESS...
HEH!

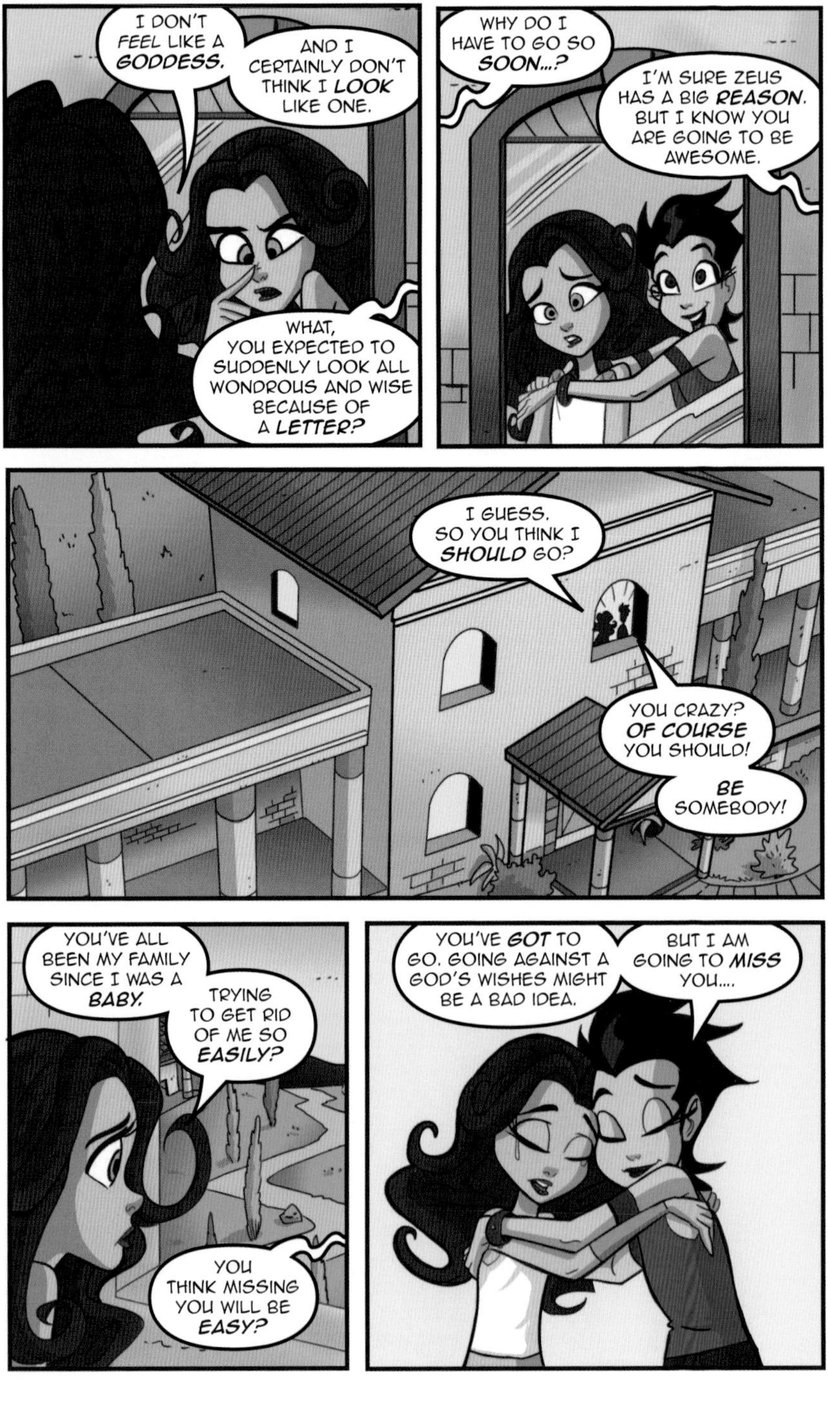
I DON'T FEEL LIKE A GODDESS.
AND I CERTAINLY DON'T THINK I LOOK LIKE ONE.
WHAT, YOU EXPECTED TO SUDDENLY LOOK ALL WONDROUS AND WISE BECAUSE OF A LETTER?
WHY DO I HAVE TO GO SO SOON...?
I'M SURE ZEUS HAS A BIG REASON. BUT I KNOW YOU ARE GOING TO BE AWESOME.
I GUESS. SO YOU THINK I SHOULD GO?
YOU CRAZY? OF COURSE YOU SHOULD!
BE SOMEBODY!
YOU'VE ALL BEEN MY FAMILY SINCE I WAS A BABY.
TRYING TO GET RID OF ME SO EASILY?
YOU THINK MISSING YOU WILL BE EASY?
YOU'VE GOT TO GO. GOING AGAINST A GOD'S WISHES MIGHT BE A BAD IDEA.
BUT I AM GOING TO MISS YOU....

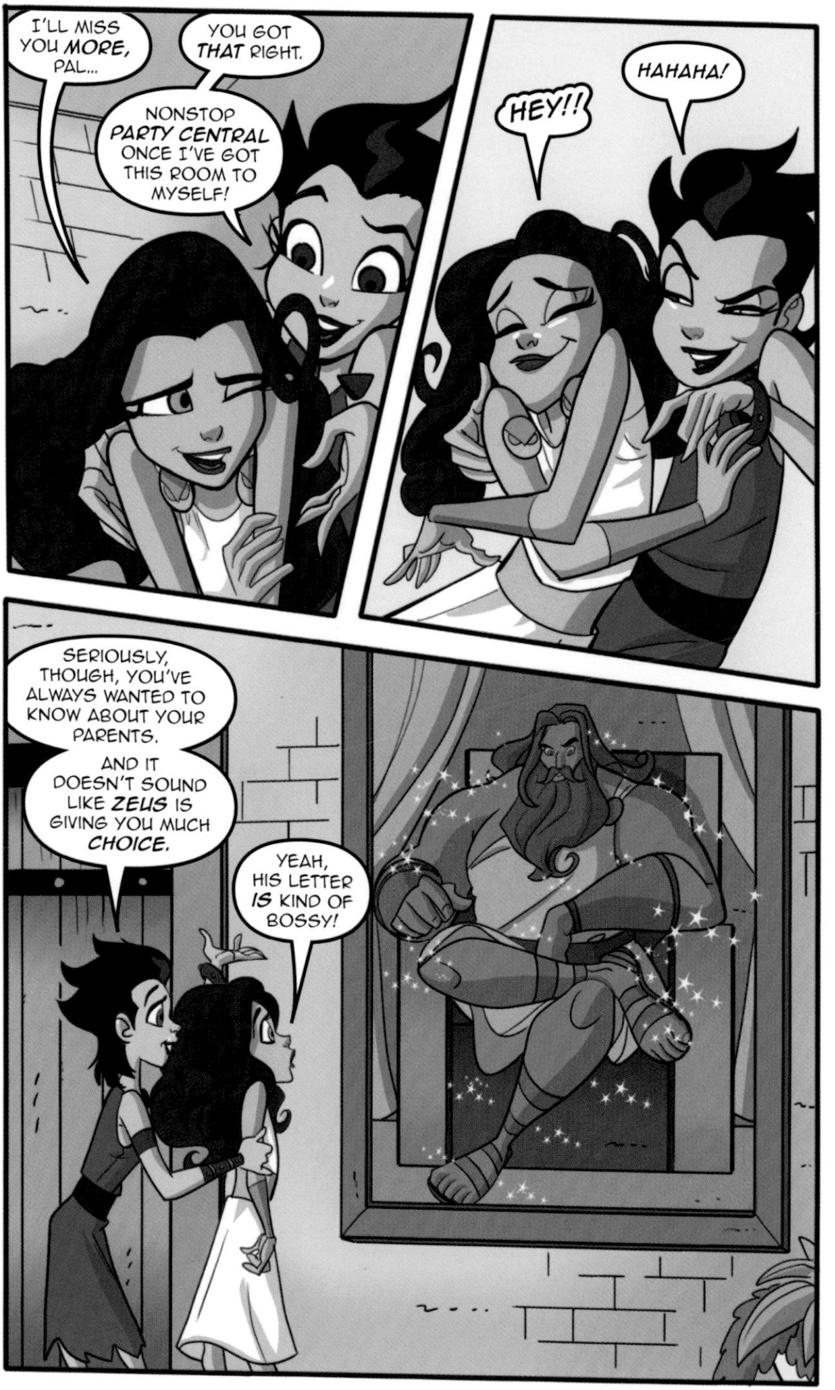
I'LL MISS YOU MORE, PAL...
YOU GOT THAT RIGHT.
NONSTOP PARTY CENTRAL ONCE I'VE GOT THIS ROOM TO MYSELF!
HEY!!
HAHAHA!
SERIOUSLY, THOUGH, YOU'VE ALWAYS WANTED TO KNOW ABOUT YOUR PARENTS.
AND IT DOESN'T SOUND LIKE ZEUS IS GIVING YOU MUCH CHOICE.
YEAH, HIS LETTER IS KIND OF BOSSY!

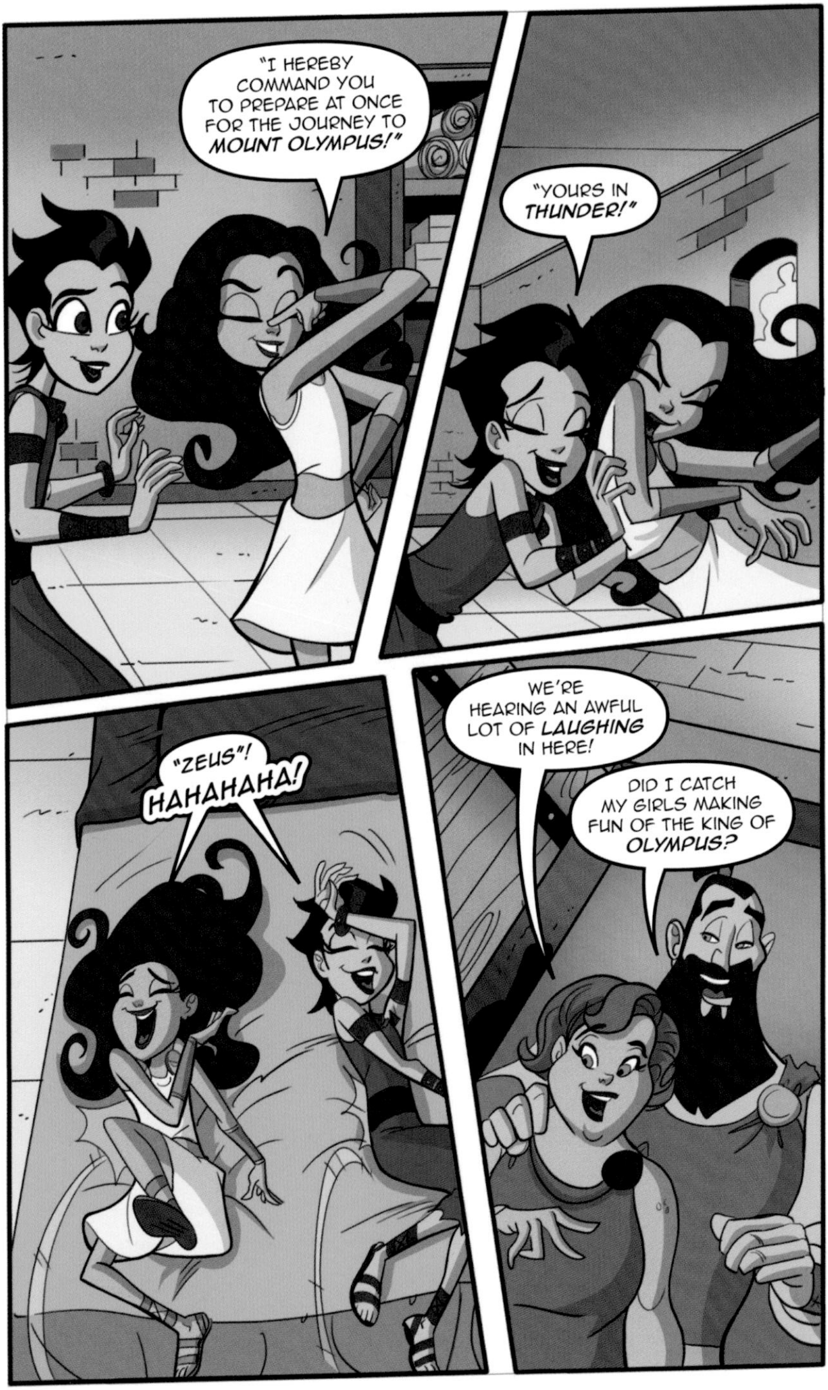
"I HEREBY COMMAND YOU TO PREPARE AT ONCE FOR THE JOURNEY TO *MOUNT OLYMPUS!*"
"YOURS IN *THUNDER!*"
"ZEUS"! HAHAHAHA!
WE'RE HEARING AN AWFUL LOT OF *LAUGHING* IN HERE!
DID I CATCH MY GIRLS MAKING FUN OF THE KING OF *OLYMPUS?*

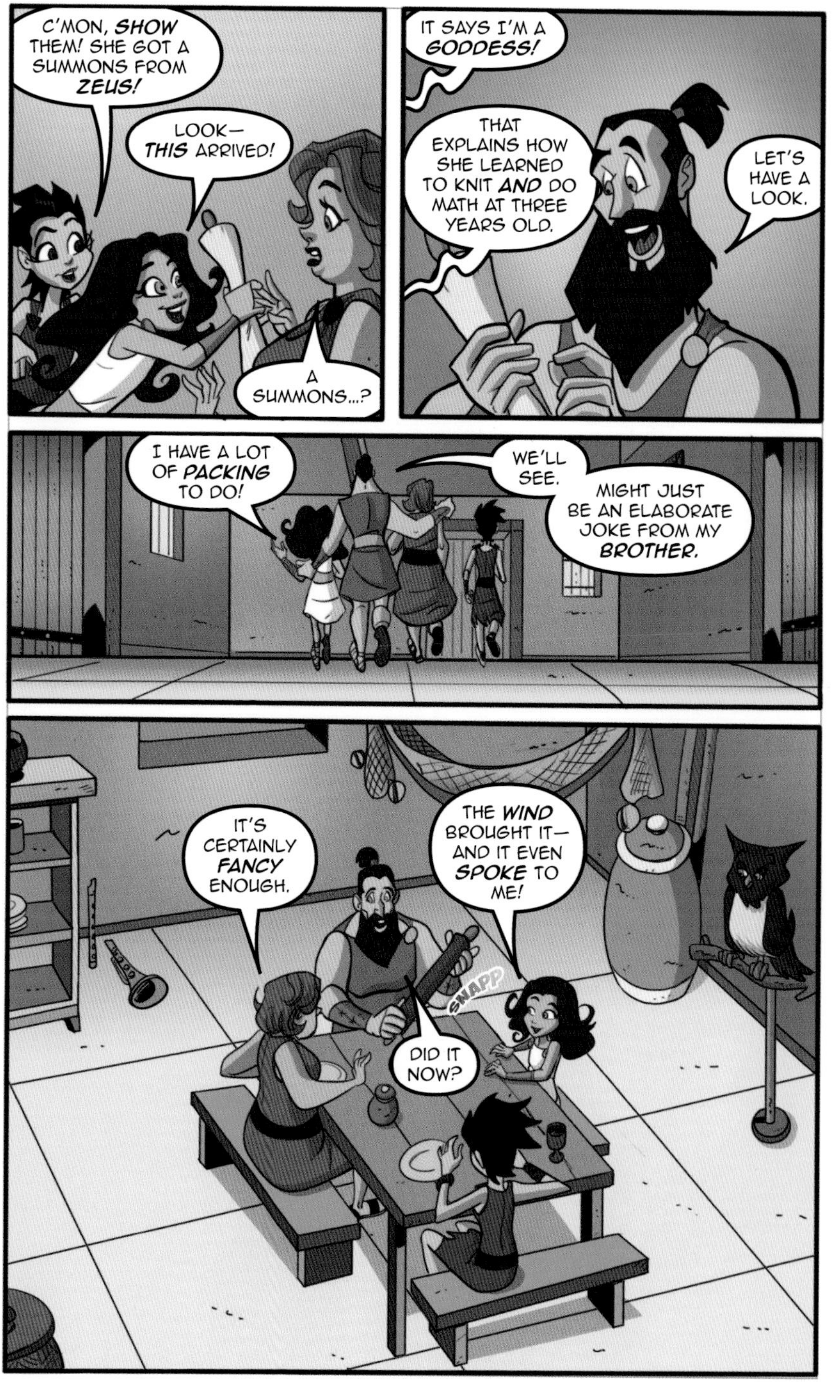
C'MON, SHOW THEM! SHE GOT A SUMMONS FROM ZEUS!
LOOK— THIS ARRIVED!
A SUMMONS...?
IT SAYS I'M A GODDESS!
THAT EXPLAINS HOW SHE LEARNED TO KNIT AND DO MATH AT THREE YEARS OLD.
LET'S HAVE A LOOK.
I HAVE A LOT OF PACKING TO DO!
WE'LL SEE.
MIGHT JUST BE AN ELABORATE JOKE FROM MY BROTHER.
IT'S CERTAINLY FANCY ENOUGH.
THE WIND BROUGHT IT— AND IT EVEN SPOKE TO ME!
SNAPP
DID IT NOW?

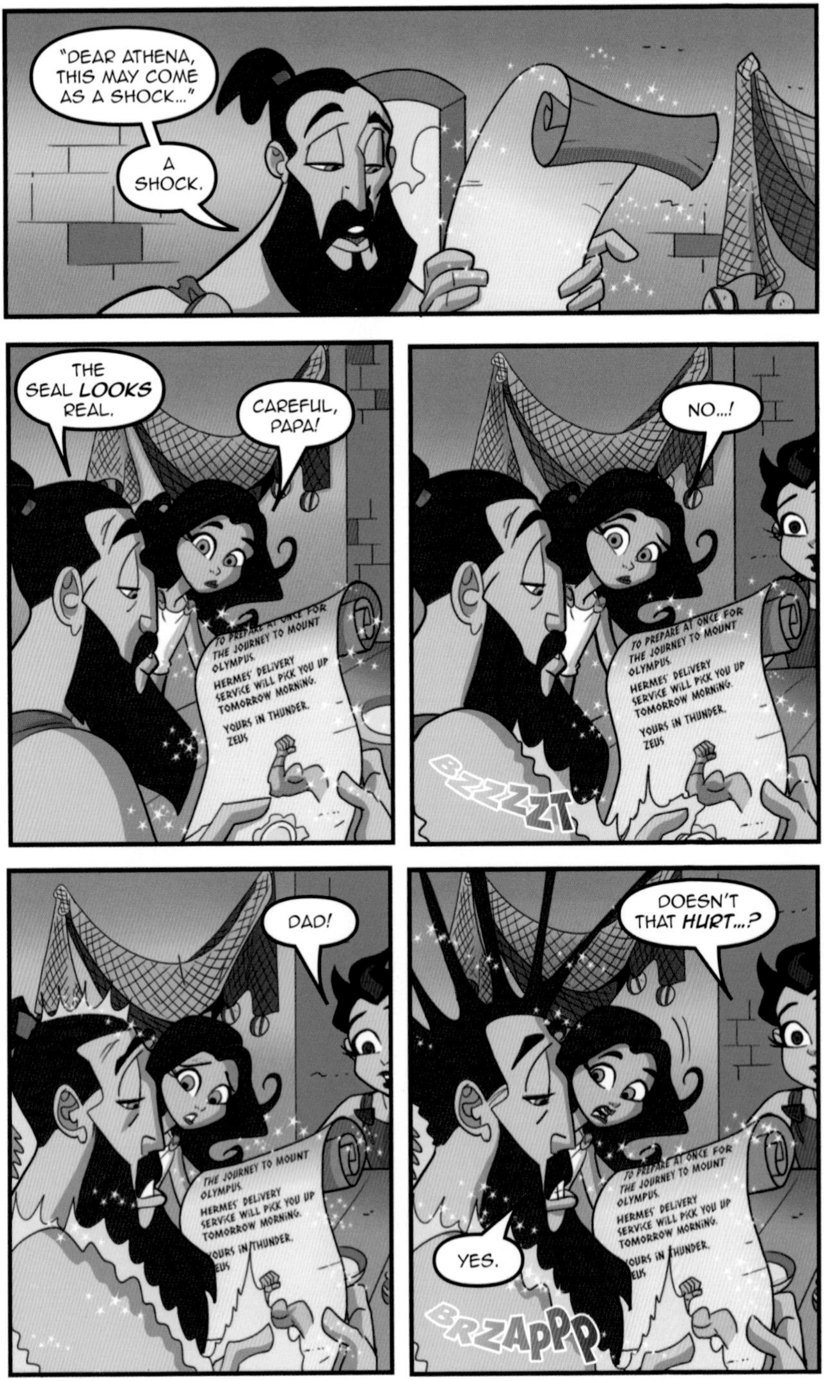
"DEAR ATHENA, THIS MAY COME AS A SHOCK..."
A SHOCK.
THE SEAL LOOKS REAL.
CAREFUL, PAPA!
TO PREPARE AT ONCE FOR THE JOURNEY TO MOUNT OLYMPUS.
HERMES' DELIVERY SERVICE WILL PICK YOU UP TOMORROW MORNING.
YOURS IN THUNDER, ZEUS
NO...!
BZZZZZT
DAD!
DOESN'T THAT HURT...?
YES.
BRZAPPP

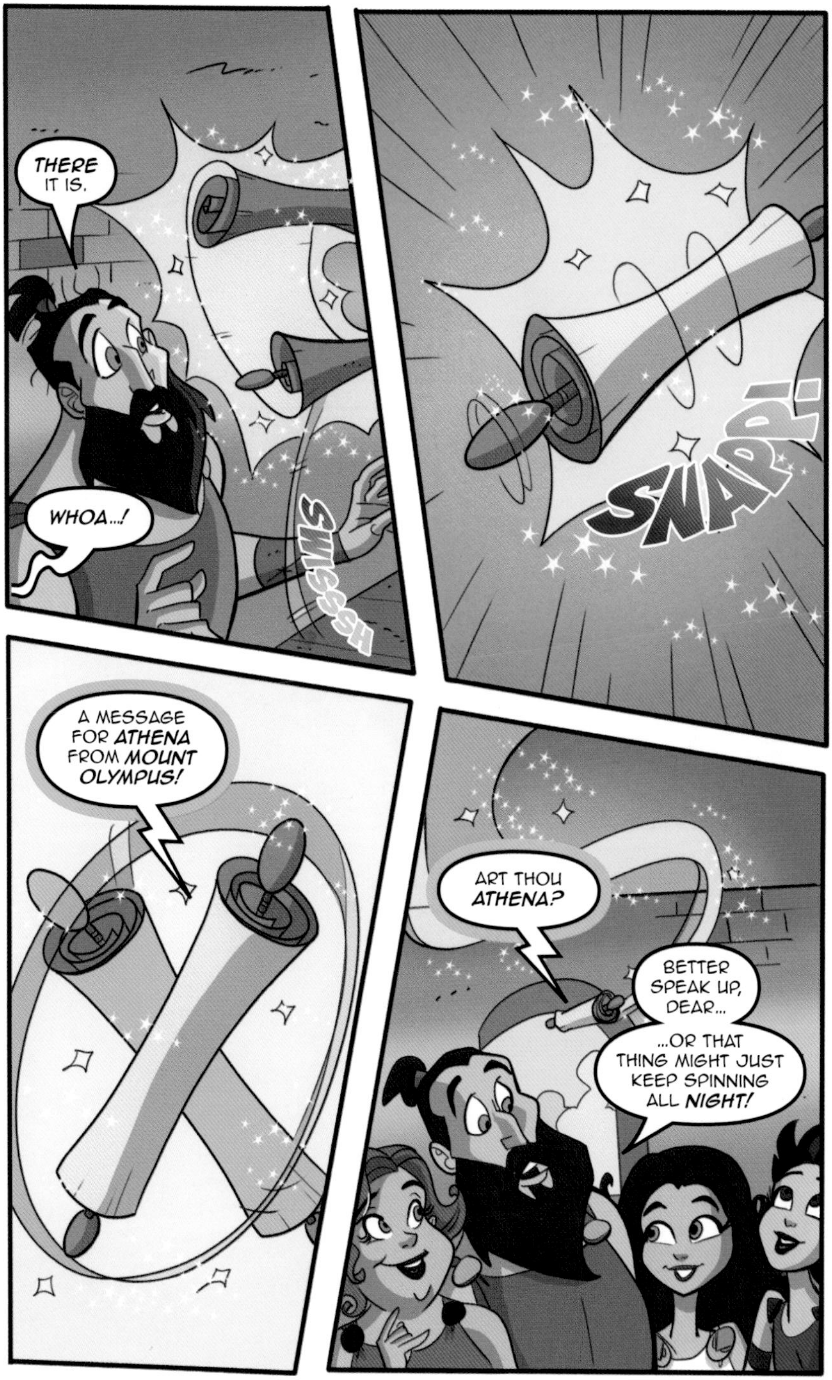
THERE IT IS.
WHOA...!
SWISSSH
SNAP!
A MESSAGE FOR ATHENA FROM MOUNT OLYMPUS!
ART THOU ATHENA?
BETTER SPEAK UP, DEAR...
...OR THAT THING MIGHT JUST KEEP SPINNING ALL NIGHT!

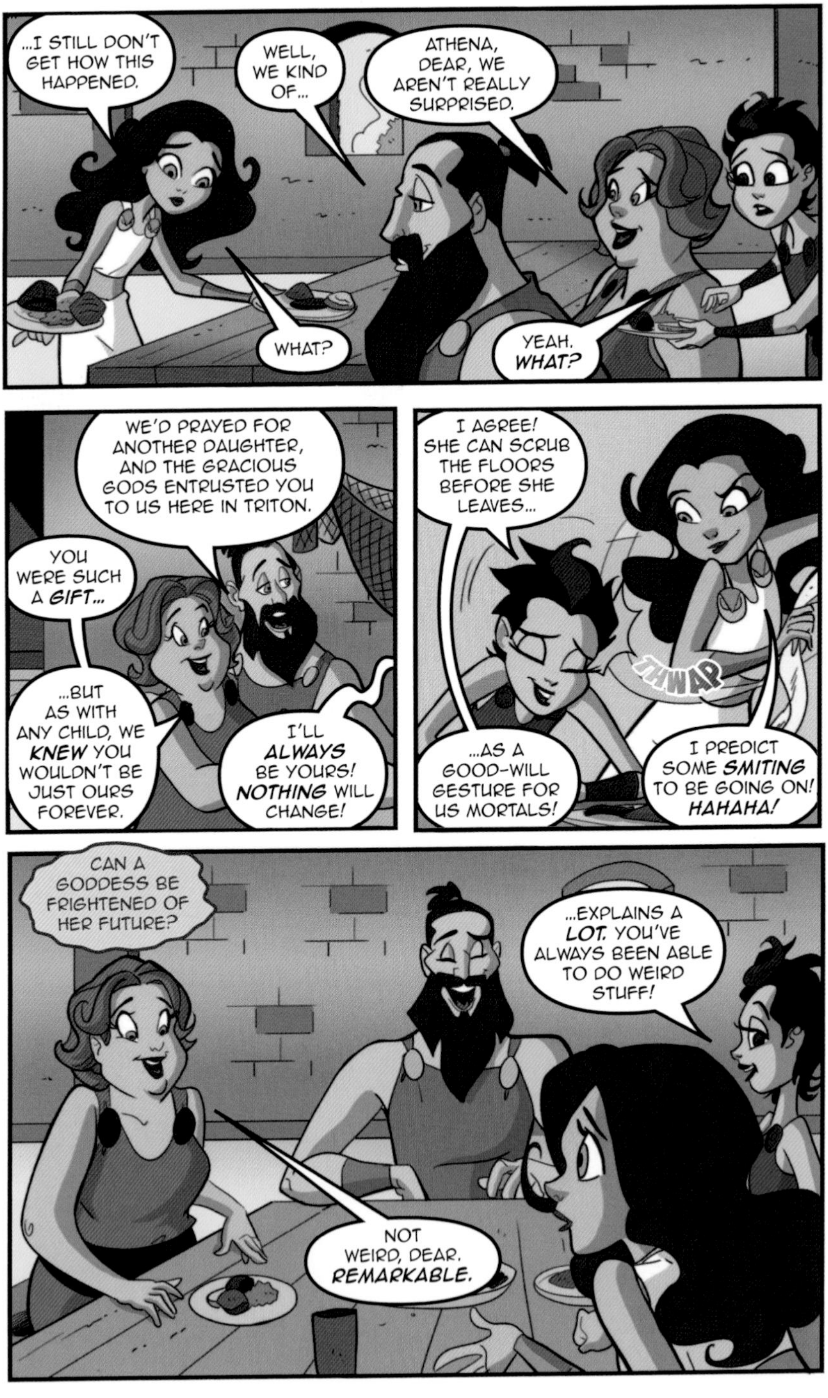
...I STILL DON'T GET HOW THIS HAPPENED.
WELL, WE KIND OF...
ATHENA, DEAR, WE AREN'T REALLY SURPRISED.
WHAT?
YEAH. WHAT?
WE'D PRAYED FOR ANOTHER DAUGHTER, AND THE GRACIOUS GODS ENTRUSTED YOU TO US HERE IN TRITON.
YOU WERE SUCH A GIFT...
...BUT AS WITH ANY CHILD, WE KNEW YOU WOULDN'T BE JUST OURS FOREVER.
I'LL ALWAYS BE YOURS! NOTHING WILL CHANGE!
I AGREE! SHE CAN SCRUB THE FLOORS BEFORE SHE LEAVES...
THWAP
...AS A GOOD-WILL GESTURE FOR US MORTALS!
I PREDICT SOME SMITING TO BE GOING ON! HAHAHA!
CAN A GODDESS BE FRIGHTENED OF HER FUTURE?
...EXPLAINS A LOT. YOU'VE ALWAYS BEEN ABLE TO DO WEIRD STUFF!
NOT WEIRD, DEAR. REMARKABLE.

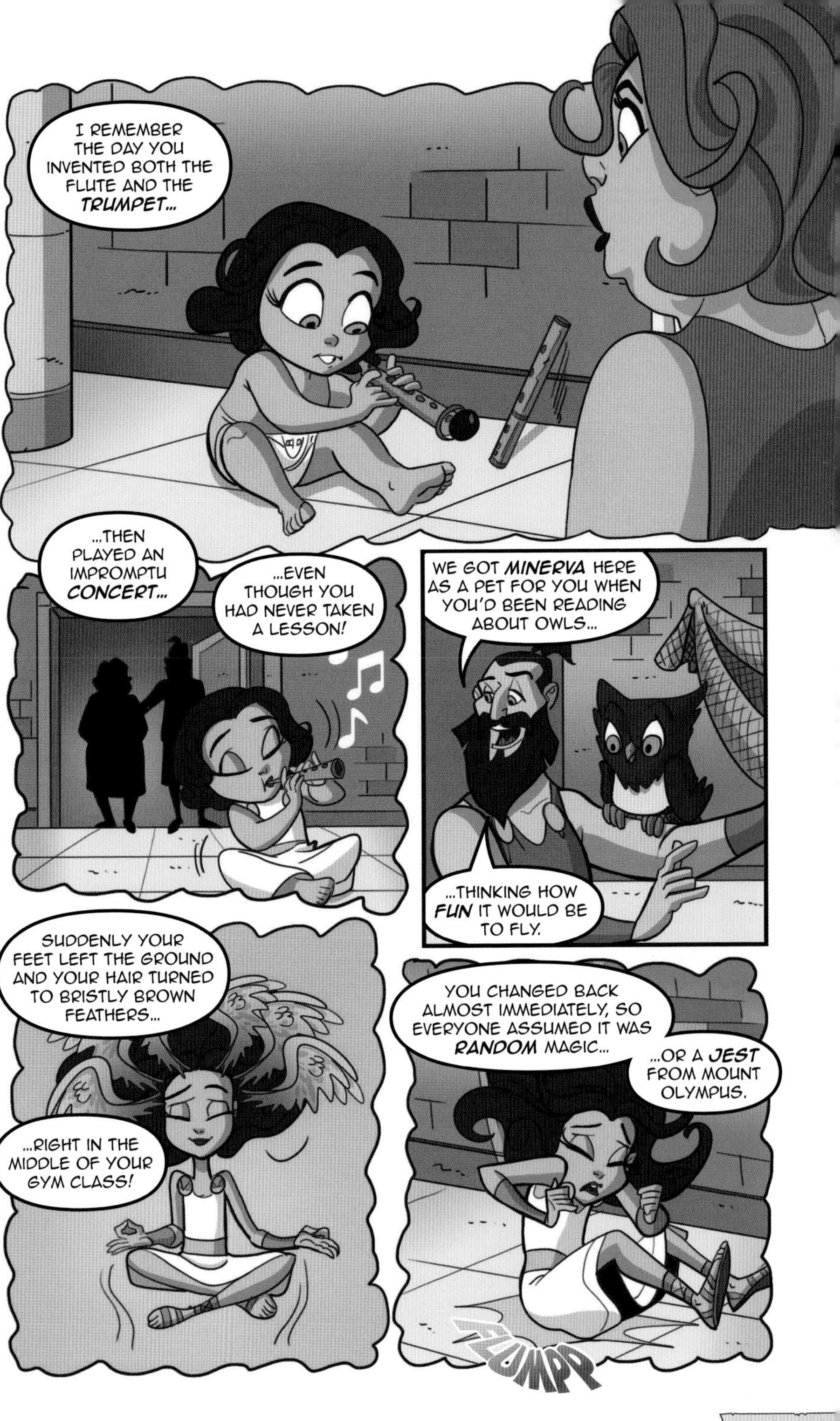
I REMEMBER THE DAY YOU INVENTED BOTH THE FLUTE AND THE *TRUMPET*...
...THEN PLAYED AN IMPROMPTU *CONCERT*...
...EVEN THOUGH YOU HAD NEVER TAKEN A LESSON!
WE GOT *MINERVA* HERE AS A PET FOR YOU WHEN YOU'D BEEN READING ABOUT OWLS...
...THINKING HOW *FUN* IT WOULD BE TO FLY.
SUDDENLY YOUR FEET LEFT THE GROUND AND YOUR HAIR TURNED TO BRISTLY BROWN FEATHERS...
...RIGHT IN THE MIDDLE OF YOUR GYM CLASS!
YOU CHANGED BACK ALMOST IMMEDIATELY, SO EVERYONE ASSUMED IT WAS *RANDOM* MAGIC...
...OR A *JEST* FROM MOUNT OLYMPUS.
FLUMPP

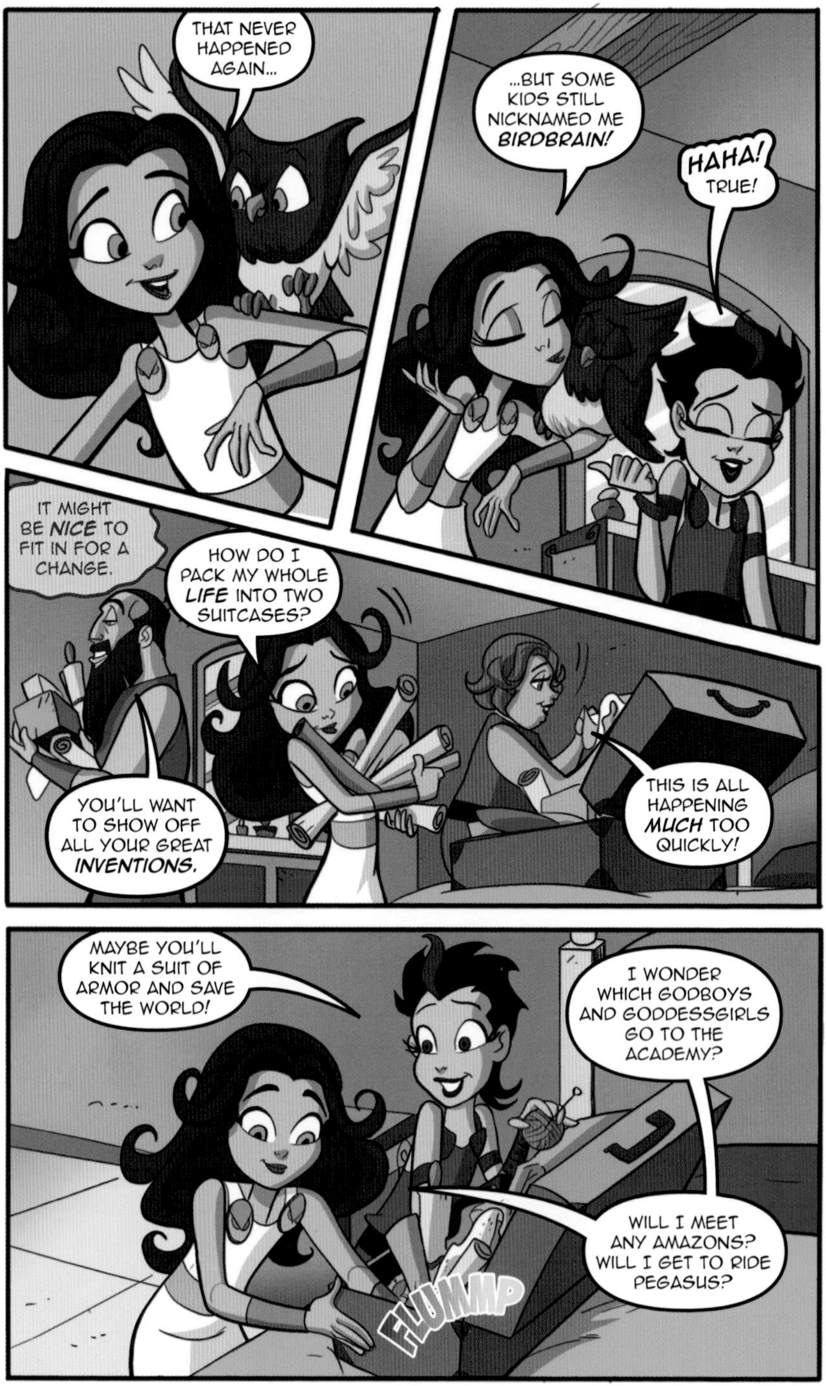

THAT NEVER HAPPENED AGAIN...
...BUT SOME KIDS STILL NICKNAMED ME *BIRDBRAIN!*
HAHA! TRUE!
IT MIGHT BE *NICE* TO FIT IN FOR A CHANGE.
HOW DO I PACK MY WHOLE *LIFE* INTO TWO SUITCASES?
YOU'LL WANT TO SHOW OFF ALL YOUR GREAT *INVENTIONS.*
THIS IS ALL HAPPENING *MUCH* TOO QUICKLY!
MAYBE YOU'LL KNIT A SUIT OF ARMOR AND SAVE THE WORLD!
I WONDER WHICH GODBOYS AND GODDESSGIRLS GO TO THE ACADEMY?
WILL I MEET ANY AMAZONS? WILL I GET TO RIDE PEGASUS?
FLUMMP

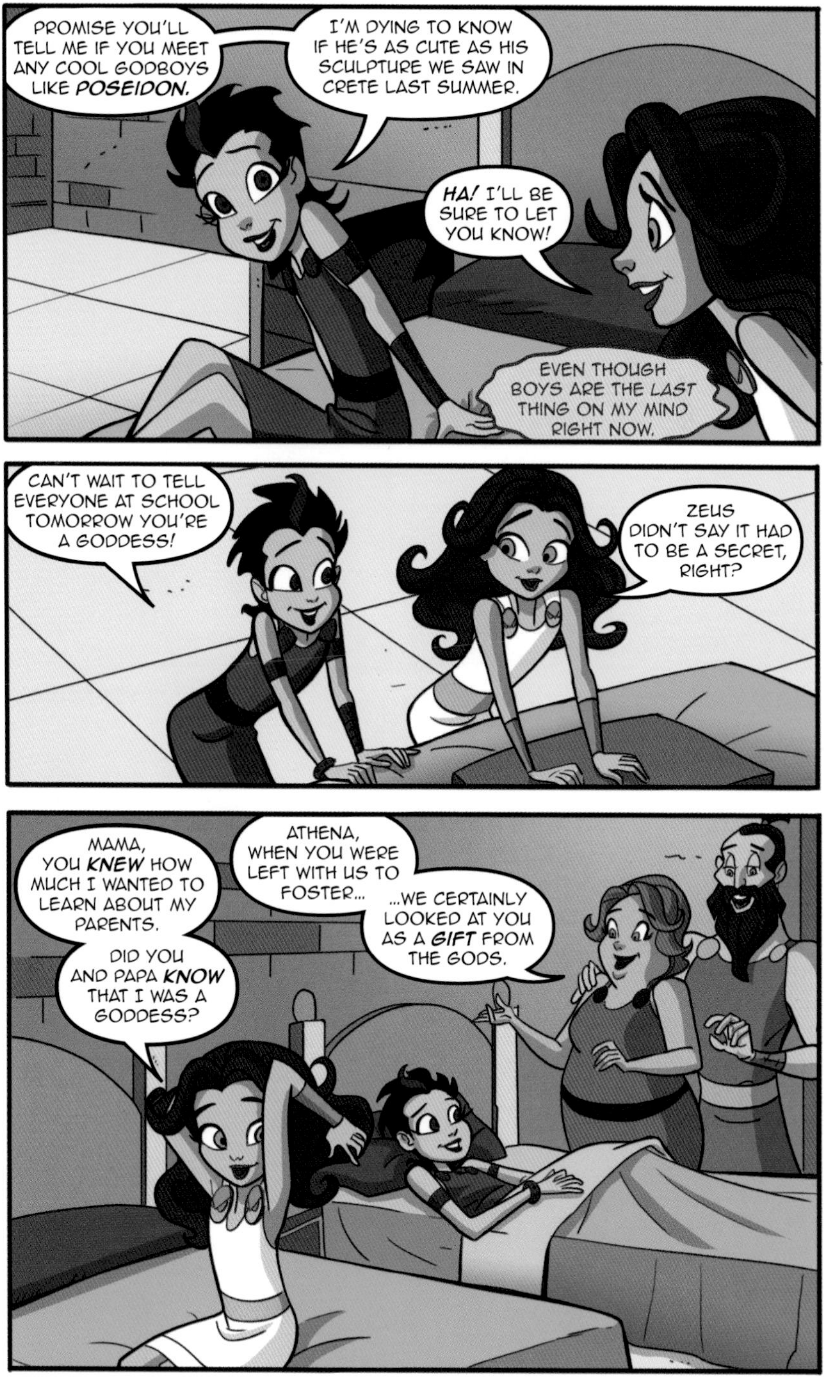
PROMISE YOU'LL TELL ME IF YOU MEET ANY COOL GODBOYS LIKE *POSEIDON.*
I'M DYING TO KNOW IF HE'S AS CUTE AS HIS SCULPTURE WE SAW IN CRETE LAST SUMMER.
HA! I'LL BE SURE TO LET YOU KNOW!
EVEN THOUGH BOYS ARE THE *LAST* THING ON MY MIND RIGHT NOW.
CAN'T WAIT TO TELL EVERYONE AT SCHOOL TOMORROW YOU'RE A GODDESS!
ZEUS DIDN'T SAY IT HAD TO BE A SECRET, RIGHT?
MAMA, YOU **KNEW** HOW MUCH I WANTED TO LEARN ABOUT MY PARENTS.
DID YOU AND PAPA **KNOW** THAT I WAS A GODDESS?
ATHENA, WHEN YOU WERE LEFT WITH US TO FOSTER...
...WE CERTAINLY LOOKED AT YOU AS A *GIFT* FROM THE GODS.

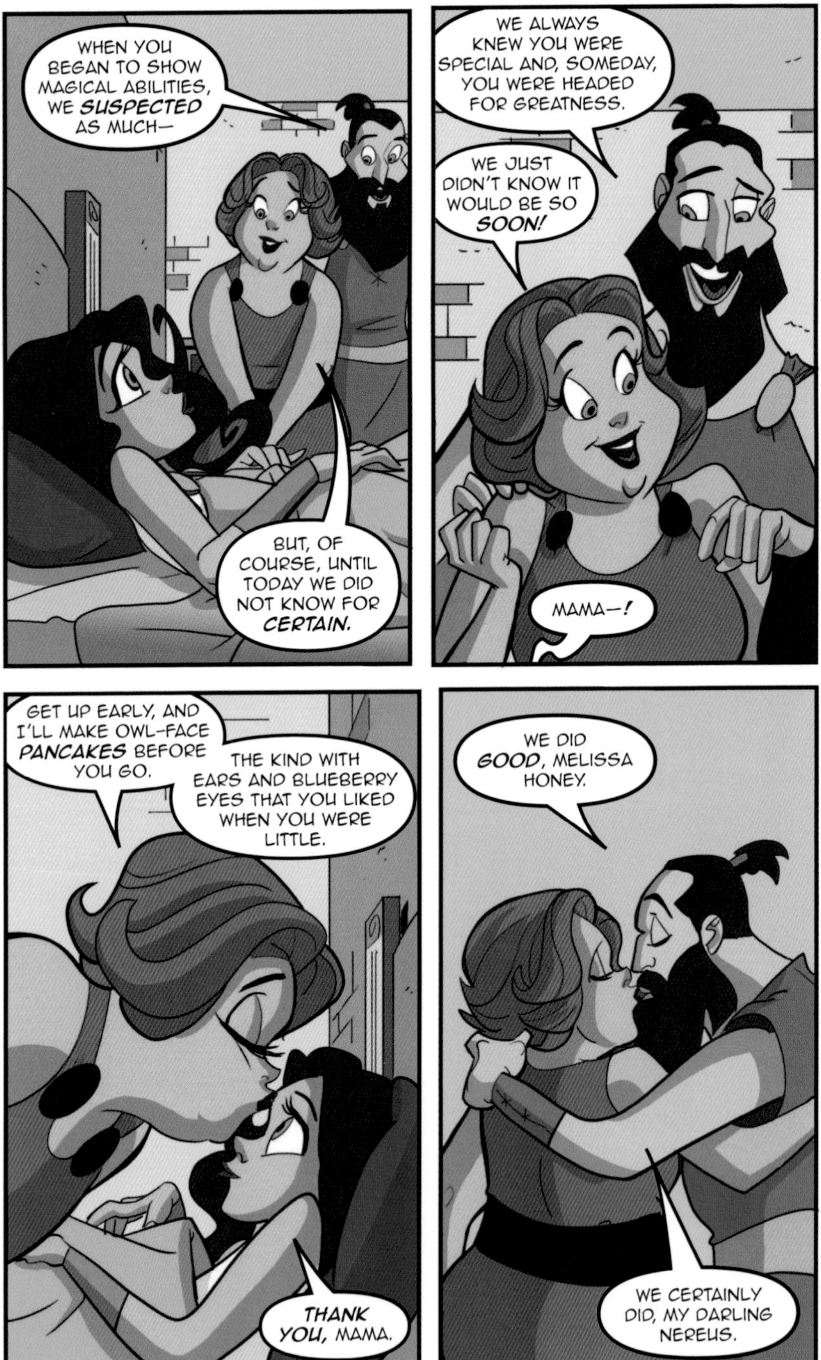
WHEN YOU BEGAN TO SHOW MAGICAL ABILITIES, WE *SUSPECTED* AS MUCH—
BUT, OF COURSE, UNTIL TODAY WE DID NOT KNOW FOR *CERTAIN.*
WE ALWAYS KNEW YOU WERE SPECIAL AND, SOMEDAY, YOU WERE HEADED FOR GREATNESS.
WE JUST DIDN'T KNOW IT WOULD BE SO *SOON!*
MAMA—!
GET UP EARLY, AND I'LL MAKE OWL-FACE *PANCAKES* BEFORE YOU GO.
THE KIND WITH EARS AND BLUEBERRY EYES THAT YOU LIKED WHEN YOU WERE LITTLE.
THANK YOU, MAMA.
WE DID *GOOD*, MELISSA HONEY.
WE CERTAINLY DID, MY DARLING NEREUS.

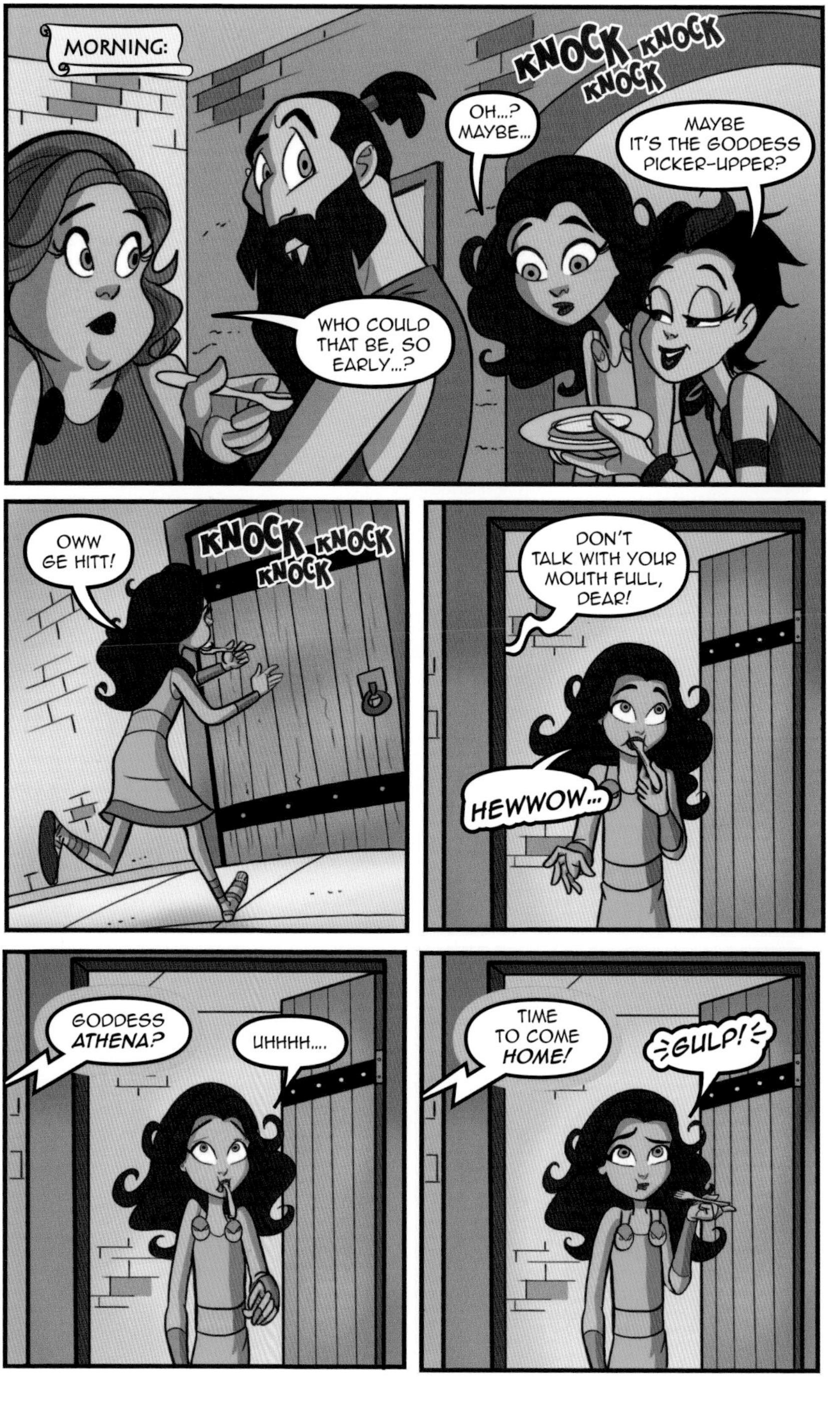
MORNING:
KNOCK KNOCK KNOCK
OH...? MAYBE...
MAYBE IT'S THE GODDESS PICKER-UPPER?
WHO COULD THAT BE, SO EARLY...?
OWW GE HITT!
KNOCK KNOCK KNOCK
DON'T TALK WITH YOUR MOUTH FULL, DEAR!
HEWWOW...
GODDESS ATHENA?
UHHHH....
TIME TO COME HOME!
GULP!

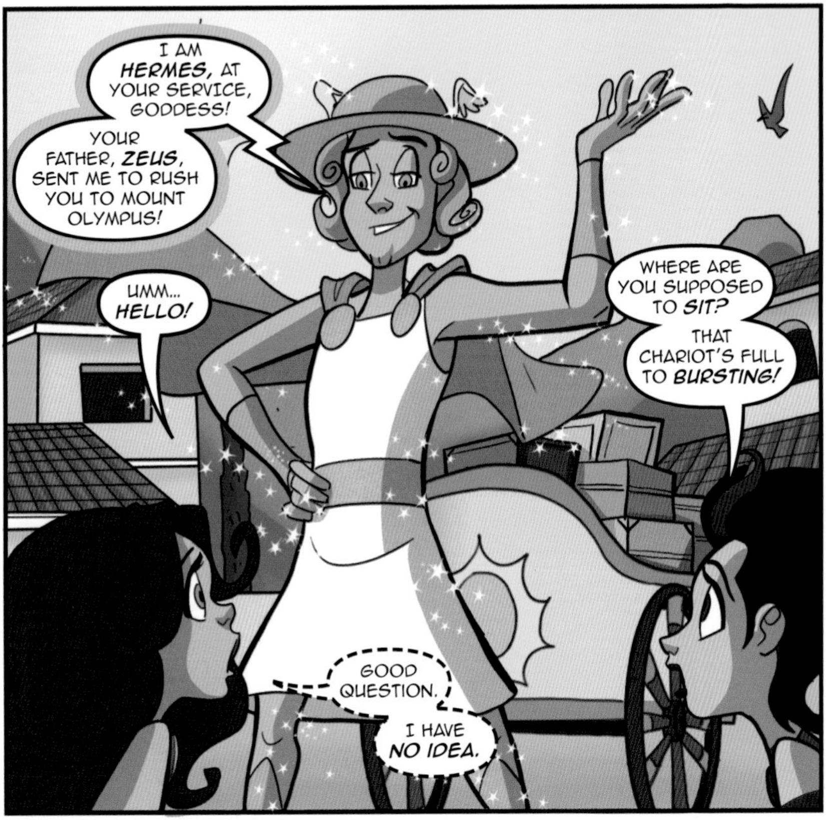
I AM HERMES, AT YOUR SERVICE, GODDESS!
YOUR FATHER, ZEUS, SENT ME TO RUSH YOU TO MOUNT OLYMPUS!
UMM... HELLO!
WHERE ARE YOU SUPPOSED TO SIT?
THAT CHARIOT'S FULL TO BURSTING!
GOOD QUESTION.
I HAVE NO IDEA.

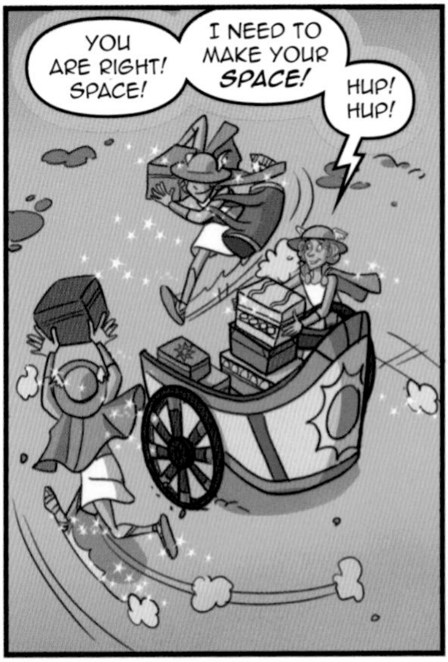
YOU ARE RIGHT! SPACE!
I NEED TO MAKE YOUR SPACE!
HUP! HUP!

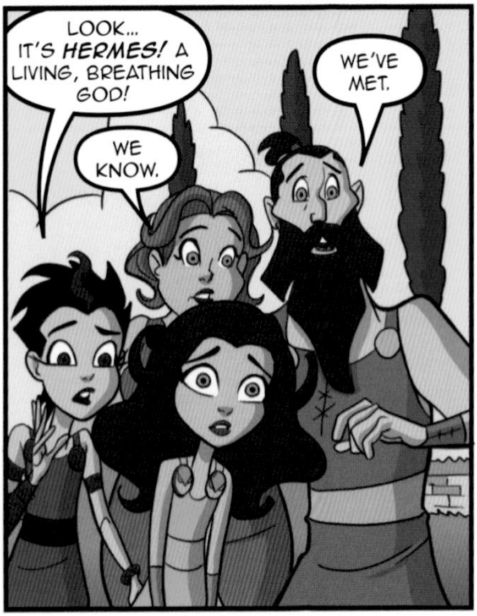
LOOK... IT'S HERMES! A LIVING, BREATHING GOD!
WE KNOW.
WE'VE MET.

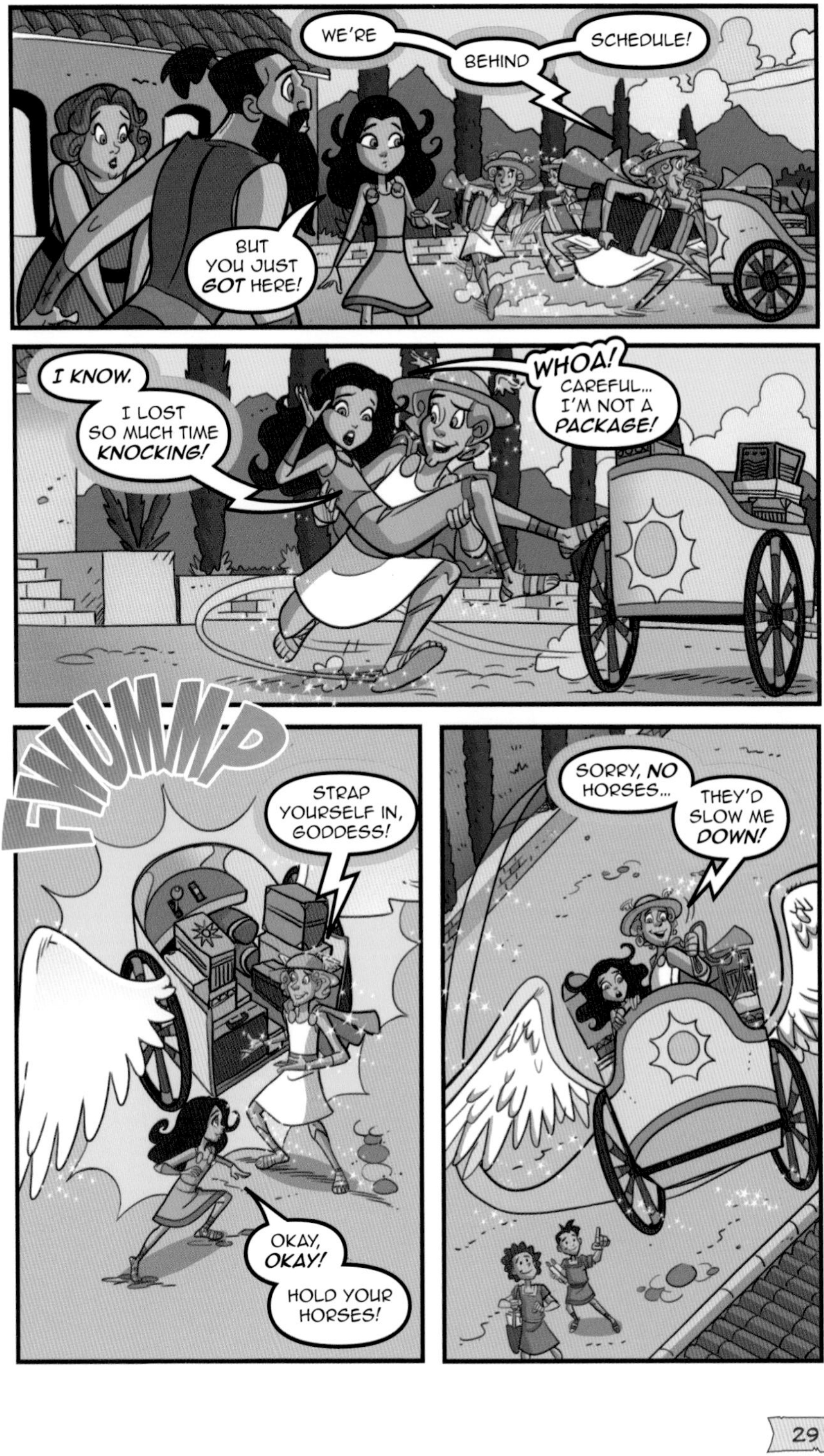
WE'RE
BEHIND
SCHEDULE!
BUT YOU JUST GOT HERE!
I KNOW.
I LOST SO MUCH TIME KNOCKING!
WHOA!
CAREFUL... I'M NOT A PACKAGE!
FWUMMP
STRAP YOURSELF IN, GODDESS!
OKAY, OKAY!
HOLD YOUR HORSES!
SORRY, NO HORSES...
THEY'D SLOW ME DOWN!

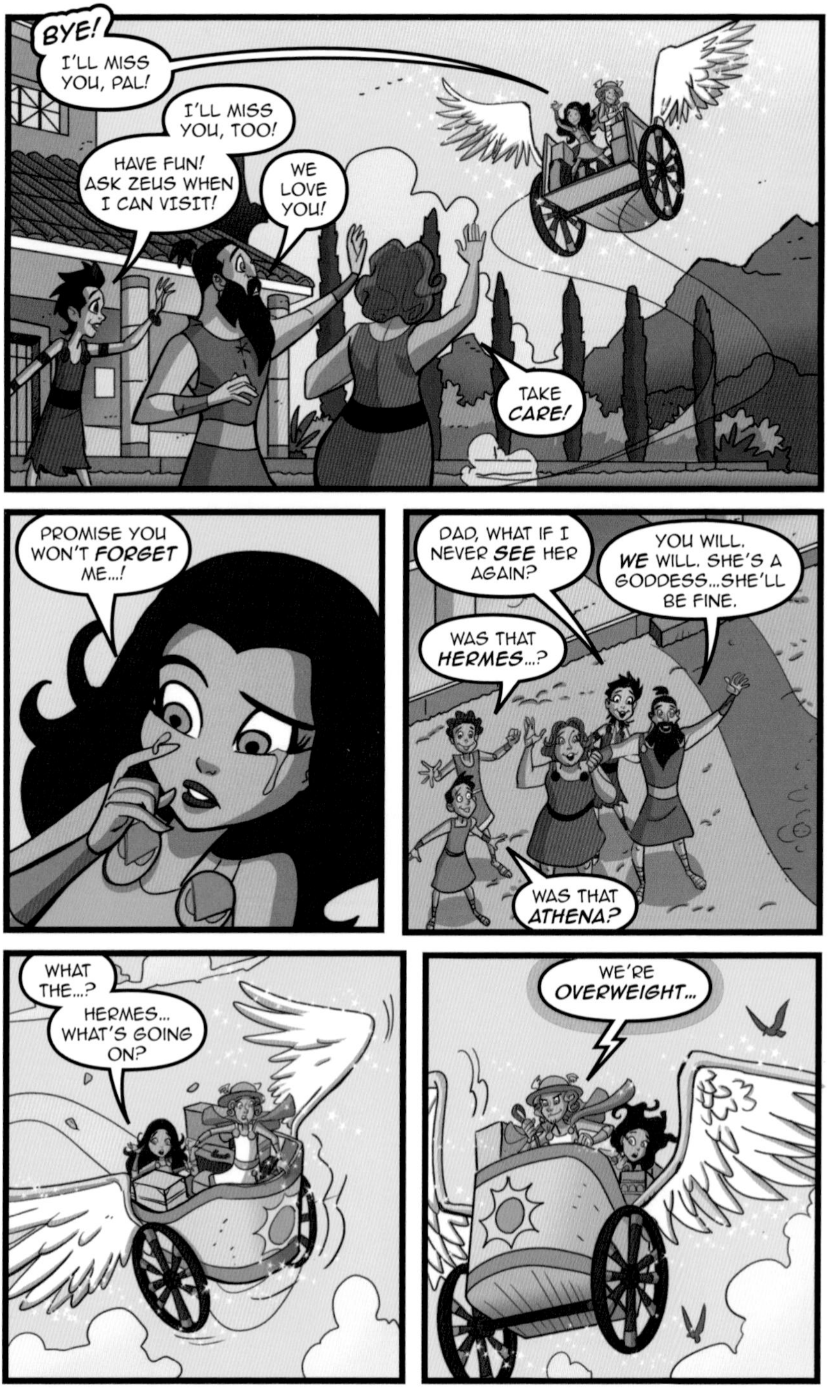
BYE!
I'LL MISS YOU, PAL!
I'LL MISS YOU, TOO!
HAVE FUN! ASK ZEUS WHEN I CAN VISIT!
WE LOVE YOU!
TAKE CARE!
PROMISE YOU WON'T FORGET ME...!
DAD, WHAT IF I NEVER SEE HER AGAIN?
YOU WILL. WE WILL. SHE'S A GODDESS...SHE'LL BE FINE.
WAS THAT HERMES...?
WAS THAT ATHENA?
WHAT THE...?
HERMES... WHAT'S GOING ON?
WE'RE OVERWEIGHT...

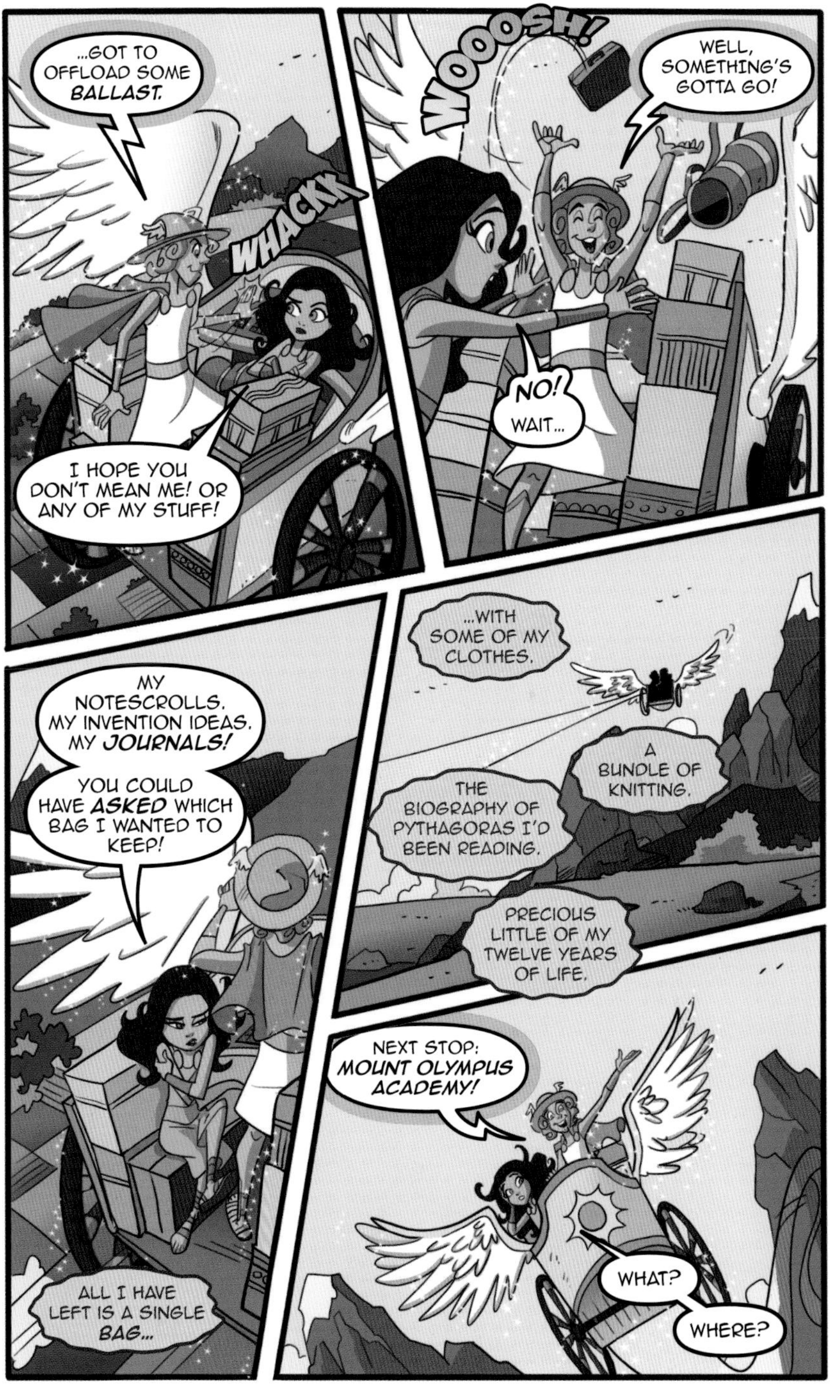

...GOT TO OFFLOAD SOME *BALLAST.*
WHACKK
I HOPE YOU DON'T MEAN ME! OR ANY OF MY STUFF!
WOOOSH!
WELL, SOMETHING'S GOTTA GO!
NO! WAIT...
...WITH SOME OF MY CLOTHES.
A BUNDLE OF KNITTING.
THE BIOGRAPHY OF PYTHAGORAS I'D BEEN READING.
PRECIOUS LITTLE OF MY TWELVE YEARS OF LIFE.
MY NOTESCROLLS. MY INVENTION IDEAS. MY *JOURNALS!*
YOU COULD HAVE *ASKED* WHICH BAG I WANTED TO KEEP!
ALL I HAVE LEFT IS A SINGLE *BAG...*
NEXT STOP: *MOUNT OLYMPUS ACADEMY!*
WHAT?
WHERE?

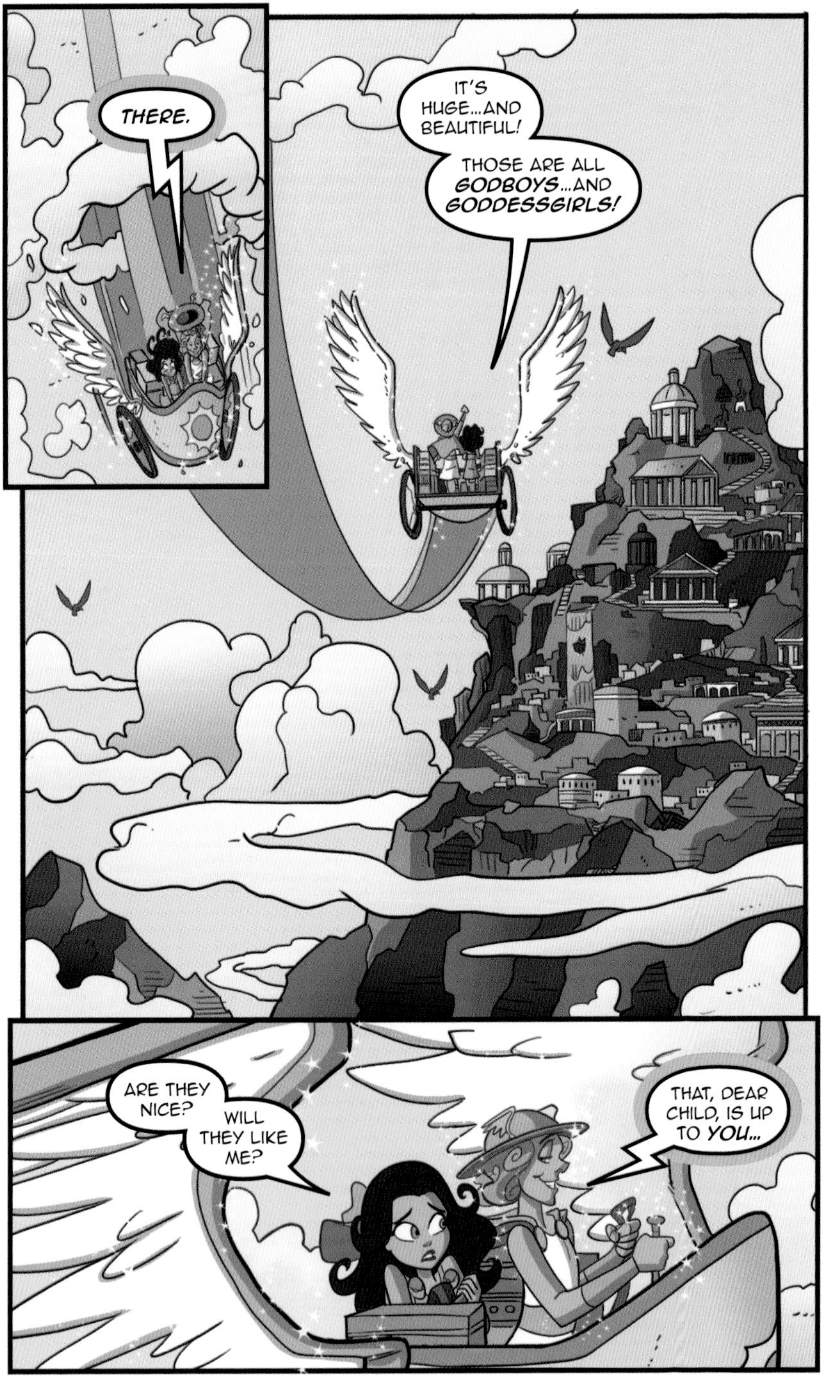
THERE.
IT'S HUGE...AND BEAUTIFUL!
THOSE ARE ALL GODBOYS...AND GODDESSGIRLS!
ARE THEY NICE?
WILL THEY LIKE ME?
THAT, DEAR CHILD, IS UP TO YOU...

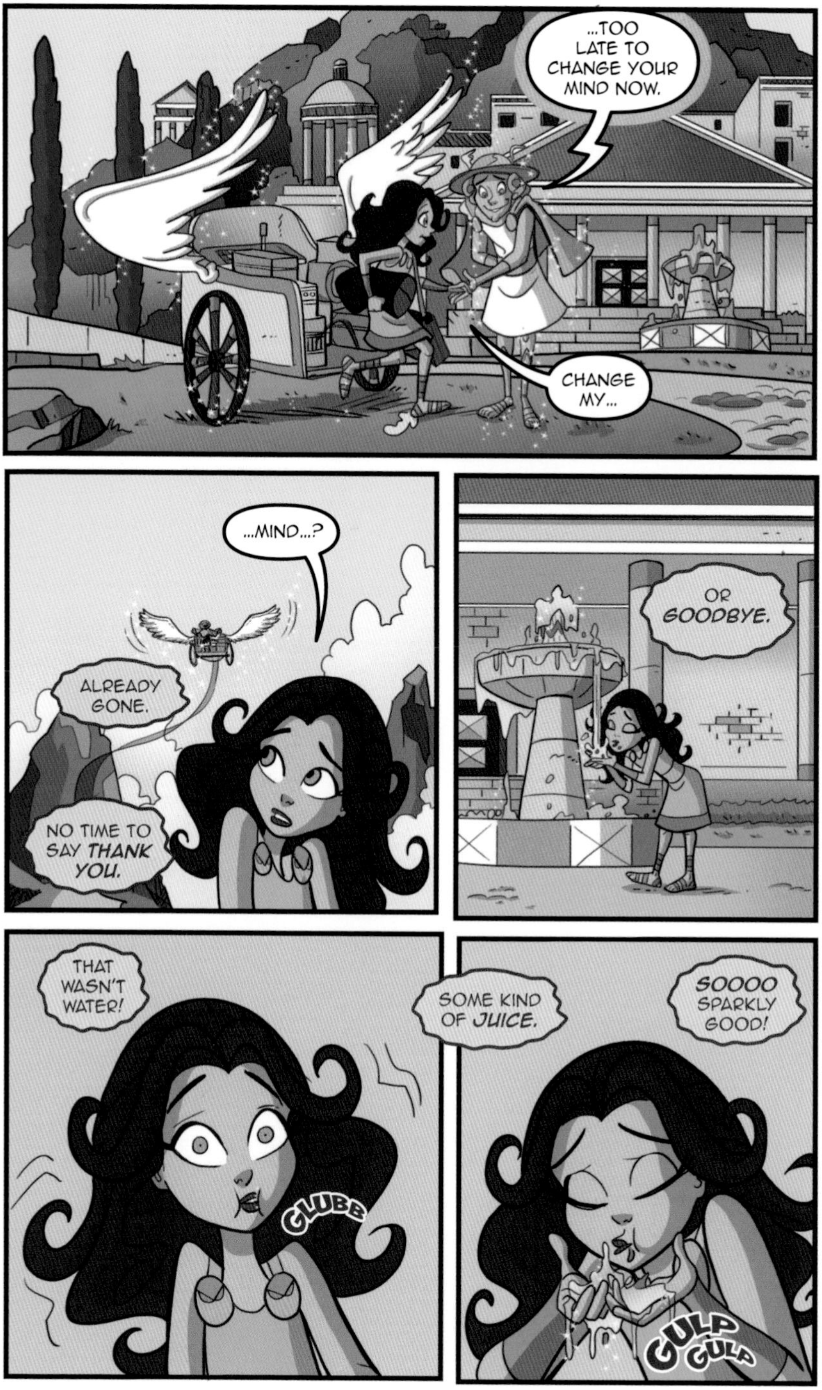
...TOO LATE TO CHANGE YOUR MIND NOW.
CHANGE MY...
...MIND...?
ALREADY GONE.
NO TIME TO SAY THANK YOU.
OR GOODBYE.
THAT WASN'T WATER!
GLUBB
SOME KIND OF JUICE.
SOOOO SPARKLY GOOD!
GULP GULP

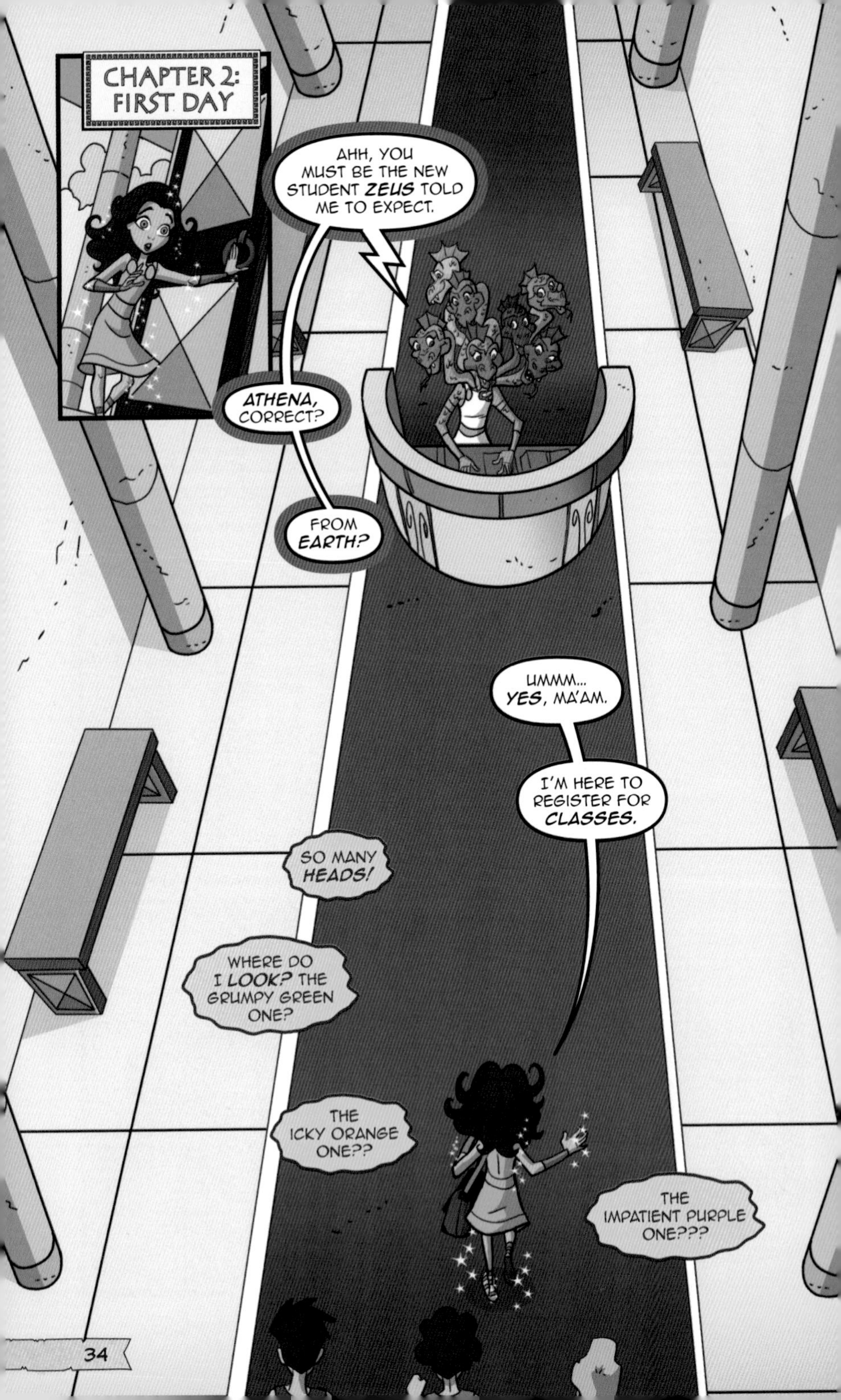

CHAPTER 2: FIRST DAY
AHH, YOU MUST BE THE NEW STUDENT ZEUS TOLD ME TO EXPECT.
ATHENA, CORRECT?
FROM EARTH?
UMMM... YES, MA'AM.
I'M HERE TO REGISTER FOR CLASSES.
SO MANY HEADS!
WHERE DO I LOOK? THE GRUMPY GREEN ONE?
THE ICKY ORANGE ONE??
THE IMPATIENT PURPLE ONE???

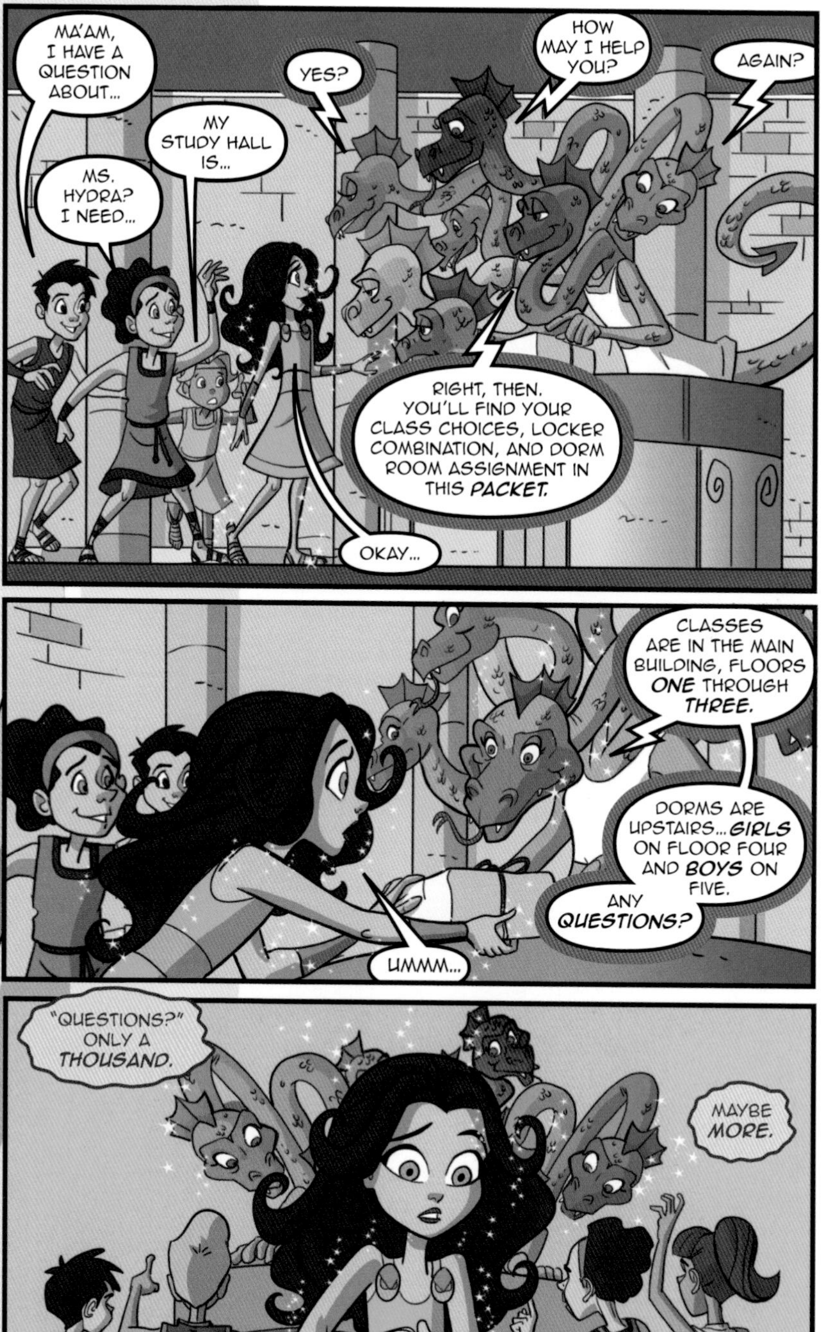
MA'AM, I HAVE A QUESTION ABOUT...
MS. HYDRA? I NEED...
MY STUDY HALL IS...
YES?
HOW MAY I HELP YOU?
AGAIN?
RIGHT, THEN. YOU'LL FIND YOUR CLASS CHOICES, LOCKER COMBINATION, AND DORM ROOM ASSIGNMENT IN THIS *PACKET.*
OKAY...
CLASSES ARE IN THE MAIN BUILDING, FLOORS *ONE* THROUGH *THREE.*
DORMS ARE UPSTAIRS...*GIRLS* ON FLOOR FOUR AND *BOYS* ON FIVE.
ANY *QUESTIONS?*
UMMM...
"QUESTIONS?" ONLY A *THOUSAND.*
MAYBE *MORE.*

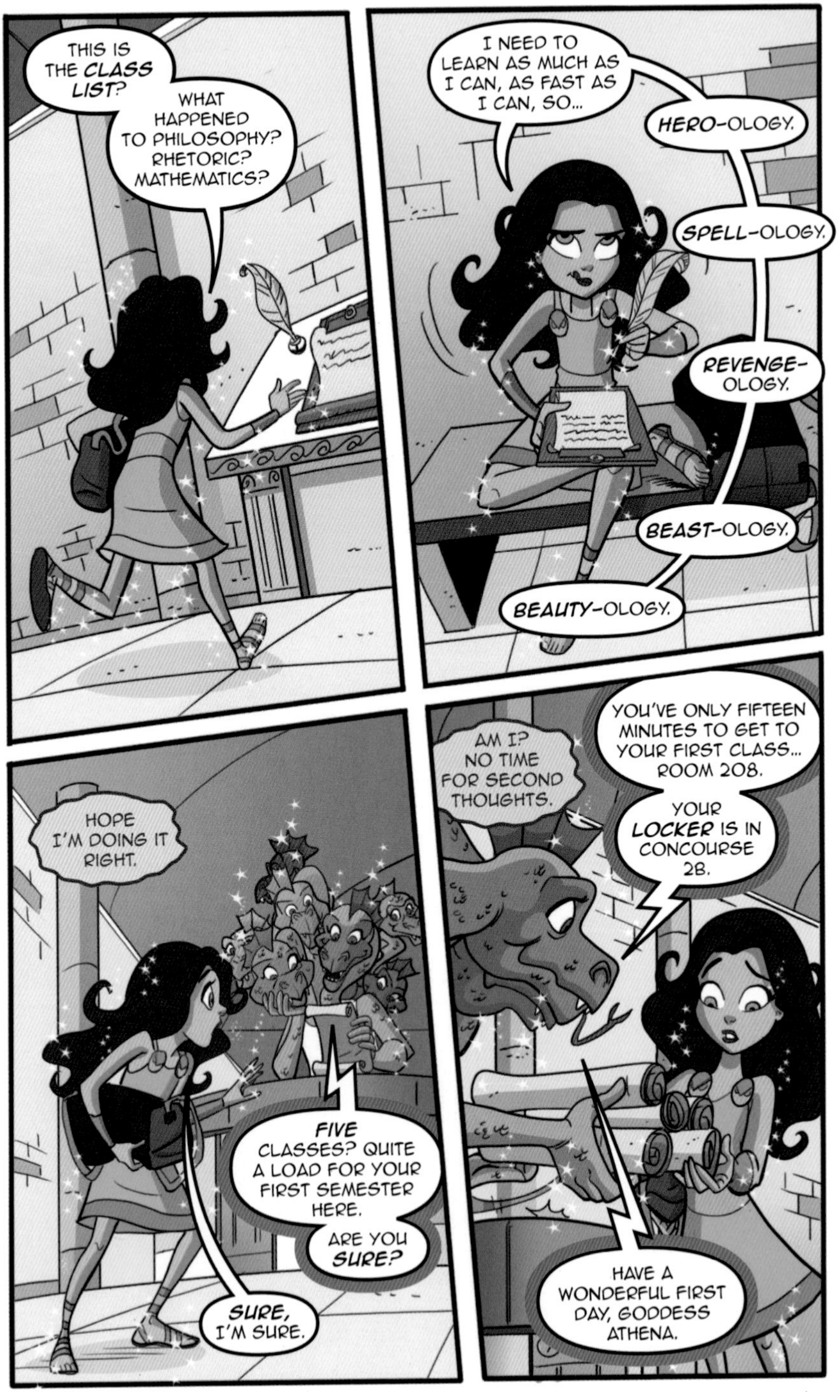
THIS IS THE CLASS LIST?
WHAT HAPPENED TO PHILOSOPHY? RHETORIC? MATHEMATICS?
I NEED TO LEARN AS MUCH AS I CAN, AS FAST AS I CAN, SO...
HERO-OLOGY.
SPELL-OLOGY.
REVENGE-OLOGY.
BEAST-OLOGY.
BEAUTY-OLOGY.
HOPE I'M DOING IT RIGHT.
FIVE CLASSES? QUITE A LOAD FOR YOUR FIRST SEMESTER HERE.
ARE YOU SURE?
SURE, I'M SURE.
AM I? NO TIME FOR SECOND THOUGHTS.
YOU'VE ONLY FIFTEEN MINUTES TO GET TO YOUR FIRST CLASS... ROOM 208.
YOUR LOCKER IS IN CONCOURSE 2B.
HAVE A WONDERFUL FIRST DAY, GODDESS ATHENA.

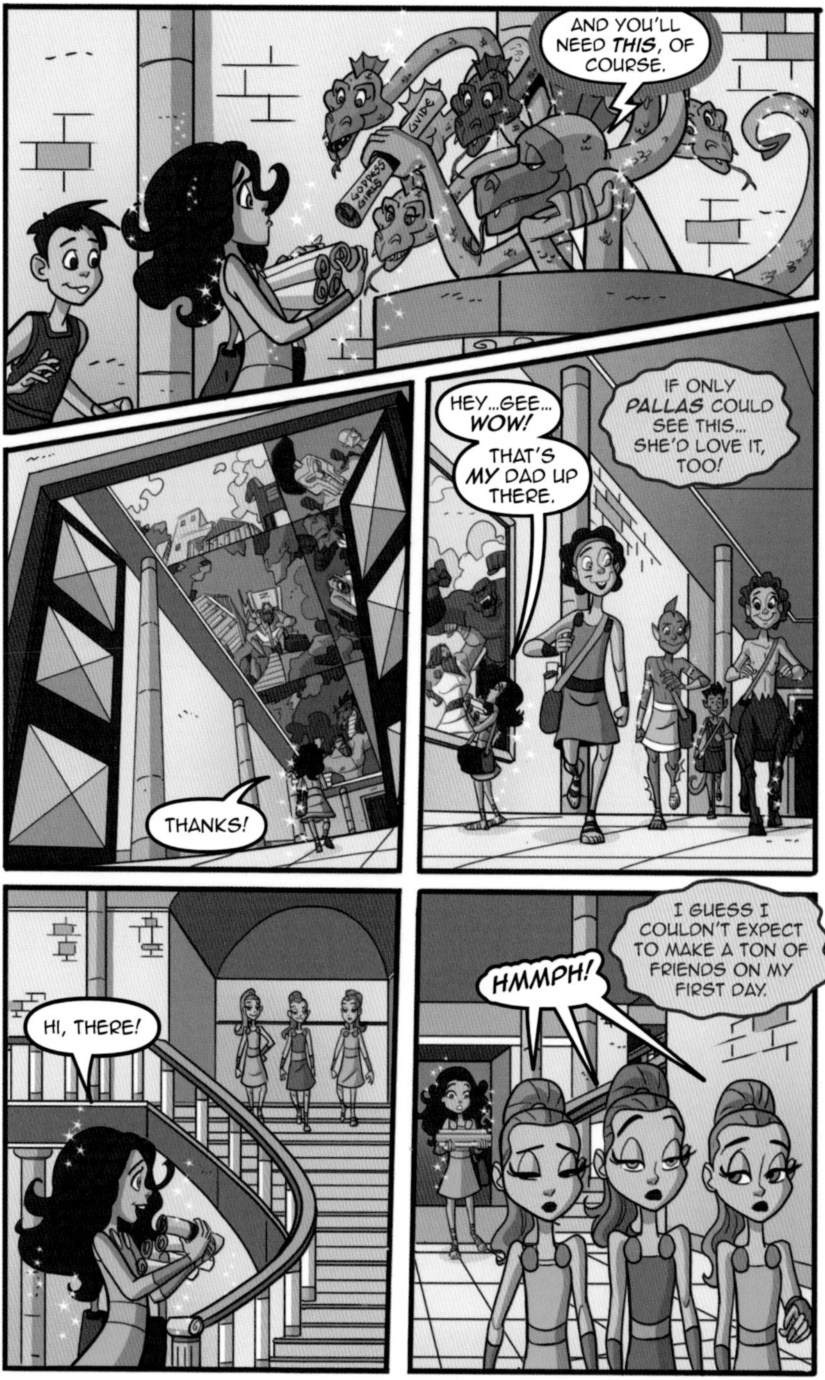
AND YOU'LL NEED THIS, OF COURSE.
GODDESS GIRLS GUIDE
THANKS!
HEY...GEE... WOW!
THAT'S MY DAD UP THERE.
IF ONLY PALLAS COULD SEE THIS... SHE'D LOVE IT, TOO!
HI, THERE!
HMMPH!
I GUESS I COULDN'T EXPECT TO MAKE A TON OF FRIENDS ON MY FIRST DAY.

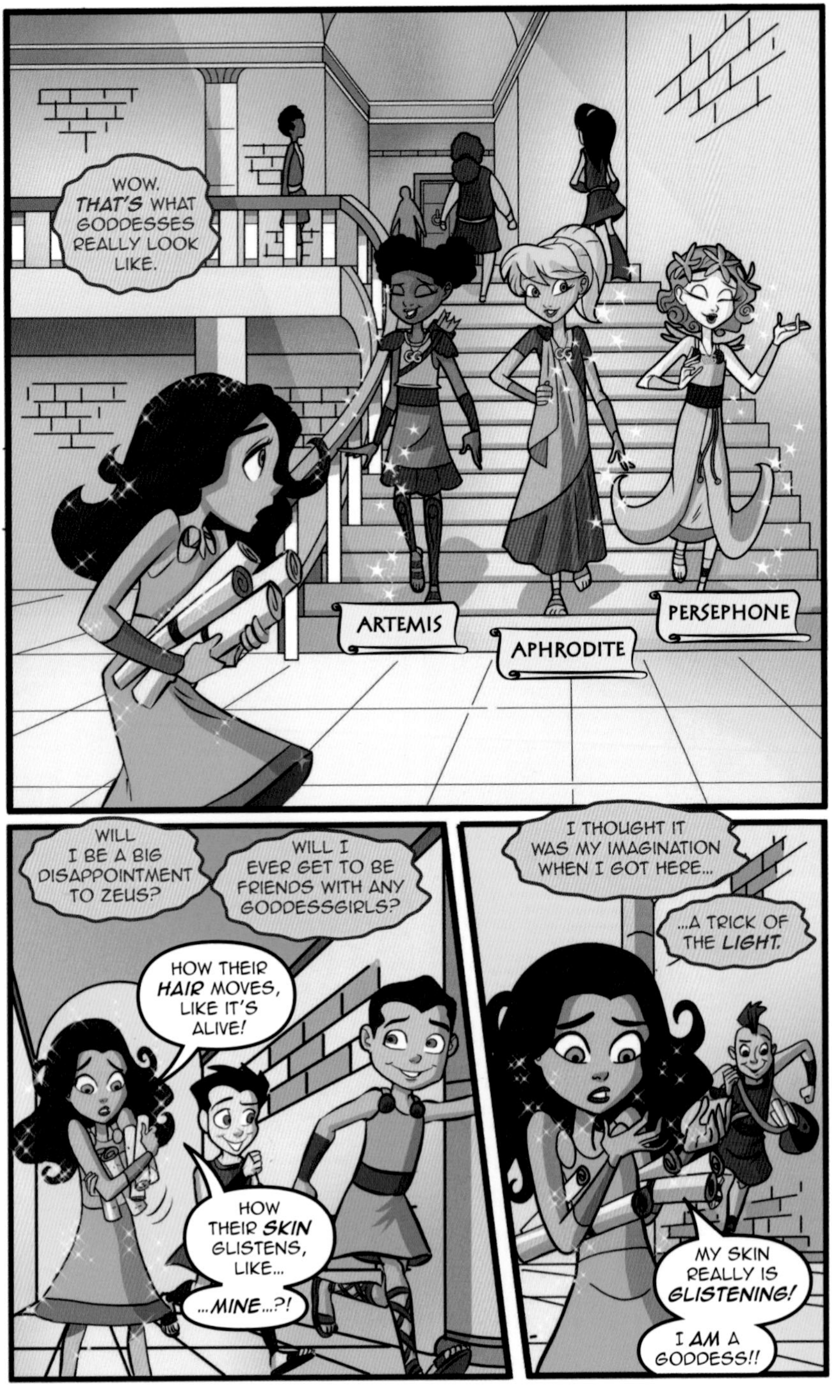
WOW. THAT'S WHAT GODDESSES REALLY LOOK LIKE.
ARTEMIS
APHRODITE
PERSEPHONE
WILL I BE A BIG DISAPPOINTMENT TO ZEUS?
WILL I EVER GET TO BE FRIENDS WITH ANY GODDESSGIRLS?
HOW THEIR HAIR MOVES, LIKE IT'S ALIVE!
HOW THEIR SKIN GLISTENS, LIKE...
...MINE...?!
I THOUGHT IT WAS MY IMAGINATION WHEN I GOT HERE...
...A TRICK OF THE LIGHT.
MY SKIN REALLY IS GLISTENING!
I AM A GODDESS!!

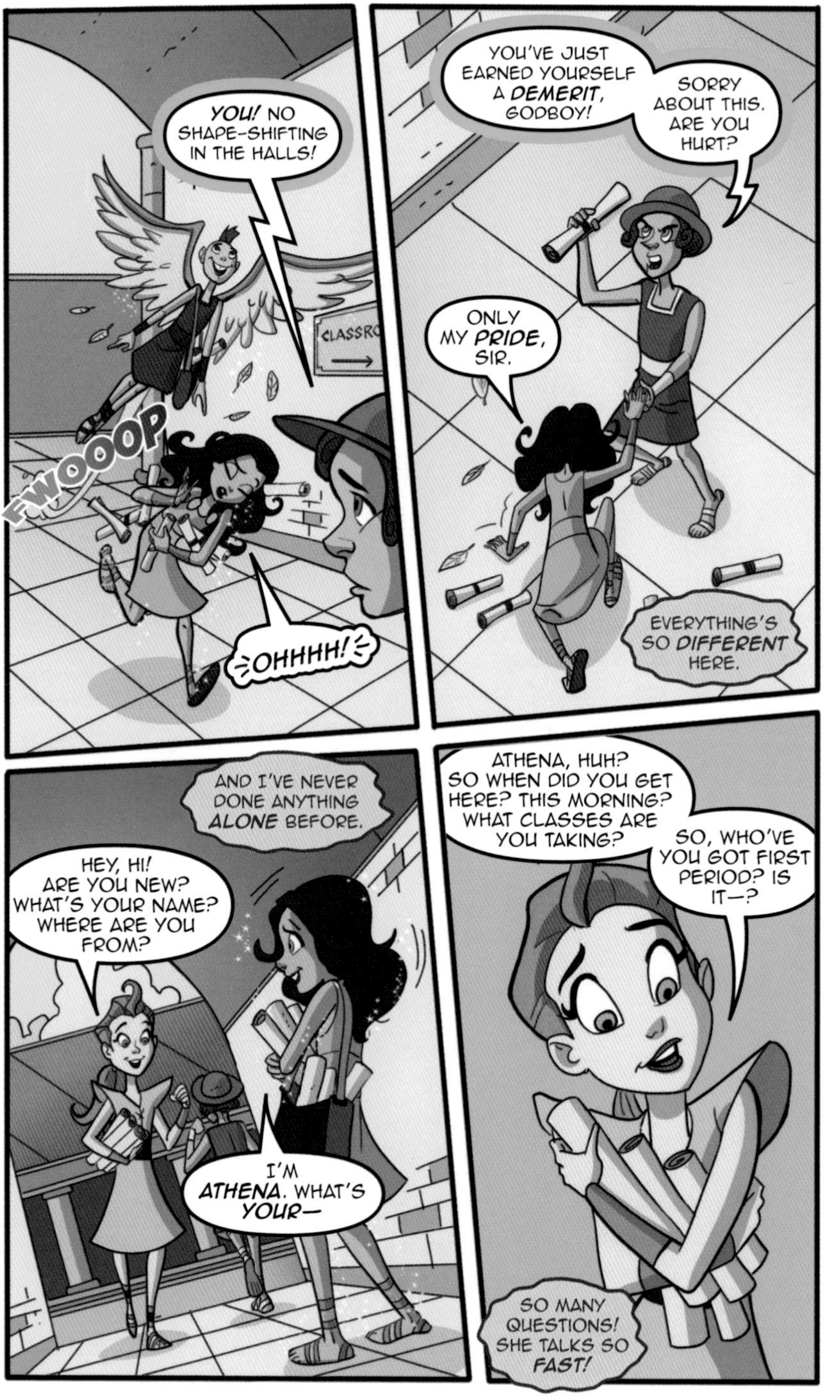
YOU! NO SHAPE-SHIFTING IN THE HALLS!
FWOOOP
OHHHH!
CLASSRO
YOU'VE JUST EARNED YOURSELF A DEMERIT, GODBOY!
SORRY ABOUT THIS. ARE YOU HURT?
ONLY MY PRIDE, SIR.
EVERYTHING'S SO DIFFERENT HERE.
AND I'VE NEVER DONE ANYTHING ALONE BEFORE.
HEY, HI! ARE YOU NEW? WHAT'S YOUR NAME? WHERE ARE YOU FROM?
I'M ATHENA. WHAT'S YOUR—
ATHENA, HUH? SO WHEN DID YOU GET HERE? THIS MORNING? WHAT CLASSES ARE YOU TAKING?
SO, WHO'VE YOU GOT FIRST PERIOD? IS IT—?
SO MANY QUESTIONS! SHE TALKS SO FAST!

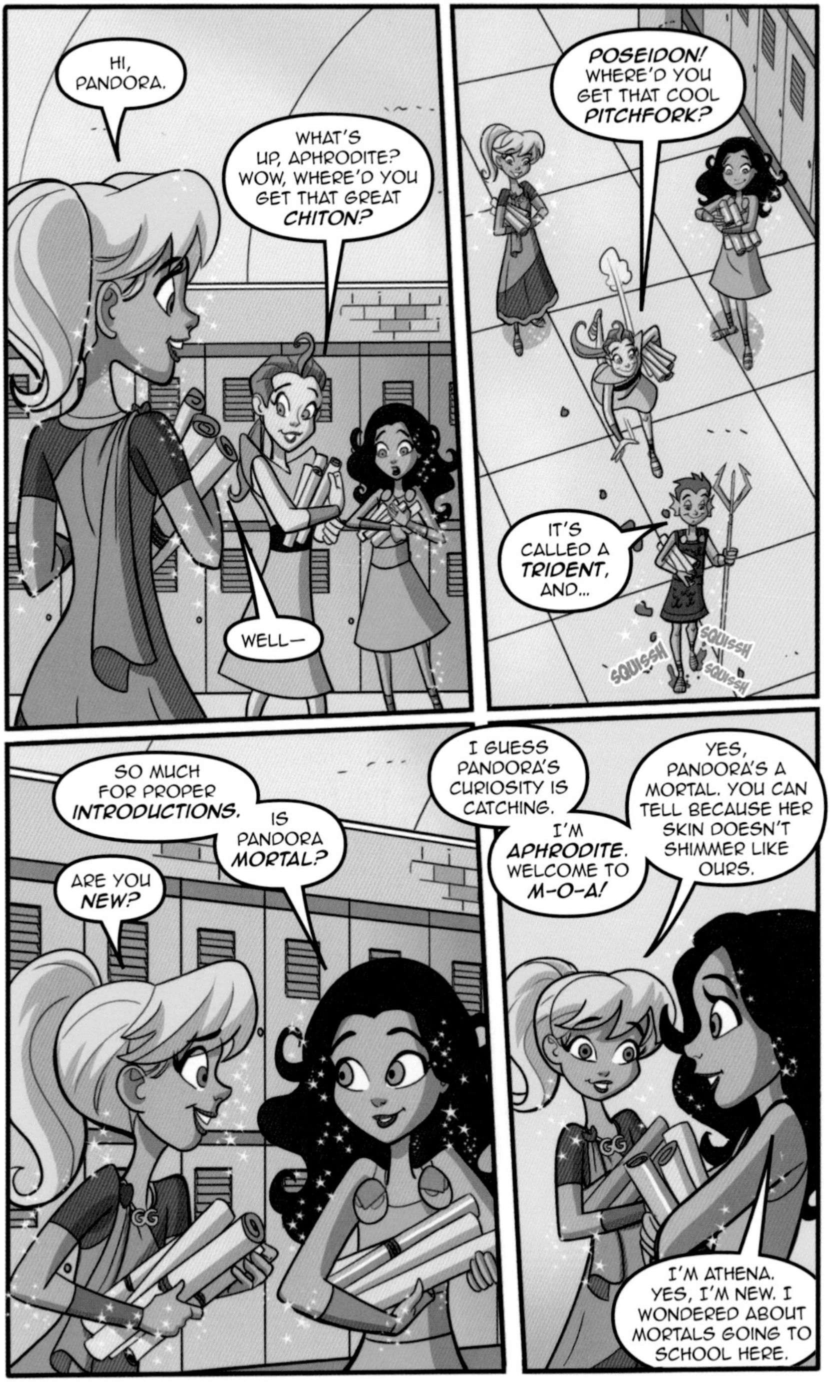

HI, PANDORA.
WHAT'S UP, APHRODITE? WOW, WHERE'D YOU GET THAT GREAT CHITON?
WELL—
POSEIDON! WHERE'D YOU GET THAT COOL PITCHFORK?
IT'S CALLED A TRIDENT, AND...
SQUISSH
SQUISSH
SQUISSH
SO MUCH FOR PROPER INTRODUCTIONS.
IS PANDORA MORTAL?
ARE YOU NEW?
I GUESS PANDORA'S CURIOSITY IS CATCHING.
I'M APHRODITE. WELCOME TO M-O-A!
YES, PANDORA'S A MORTAL. YOU CAN TELL BECAUSE HER SKIN DOESN'T SHIMMER LIKE OURS.
I'M ATHENA. YES, I'M NEW. I WONDERED ABOUT MORTALS GOING TO SCHOOL HERE.

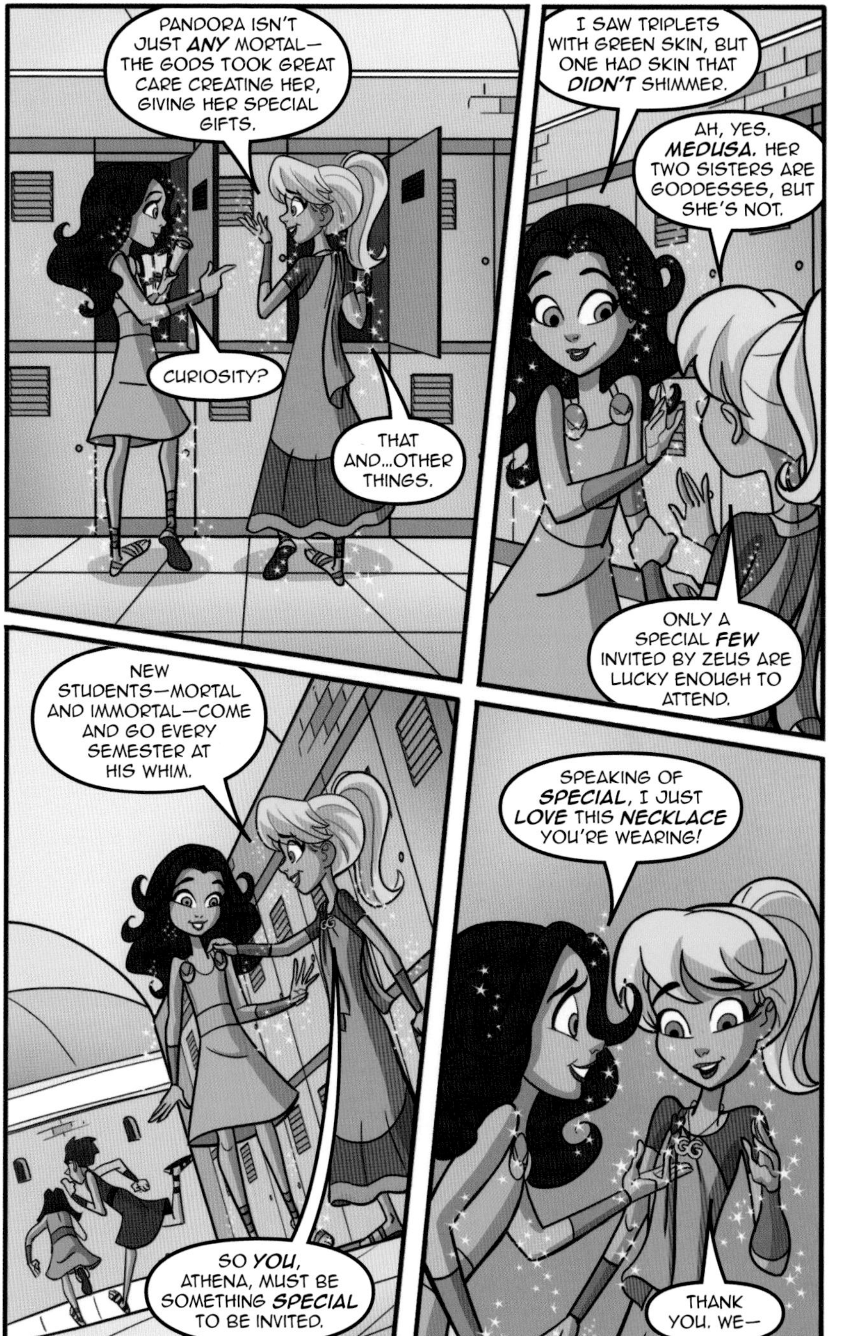
PANDORA ISN'T JUST *ANY* MORTAL—THE GODS TOOK GREAT CARE CREATING HER, GIVING HER SPECIAL GIFTS.
CURIOSITY?
THAT AND...OTHER THINGS.
I SAW TRIPLETS WITH GREEN SKIN, BUT ONE HAD SKIN THAT *DIDN'T* SHIMMER.
AH, YES. *MEDUSA.* HER TWO SISTERS ARE GODDESSES, BUT SHE'S NOT.
ONLY A SPECIAL *FEW* INVITED BY ZEUS ARE LUCKY ENOUGH TO ATTEND.
NEW STUDENTS—MORTAL AND IMMORTAL—COME AND GO EVERY SEMESTER AT HIS WHIM.
SO *YOU*, ATHENA, MUST BE SOMETHING *SPECIAL* TO BE INVITED.
SPEAKING OF *SPECIAL*, I JUST *LOVE* THIS *NECKLACE* YOU'RE WEARING!
THANK YOU. WE—

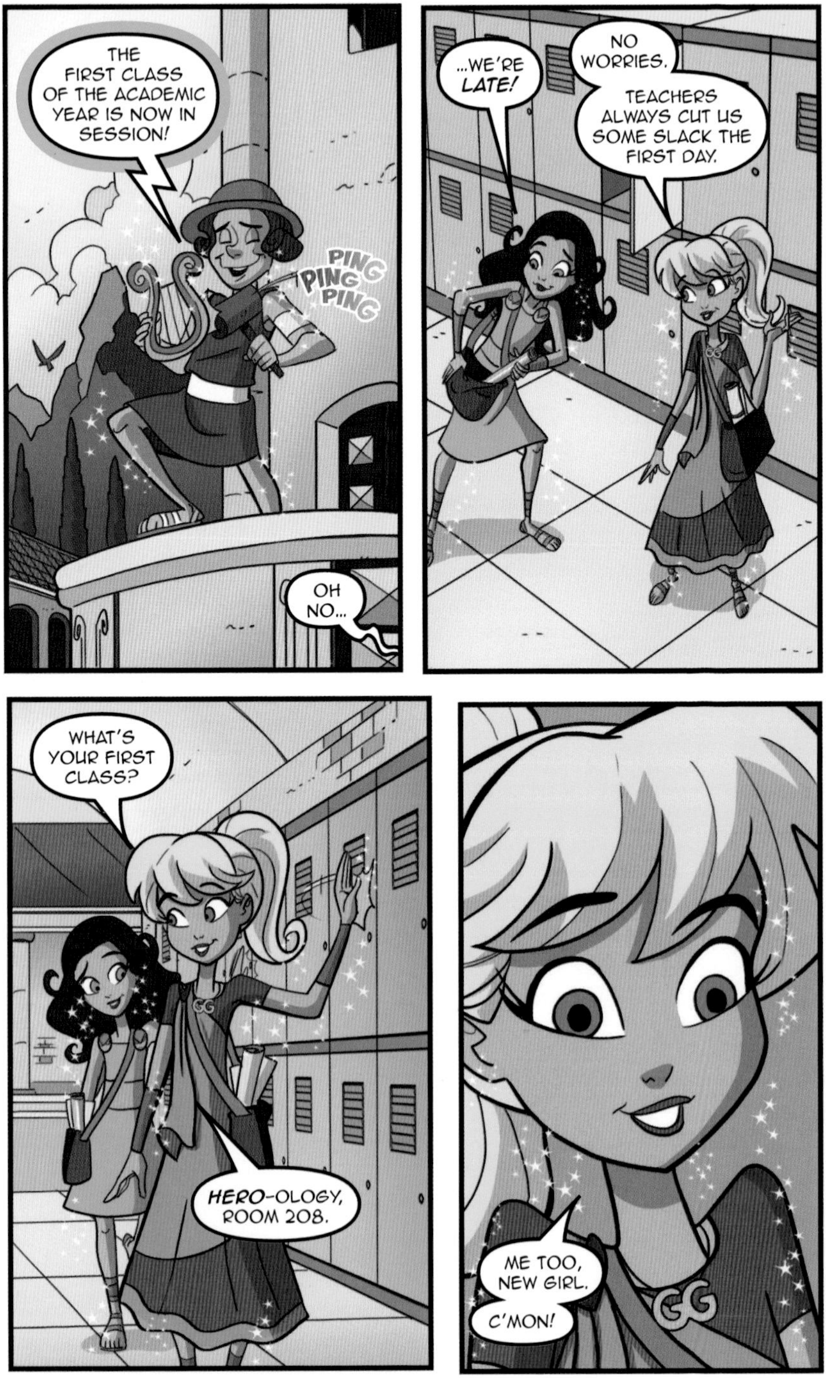
THE FIRST CLASS OF THE ACADEMIC YEAR IS NOW IN SESSION!
PING PING PING
OH NO...
...WE'RE *LATE!*
NO WORRIES.
TEACHERS ALWAYS CUT US SOME SLACK THE FIRST DAY.
WHAT'S YOUR FIRST CLASS?
HERO-OLOGY, ROOM 208.
ME TOO, NEW GIRL.
C'MON!

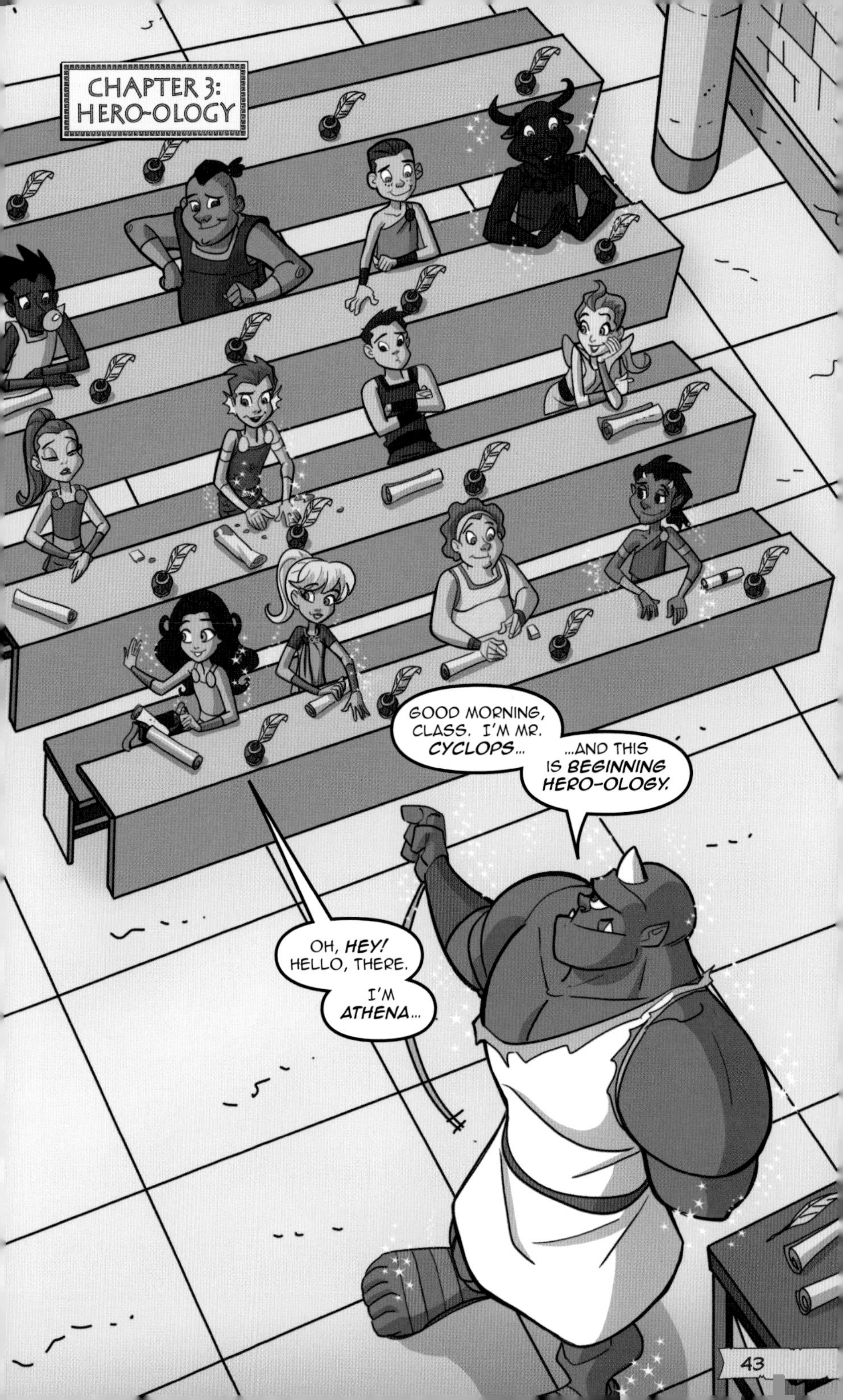

CHAPTER 3:
HERO-OLOGY
GOOD MORNING, CLASS. I'M MR. CYCLOPS...
...AND THIS IS BEGINNING HERO-OLOGY.
OH, HEY! HELLO, THERE.
I'M ATHENA...

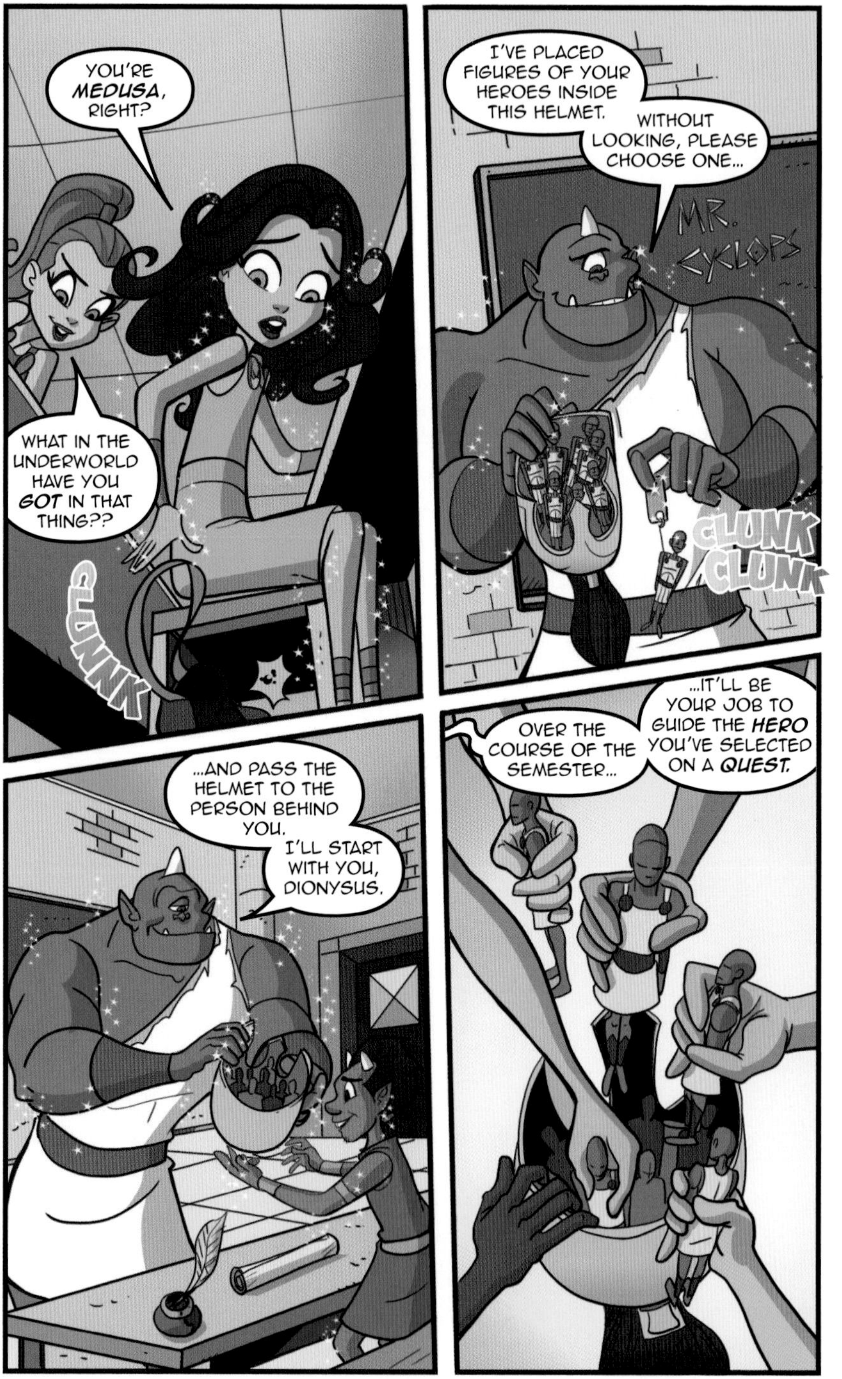
YOU'RE MEDUSA, RIGHT?
WHAT IN THE UNDERWORLD HAVE YOU GOT IN THAT THING??
CLUNNK
I'VE PLACED FIGURES OF YOUR HEROES INSIDE THIS HELMET.
WITHOUT LOOKING, PLEASE CHOOSE ONE...
MR. CYCLOPS
CLUNK CLUNK
...AND PASS THE HELMET TO THE PERSON BEHIND YOU.
I'LL START WITH YOU, DIONYSUS.
OVER THE COURSE OF THE SEMESTER...
...IT'LL BE YOUR JOB TO GUIDE THE HERO YOU'VE SELECTED ON A QUEST.

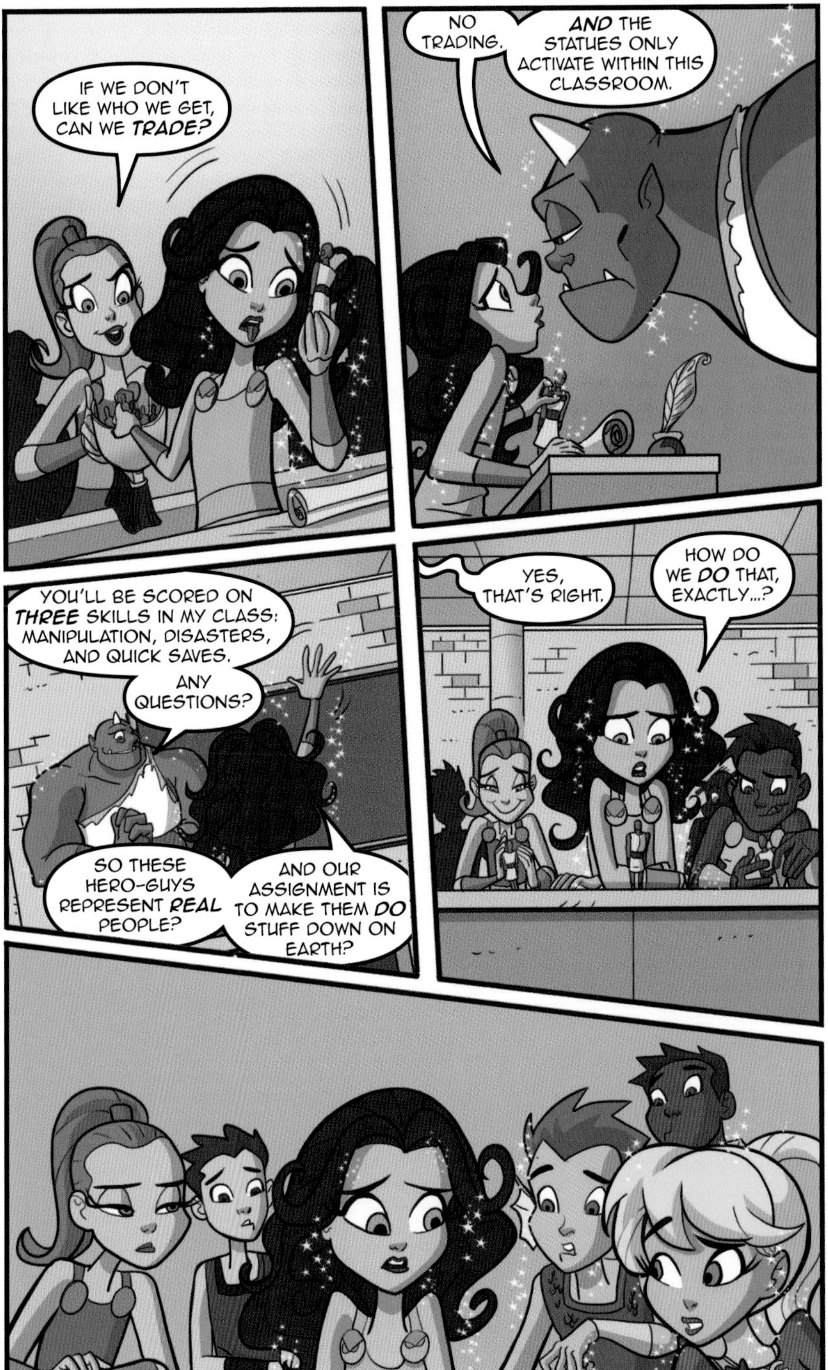
IF WE DON'T LIKE WHO WE GET, CAN WE *TRADE?*
NO TRADING.
AND THE STATUES ONLY ACTIVATE WITHIN THIS CLASSROOM.
YOU'LL BE SCORED ON *THREE* SKILLS IN MY CLASS: MANIPULATION, DISASTERS, AND QUICK SAVES.
ANY QUESTIONS?
SO THESE HERO-GUYS REPRESENT *REAL* PEOPLE?
AND OUR ASSIGNMENT IS TO MAKE THEM *DO* STUFF DOWN ON EARTH?
YES, THAT'S RIGHT.
HOW DO WE *DO* THAT, EXACTLY...?

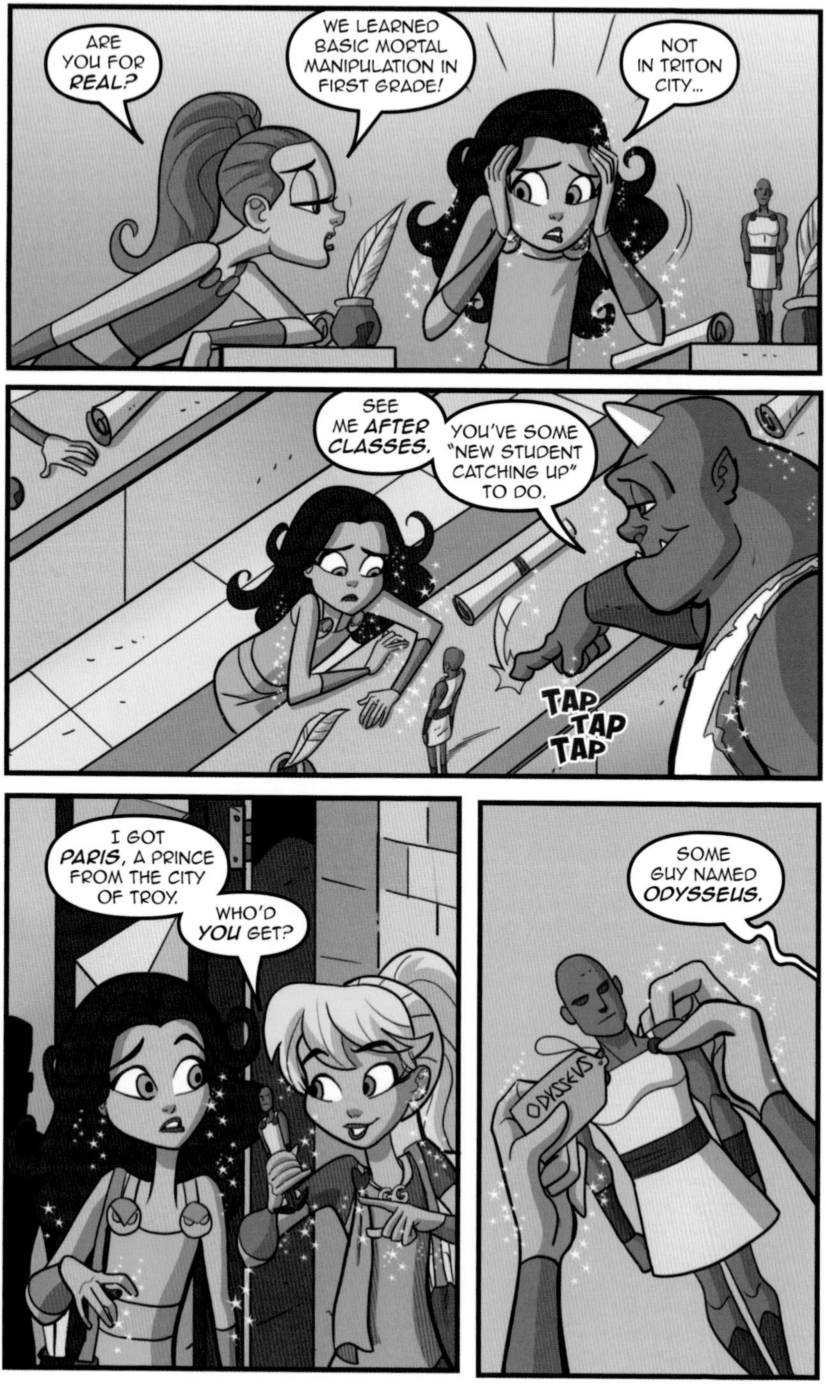

ARE YOU FOR REAL?
WE LEARNED BASIC MORTAL MANIPULATION IN FIRST GRADE!
NOT IN TRITON CITY...
SEE ME AFTER CLASSES.
YOU'VE SOME "NEW STUDENT CATCHING UP" TO DO.
TAP TAP TAP
I GOT PARIS, A PRINCE FROM THE CITY OF TROY.
WHO'D YOU GET?
SOME GUY NAMED ODYSSEUS.
ODYSSEUS

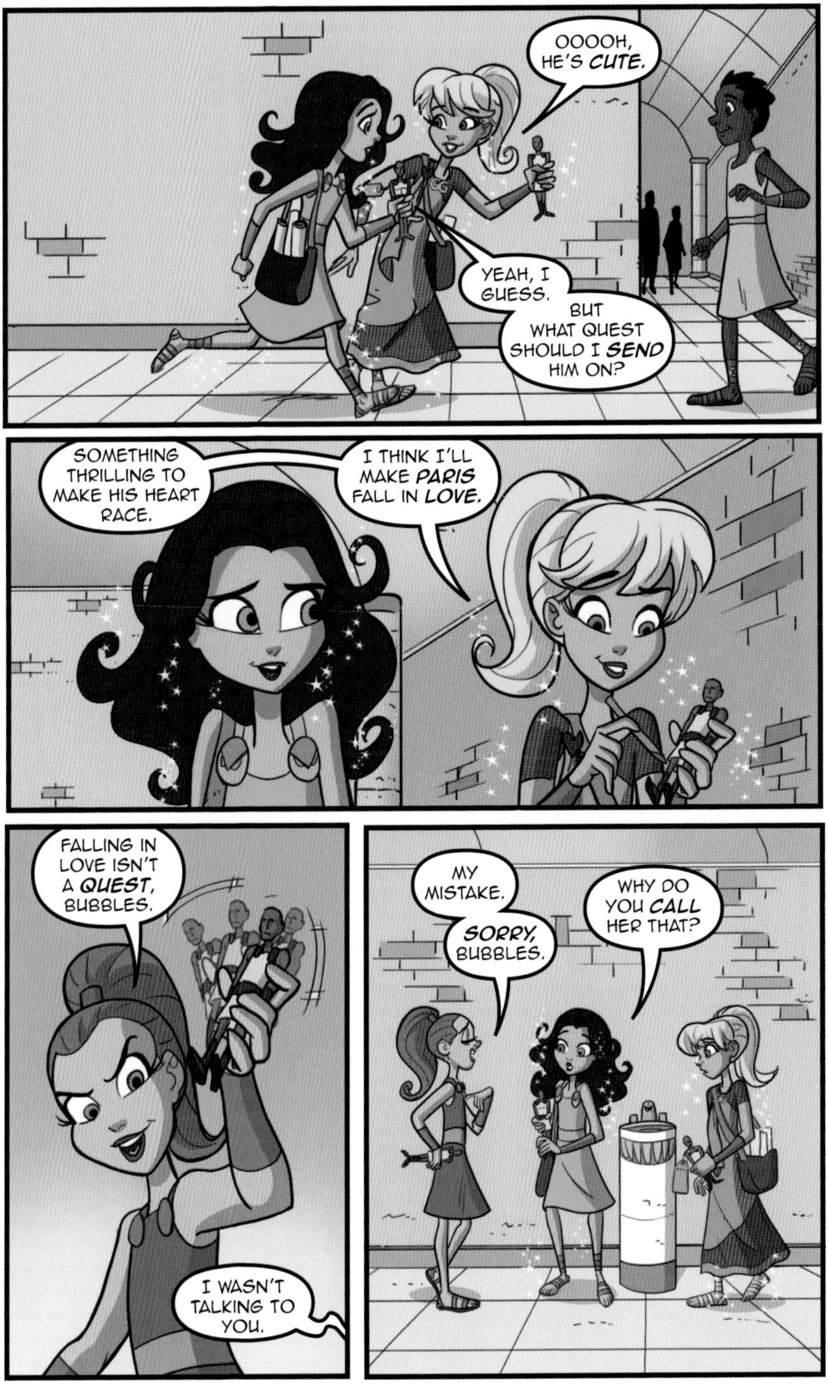
OOOOH, HE'S CUTE.
YEAH, I GUESS.
BUT WHAT QUEST SHOULD I SEND HIM ON?
SOMETHING THRILLING TO MAKE HIS HEART RACE.
I THINK I'LL MAKE PARIS FALL IN LOVE.
FALLING IN LOVE ISN'T A QUEST, BUBBLES.
I WASN'T TALKING TO YOU.
MY MISTAKE.
SORRY, BUBBLES.
WHY DO YOU CALL HER THAT?

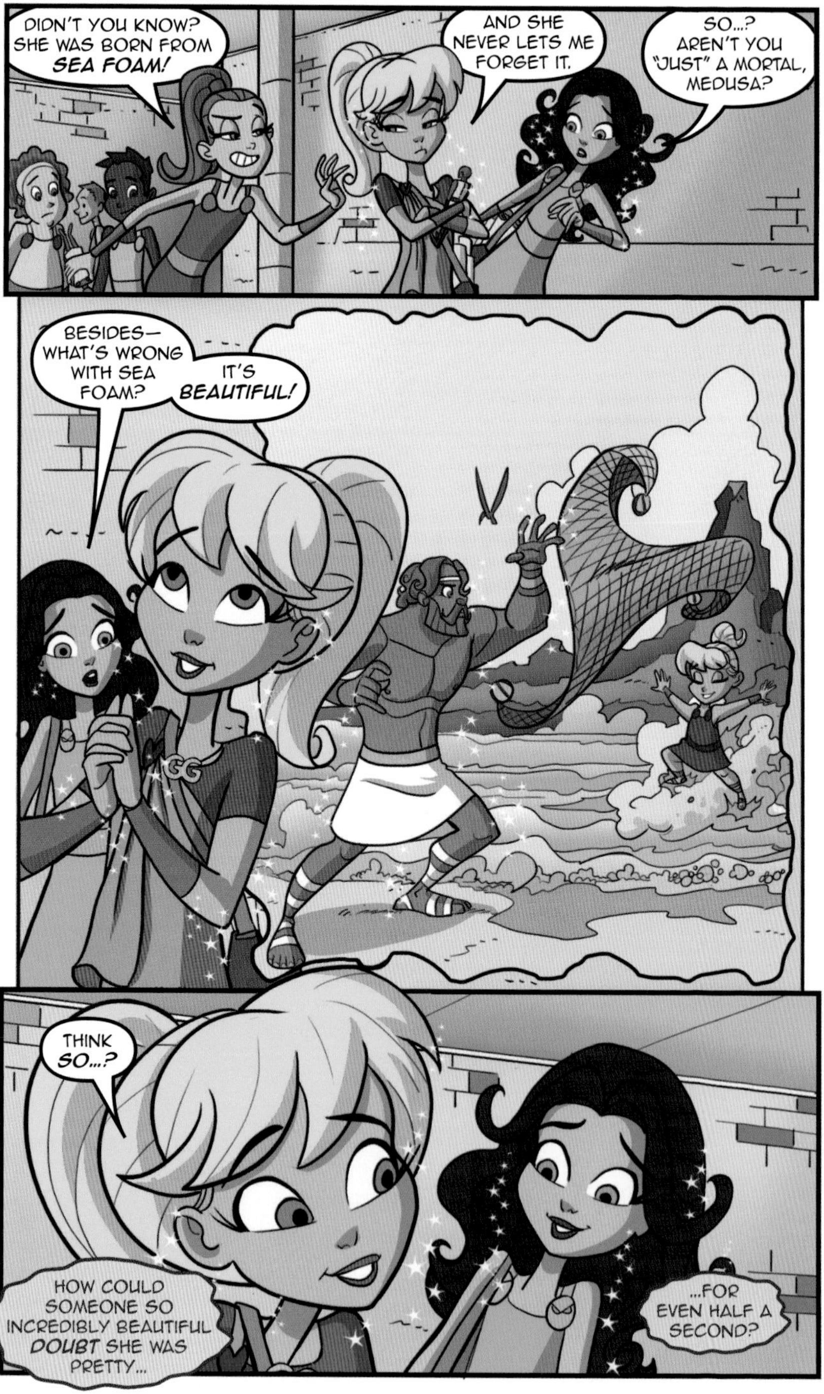
DIDN'T YOU KNOW? SHE WAS BORN FROM *SEA FOAM!*
AND SHE NEVER LETS ME FORGET IT.
SO...? AREN'T YOU "JUST" A MORTAL, MEDUSA?
BESIDES— WHAT'S WRONG WITH SEA FOAM?
IT'S *BEAUTIFUL!*
THINK *SO...?*
HOW COULD SOMEONE SO INCREDIBLY BEAUTIFUL *DOUBT* SHE WAS PRETTY...
...FOR EVEN HALF A SECOND?

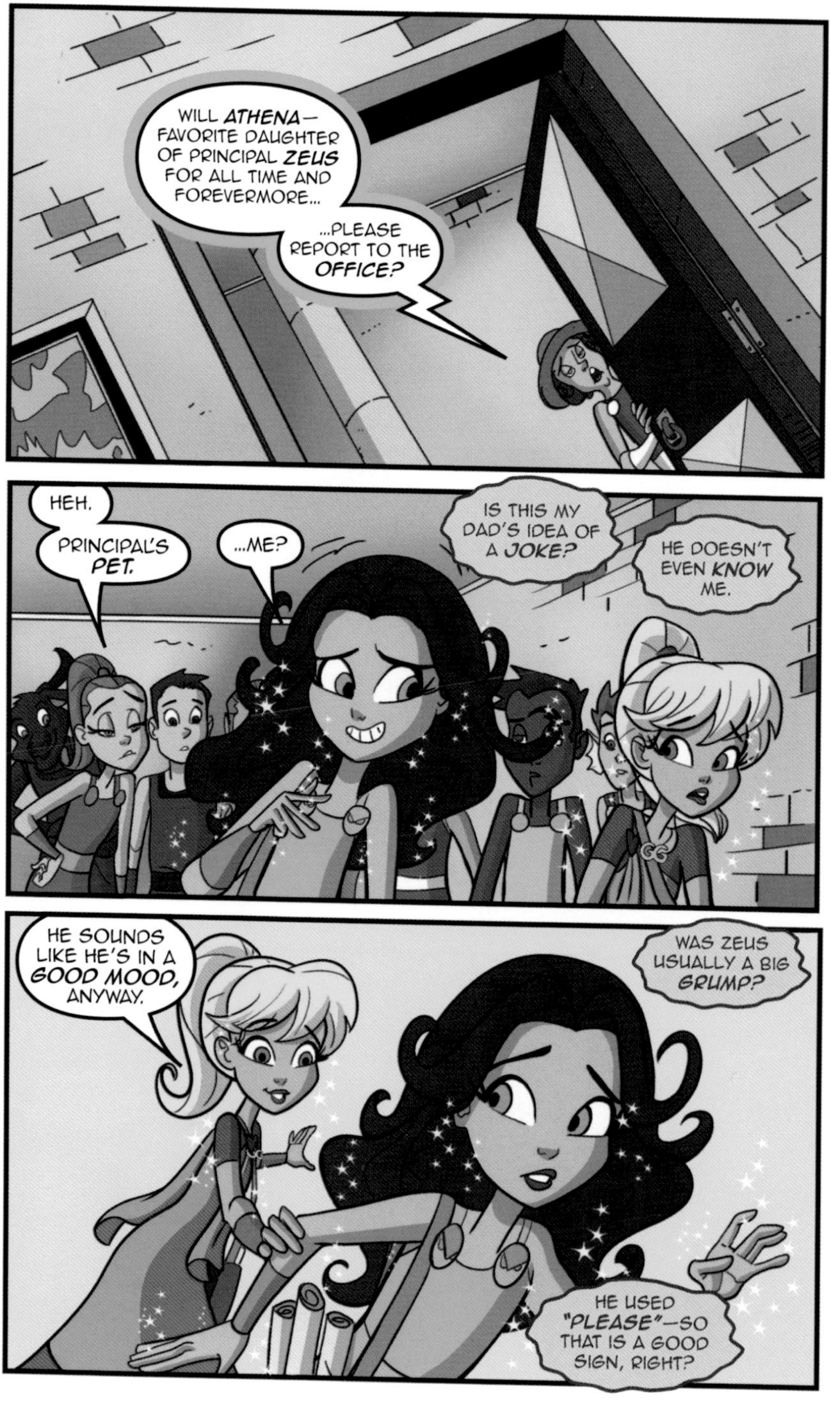
WILL ATHENA—FAVORITE DAUGHTER OF PRINCIPAL ZEUS FOR ALL TIME AND FOREVERMORE...
...PLEASE REPORT TO THE OFFICE?
HEH.
PRINCIPAL'S PET.
...ME?
IS THIS MY DAD'S IDEA OF A JOKE?
HE DOESN'T EVEN KNOW ME.
HE SOUNDS LIKE HE'S IN A GOOD MOOD, ANYWAY.
WAS ZEUS USUALLY A BIG GRUMP?
HE USED "PLEASE"—SO THAT IS A GOOD SIGN, RIGHT?

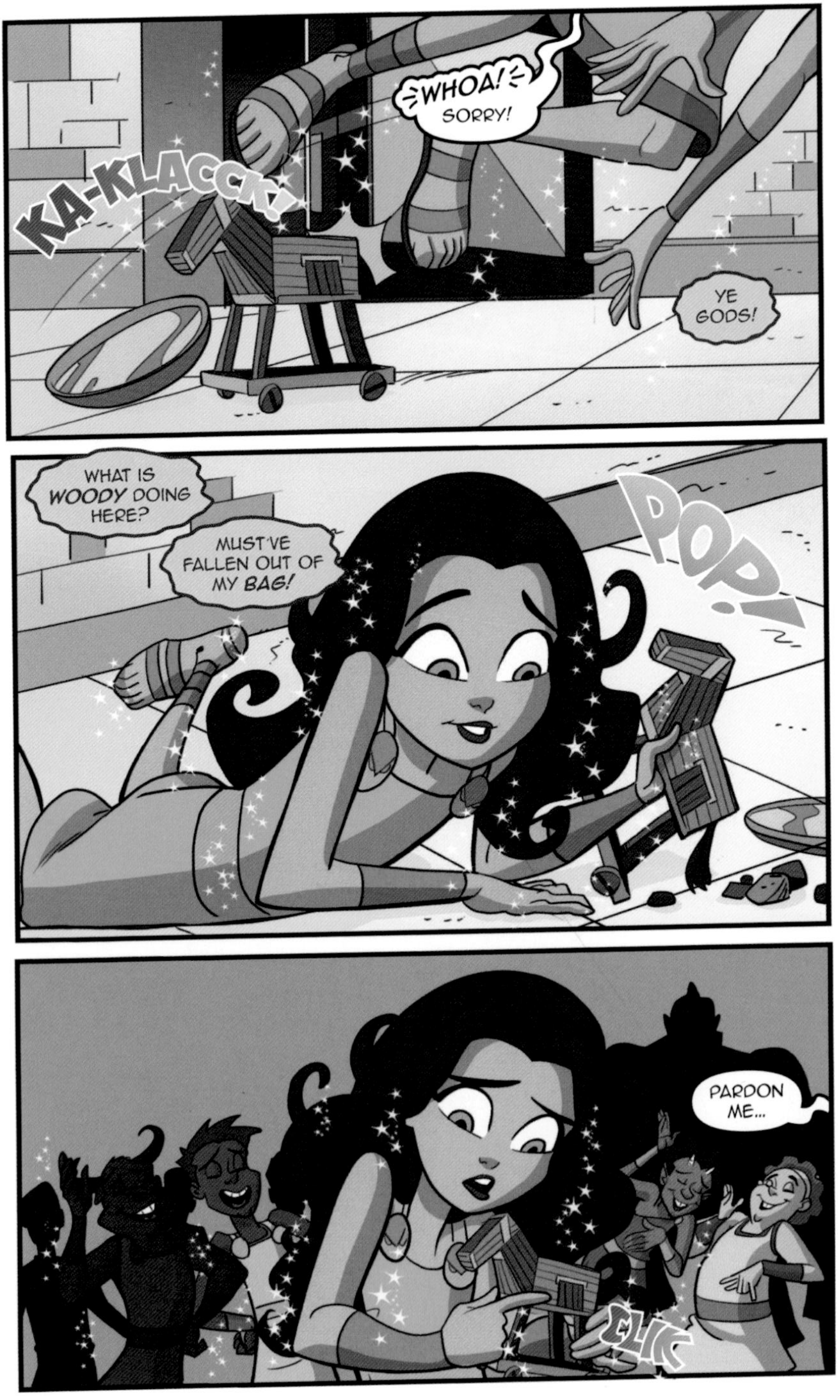

WHOA! SORRY!
KA-KLACCK!
YE GODS!
WHAT IS WOODY DOING HERE?
MUST'VE FALLEN OUT OF MY BAG!
POP!
PARDON ME...
CLIC

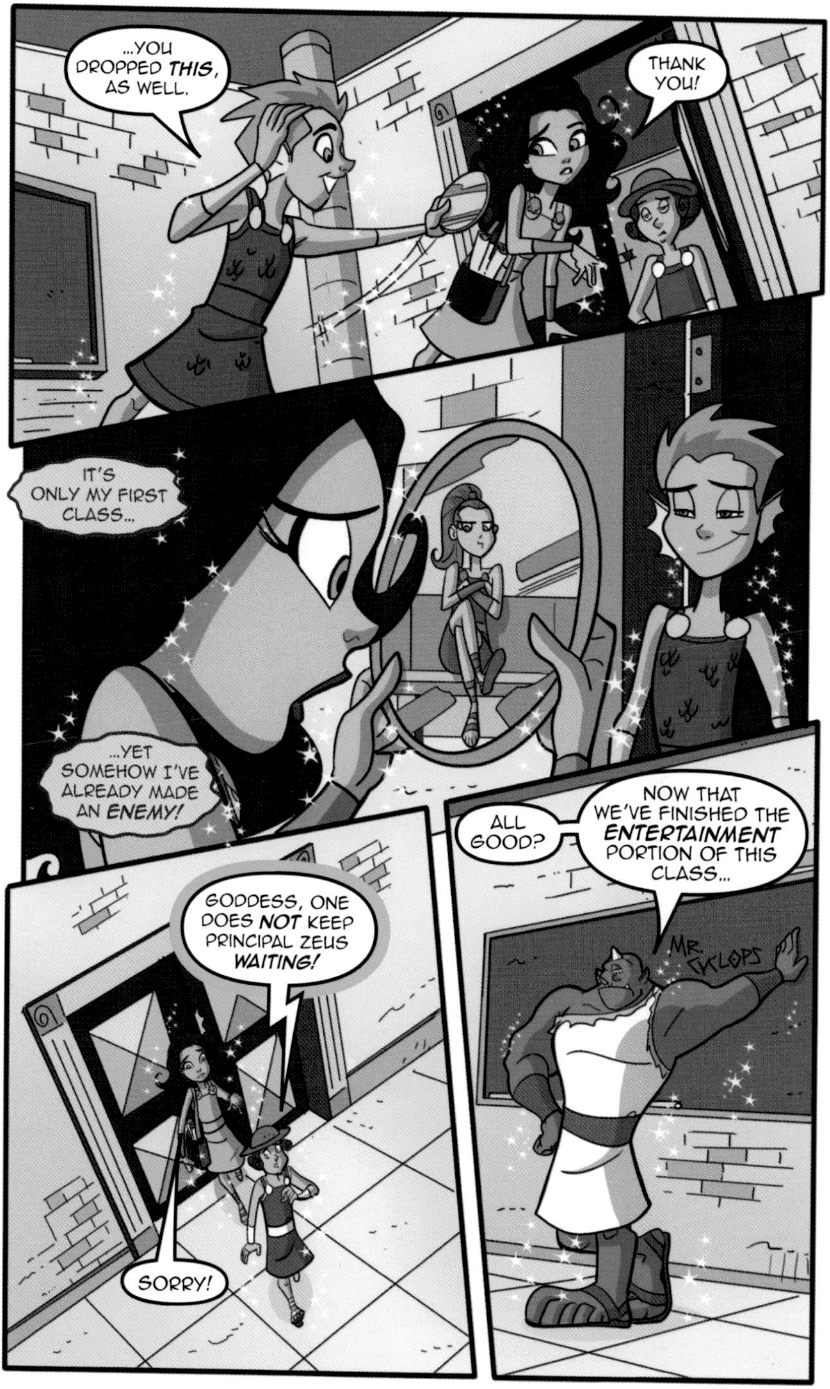
...YOU DROPPED *THIS*, AS WELL.
THANK YOU!
IT'S ONLY MY FIRST CLASS...
...YET SOMEHOW I'VE ALREADY MADE AN *ENEMY!*
GODDESS, ONE DOES *NOT* KEEP PRINCIPAL ZEUS *WAITING!*
SORRY!
ALL GOOD?
NOW THAT WE'VE FINISHED THE *ENTERTAINMENT* PORTION OF THIS CLASS...
MR. CYCLOPS

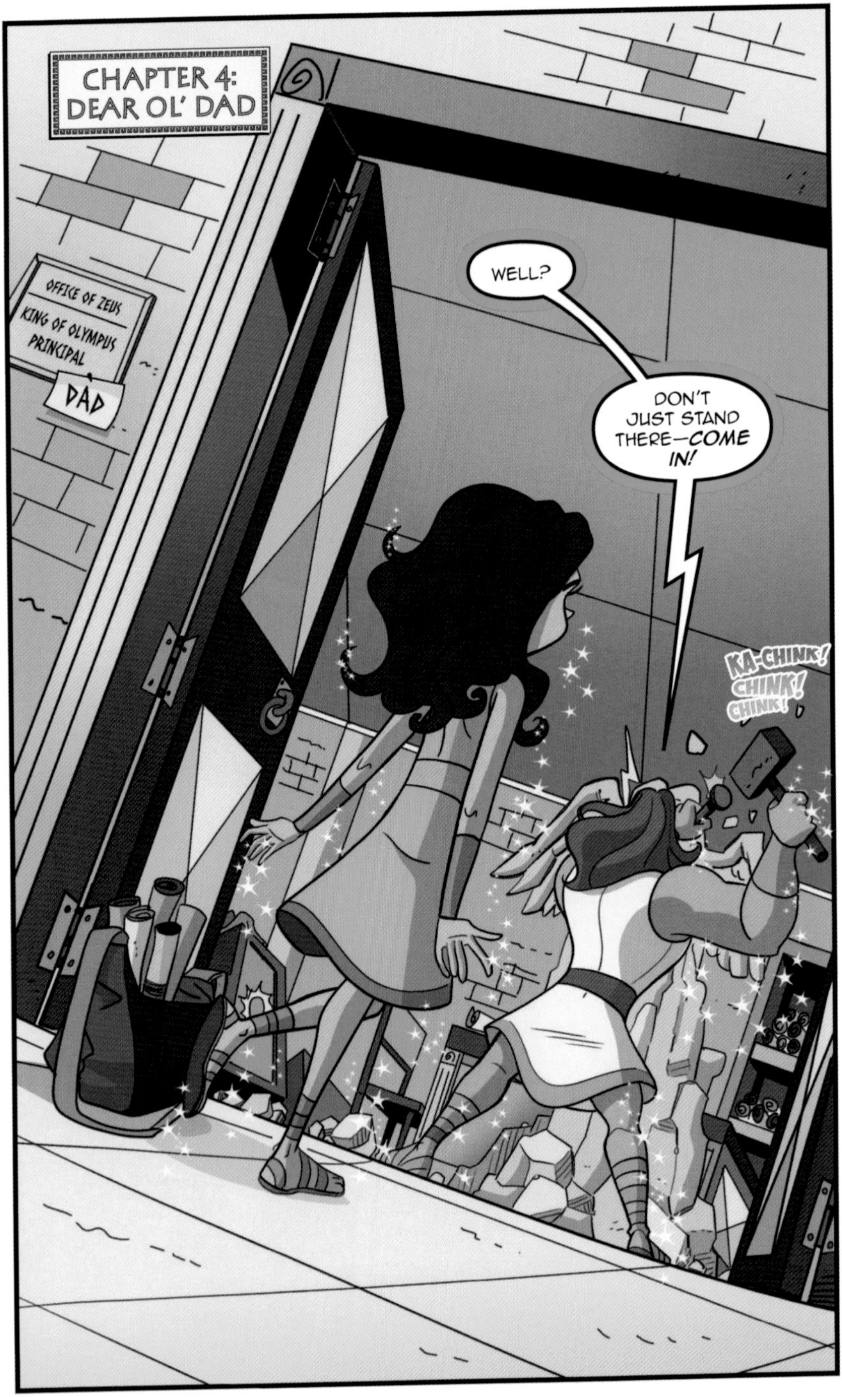
CHAPTER 4:
DEAR OL' DAD
OFFICE OF ZEUS
KING OF OLYMPUS
PRINCIPAL
DAD
WELL?
DON'T JUST STAND THERE—*COME IN!*
KA-CHINK! CHINK! CHINK!

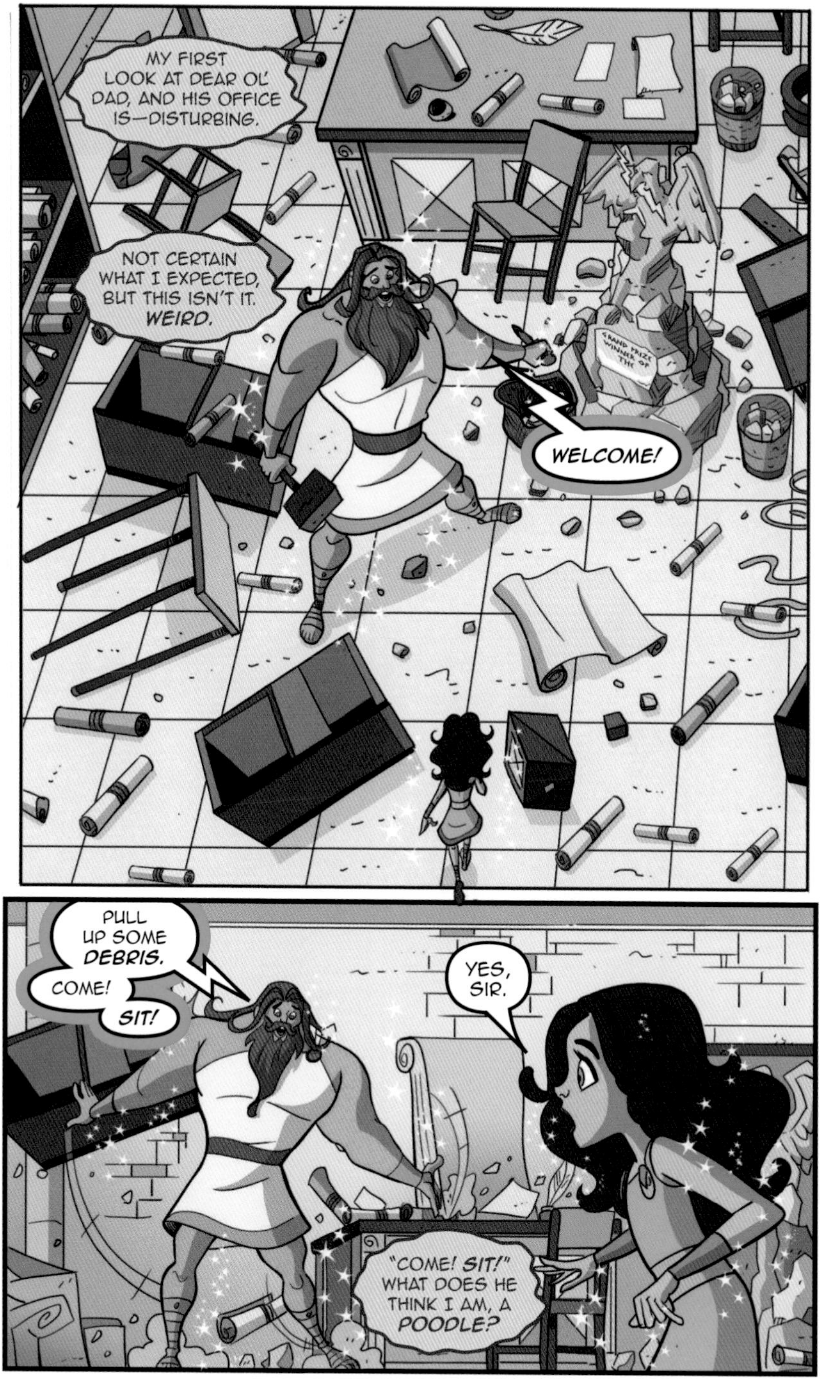
MY FIRST LOOK AT DEAR OL' DAD, AND HIS OFFICE IS—DISTURBING.
NOT CERTAIN WHAT I EXPECTED, BUT THIS ISN'T IT. *WEIRD.*
WELCOME!
PULL UP SOME *DEBRIS.*
COME!
SIT!
YES, SIR.
"COME! *SIT!*" WHAT DOES HE THINK I AM, A *POODLE?*

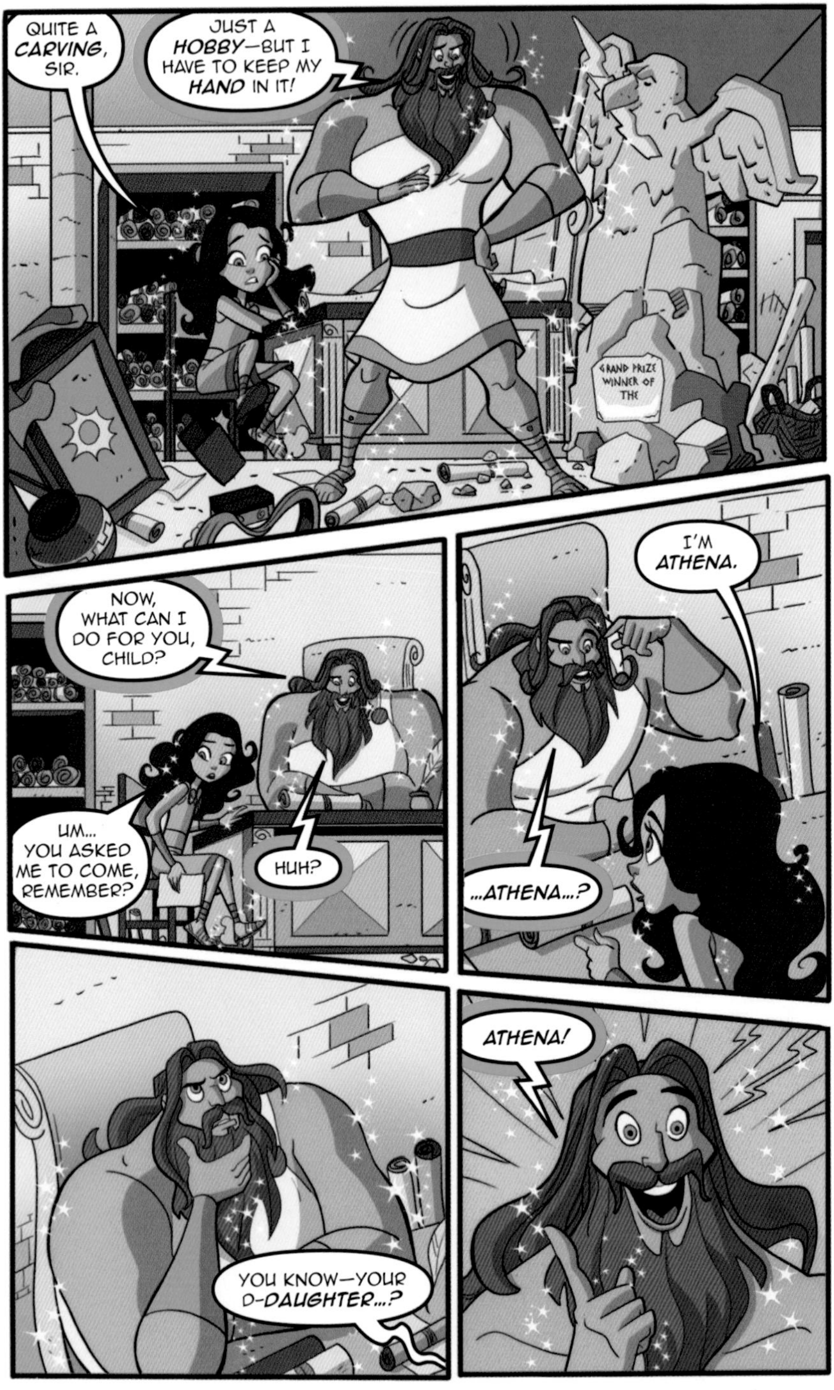
QUITE A CARVING, SIR.
JUST A HOBBY—BUT I HAVE TO KEEP MY HAND IN IT!
GRAND PRIZE WINNER OF THE
NOW, WHAT CAN I DO FOR YOU, CHILD?
UM... YOU ASKED ME TO COME, REMEMBER?
HUH?
I'M ATHENA.
...ATHENA...?
YOU KNOW—YOUR D-DAUGHTER...?
ATHENA!

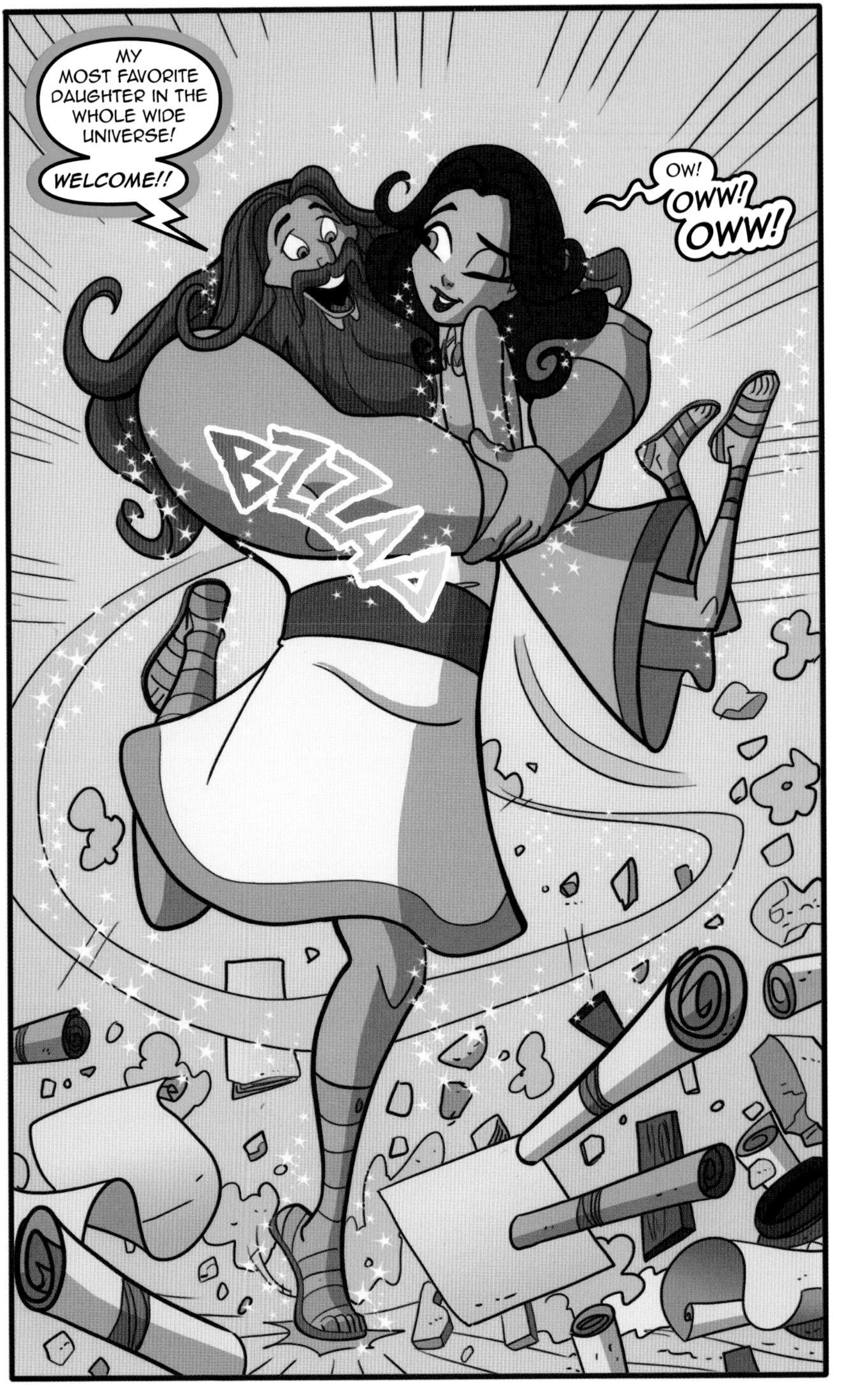
MY MOST FAVORITE DAUGHTER IN THE WHOLE WIDE UNIVERSE!
WELCOME!!
OW! OWW! OWW!
BZZAP

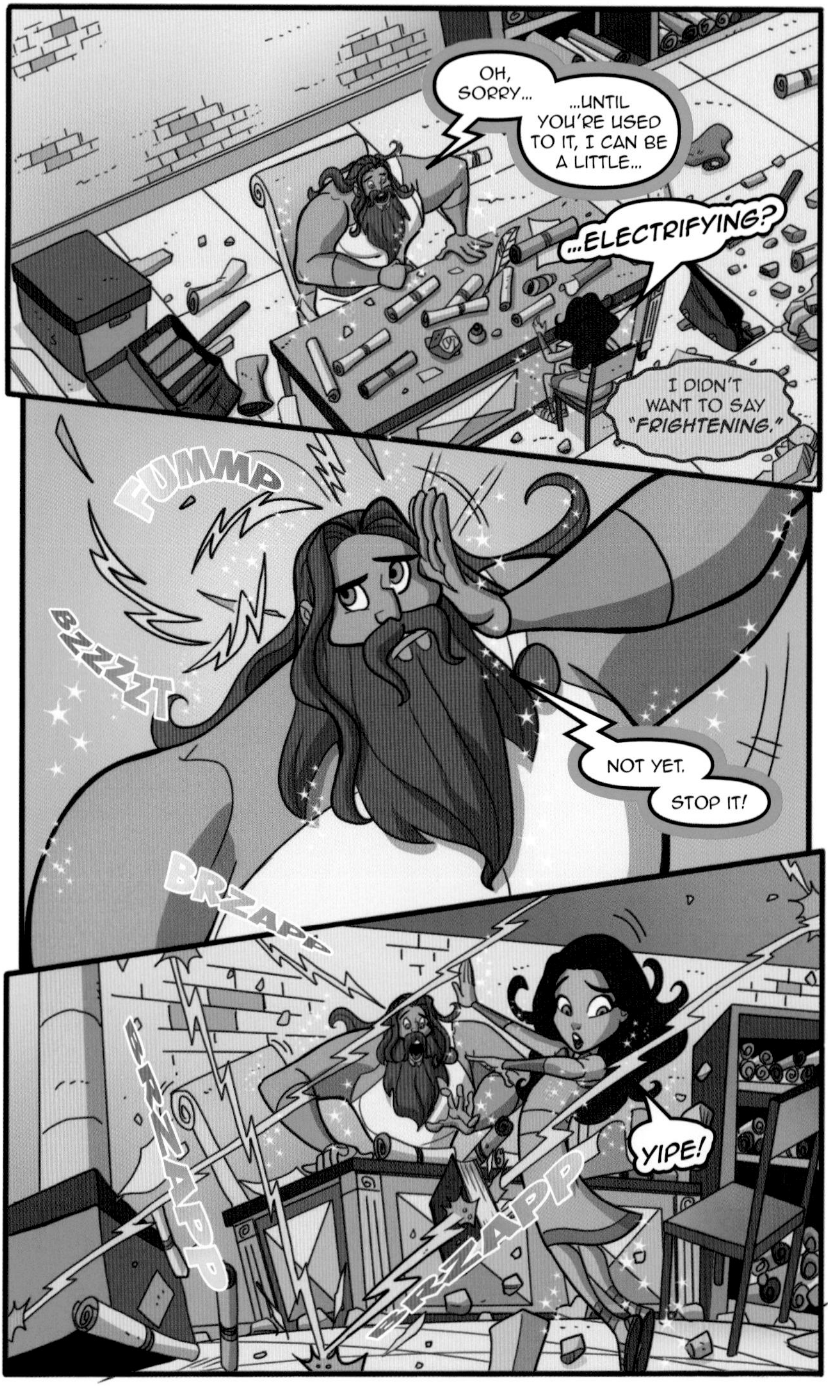
OH, SORRY...
...UNTIL YOU'RE USED TO IT, I CAN BE A LITTLE...
...ELECTRIFYING?
I DIDN'T WANT TO SAY "FRIGHTENING."
FUMMP
BZZZZT
NOT YET.
STOP IT!
BRZAPP
BRZAPP
YIPE!
BRZAPP

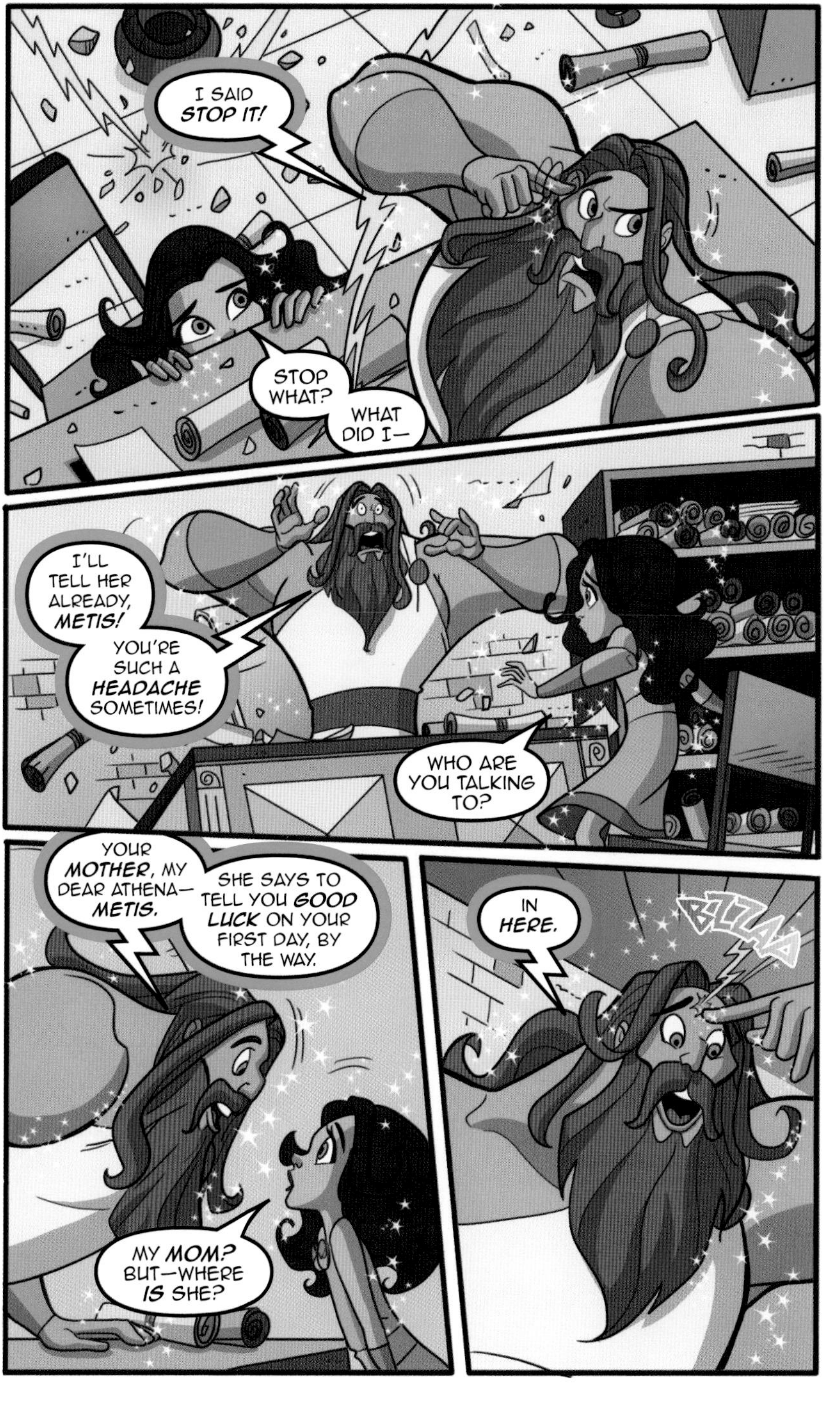
I SAID STOP IT!
STOP WHAT?
WHAT DID I—
I'LL TELL HER ALREADY, METIS!
YOU'RE SUCH A HEADACHE SOMETIMES!
WHO ARE YOU TALKING TO?
YOUR MOTHER, MY DEAR ATHENA—METIS.
SHE SAYS TO TELL YOU GOOD LUCK ON YOUR FIRST DAY, BY THE WAY.
MY MOM? BUT—WHERE IS SHE?
IN HERE.
BZZAP

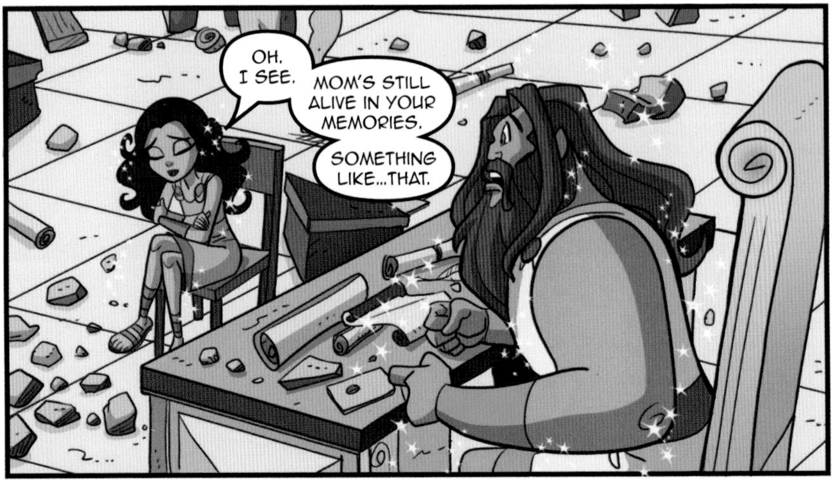
OH. I SEE.
MOM'S STILL ALIVE IN YOUR MEMORIES.
SOMETHING LIKE...THAT.

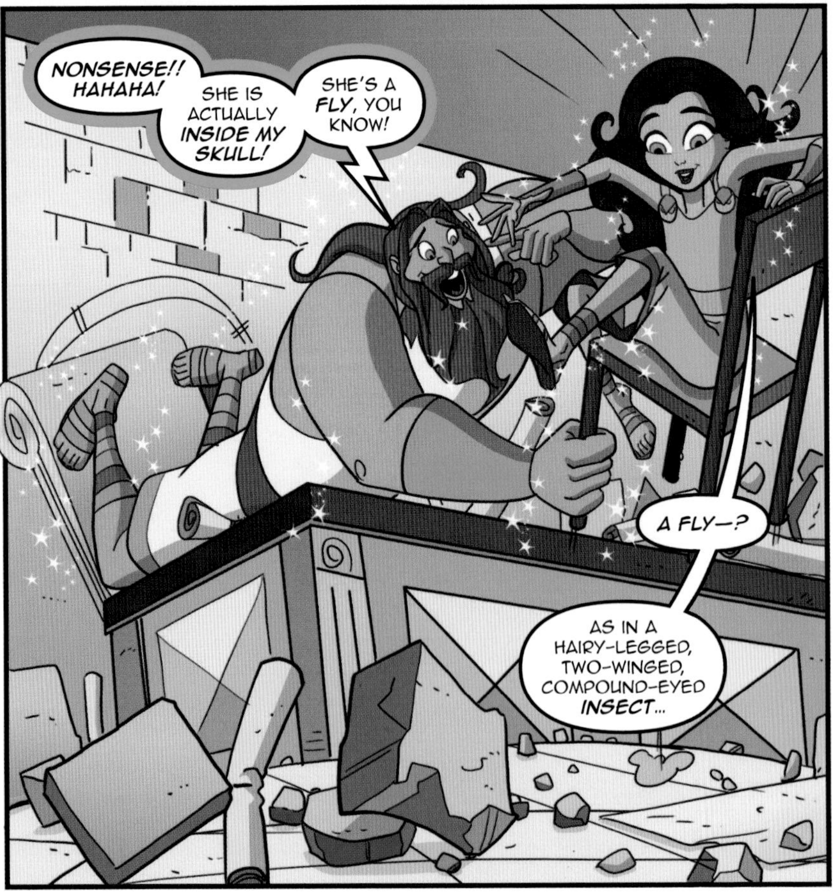
NONSENSE!! HAHAHA!
SHE IS ACTUALLY INSIDE MY SKULL!
SHE'S A FLY, YOU KNOW!
A FLY—?
AS IN A HAIRY-LEGGED, TWO-WINGED, COMPOUND-EYED INSECT...

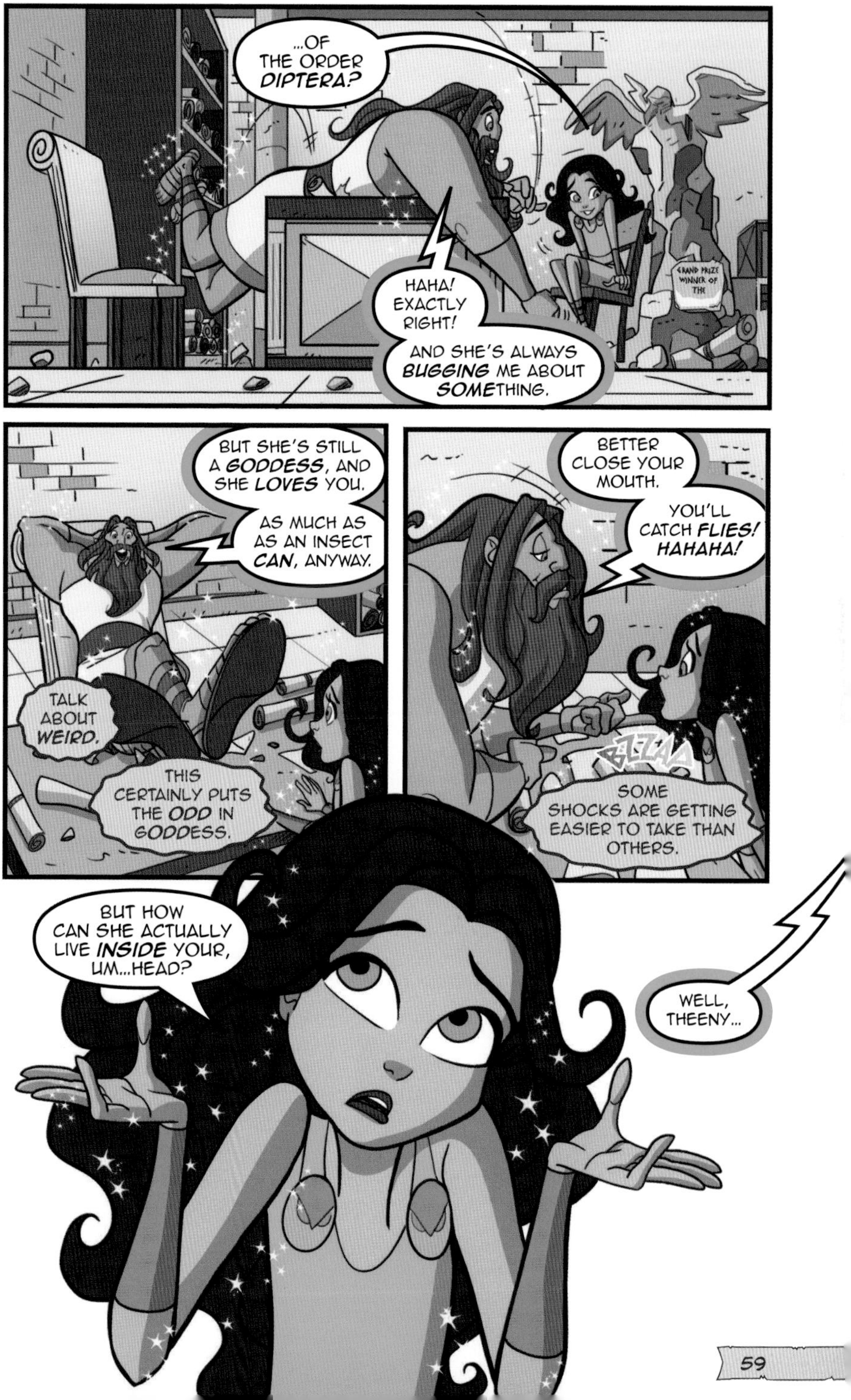
...OF THE ORDER DIPTERA?
HAHA! EXACTLY RIGHT!
AND SHE'S ALWAYS BUGGING ME ABOUT SOMETHING.
GRAND PRIZE WINNER OF THE
BUT SHE'S STILL A GODDESS, AND SHE LOVES YOU.
AS MUCH AS AS AN INSECT CAN, ANYWAY.
TALK ABOUT WEIRD.
THIS CERTAINLY PUTS THE ODD IN GODDESS.
BETTER CLOSE YOUR MOUTH.
YOU'LL CATCH FLIES! HAHAHA!
BZZAA
SOME SHOCKS ARE GETTING EASIER TO TAKE THAN OTHERS.
BUT HOW CAN SHE ACTUALLY LIVE INSIDE YOUR, UM...HEAD?
WELL, THEENY...

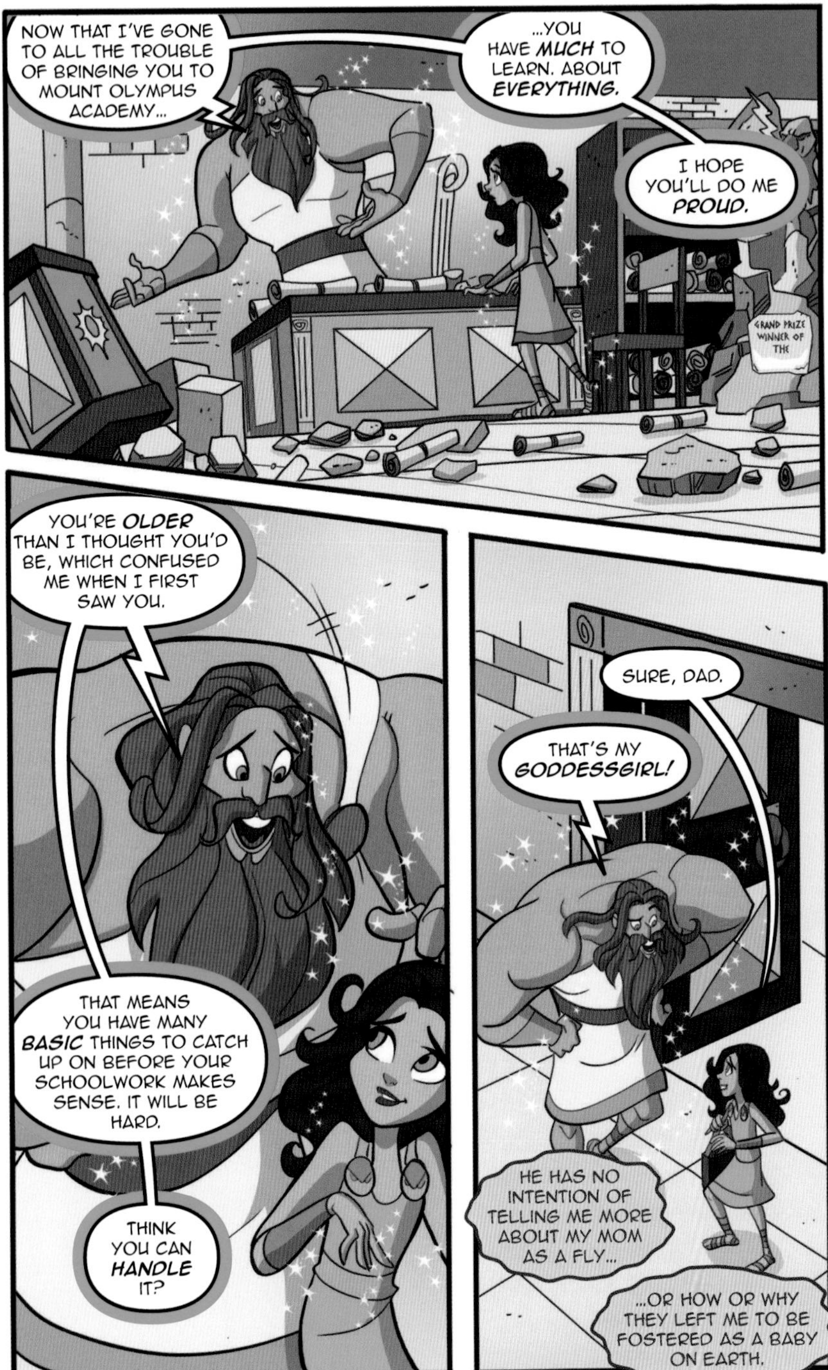
NOW THAT I'VE GONE TO ALL THE TROUBLE OF BRINGING YOU TO MOUNT OLYMPUS ACADEMY...
...YOU HAVE MUCH TO LEARN. ABOUT EVERYTHING.
I HOPE YOU'LL DO ME PROUD.
GRAND PRIZE WINNER OF THE
YOU'RE OLDER THAN I THOUGHT YOU'D BE, WHICH CONFUSED ME WHEN I FIRST SAW YOU.
THAT MEANS YOU HAVE MANY BASIC THINGS TO CATCH UP ON BEFORE YOUR SCHOOLWORK MAKES SENSE. IT WILL BE HARD.
THINK YOU CAN HANDLE IT?
SURE, DAD.
THAT'S MY GODDESSGIRL!
HE HAS NO INTENTION OF TELLING ME MORE ABOUT MY MOM AS A FLY...
...OR HOW OR WHY THEY LEFT ME TO BE FOSTERED AS A BABY ON EARTH.

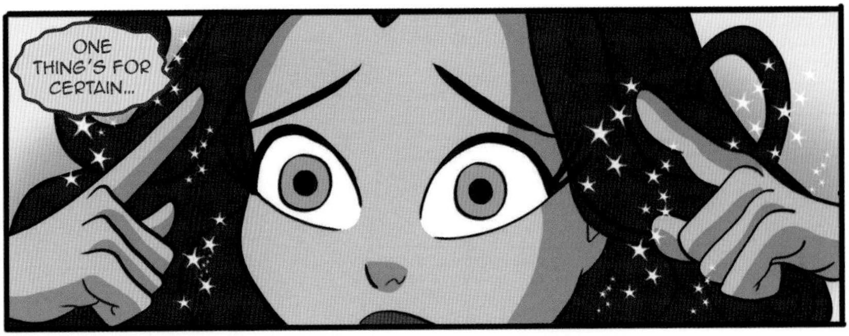
ONE THING'S FOR CERTAIN...

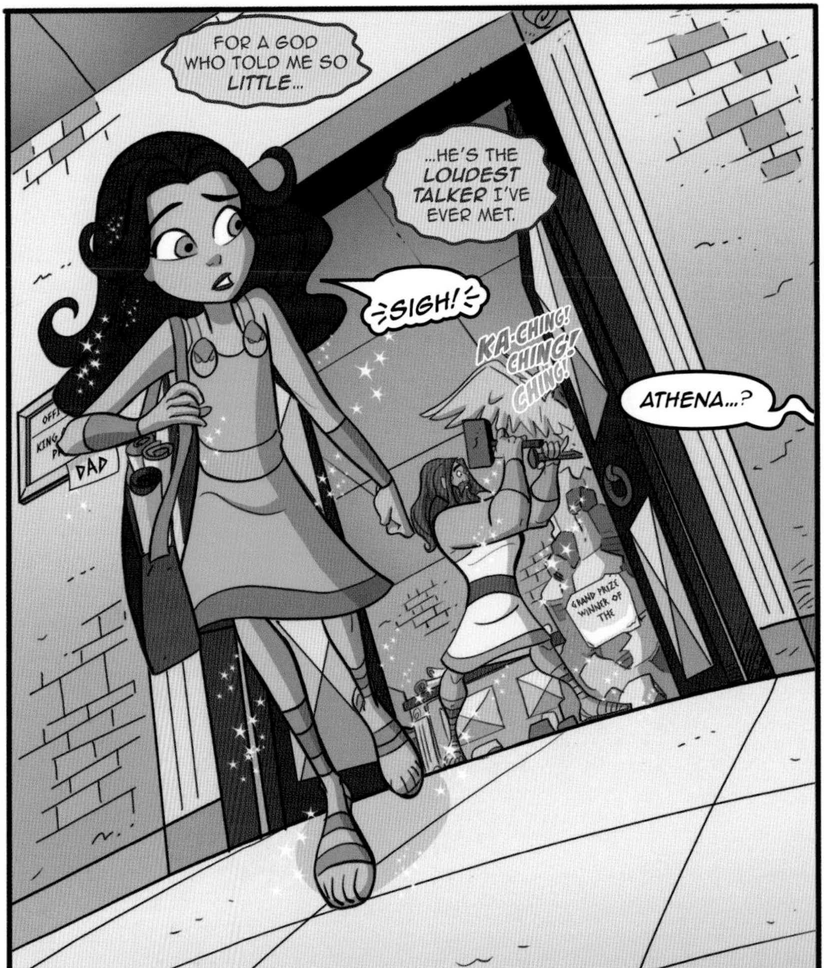
FOR A GOD WHO TOLD ME SO LITTLE...
...HE'S THE LOUDEST TALKER I'VE EVER MET.
SIGH!
KA-CHING! CHING! CHING!
ATHENA...?
DAD
GRAND PRIZE WINNER OF THE

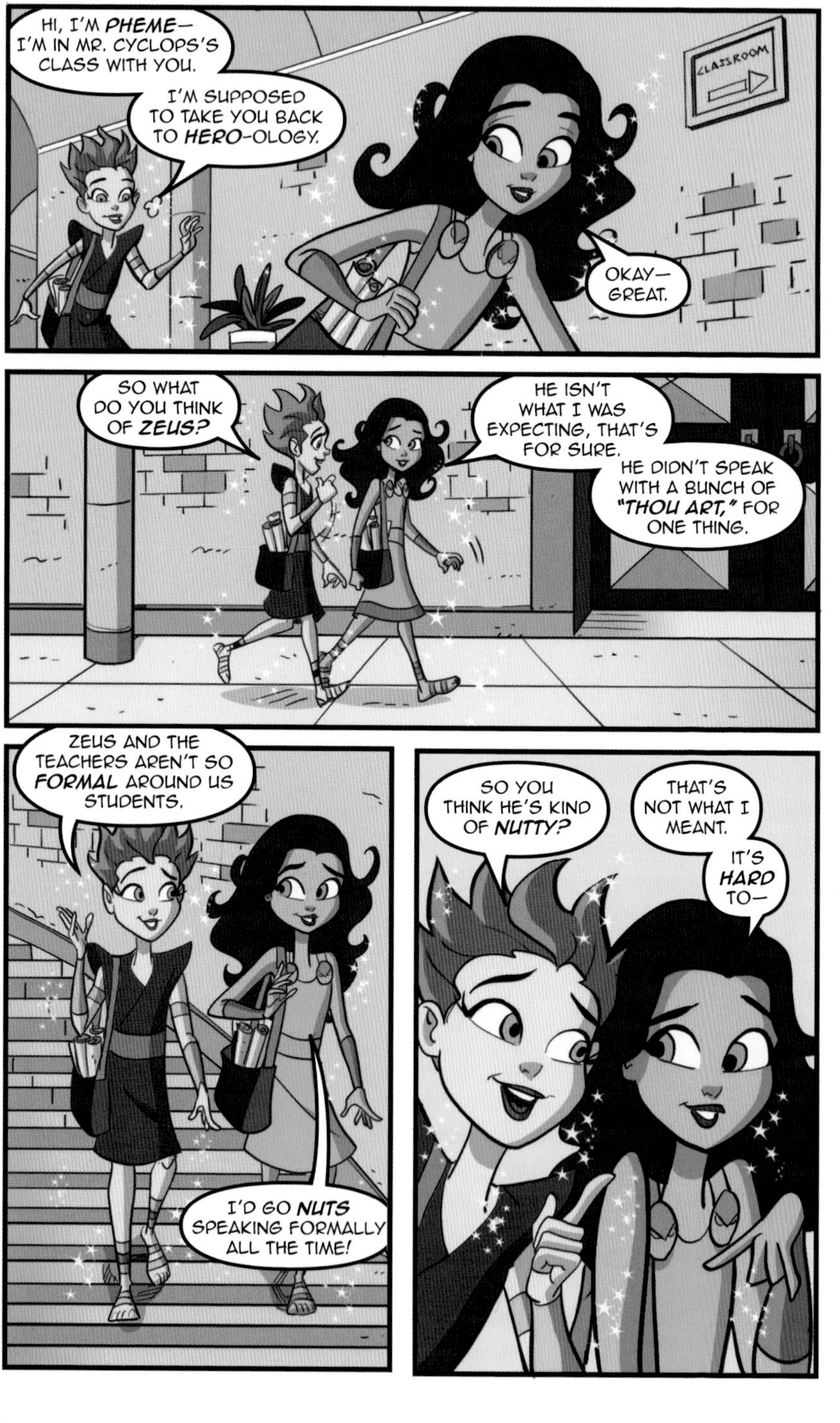

HI, I'M PHEME—
I'M IN MR. CYCLOPS'S CLASS WITH YOU.
I'M SUPPOSED TO TAKE YOU BACK TO HERO-OLOGY.
CLASSROOM
OKAY—GREAT.
SO WHAT DO YOU THINK OF ZEUS?
HE ISN'T WHAT I WAS EXPECTING, THAT'S FOR SURE.
HE DIDN'T SPEAK WITH A BUNCH OF "THOU ART," FOR ONE THING.
ZEUS AND THE TEACHERS AREN'T SO FORMAL AROUND US STUDENTS.
I'D GO NUTS SPEAKING FORMALLY ALL THE TIME!
SO YOU THINK HE'S KIND OF NUTTY?
THAT'S NOT WHAT I MEANT.
IT'S HARD TO—

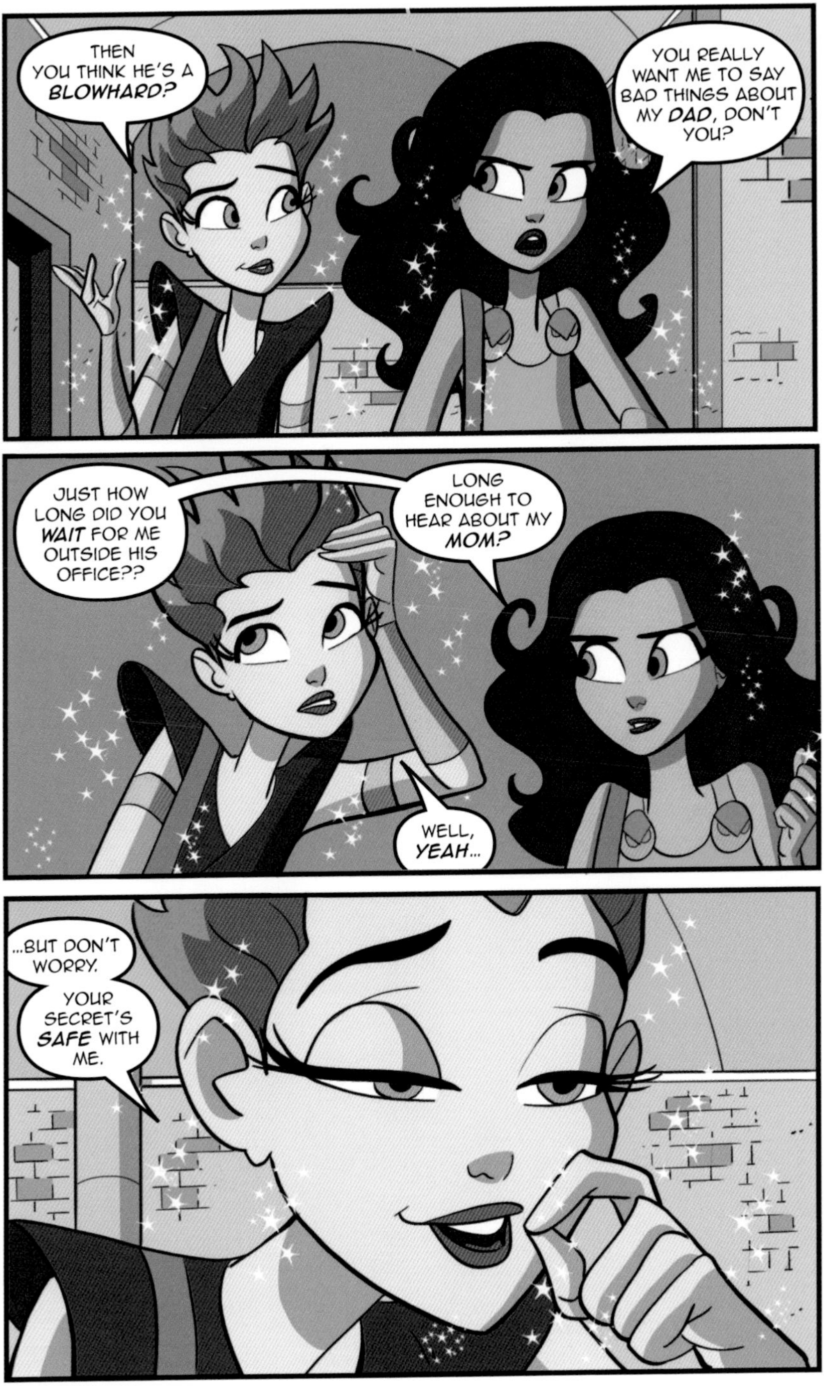
THEN YOU THINK HE'S A *BLOWHARD?*
YOU REALLY WANT ME TO SAY BAD THINGS ABOUT MY *DAD*, DON'T YOU?
JUST HOW LONG DID YOU *WAIT* FOR ME OUTSIDE HIS OFFICE??
LONG ENOUGH TO HEAR ABOUT MY *MOM?*
WELL, *YEAH*...
...BUT DON'T WORRY.
YOUR SECRET'S *SAFE* WITH ME.

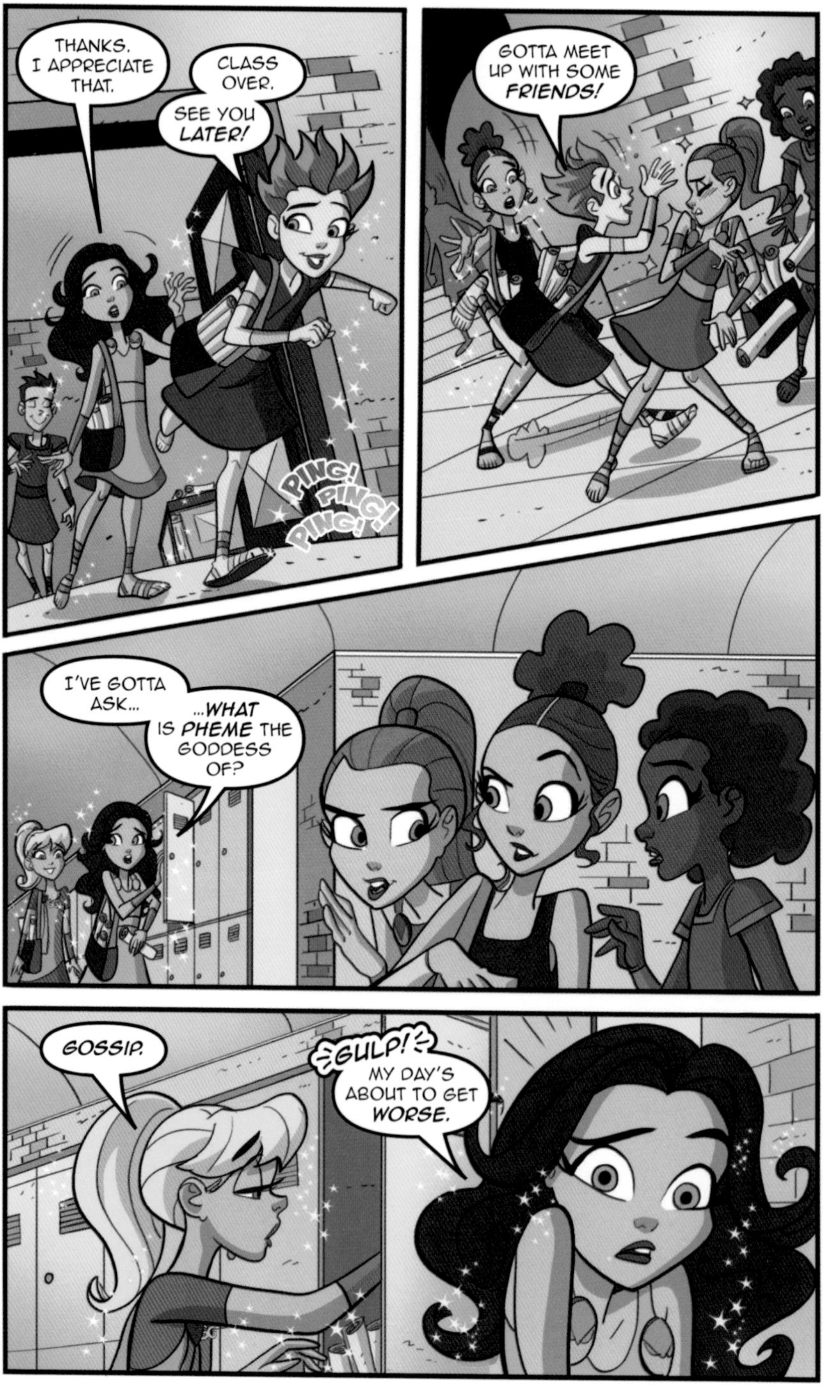
THANKS. I APPRECIATE THAT.
CLASS OVER.
SEE YOU LATER!
PING! PING! PING!
GOTTA MEET UP WITH SOME FRIENDS!
I'VE GOTTA ASK...
...WHAT IS PHEME THE GODDESS OF?
GOSSIP.
GULP!
MY DAY'S ABOUT TO GET WORSE.

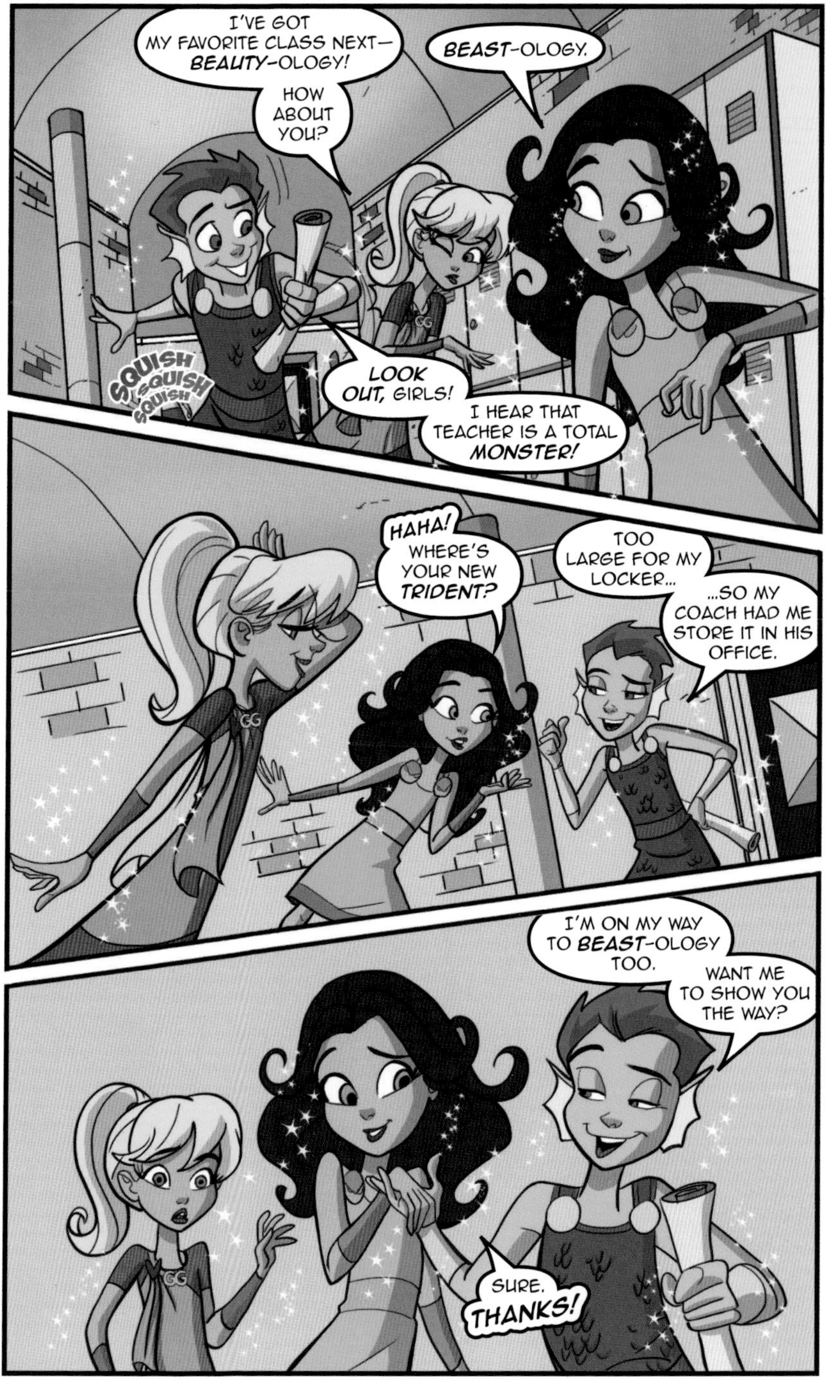
I'VE GOT MY FAVORITE CLASS NEXT—BEAUTY-OLOGY!
HOW ABOUT YOU?
BEAST-OLOGY.
SQUISH SQUISH SQUISH
LOOK OUT, GIRLS!
I HEAR THAT TEACHER IS A TOTAL MONSTER!
HAHA! WHERE'S YOUR NEW TRIDENT?
TOO LARGE FOR MY LOCKER...
...SO MY COACH HAD ME STORE IT IN HIS OFFICE.
I'M ON MY WAY TO BEAST-OLOGY TOO.
WANT ME TO SHOW YOU THE WAY?
SURE. THANKS!

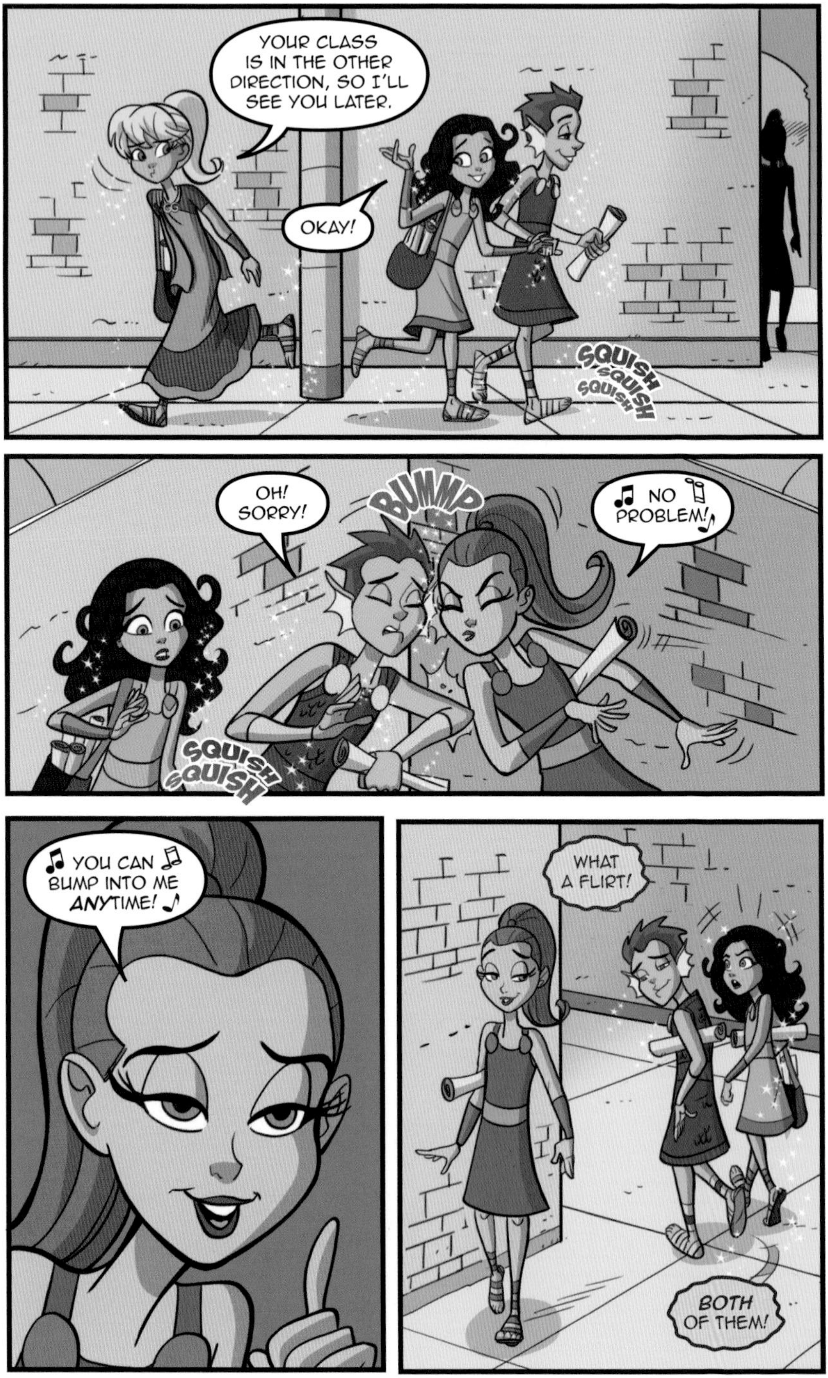
YOUR CLASS IS IN THE OTHER DIRECTION, SO I'LL SEE YOU LATER.
OKAY!
SQUISH SQUISH SQUISH
OH! SORRY!
BUMMP
NO PROBLEM!
SQUISH SQUISH
YOU CAN BUMP INTO ME ANYTIME!
WHAT A FLIRT!
BOTH OF THEM!

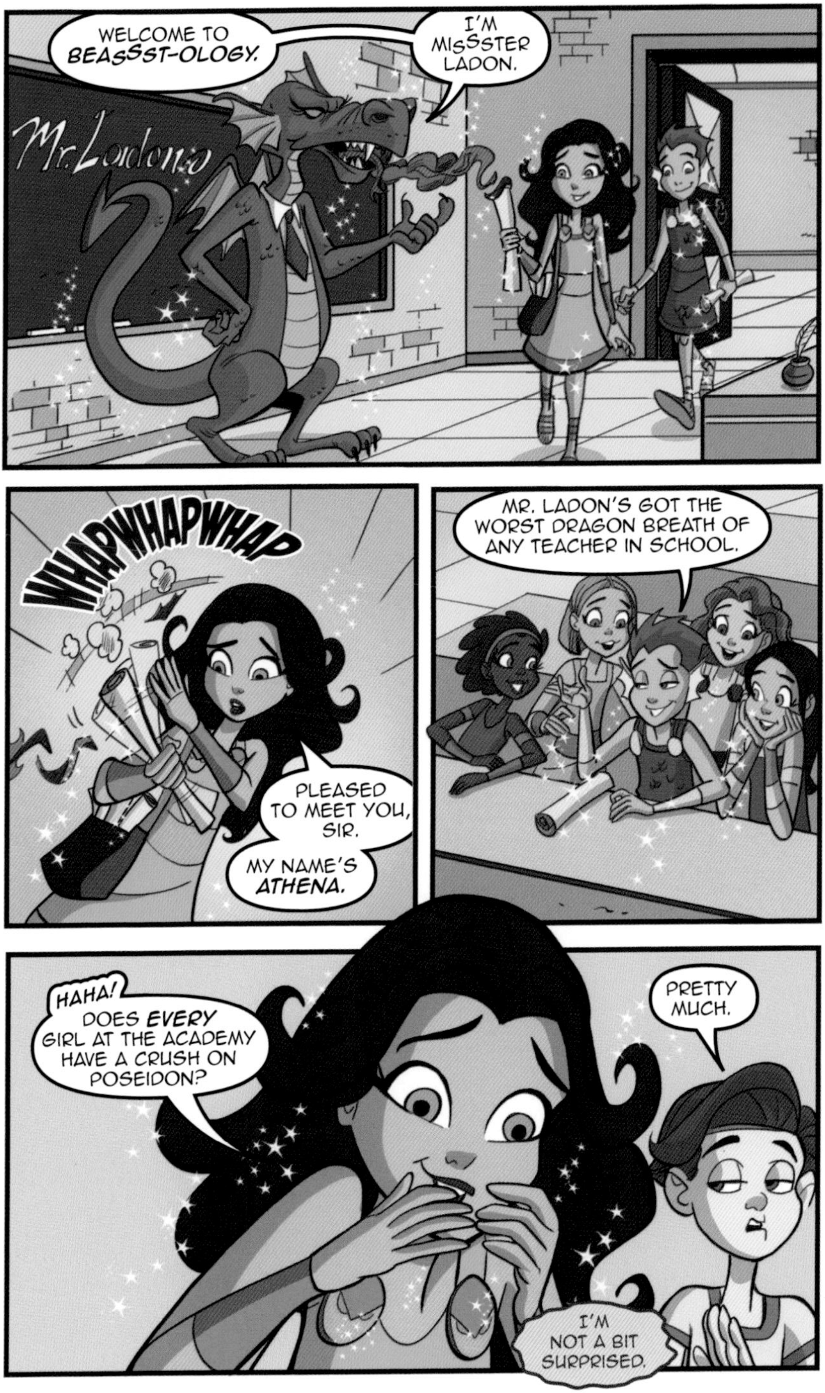

WELCOME TO BEASSST-OLOGY.
I'M MISSSTER LADON.
Mr. Ladon
WHAPWHAPWHAP
PLEASED TO MEET YOU, SIR.
MY NAME'S ATHENA.
MR. LADON'S GOT THE WORST DRAGON BREATH OF ANY TEACHER IN SCHOOL.
HAHA! DOES EVERY GIRL AT THE ACADEMY HAVE A CRUSH ON POSEIDON?
PRETTY MUCH.
I'M NOT A BIT SURPRISED.

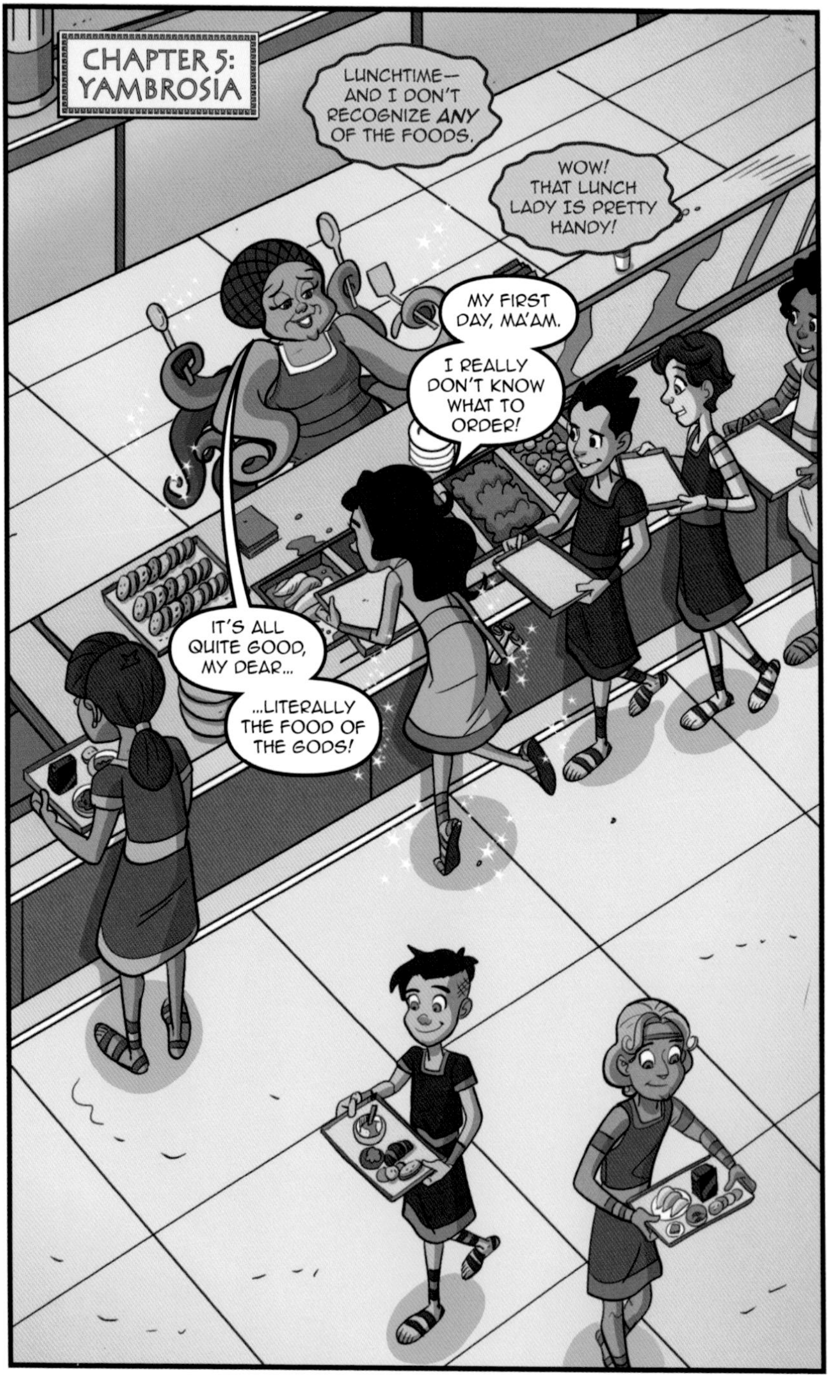
CHAPTER 5: YAMBROSIA
LUNCHTIME— AND I DON'T RECOGNIZE ANY OF THE FOODS.
WOW! THAT LUNCH LADY IS PRETTY HANDY!
MY FIRST DAY, MA'AM.
I REALLY DON'T KNOW WHAT TO ORDER!
IT'S ALL QUITE GOOD, MY DEAR...
...LITERALLY THE FOOD OF THE GODS!

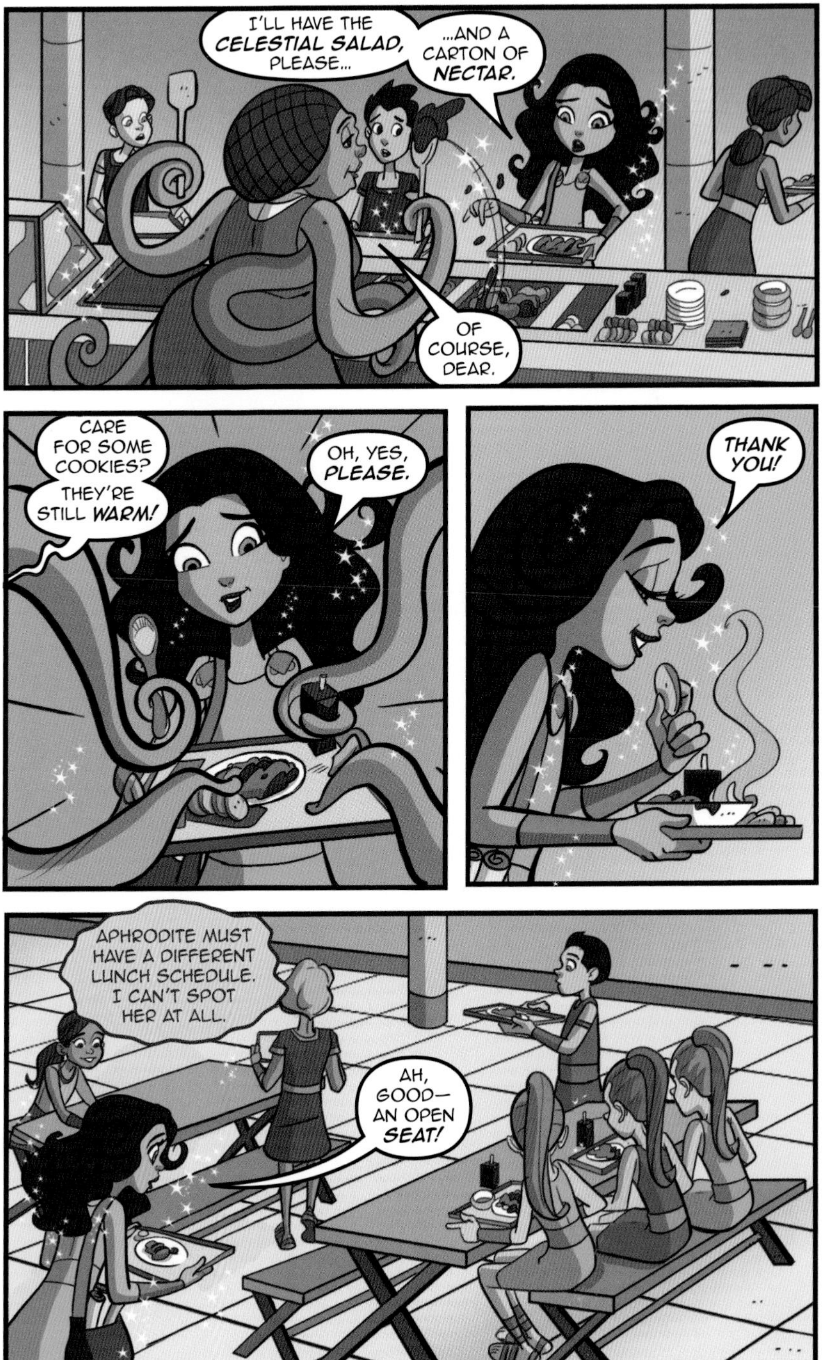
I'LL HAVE THE CELESTIAL SALAD, PLEASE...
...AND A CARTON OF NECTAR.
OF COURSE, DEAR.
CARE FOR SOME COOKIES?
THEY'RE STILL WARM!
OH, YES, PLEASE.
THANK YOU!
APHRODITE MUST HAVE A DIFFERENT LUNCH SCHEDULE. I CAN'T SPOT HER AT ALL.
AH, GOOD— AN OPEN SEAT!

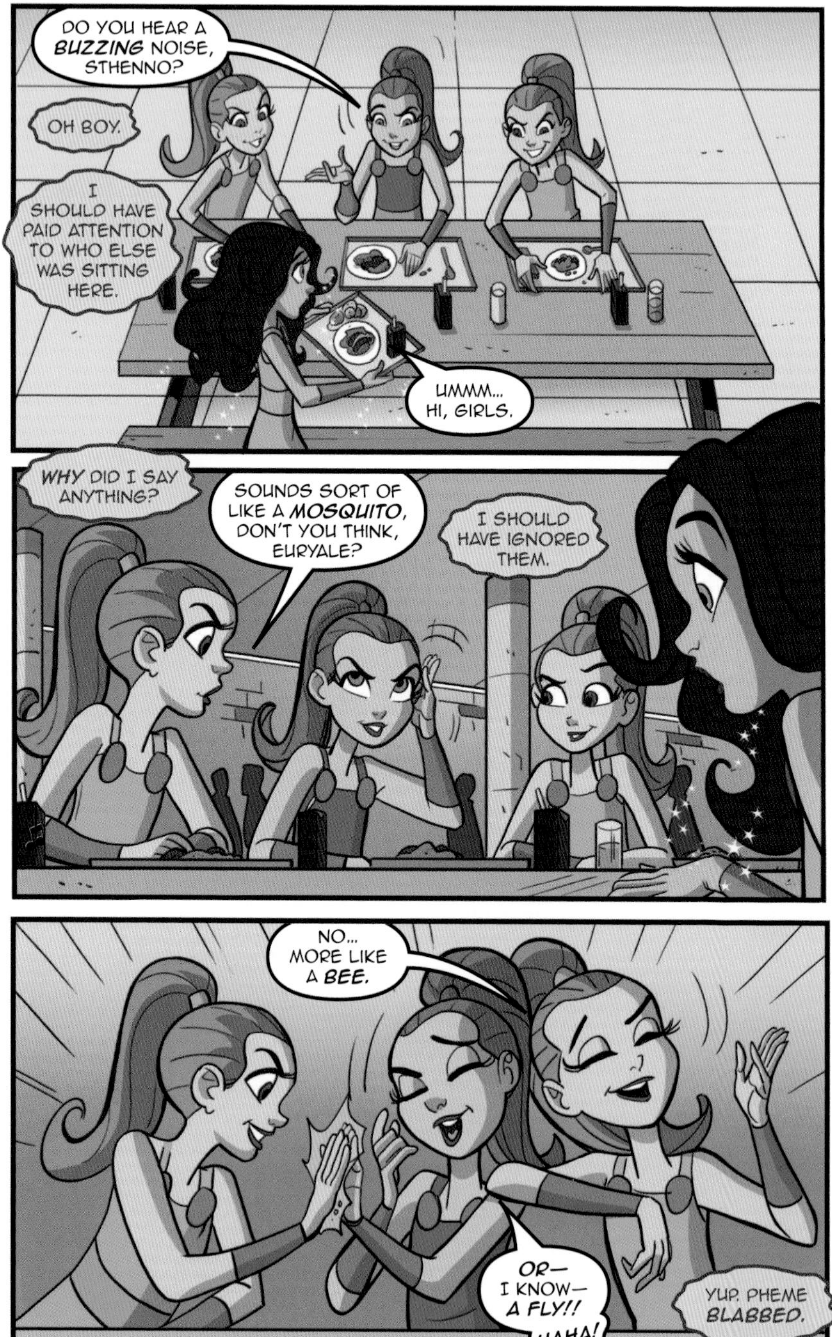
DO YOU HEAR A *BUZZING* NOISE, STHENNO?
OH BOY.
I SHOULD HAVE PAID ATTENTION TO WHO ELSE WAS SITTING HERE.
UMMM... HI, GIRLS.
WHY DID I SAY ANYTHING?
SOUNDS SORT OF LIKE A *MOSQUITO*, DON'T YOU THINK, EURYALE?
I SHOULD HAVE IGNORED THEM.
NO... MORE LIKE A *BEE*.
OR— I KNOW— A FLY!!
HAHA!
YUP. PHEME *BLABBED*.

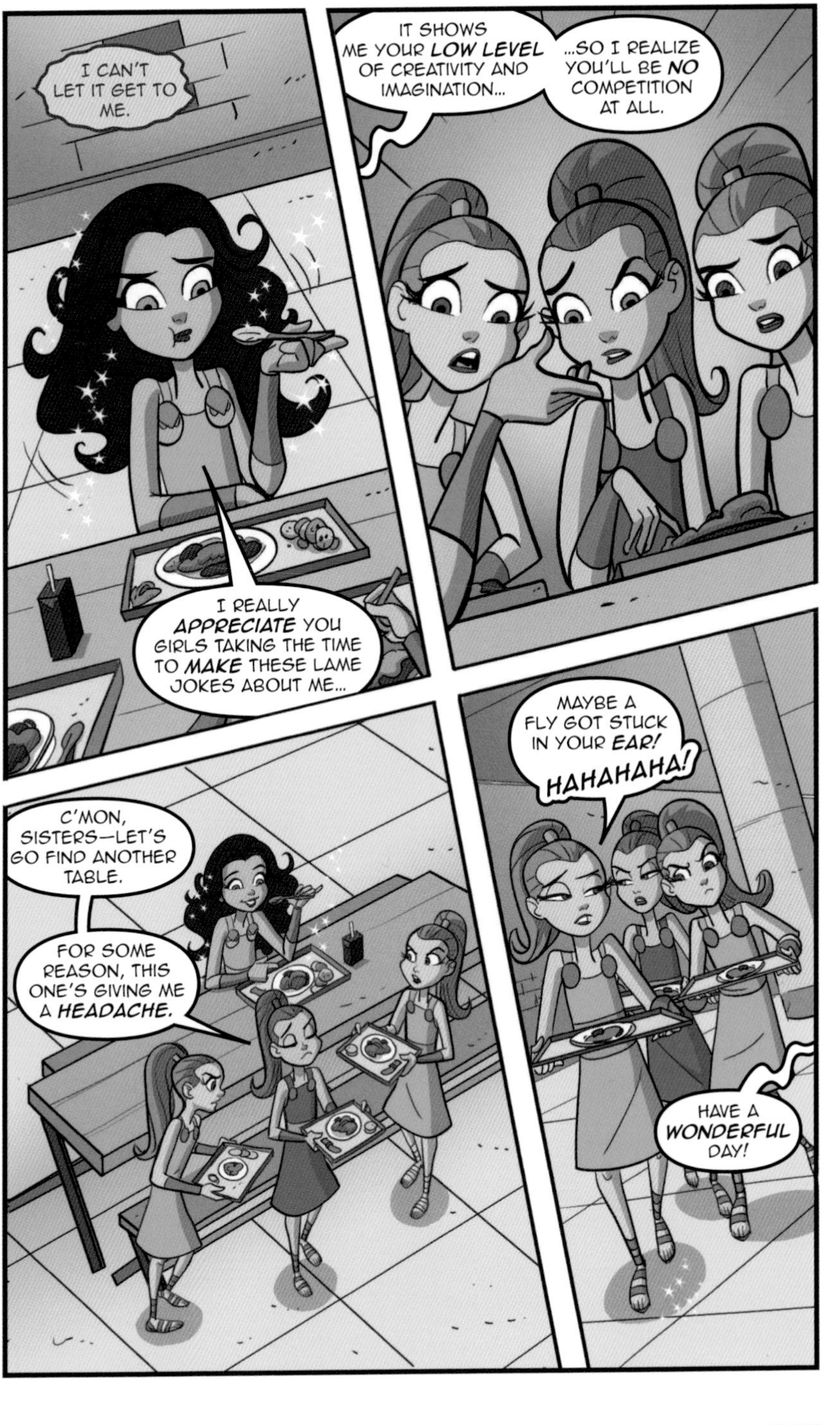

I CAN'T LET IT GET TO ME.
I REALLY APPRECIATE YOU GIRLS TAKING THE TIME TO MAKE THESE LAME JOKES ABOUT ME...
IT SHOWS ME YOUR LOW LEVEL OF CREATIVITY AND IMAGINATION...
...SO I REALIZE YOU'LL BE NO COMPETITION AT ALL.
C'MON, SISTERS—LET'S GO FIND ANOTHER TABLE.
FOR SOME REASON, THIS ONE'S GIVING ME A HEADACHE.
MAYBE A FLY GOT STUCK IN YOUR EAR!
HAHAHAHA!
HAVE A WONDERFUL DAY!

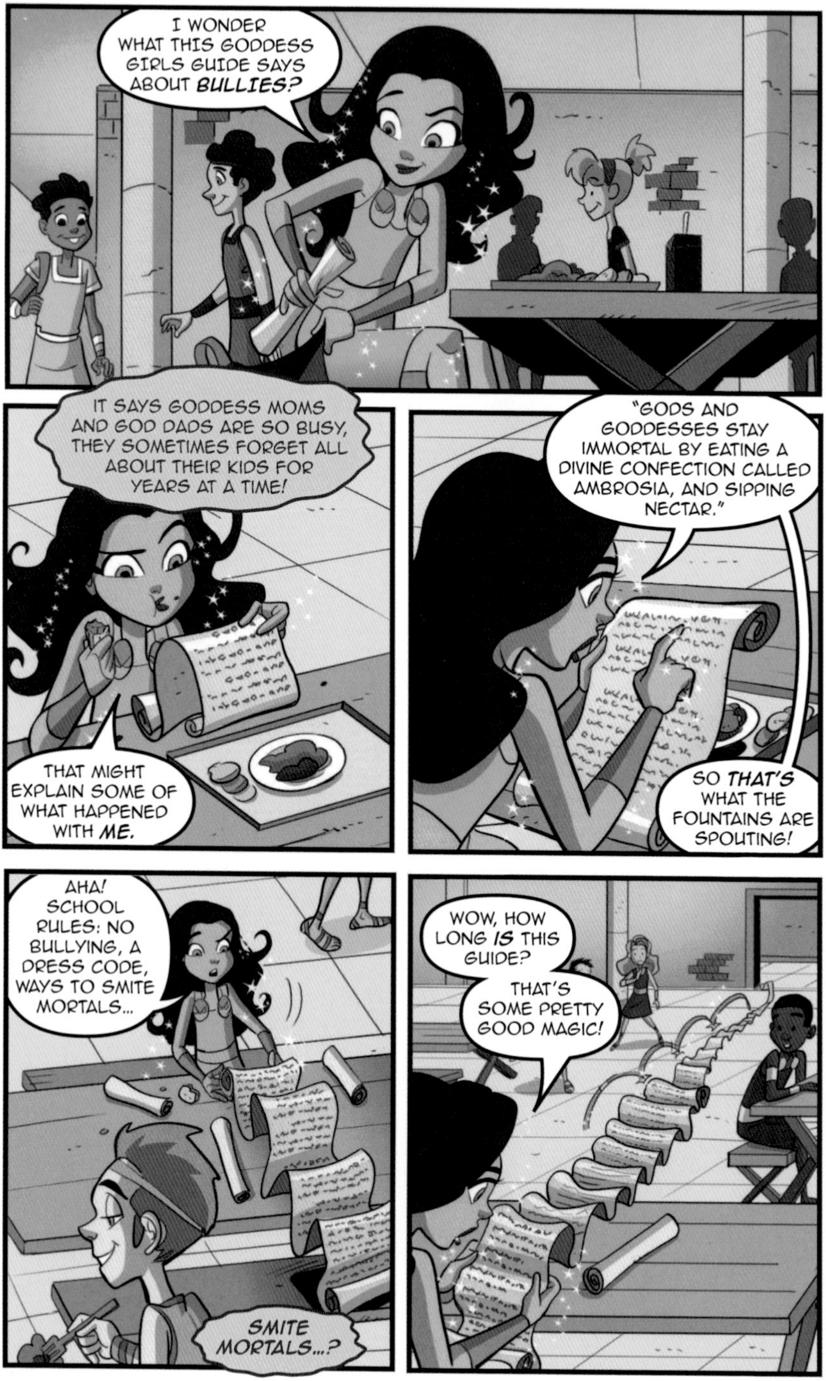
I WONDER WHAT THIS GODDESS GIRLS GUIDE SAYS ABOUT *BULLIES?*
IT SAYS GODDESS MOMS AND GOD DADS ARE SO BUSY, THEY SOMETIMES FORGET ALL ABOUT THEIR KIDS FOR YEARS AT A TIME!
THAT MIGHT EXPLAIN SOME OF WHAT HAPPENED WITH *ME.*
"GODS AND GODDESSES STAY IMMORTAL BY EATING A DIVINE CONFECTION CALLED AMBROSIA, AND SIPPING NECTAR."
SO *THAT'S* WHAT THE FOUNTAINS ARE SPOUTING!
AHA! SCHOOL RULES: NO BULLYING, A DRESS CODE, WAYS TO SMITE MORTALS...
SMITE MORTALS...?
WOW, HOW LONG *IS* THIS GUIDE?
THAT'S SOME PRETTY GOOD MAGIC!

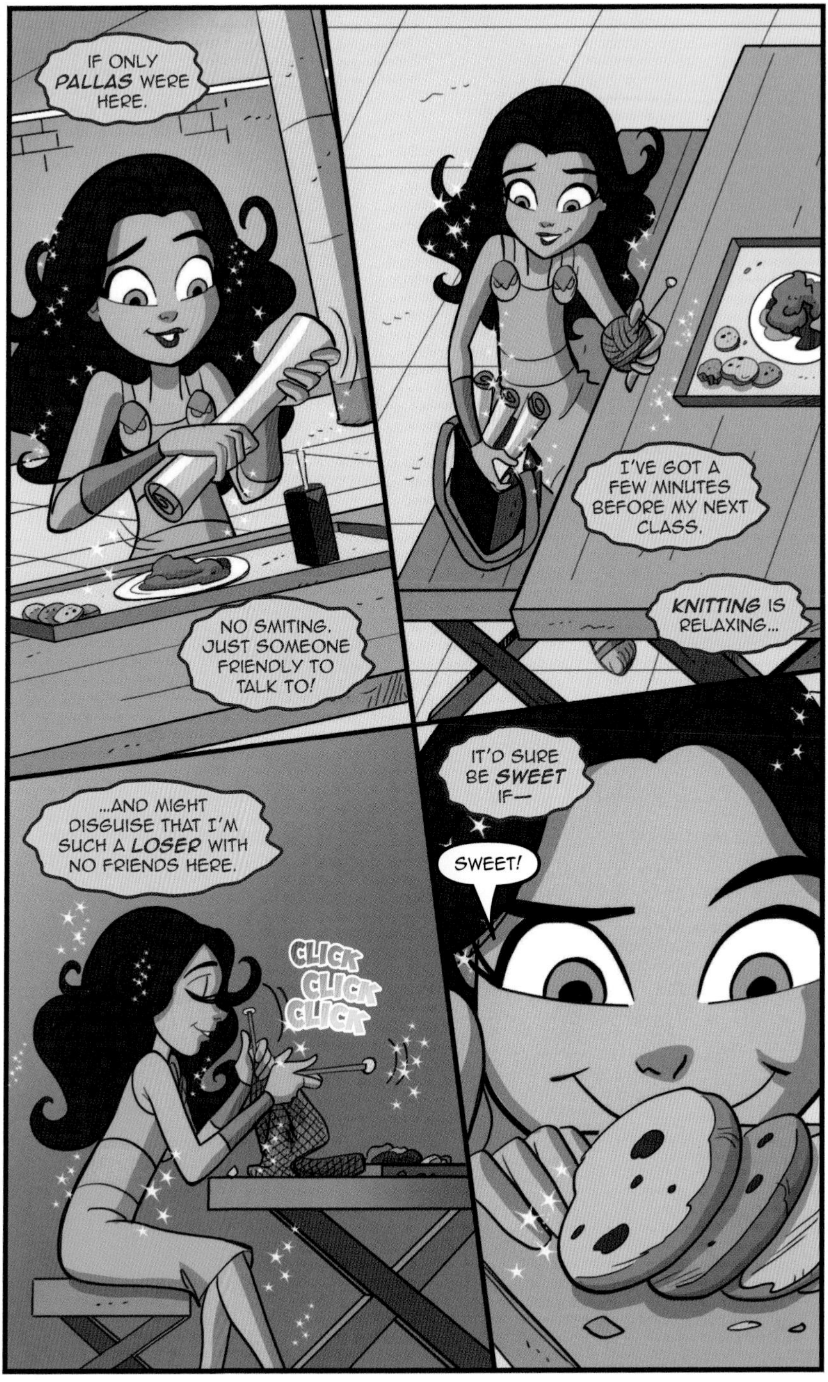
IF ONLY PALLAS WERE HERE.
NO SMITING. JUST SOMEONE FRIENDLY TO TALK TO!
I'VE GOT A FEW MINUTES BEFORE MY NEXT CLASS.
KNITTING IS RELAXING...
...AND MIGHT DISGUISE THAT I'M SUCH A LOSER WITH NO FRIENDS HERE.
CLICK CLICK CLICK
IT'D SURE BE SWEET IF—
SWEET!

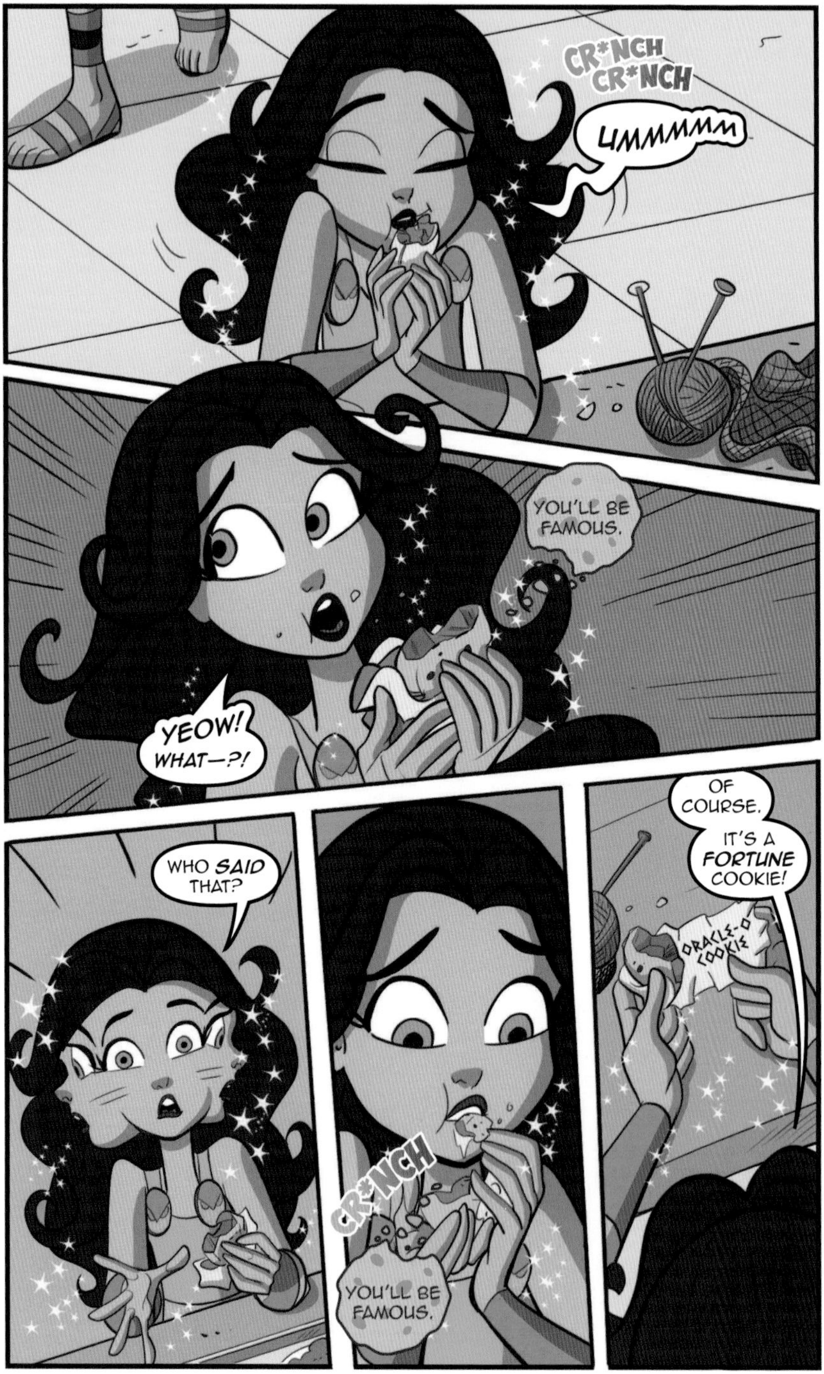
CR*NCH CR*NCH
UMMMMM
YOU'LL BE FAMOUS.
YEOW! WHAT—?!
WHO SAID THAT?
CR*NCH
YOU'LL BE FAMOUS.
OF COURSE.
IT'S A FORTUNE COOKIE!
ORACLE-O COOKIE

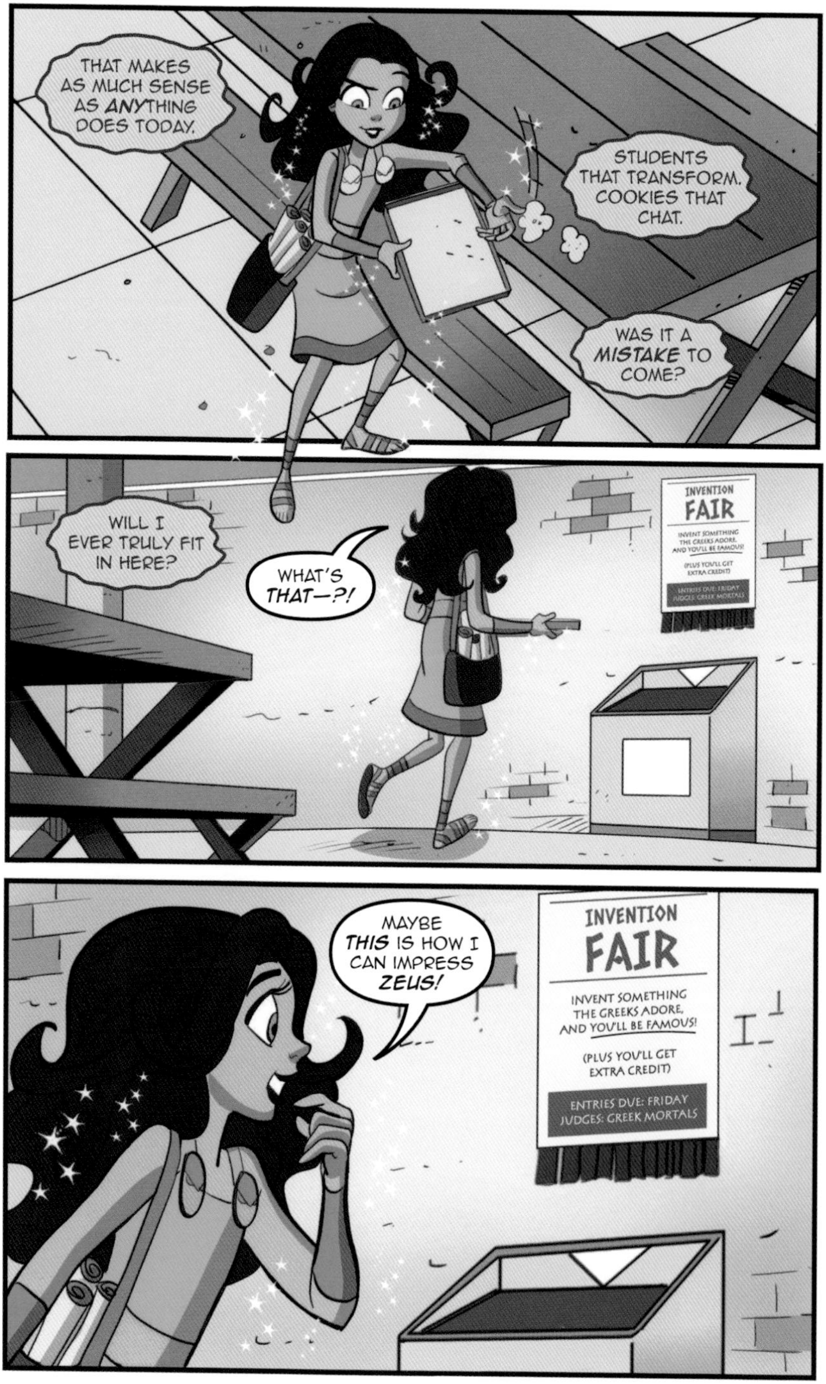
THAT MAKES AS MUCH SENSE AS ANYTHING DOES TODAY.
STUDENTS THAT TRANSFORM. COOKIES THAT CHAT.
WAS IT A MISTAKE TO COME?
WILL I EVER TRULY FIT IN HERE?
WHAT'S THAT—?!
INVENTION FAIR
MAYBE THIS IS HOW I CAN IMPRESS ZEUS!
INVENTION FAIR
INVENT SOMETHING THE GREEKS ADORE, AND YOU'LL BE FAMOUS!
(PLUS YOU'LL GET EXTRA CREDIT)
ENTRIES DUE: FRIDAY
JUDGES: GREEK MORTALS

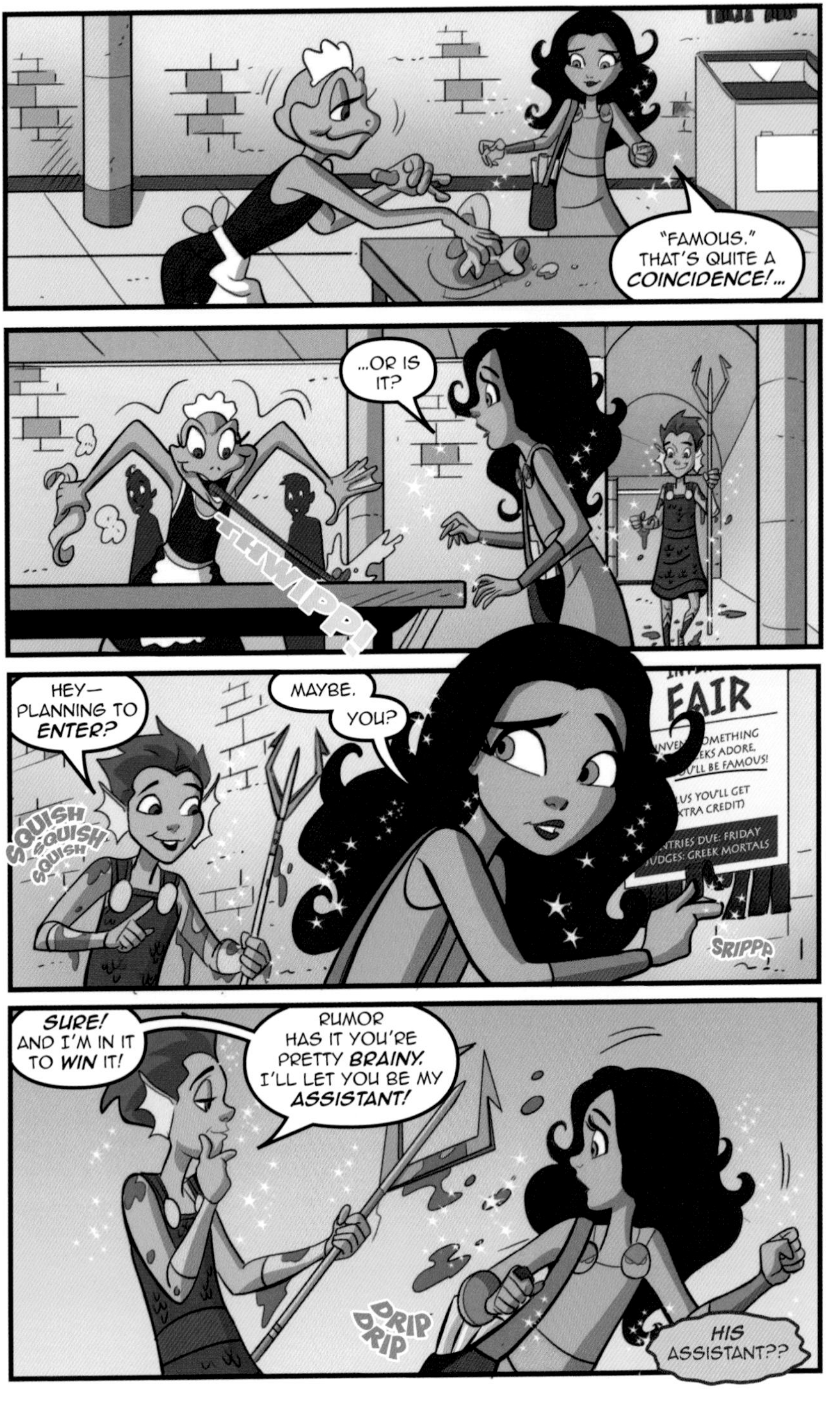
"FAMOUS." THAT'S QUITE A COINCIDENCE!...
...OR IS IT?
THWIPP!
HEY— PLANNING TO ENTER?
MAYBE.
YOU?
FAIR
SQUISH SQUISH SQUISH
SRIPPP
SURE! AND I'M IN IT TO WIN IT!
RUMOR HAS IT YOU'RE PRETTY BRAINY. I'LL LET YOU BE MY ASSISTANT!
DRIP DRIP
HIS ASSISTANT??

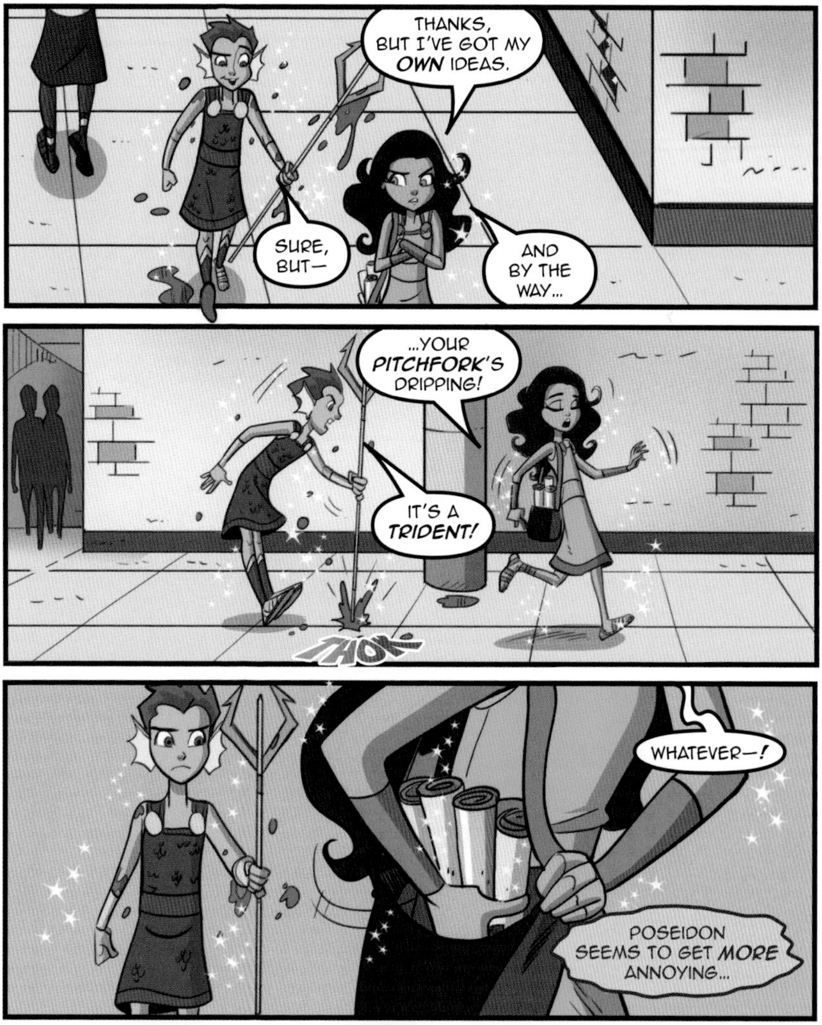

THANKS, BUT I'VE GOT MY OWN IDEAS.
SURE, BUT—
AND BY THE WAY...
...YOUR PITCHFORK'S DRIPPING!
IT'S A TRIDENT!
THOK
WHATEVER—!
POSEIDON SEEMS TO GET MORE ANNOYING...
...EVERY TIME I SEE HIM!
HI! THINKING OF TRYING OUT?
FOR WHAT?

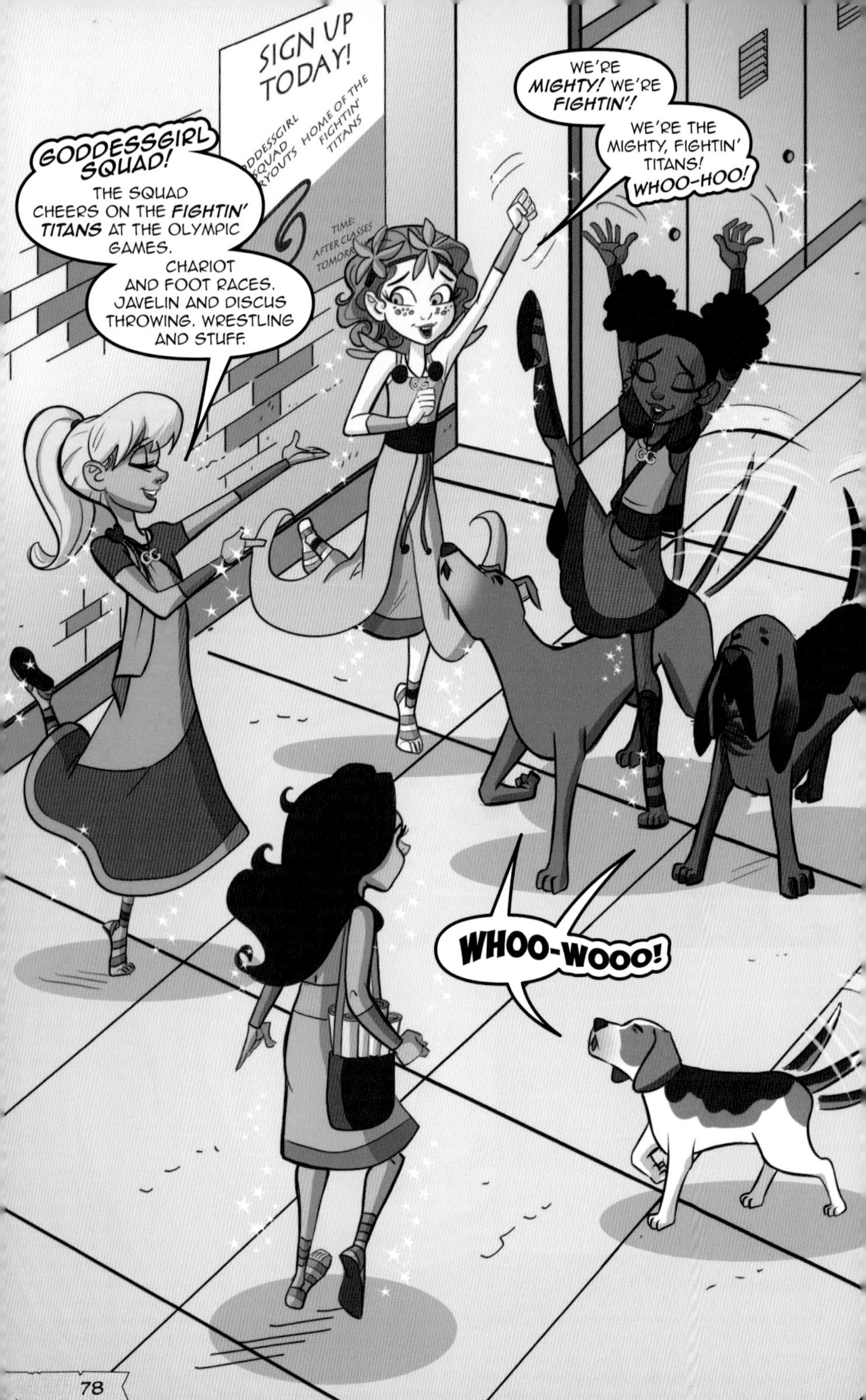
SIGN UP TODAY!
ODDESSGIRL SQUAD RYOUTS
HOME OF THE FIGHTIN' TITANS
TIME: AFTER CLASSES
GODDESSGIRL SQUAD!
THE SQUAD CHEERS ON THE ***FIGHTIN' TITANS*** AT THE OLYMPIC GAMES.
CHARIOT AND FOOT RACES. JAVELIN AND DISCUS THROWING. WRESTLING AND STUFF.
WE'RE ***MIGHTY!*** WE'RE ***FIGHTIN'!***
WE'RE THE MIGHTY, FIGHTIN' TITANS! ***WHOO-HOO!***
WHOO-WOOO!

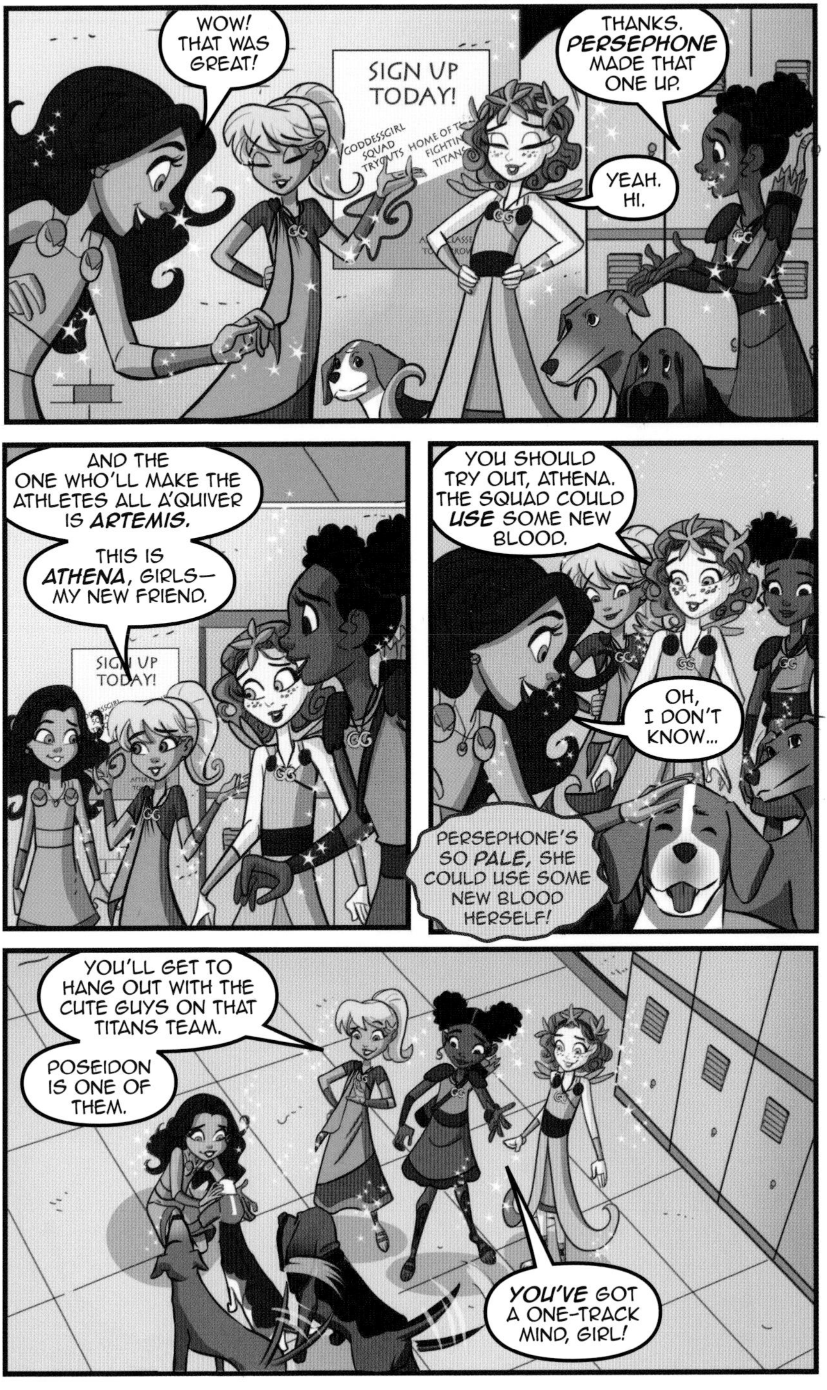

WOW! THAT WAS GREAT!
SIGN UP TODAY!
GODDESSGIRL SQUAD TRYOUTS
THANKS. *PERSEPHONE* MADE THAT ONE UP.
YEAH. HI.
AND THE ONE WHO'LL MAKE THE ATHLETES ALL A'QUIVER IS *ARTEMIS.*
THIS IS *ATHENA*, GIRLS— MY NEW FRIEND.
YOU SHOULD TRY OUT, ATHENA. THE SQUAD COULD *USE* SOME NEW BLOOD.
OH, I DON'T KNOW...
PERSEPHONE'S SO *PALE*, SHE COULD USE SOME NEW BLOOD HERSELF!
YOU'LL GET TO HANG OUT WITH THE CUTE GUYS ON THAT TITANS TEAM.
POSEIDON IS ONE OF THEM.
YOU'VE GOT A ONE-TRACK MIND, GIRL!

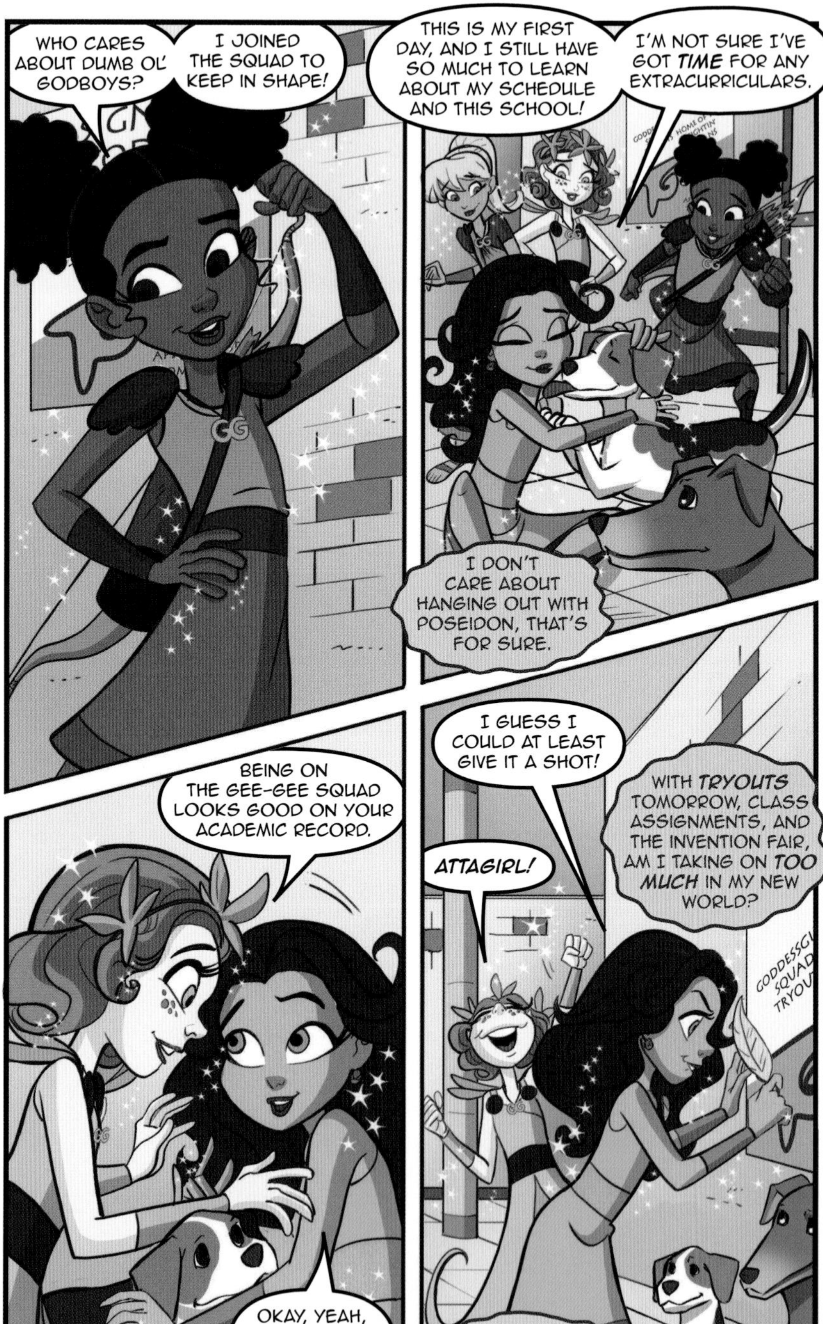
WHO CARES ABOUT DUMB OL' GODBOYS?
I JOINED THE SQUAD TO KEEP IN SHAPE!
THIS IS MY FIRST DAY, AND I STILL HAVE SO MUCH TO LEARN ABOUT MY SCHEDULE AND THIS SCHOOL!
I'M NOT SURE I'VE GOT *TIME* FOR ANY EXTRACURRICULARS.
I DON'T CARE ABOUT HANGING OUT WITH POSEIDON, THAT'S FOR SURE.
BEING ON THE GEE-GEE SQUAD LOOKS GOOD ON YOUR ACADEMIC RECORD.
OKAY, YEAH, MY DAD WOULD PROBABLY LIKE THAT.
I GUESS I COULD AT LEAST GIVE IT A SHOT!
ATTAGIRL!
WITH *TRYOUTS* TOMORROW, CLASS ASSIGNMENTS, AND THE INVENTION FAIR, AM I TAKING ON *TOO MUCH* IN MY NEW WORLD?
I'LL FIND OUT SOON *ENOUGH!*

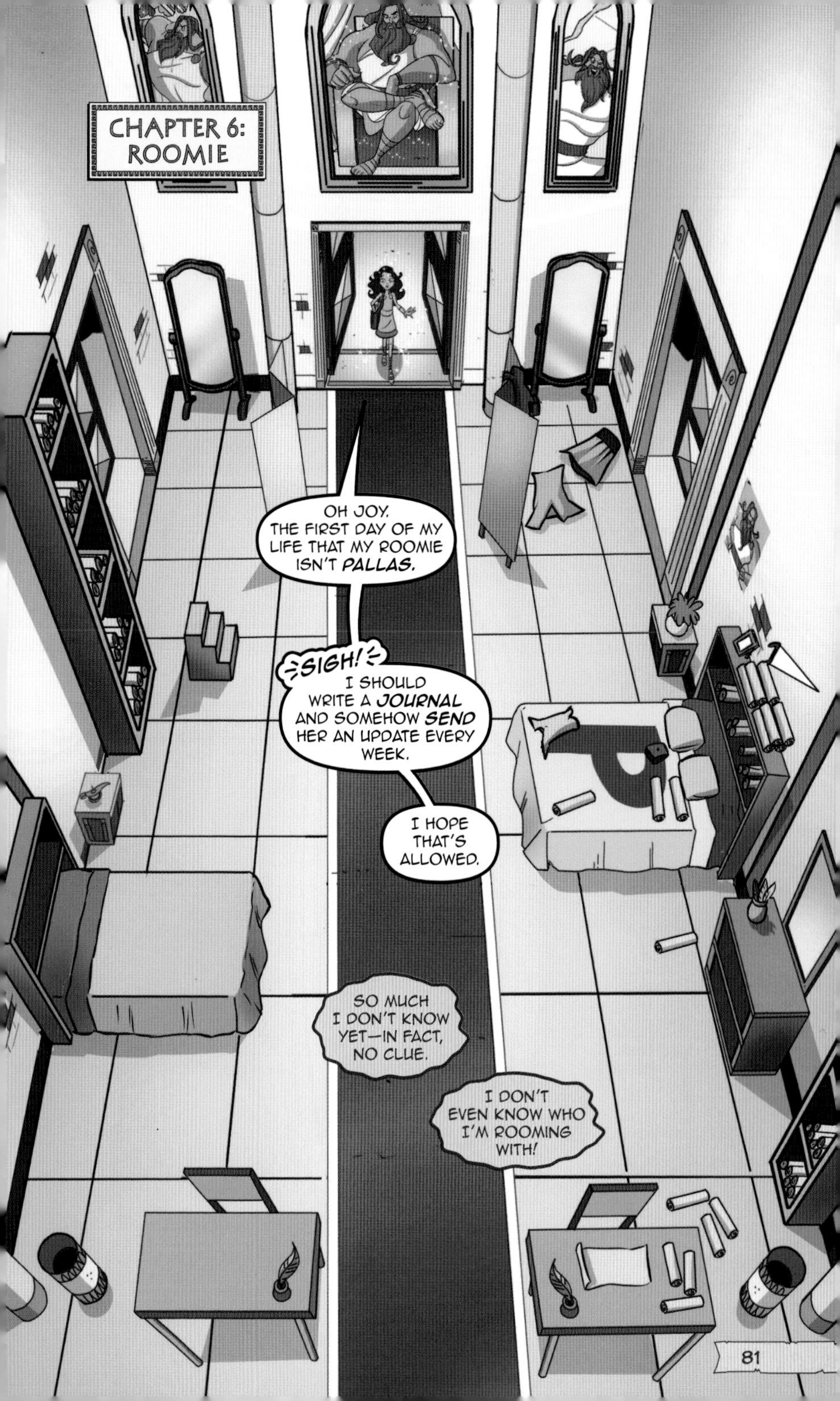
CHAPTER 6: ROOMIE
OH JOY. THE FIRST DAY OF MY LIFE THAT MY ROOMIE ISN'T PALLAS.
SIGH!
I SHOULD WRITE A JOURNAL AND SOMEHOW SEND HER AN UPDATE EVERY WEEK.
I HOPE THAT'S ALLOWED.
SO MUCH I DON'T KNOW YET—IN FACT, NO CLUE.
I DON'T EVEN KNOW WHO I'M ROOMING WITH!

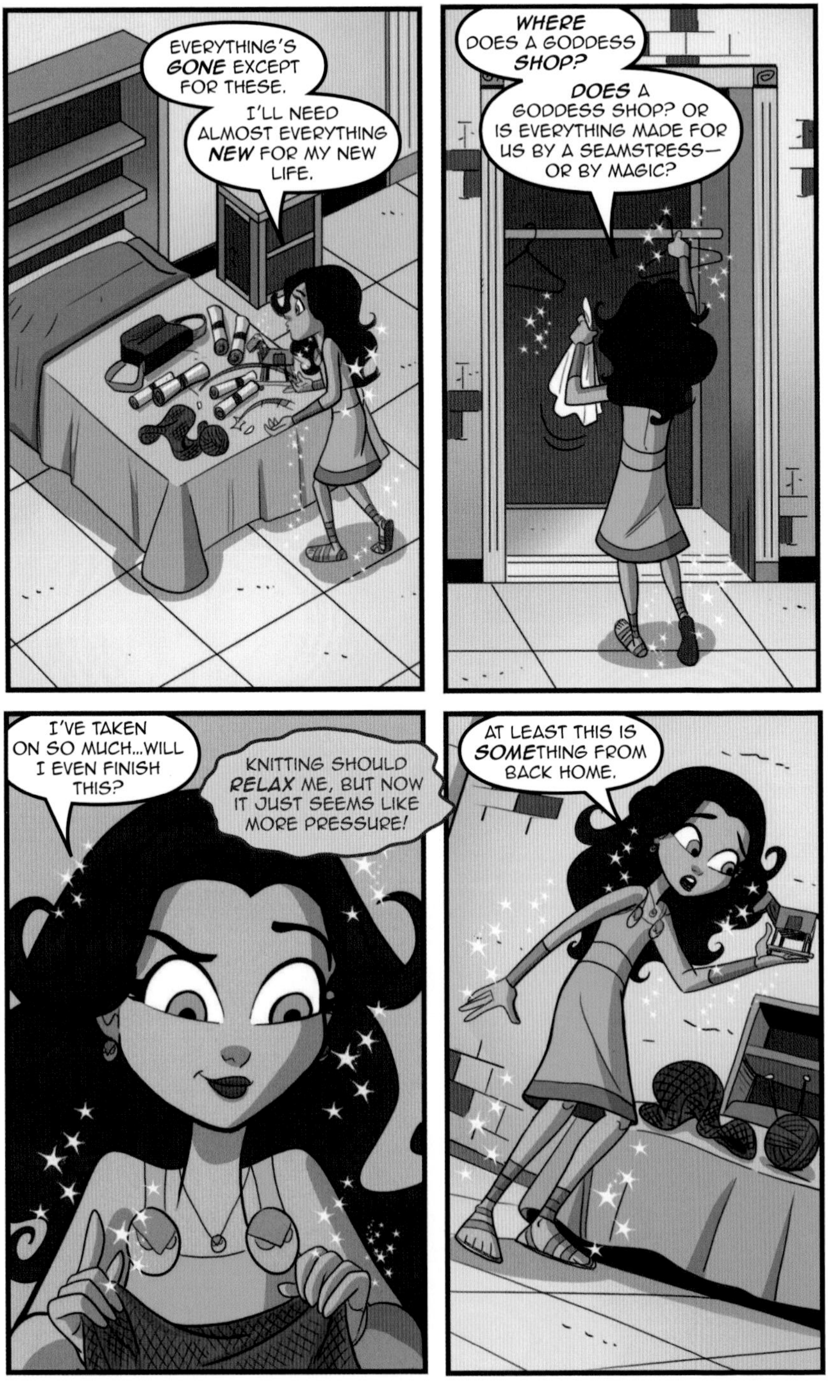

EVERYTHING'S **GONE** EXCEPT FOR THESE.
I'LL NEED ALMOST EVERYTHING **NEW** FOR MY NEW LIFE.
WHERE DOES A GODDESS **SHOP?**
DOES A GODDESS SHOP? OR IS EVERYTHING MADE FOR US BY A SEAMSTRESS— OR BY MAGIC?
I'VE TAKEN ON SO MUCH...WILL I EVEN FINISH THIS?
KNITTING SHOULD **RELAX** ME, BUT NOW IT JUST SEEMS LIKE MORE PRESSURE!
AT LEAST THIS IS **SOME**THING FROM BACK HOME.

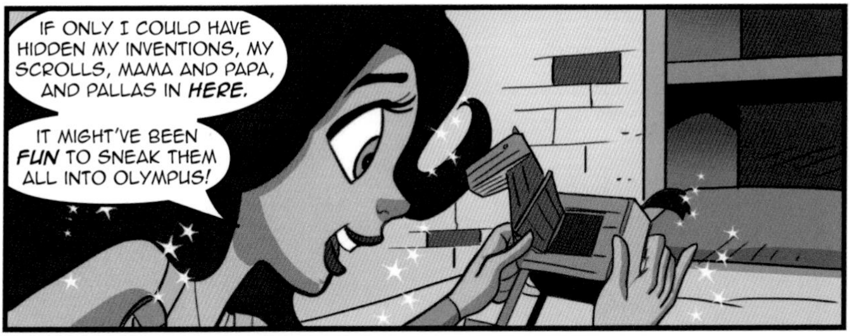
IF ONLY I COULD HAVE HIDDEN MY INVENTIONS, MY SCROLLS, MAMA AND PAPA, AND PALLAS IN *HERE.*
IT MIGHT'VE BEEN *FUN* TO SNEAK THEM ALL INTO OLYMPUS!

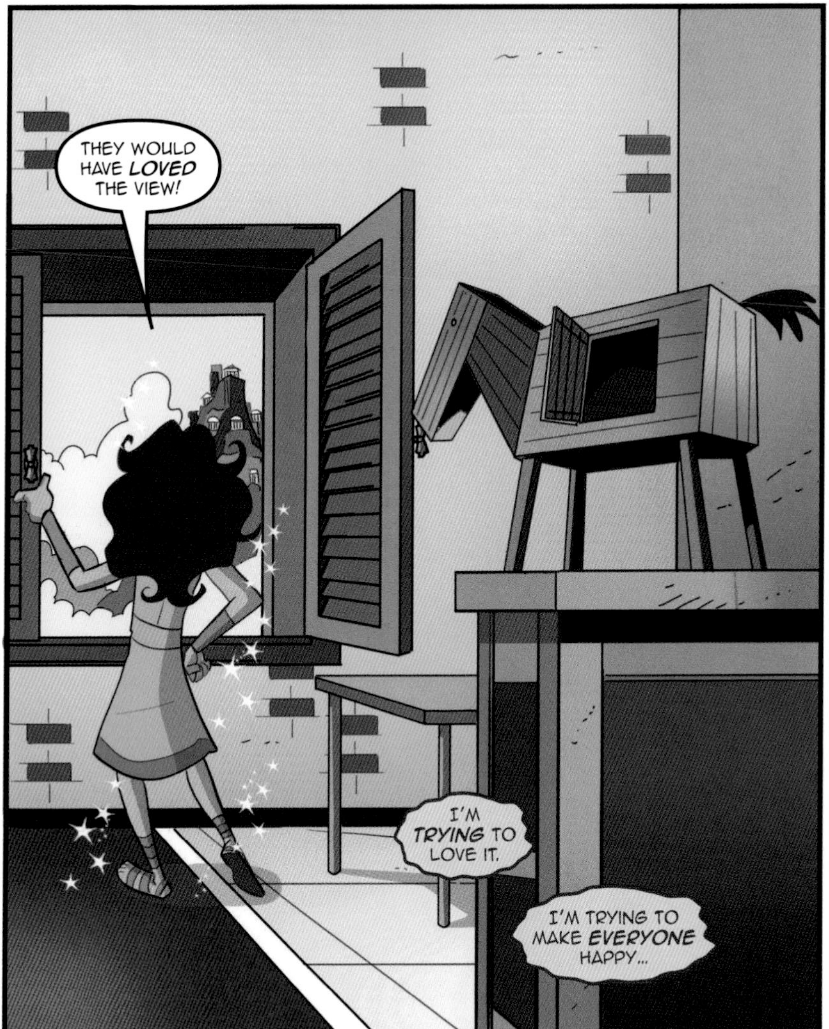
THEY WOULD HAVE *LOVED* THE VIEW!
I'M *TRYING* TO LOVE IT.
I'M TRYING TO MAKE *EVERYONE* HAPPY...

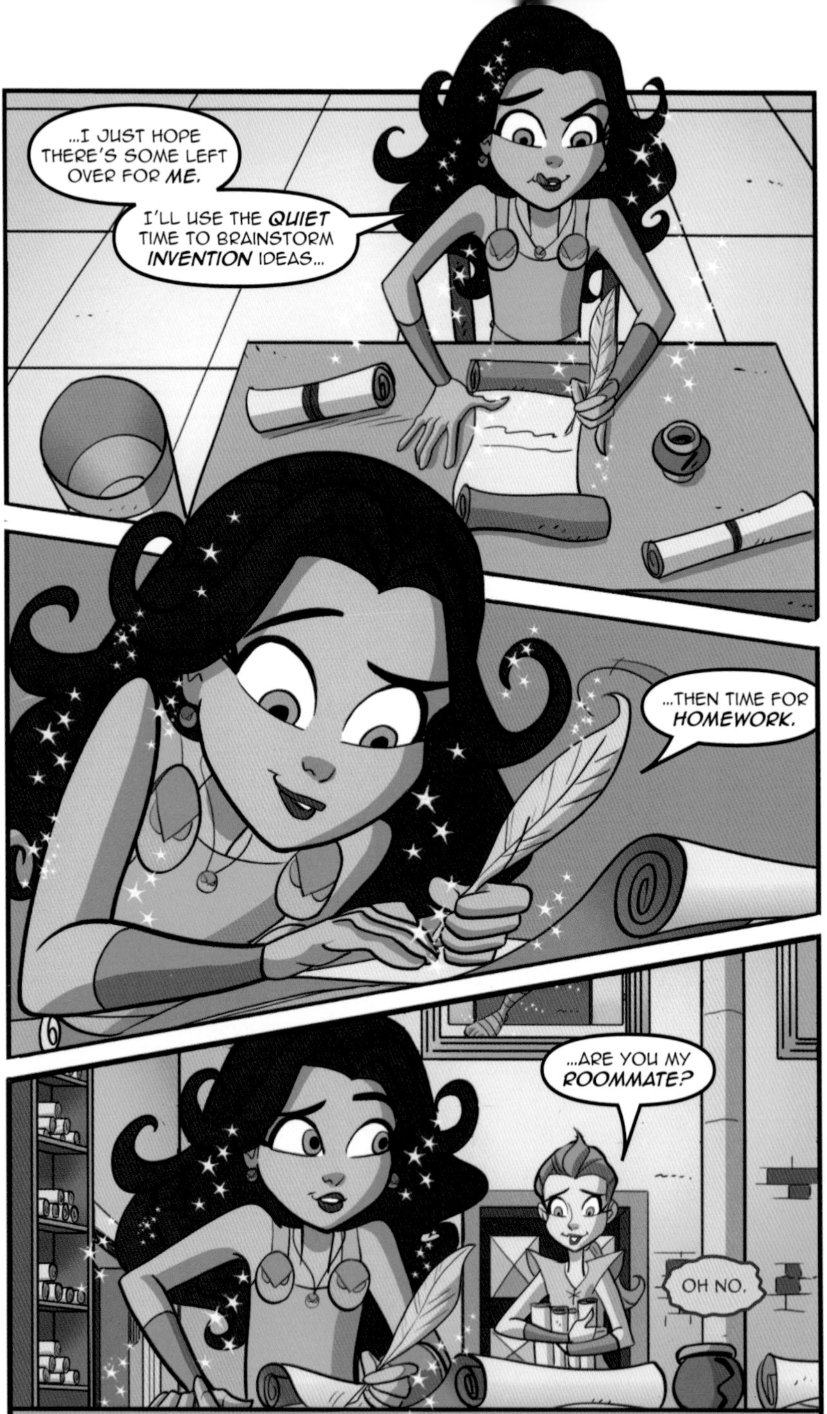
...I JUST HOPE THERE'S SOME LEFT OVER FOR ME.
I'LL USE THE QUIET TIME TO BRAINSTORM INVENTION IDEAS...
...THEN TIME FOR HOMEWORK.
...ARE YOU MY ROOMMATE?
OH NO.

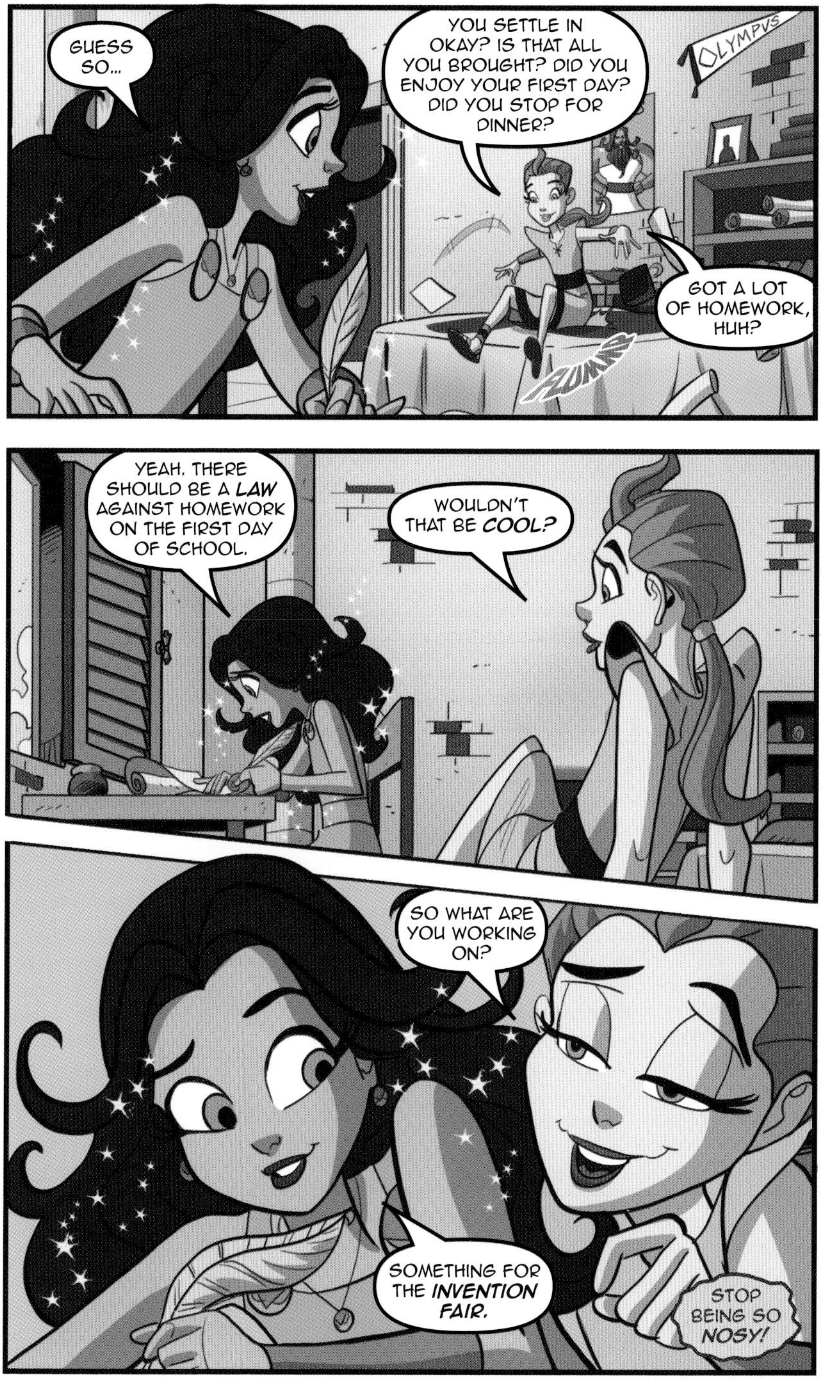
GUESS SO...
YOU SETTLE IN OKAY? IS THAT ALL YOU BROUGHT? DID YOU ENJOY YOUR FIRST DAY? DID YOU STOP FOR DINNER?
OLYMPVS
GOT A LOT OF HOMEWORK, HUH?
YEAH. THERE SHOULD BE A *LAW* AGAINST HOMEWORK ON THE FIRST DAY OF SCHOOL.
WOULDN'T THAT BE *COOL?*
SO WHAT ARE YOU WORKING ON?
SOMETHING FOR THE *INVENTION FAIR.*
STOP BEING SO *NOSY!*

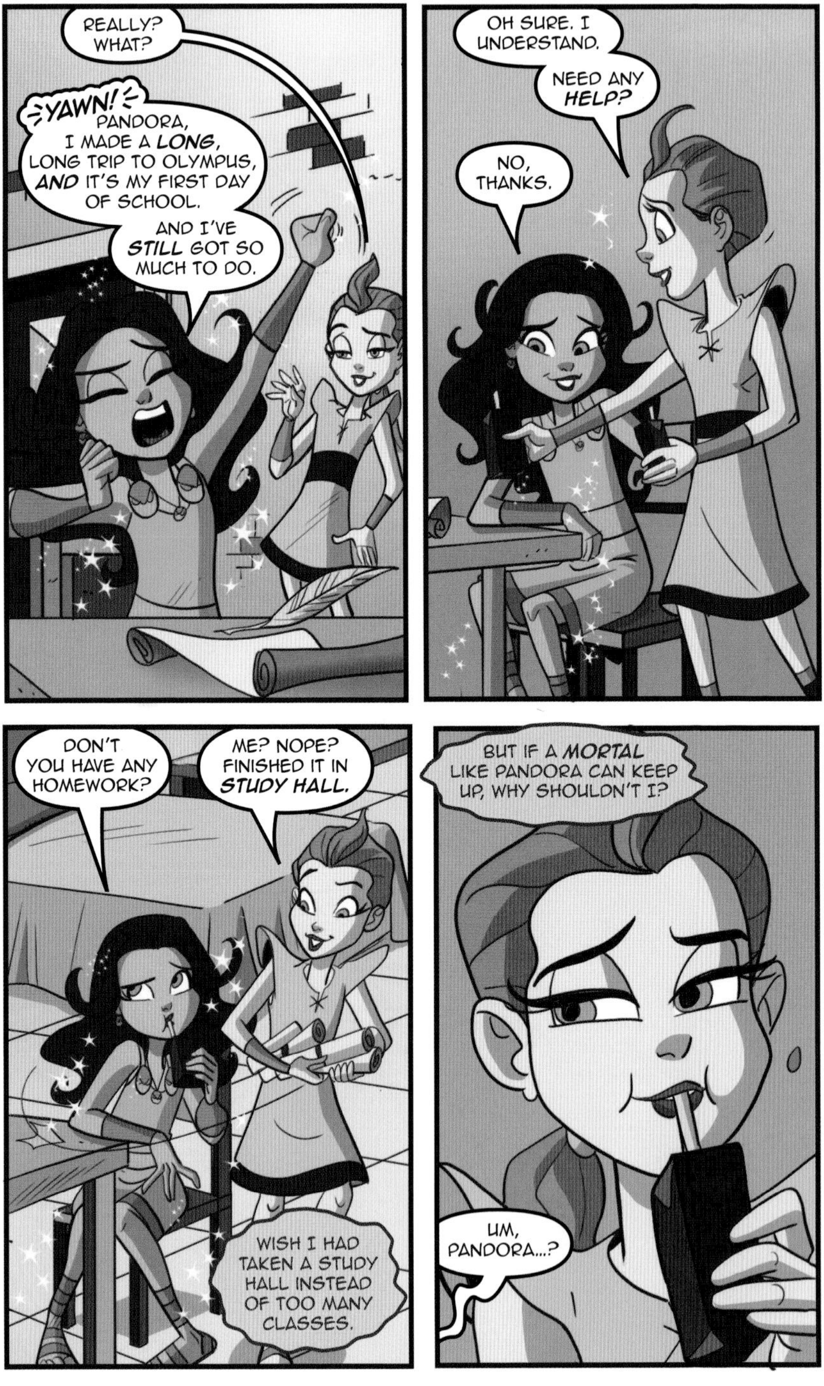

REALLY? WHAT?
YAWN!
PANDORA, I MADE A LONG, LONG TRIP TO OLYMPUS, AND IT'S MY FIRST DAY OF SCHOOL.
AND I'VE STILL GOT SO MUCH TO DO.
OH SURE. I UNDERSTAND.
NEED ANY HELP?
NO, THANKS.
DON'T YOU HAVE ANY HOMEWORK?
ME? NOPE? FINISHED IT IN STUDY HALL.
WISH I HAD TAKEN A STUDY HALL INSTEAD OF TOO MANY CLASSES.
BUT IF A MORTAL LIKE PANDORA CAN KEEP UP, WHY SHOULDN'T I?
UM, PANDORA...?

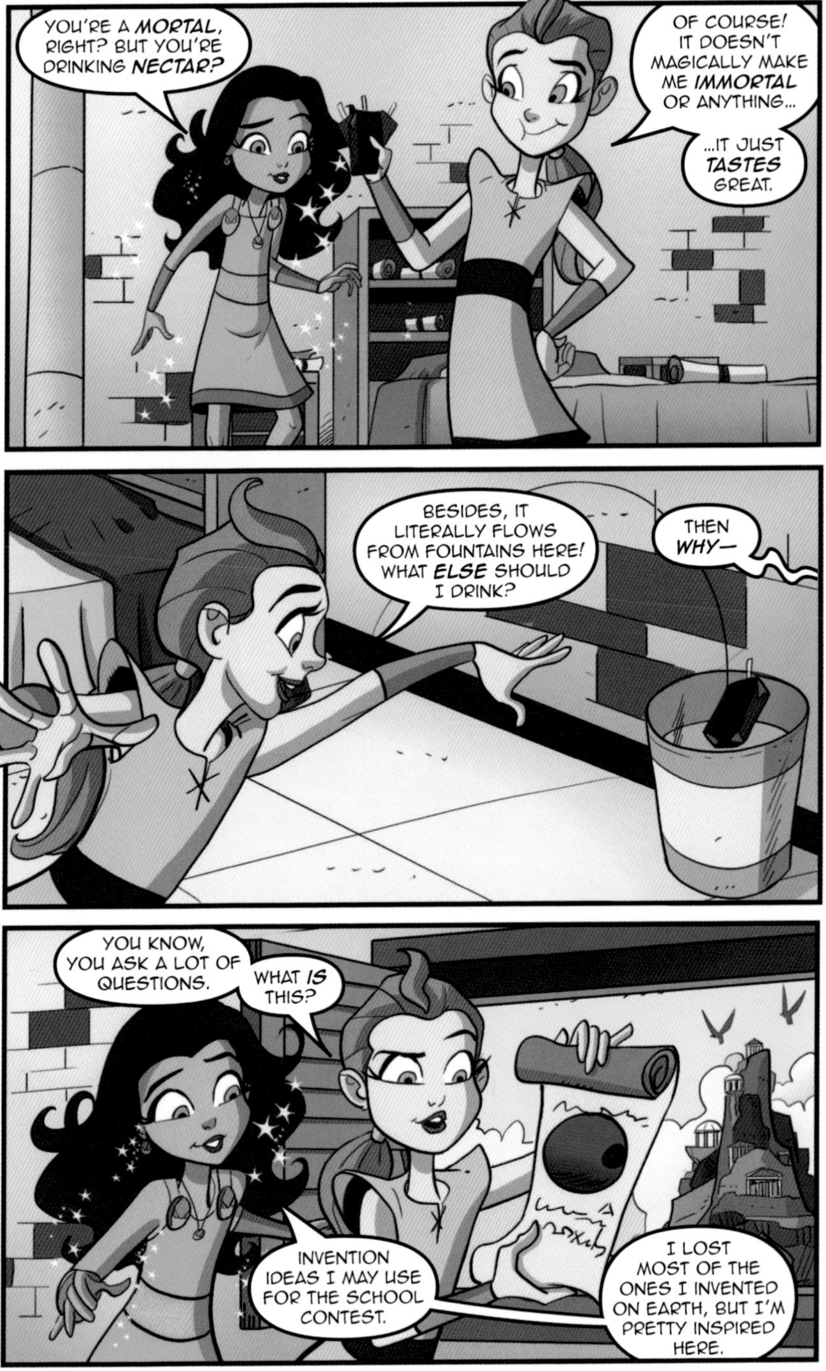
YOU'RE A **MORTAL**, RIGHT? BUT YOU'RE DRINKING **NECTAR?**
OF COURSE! IT DOESN'T MAGICALLY MAKE ME **IMMORTAL** OR ANYTHING...
...IT JUST **TASTES** GREAT.
BESIDES, IT LITERALLY FLOWS FROM FOUNTAINS HERE! WHAT **ELSE** SHOULD I DRINK?
THEN **WHY—**
YOU KNOW, YOU ASK A LOT OF QUESTIONS.
WHAT **IS** THIS?
INVENTION IDEAS I MAY USE FOR THE SCHOOL CONTEST.
I LOST MOST OF THE ONES I INVENTED ON EARTH, BUT I'M PRETTY INSPIRED HERE.

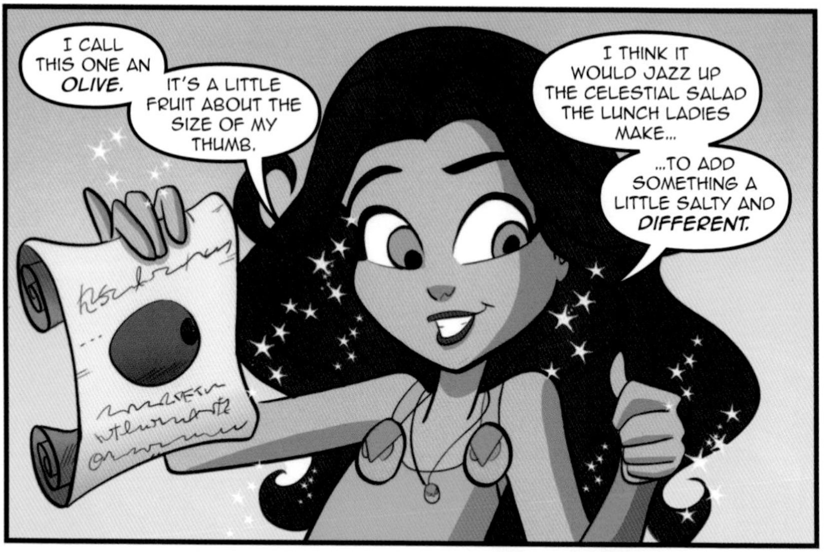
I CALL THIS ONE AN OLIVE.
IT'S A LITTLE FRUIT ABOUT THE SIZE OF MY THUMB.
I THINK IT WOULD JAZZ UP THE CELESTIAL SALAD THE LUNCH LADIES MAKE...
...TO ADD SOMETHING A LITTLE SALTY AND DIFFERENT.

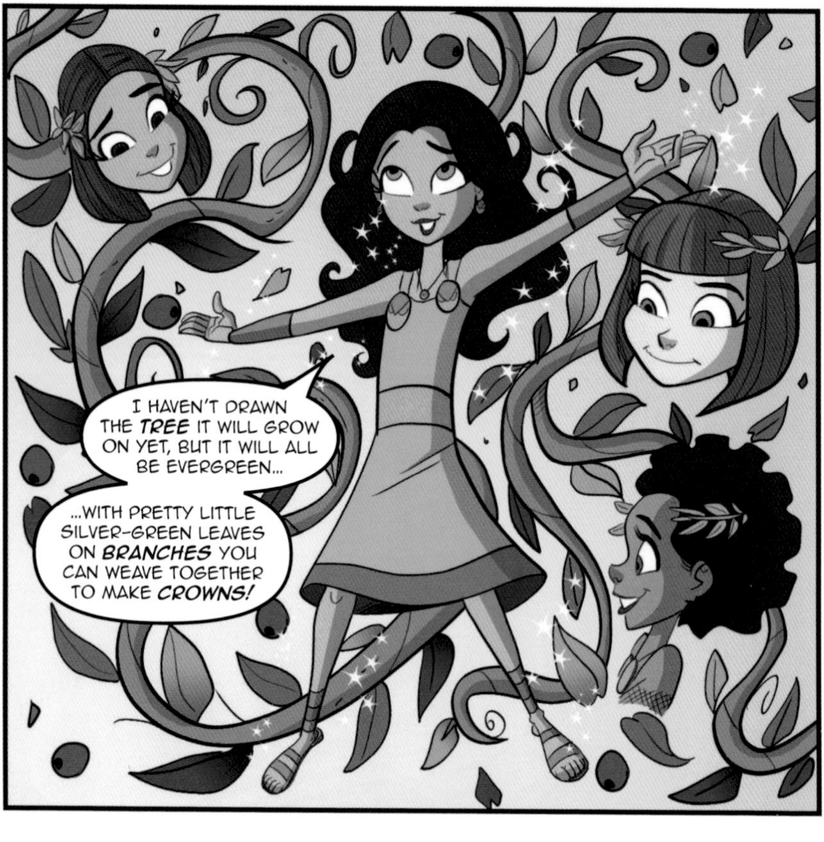
I HAVEN'T DRAWN THE TREE IT WILL GROW ON YET, BUT IT WILL ALL BE EVERGREEN...
...WITH PRETTY LITTLE SILVER-GREEN LEAVES ON BRANCHES YOU CAN WEAVE TOGETHER TO MAKE CROWNS!

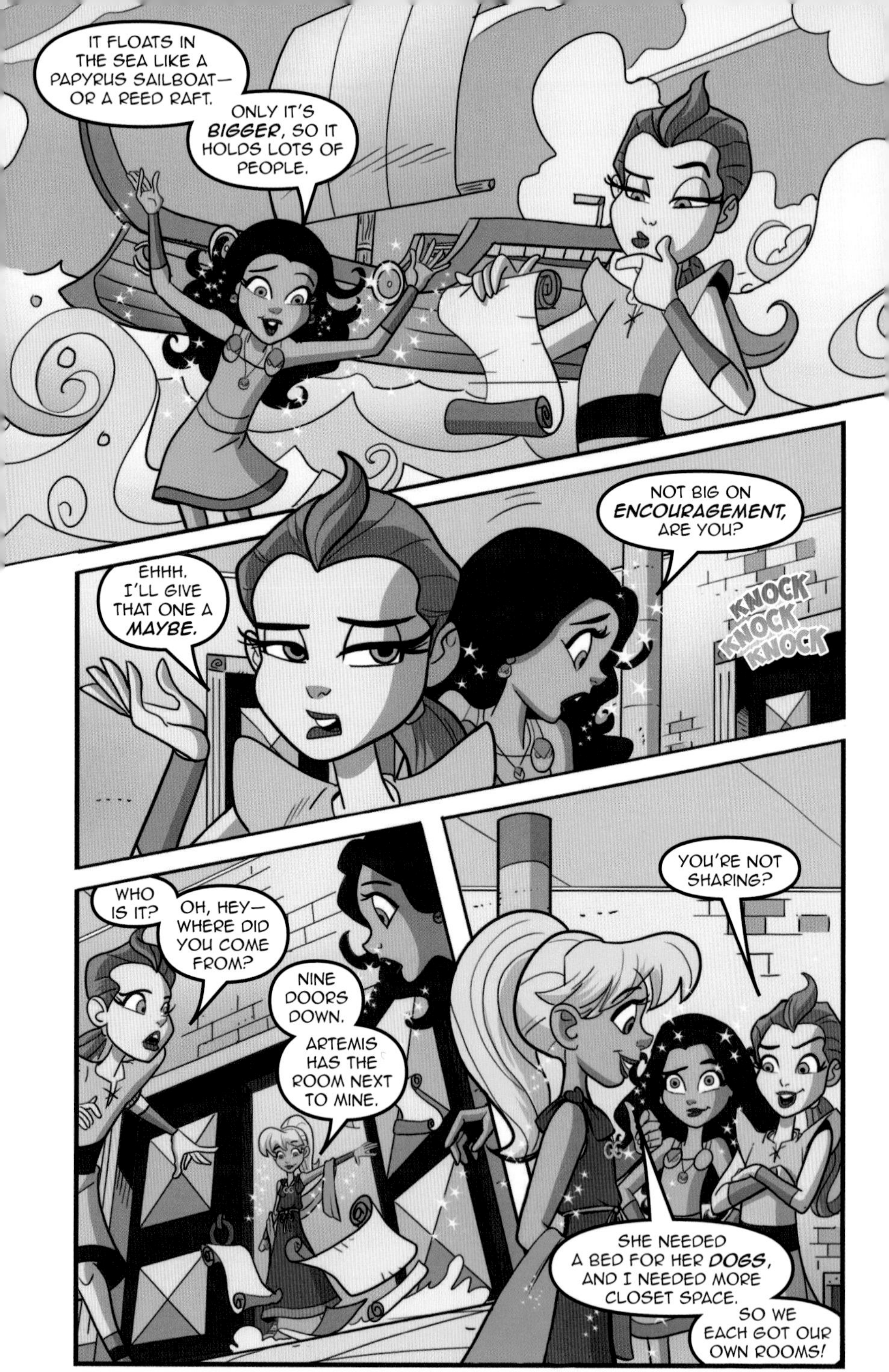
IT FLOATS IN THE SEA LIKE A PAPYRUS SAILBOAT— OR A REED RAFT.
ONLY IT'S *BIGGER*, SO IT HOLDS LOTS OF PEOPLE.
NOT BIG ON *ENCOURAGEMENT,* ARE YOU?
EHHH. I'LL GIVE THAT ONE A *MAYBE.*
KNOCK KNOCK KNOCK
WHO IS IT?
OH, HEY— WHERE DID YOU COME FROM?
NINE DOORS DOWN.
ARTEMIS HAS THE ROOM NEXT TO MINE.
YOU'RE NOT SHARING?
SHE NEEDED A BED FOR HER *DOGS*, AND I NEEDED MORE CLOSET SPACE.
SO WE EACH GOT OUR OWN ROOMS!

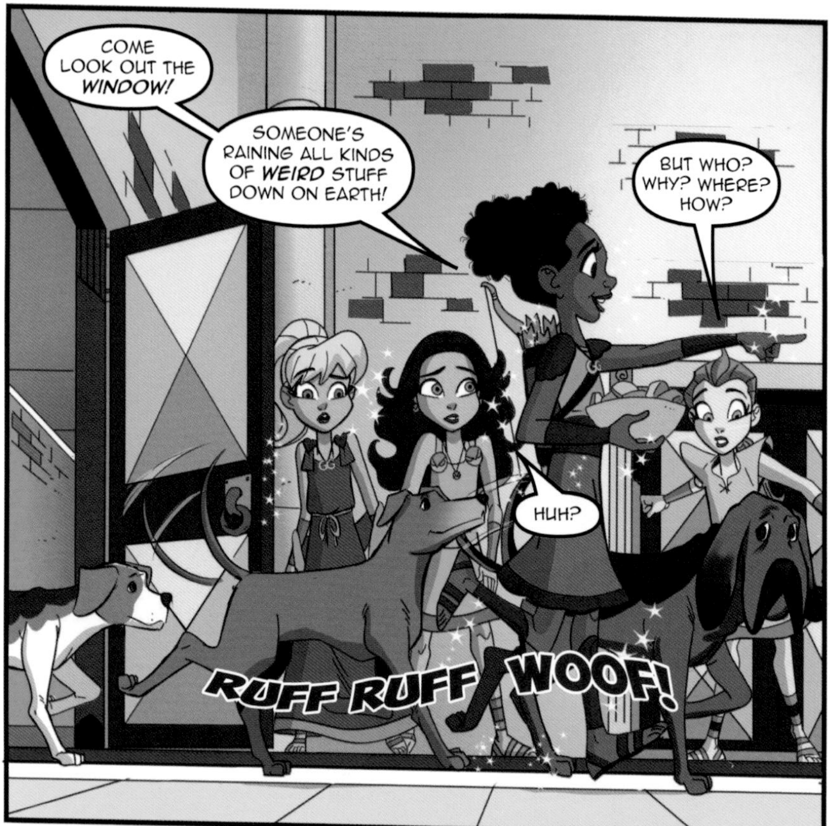
COME LOOK OUT THE *WINDOW!*
SOMEONE'S RAINING ALL KINDS OF *WEIRD* STUFF DOWN ON EARTH!
BUT WHO? WHY? WHERE? HOW?
HUH?
RUFF RUFF WOOF!

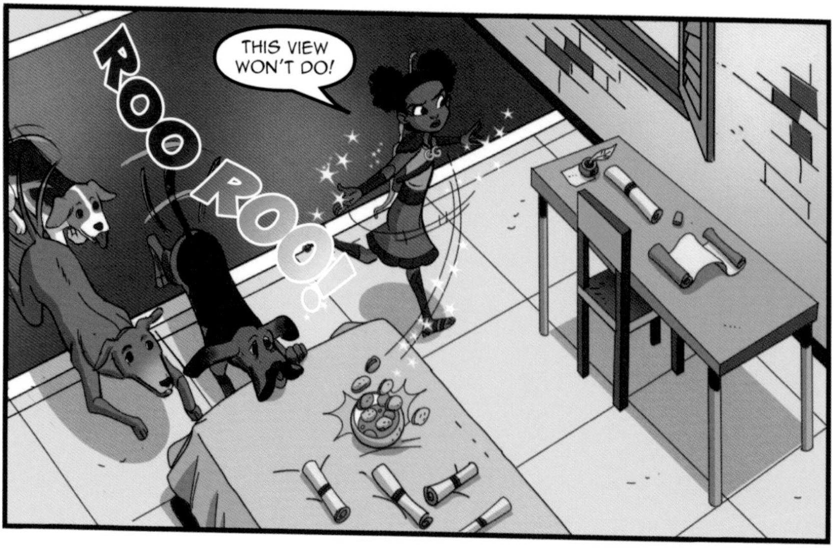
THIS VIEW WON'T DO!
ROO ROO!

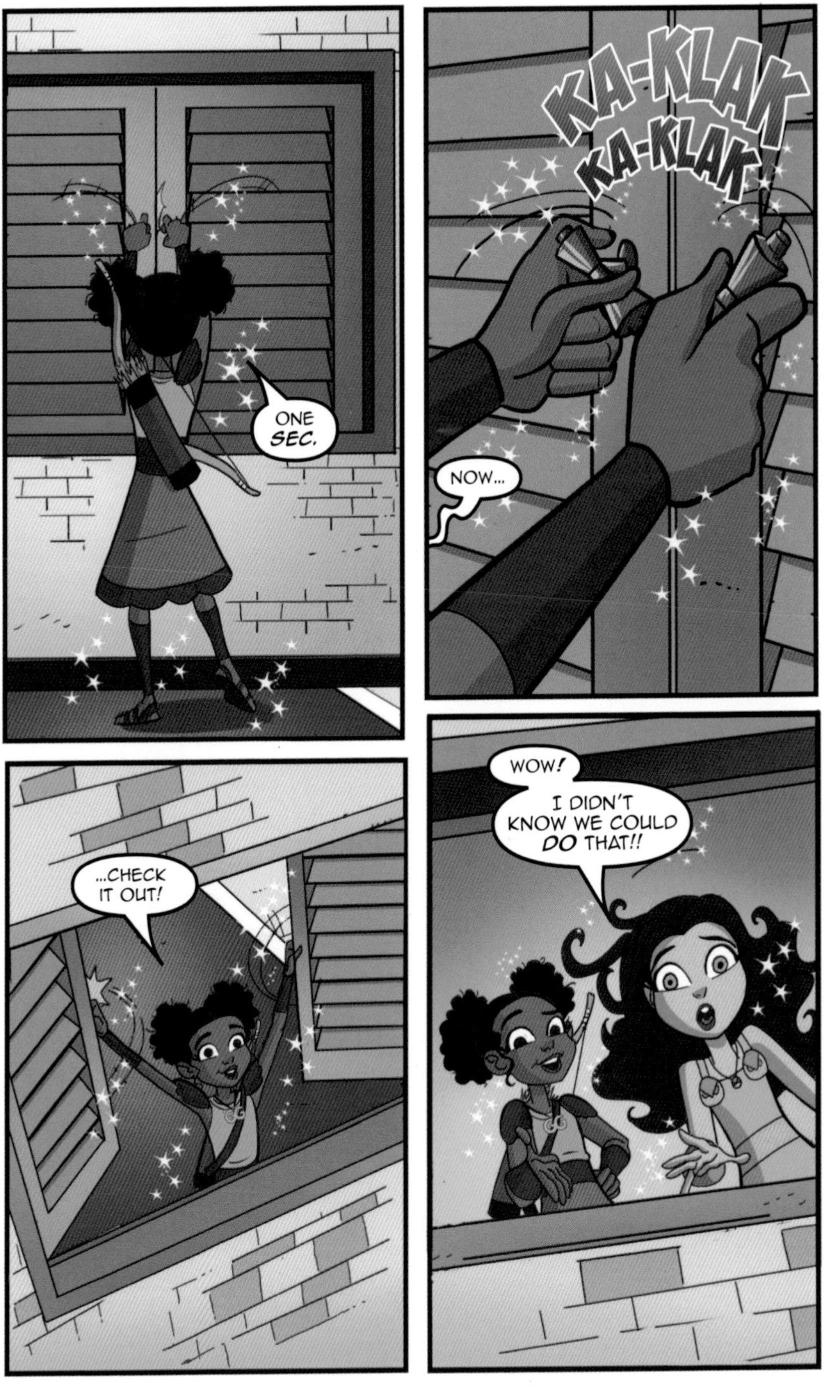

ONE SEC.
KA-KLAK KA-KLAK
NOW...
...CHECK IT OUT!
WOW!
I DIDN'T KNOW WE COULD DO THAT!!

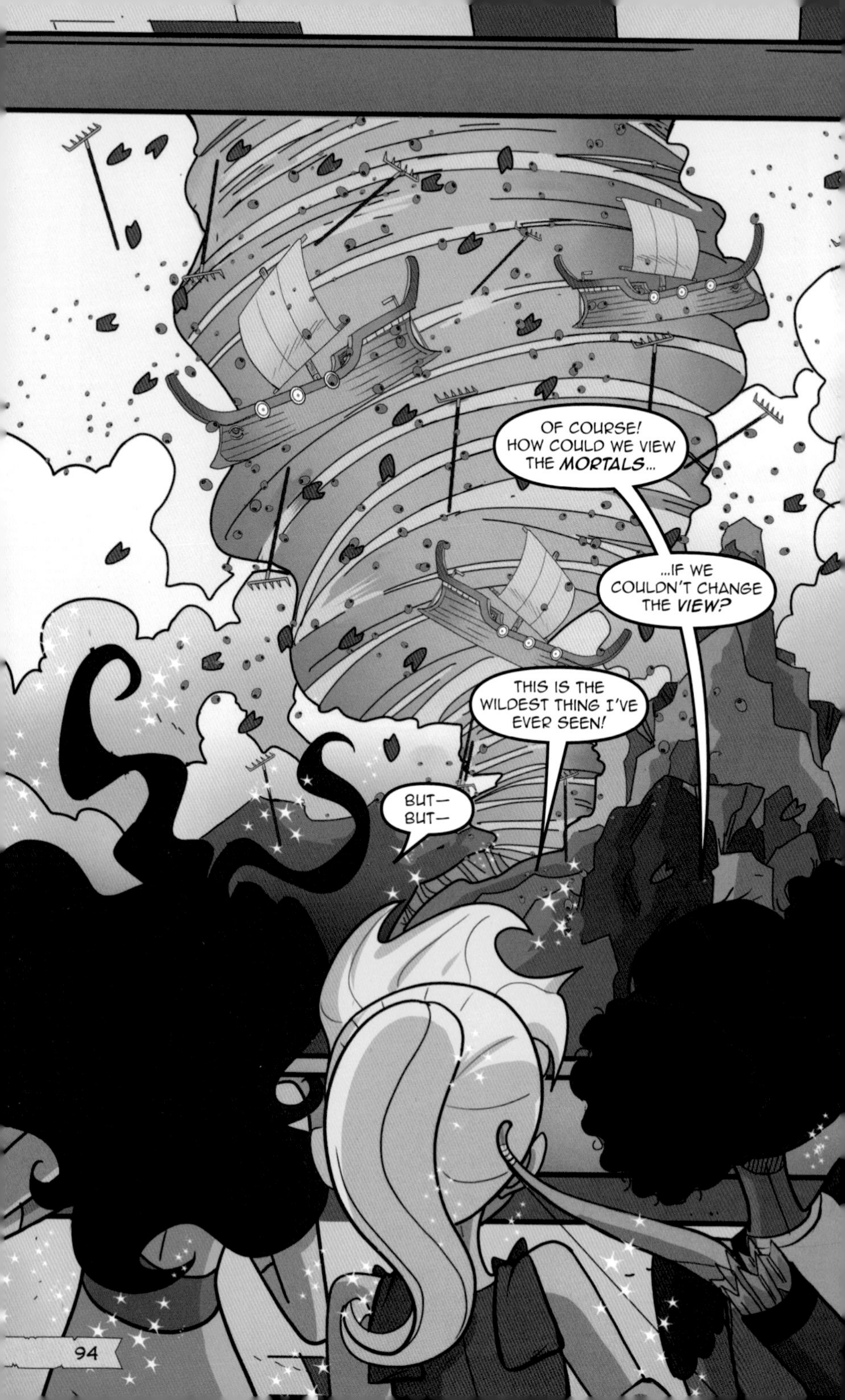
OF COURSE! HOW COULD WE VIEW THE *MORTALS*...
...IF WE COULDN'T CHANGE THE *VIEW?*
THIS IS THE WILDEST THING I'VE EVER SEEN!
BUT— BUT—

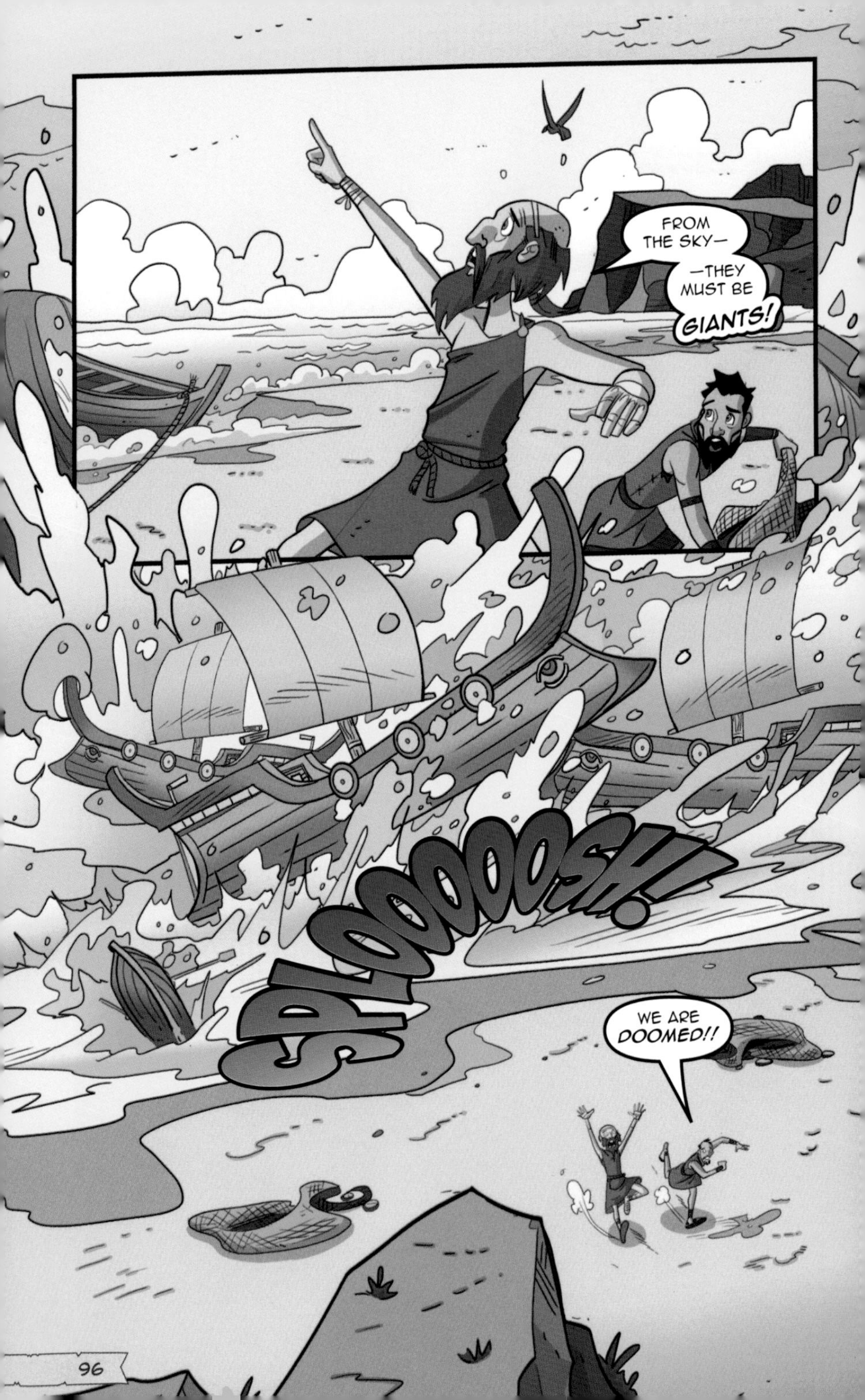
FROM THE SKY—
—THEY MUST BE GIANTS!
SPLOOOOOSH!
WE ARE DOOMED!!

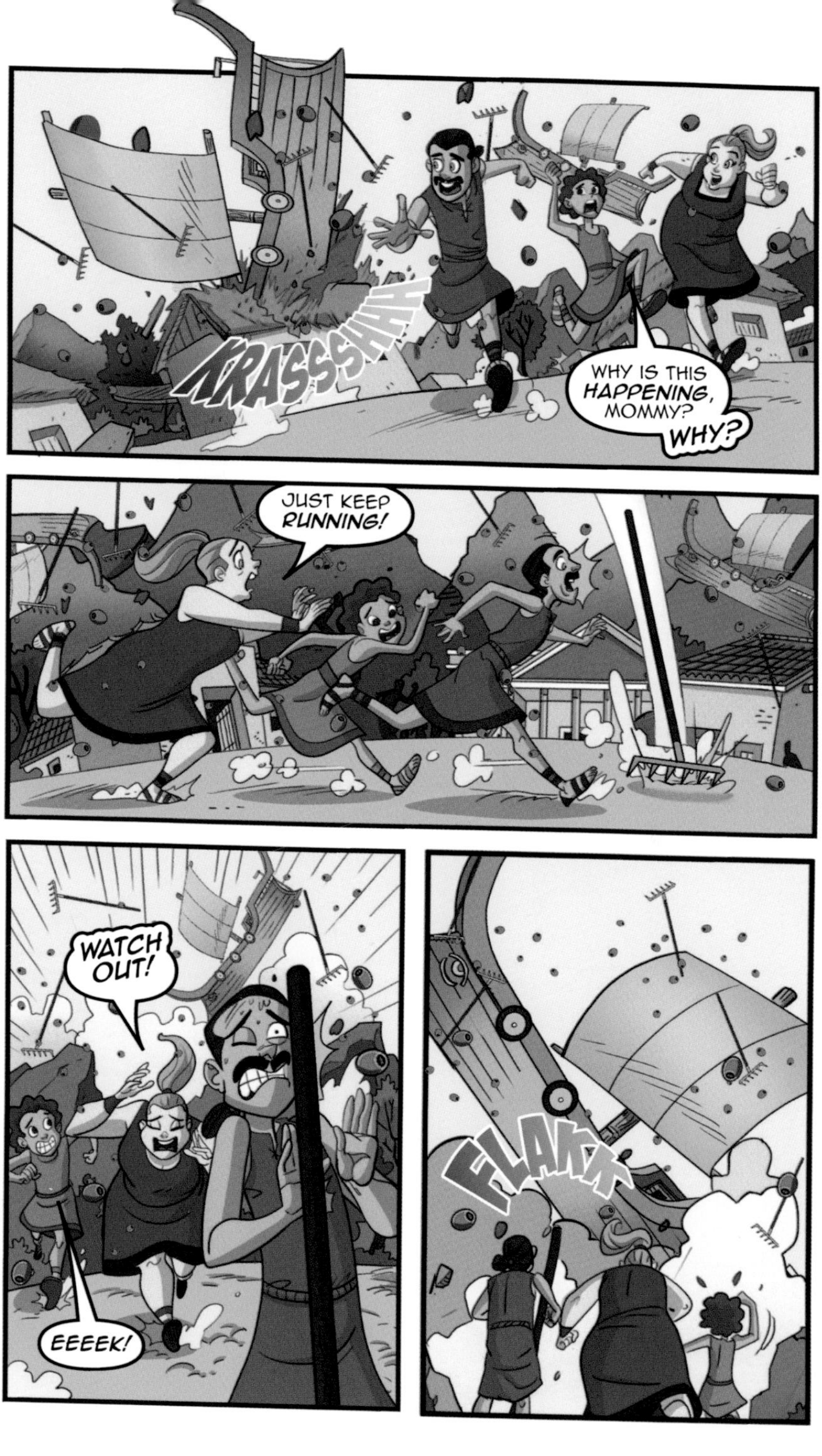
KRASSSHHH
WHY IS THIS HAPPENING, MOMMY? WHY?
JUST KEEP RUNNING!
WATCH OUT!
EEEEK!
FLAKK

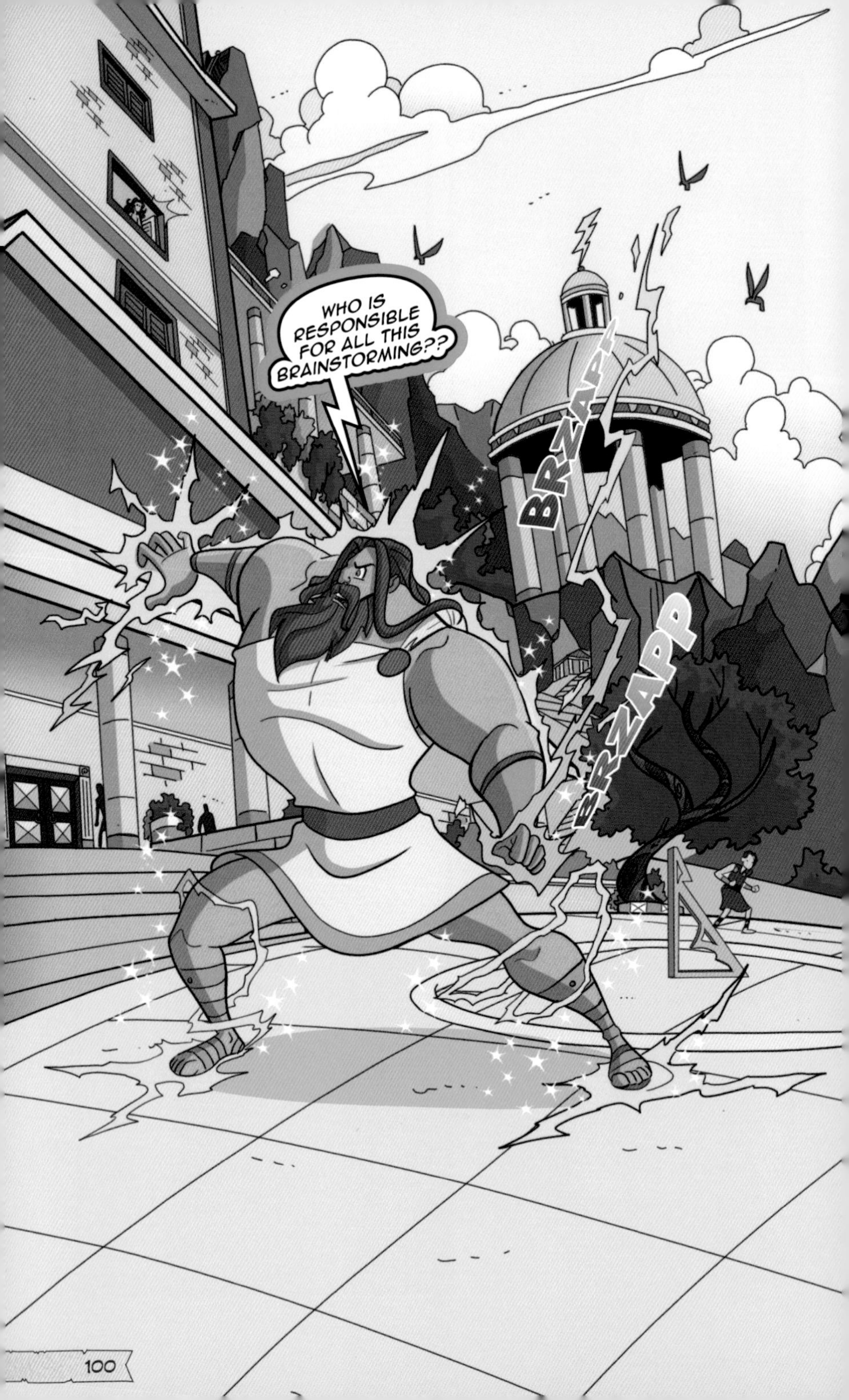
WHO IS RESPONSIBLE FOR ALL THIS BRAINSTORMING??
BRZAPP
BRZAPP

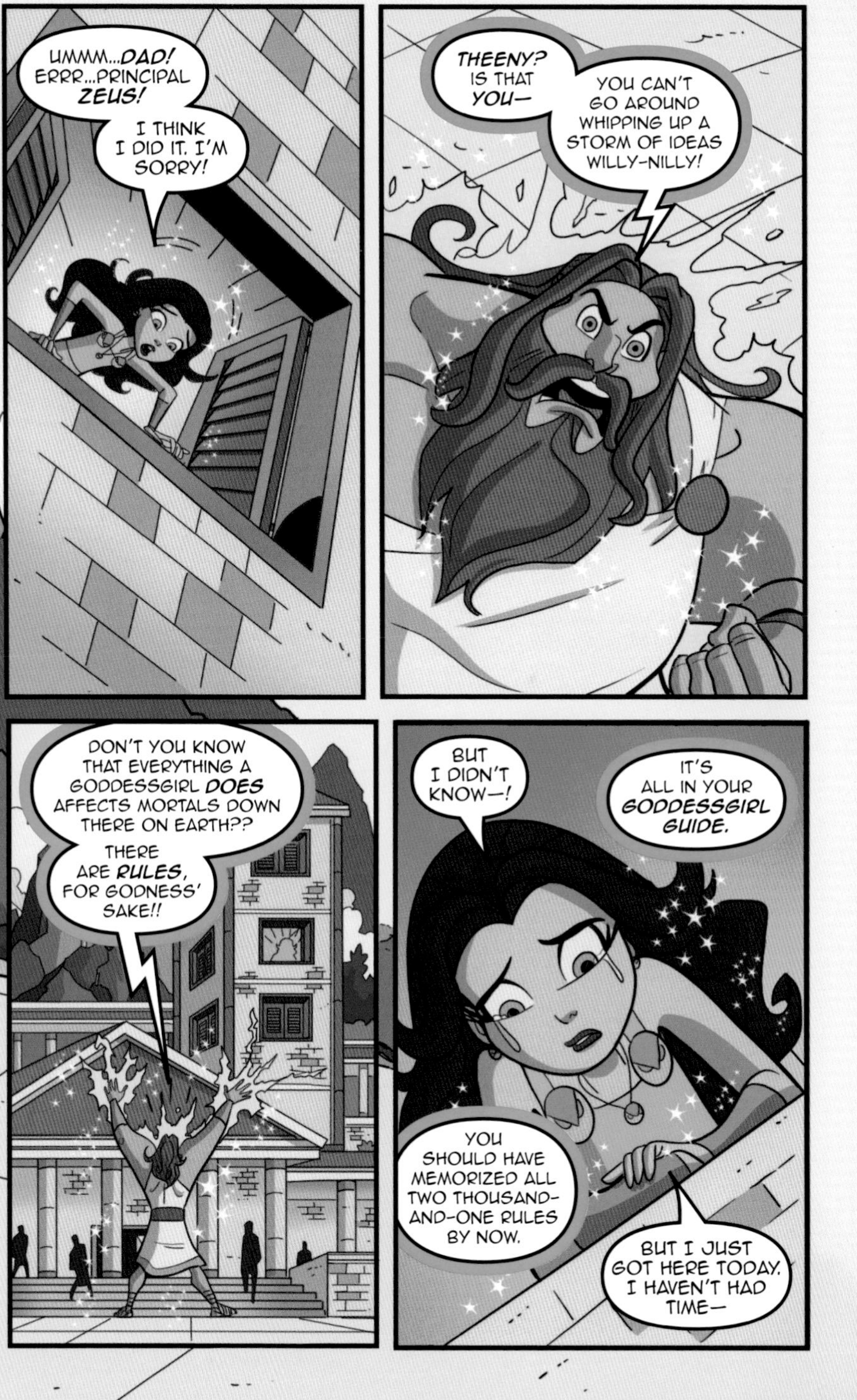
UMMM...DAD! ERRR...PRINCIPAL ZEUS!
I THINK I DID IT. I'M SORRY!
THEENY? IS THAT YOU—
YOU CAN'T GO AROUND WHIPPING UP A STORM OF IDEAS WILLY-NILLY!
DON'T YOU KNOW THAT EVERYTHING A GODDESSGIRL DOES AFFECTS MORTALS DOWN THERE ON EARTH??
THERE ARE RULES, FOR GODNESS' SAKE!!
BUT I DIDN'T KNOW—!
IT'S ALL IN YOUR GODDESSGIRL GUIDE.
YOU SHOULD HAVE MEMORIZED ALL TWO THOUSAND-AND-ONE RULES BY NOW.
BUT I JUST GOT HERE TODAY. I HAVEN'T HAD TIME—

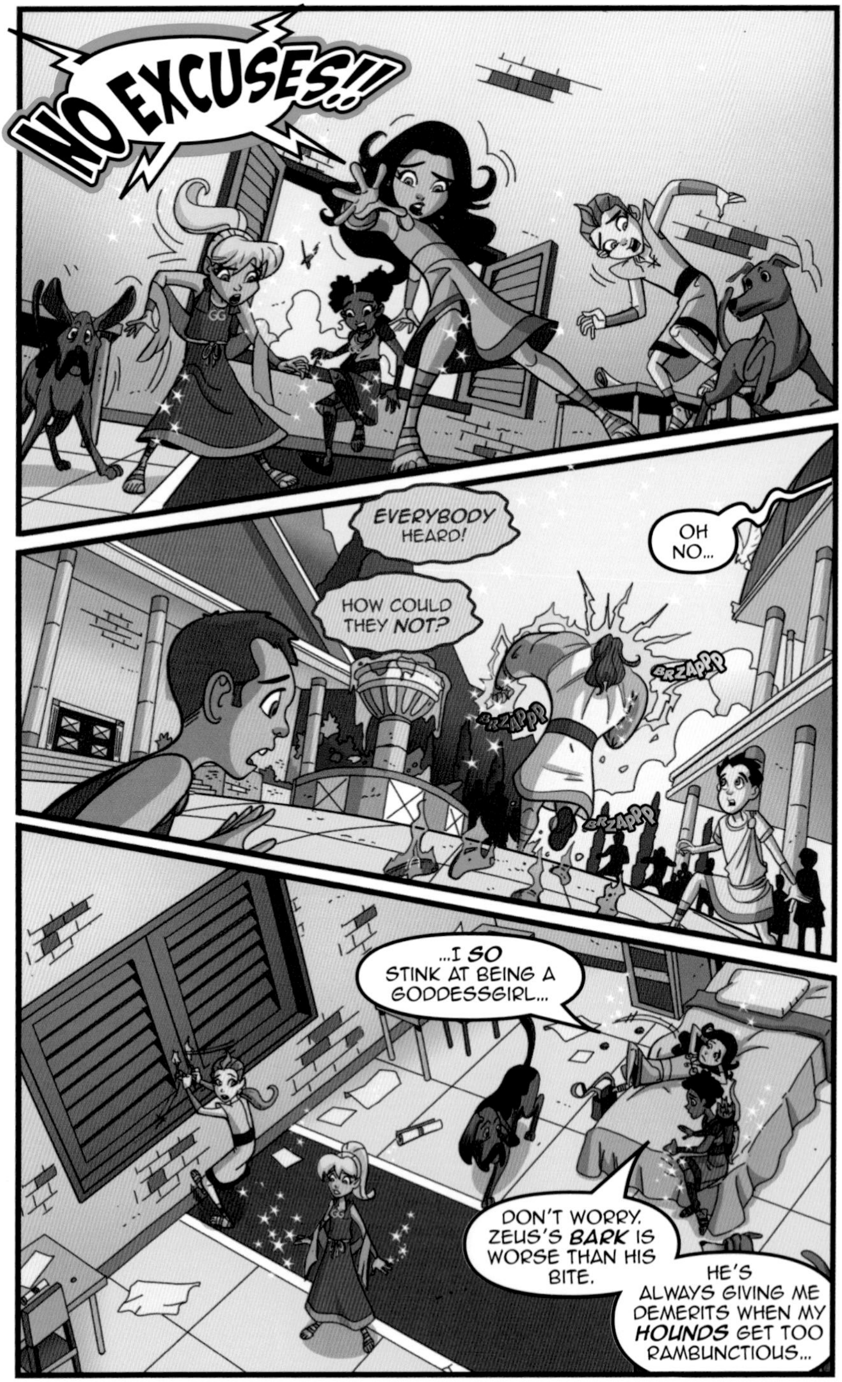
NO EXCUSES!!
EVERYBODY HEARD!
HOW COULD THEY NOT?
OH NO...
BRZAPPP
BRZAPPP
BRZAPPP
...I SO STINK AT BEING A GODDESSGIRL...
DON'T WORRY. ZEUS'S BARK IS WORSE THAN HIS BITE.
HE'S ALWAYS GIVING ME DEMERITS WHEN MY HOUNDS GET TOO RAMBUNCTIOUS...

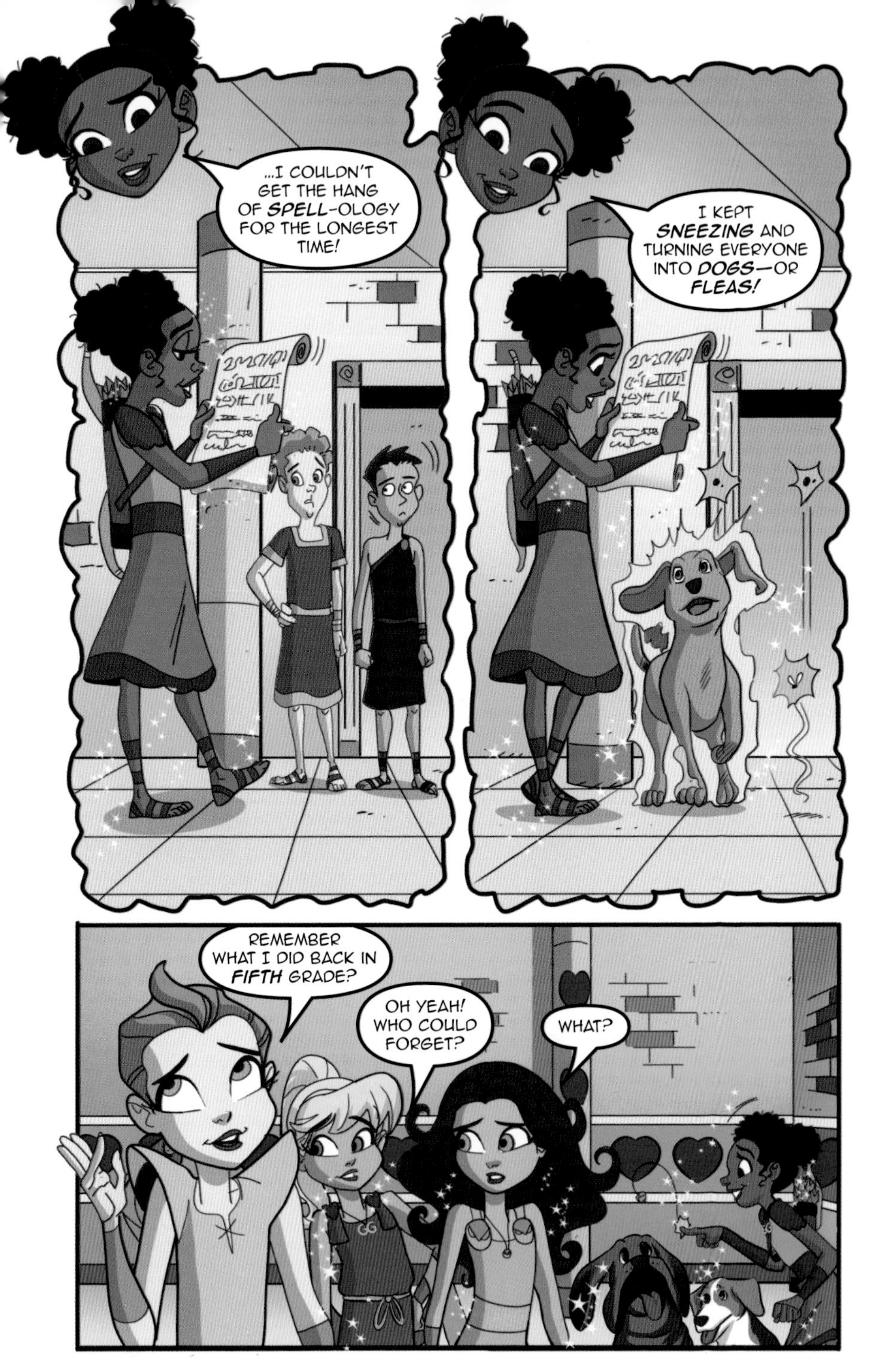
...I COULDN'T GET THE HANG OF SPELL-OLOGY FOR THE LONGEST TIME!
I KEPT SNEEZING AND TURNING EVERYONE INTO DOGS—OR FLEAS!
REMEMBER WHAT I DID BACK IN FIFTH GRADE?
OH YEAH! WHO COULD FORGET?
WHAT?

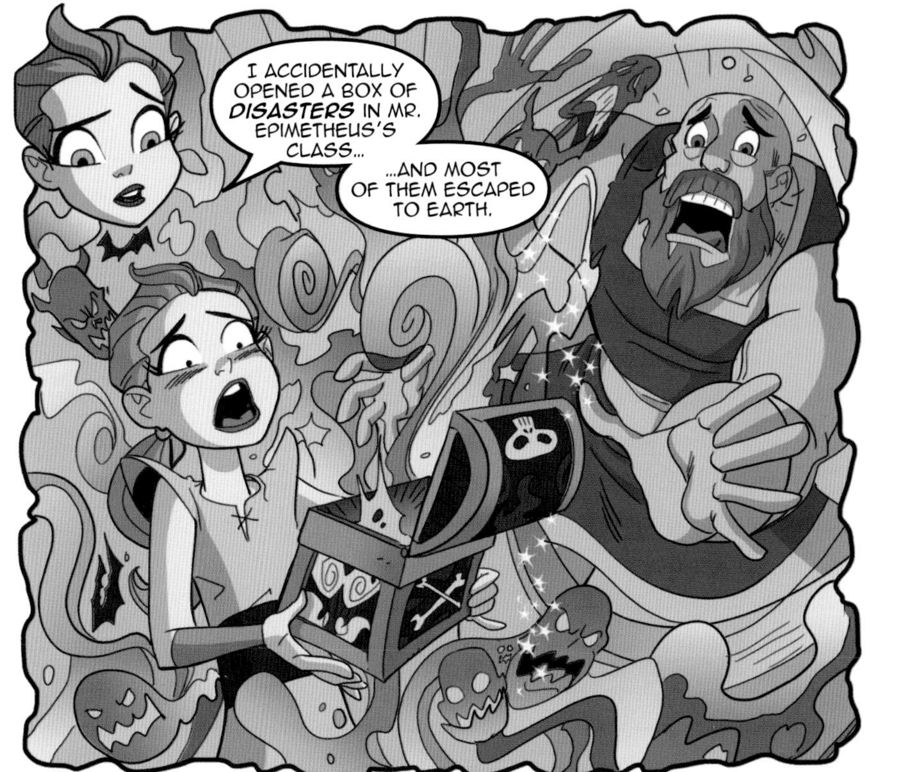
I ACCIDENTALLY OPENED A BOX OF DISASTERS IN MR. EPIMETHEUS'S CLASS...
...AND MOST OF THEM ESCAPED TO EARTH.

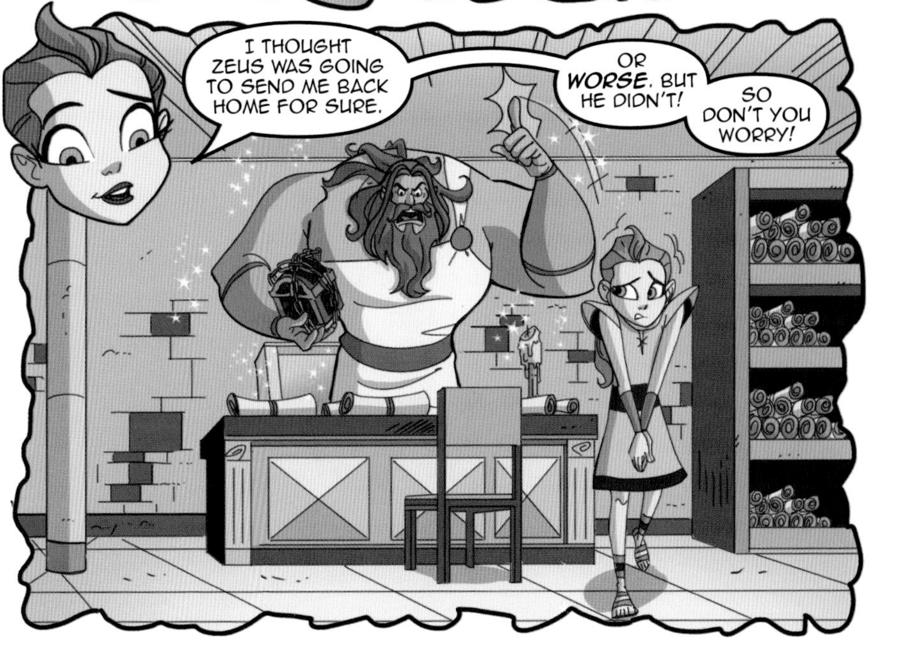
I THOUGHT ZEUS WAS GOING TO SEND ME BACK HOME FOR SURE.
OR WORSE. BUT HE DIDN'T!
SO DON'T YOU WORRY!

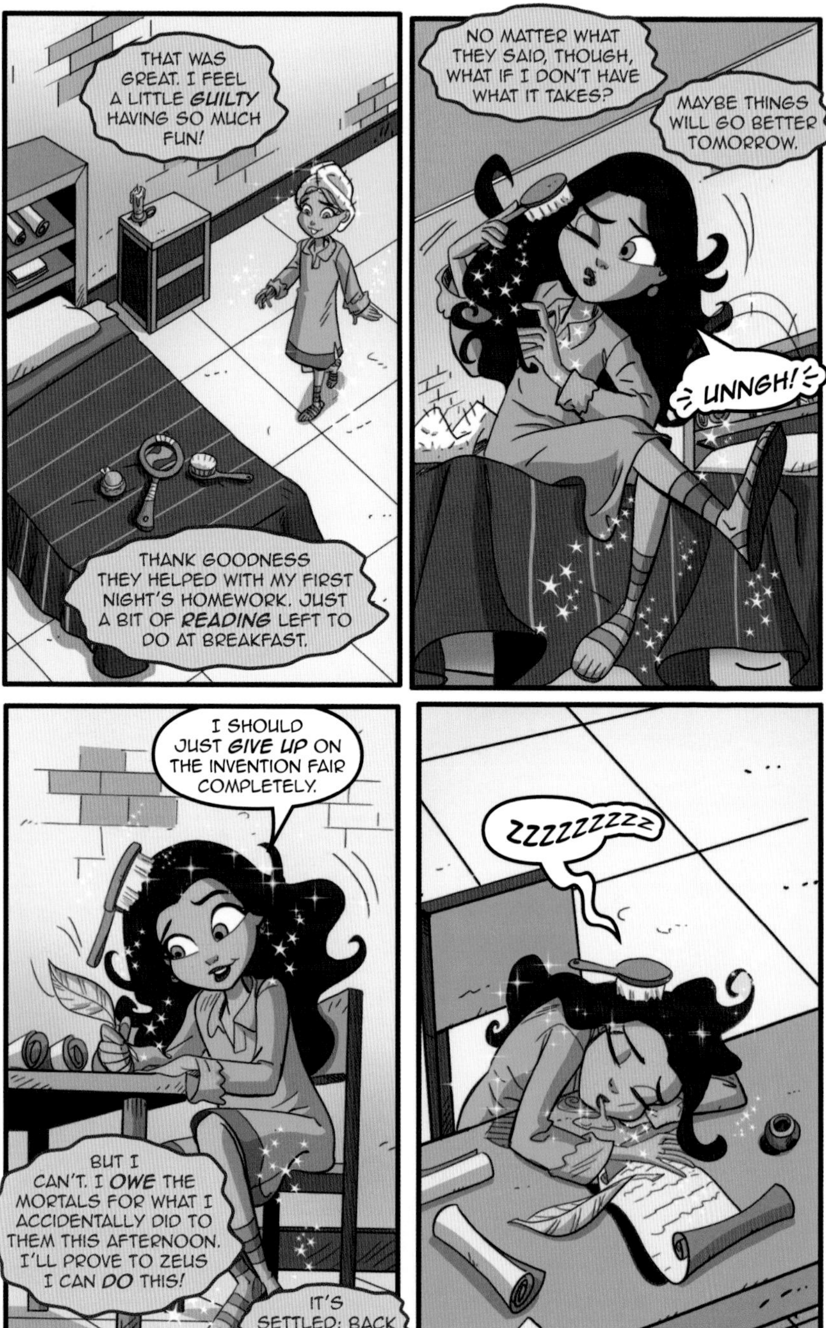
THAT WAS GREAT. I FEEL A LITTLE GUILTY HAVING SO MUCH FUN!
THANK GOODNESS THEY HELPED WITH MY FIRST NIGHT'S HOMEWORK. JUST A BIT OF READING LEFT TO DO AT BREAKFAST.
NO MATTER WHAT THEY SAID, THOUGH, WHAT IF I DON'T HAVE WHAT IT TAKES?
MAYBE THINGS WILL GO BETTER TOMORROW.
UNNGH!
I SHOULD JUST GIVE UP ON THE INVENTION FAIR COMPLETELY.
BUT I CAN'T. I OWE THE MORTALS FOR WHAT I ACCIDENTALLY DID TO THEM THIS AFTERNOON. I'LL PROVE TO ZEUS I CAN DO THIS!
IT'S SETTLED: BACK TO WORK!
ZZZZZZZZZ

CHAPTER 7: DROWNING

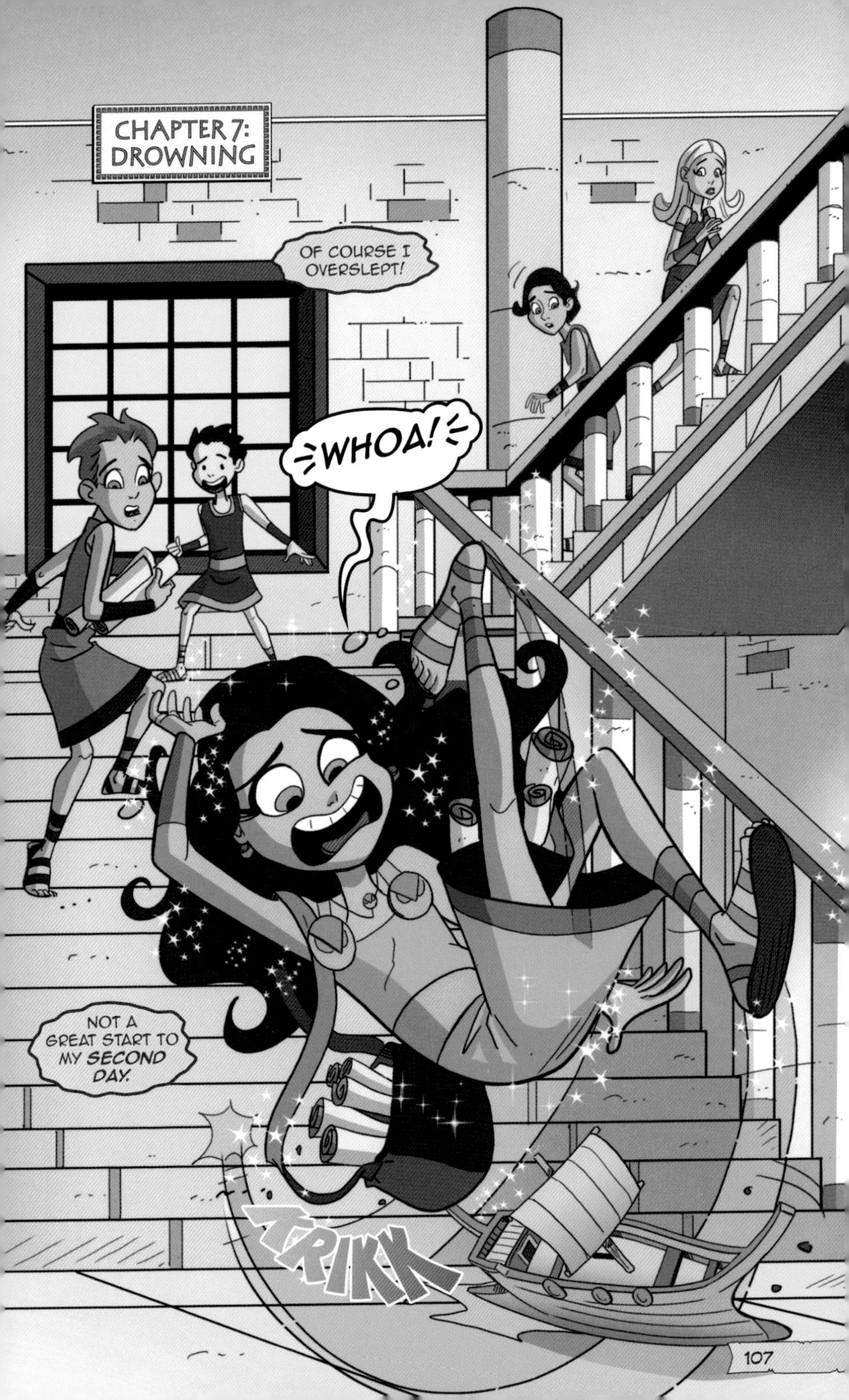
OF COURSE I OVERSLEPT!
WHOA!
NOT A GREAT START TO MY SECOND DAY.
KRIKK

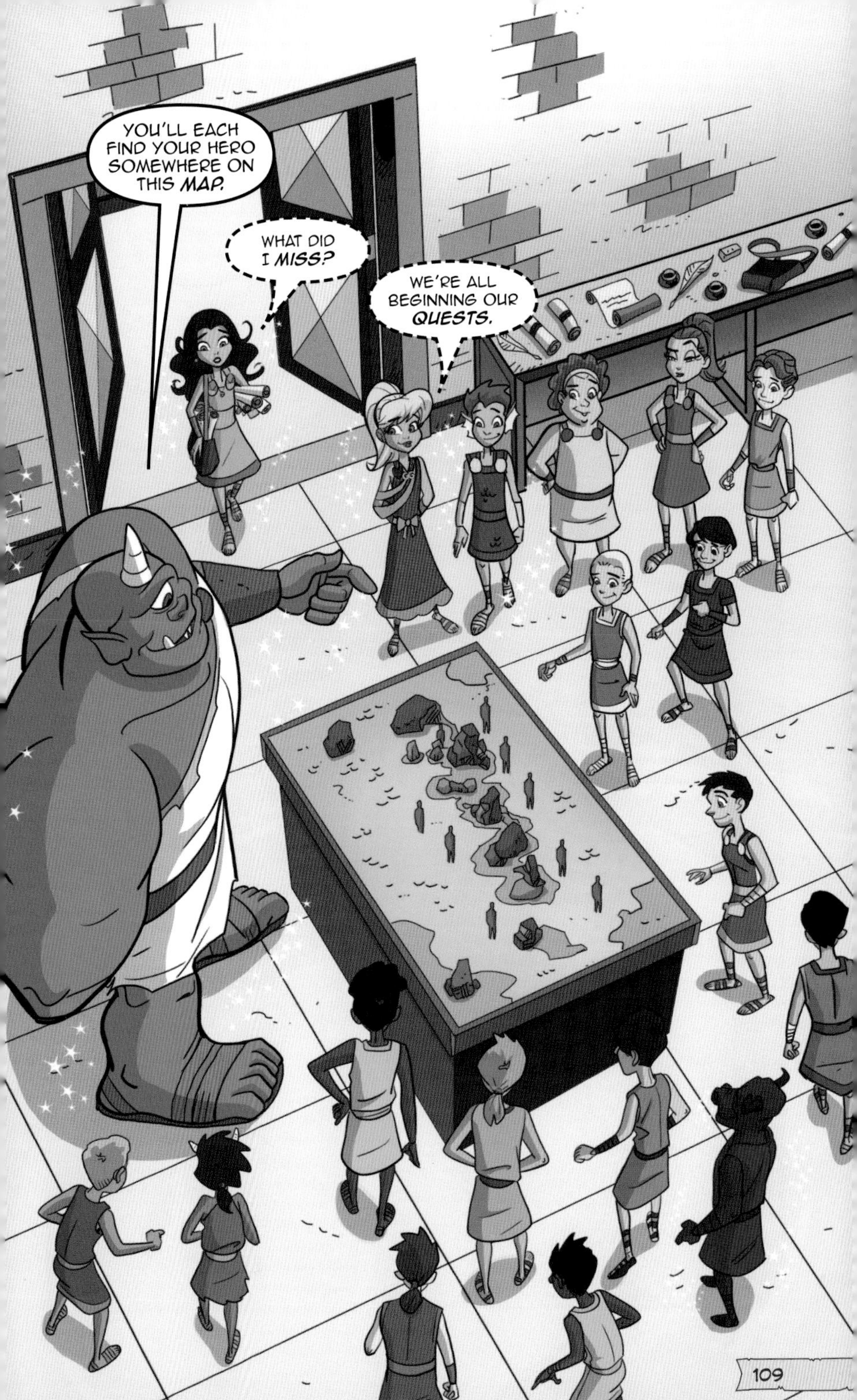
YOU'LL EACH FIND YOUR HERO SOMEWHERE ON THIS *MAP.*
WHAT DID I *MISS?*
WE'RE ALL BEGINNING OUR *QUESTS.*

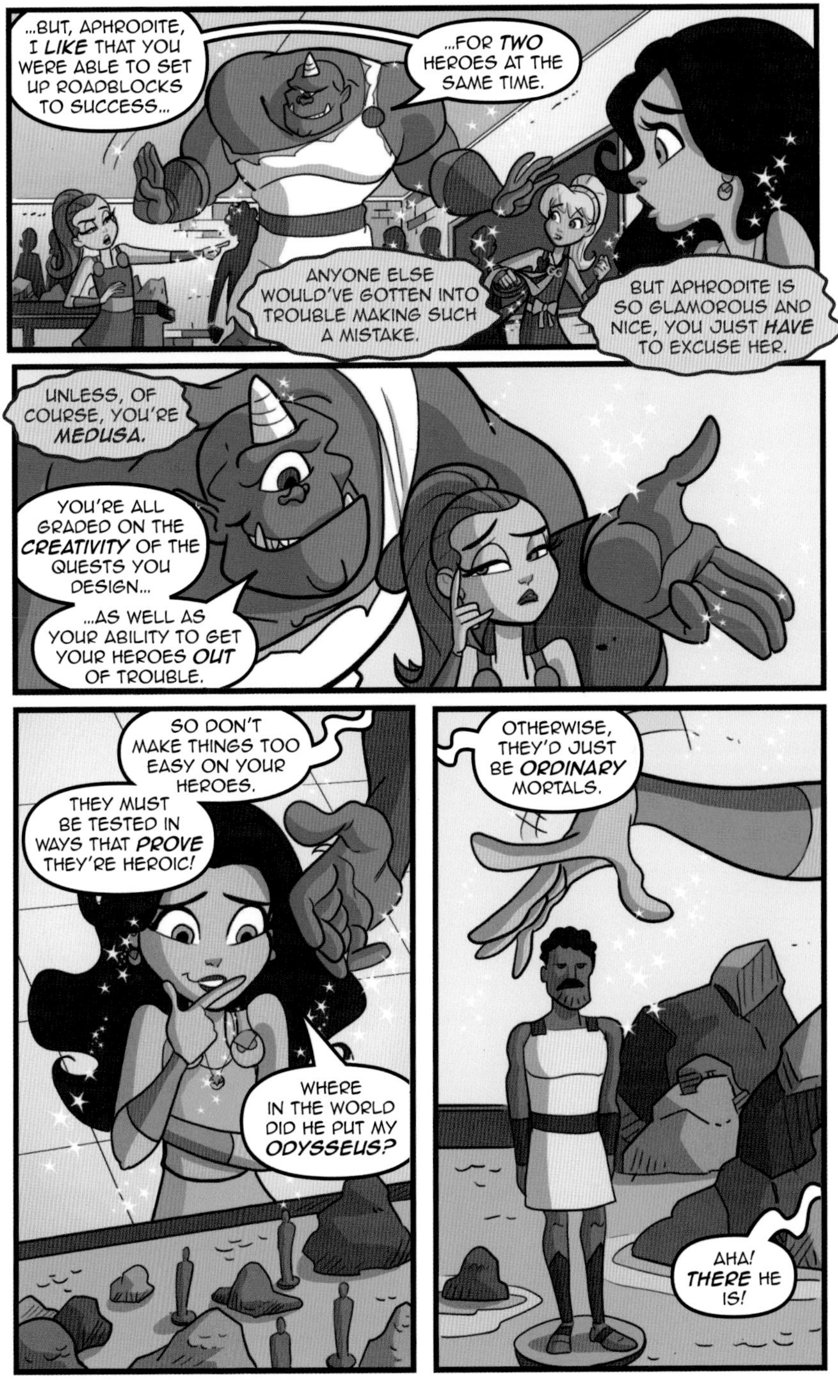
...BUT, APHRODITE, I *LIKE* THAT YOU WERE ABLE TO SET UP ROADBLOCKS TO SUCCESS...
...FOR *TWO* HEROES AT THE SAME TIME.
ANYONE ELSE WOULD'VE GOTTEN INTO TROUBLE MAKING SUCH A MISTAKE.
BUT APHRODITE IS SO GLAMOROUS AND NICE, YOU JUST *HAVE* TO EXCUSE HER.
UNLESS, OF COURSE, YOU'RE *MEDUSA.*
YOU'RE ALL GRADED ON THE *CREATIVITY* OF THE QUESTS YOU DESIGN...
...AS WELL AS YOUR ABILITY TO GET YOUR HEROES *OUT* OF TROUBLE.
SO DON'T MAKE THINGS TOO EASY ON YOUR HEROES.
THEY MUST BE TESTED IN WAYS THAT *PROVE* THEY'RE HEROIC!
WHERE IN THE WORLD DID HE PUT MY *ODYSSEUS?*
OTHERWISE, THEY'D JUST BE *ORDINARY* MORTALS.
AHA! *THERE* HE IS!

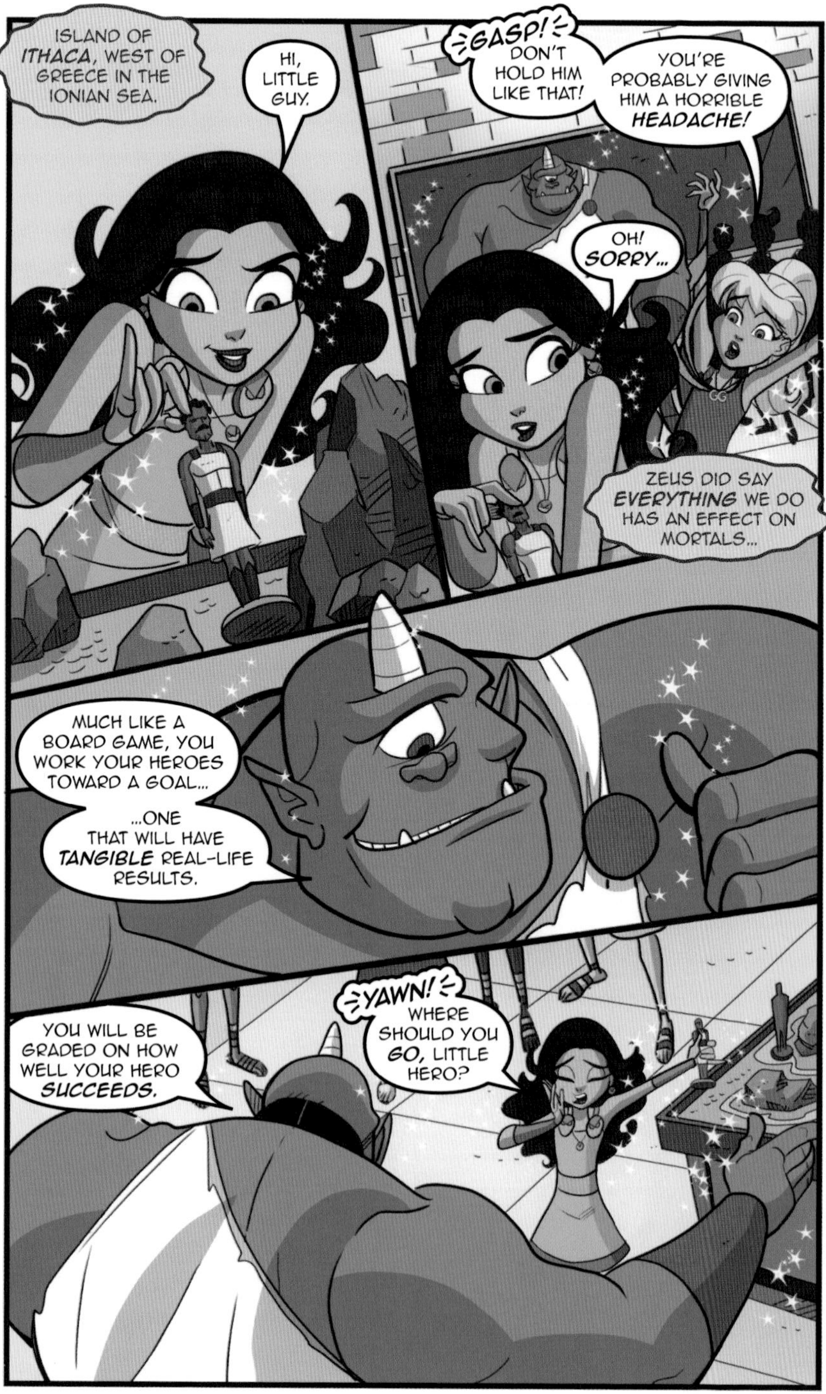
ISLAND OF ITHACA, WEST OF GREECE IN THE IONIAN SEA.
HI, LITTLE GUY.
GASP!
DON'T HOLD HIM LIKE THAT!
YOU'RE PROBABLY GIVING HIM A HORRIBLE HEADACHE!
OH! SORRY...
ZEUS DID SAY EVERYTHING WE DO HAS AN EFFECT ON MORTALS...
MUCH LIKE A BOARD GAME, YOU WORK YOUR HEROES TOWARD A GOAL...
...ONE THAT WILL HAVE TANGIBLE REAL-LIFE RESULTS.
YOU WILL BE GRADED ON HOW WELL YOUR HERO SUCCEEDS.
YAWN!
WHERE SHOULD YOU GO, LITTLE HERO?

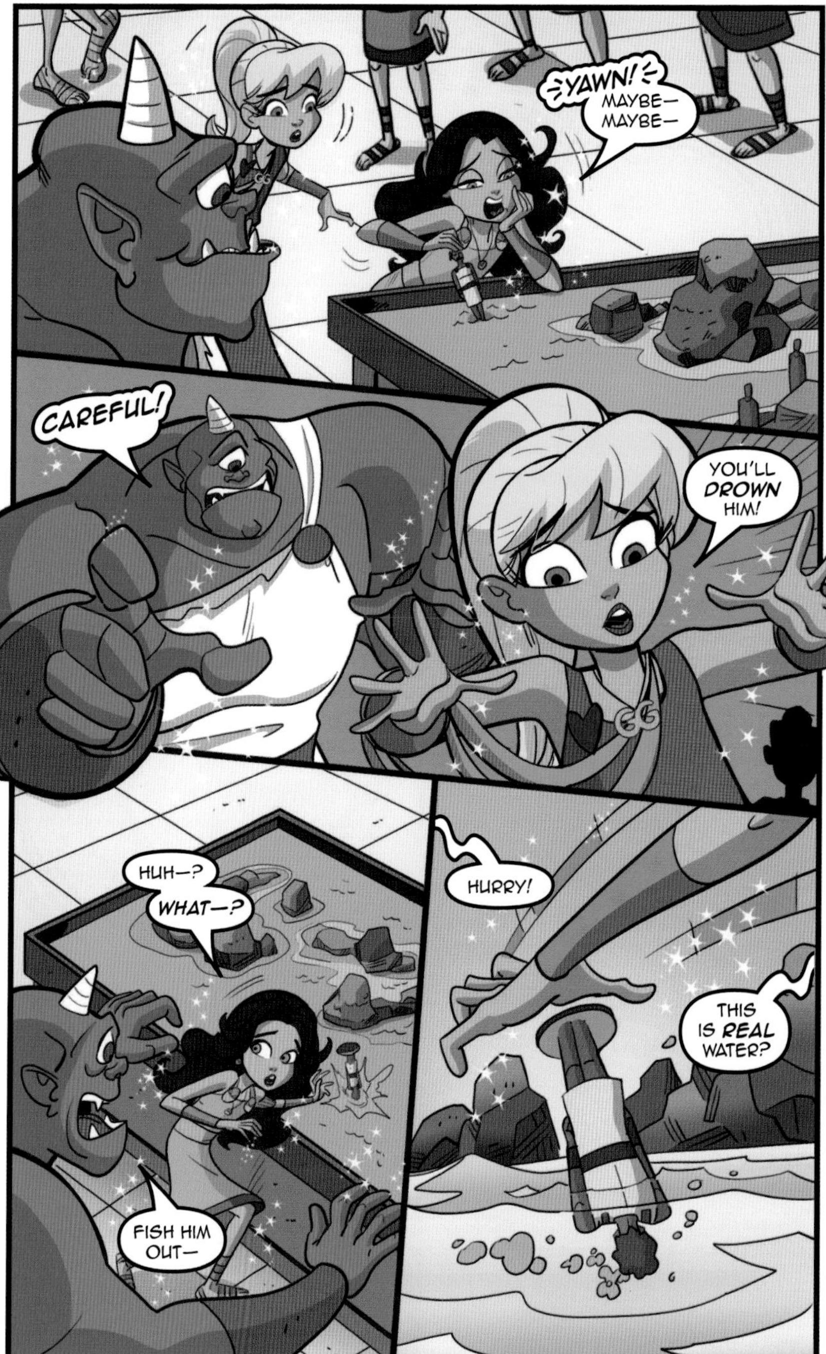
YAWN! MAYBE— MAYBE—
CAREFUL!
YOU'LL DROWN HIM!
HUH—?
WHAT—?
FISH HIM OUT—
HURRY!
THIS IS REAL WATER?

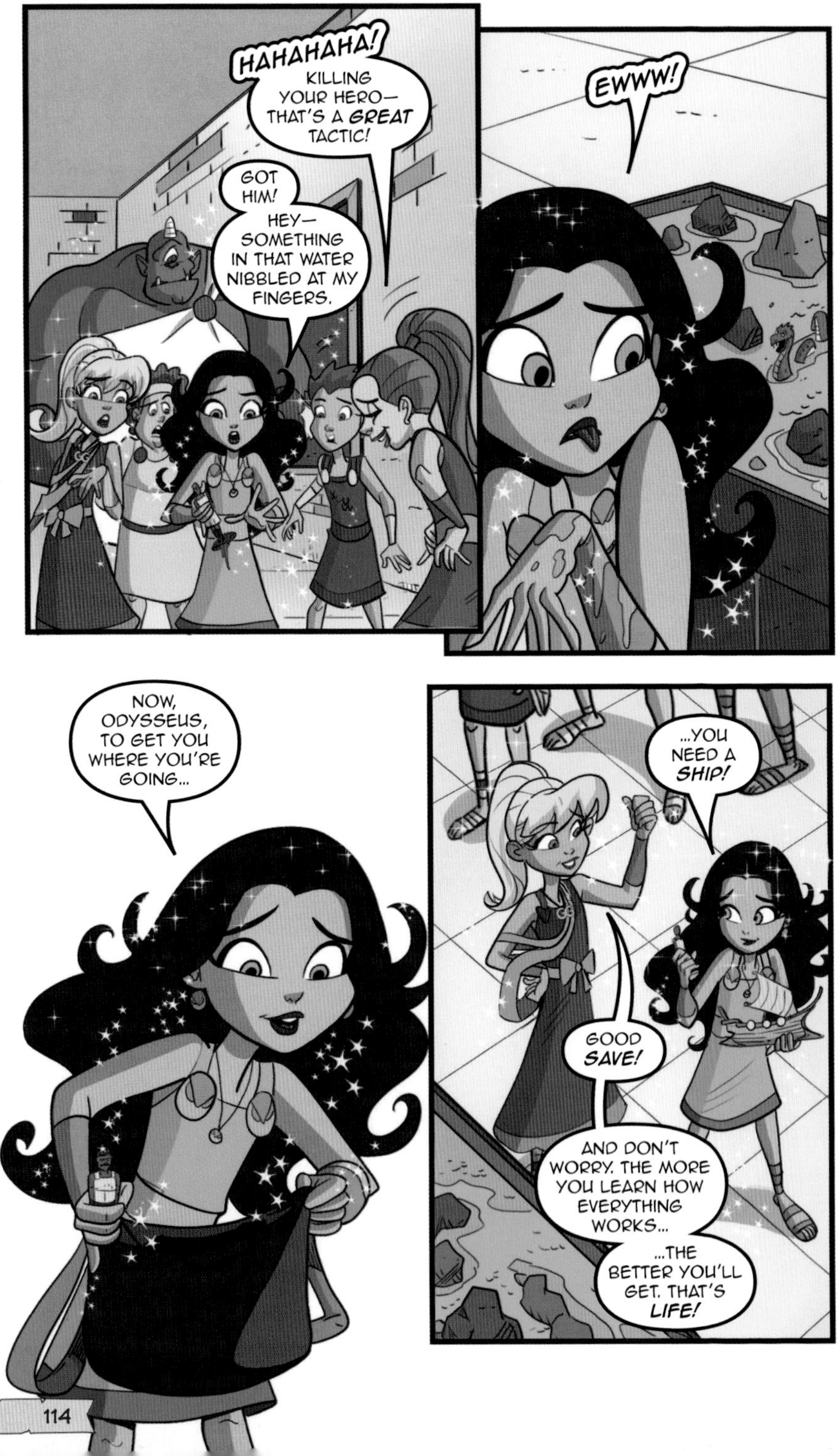
HAHAHAHA!
KILLING YOUR HERO— THAT'S A GREAT TACTIC!
GOT HIM!
HEY— SOMETHING IN THAT WATER NIBBLED AT MY FINGERS.
EWWW!
NOW, ODYSSEUS, TO GET YOU WHERE YOU'RE GOING...
...YOU NEED A SHIP!
GOOD SAVE!
AND DON'T WORRY. THE MORE YOU LEARN HOW EVERYTHING WORKS...
...THE BETTER YOU'LL GET. THAT'S LIFE!

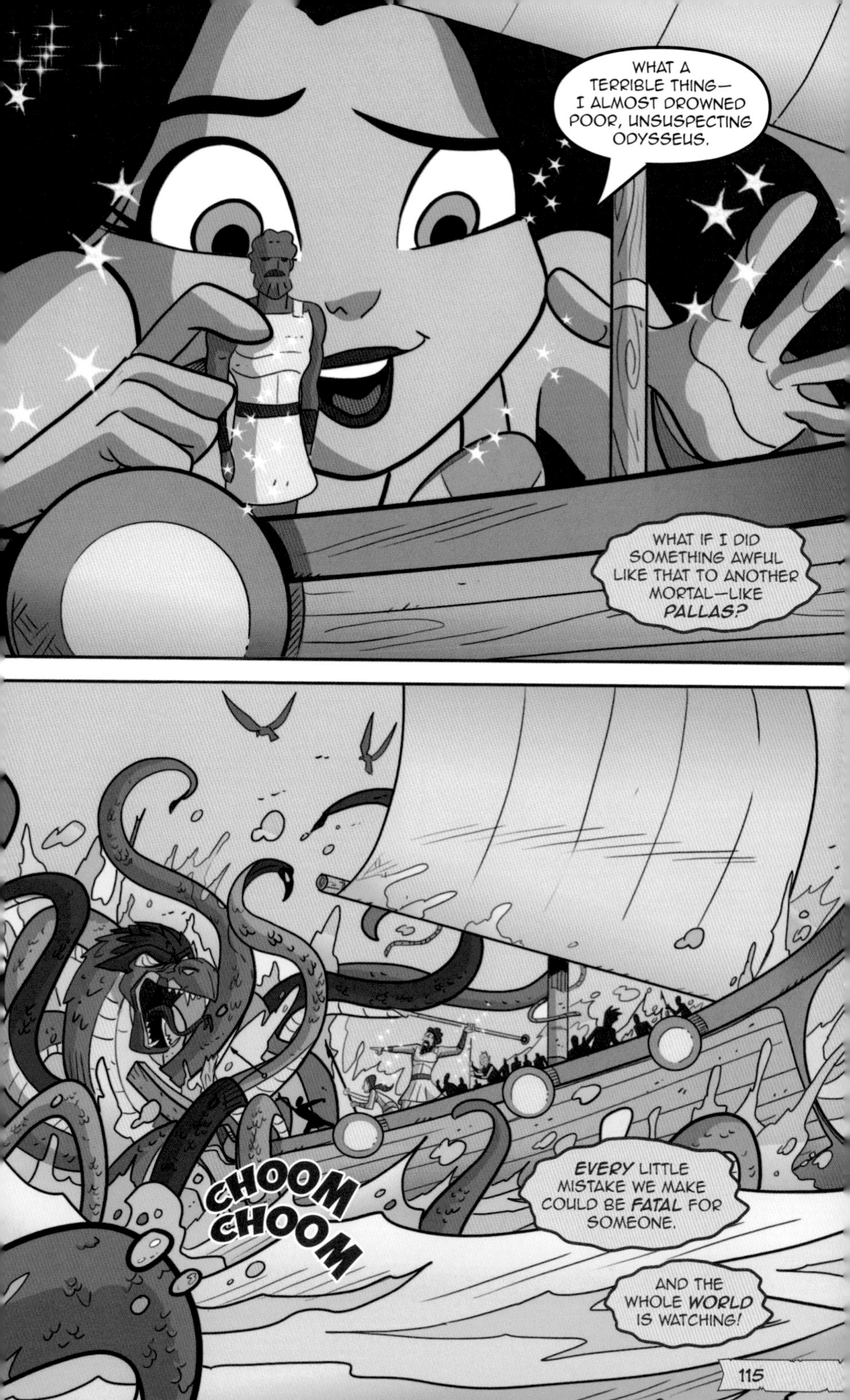
WHAT A TERRIBLE THING— I ALMOST DROWNED POOR, UNSUSPECTING ODYSSEUS.
WHAT IF I DID SOMETHING AWFUL LIKE THAT TO ANOTHER MORTAL—LIKE PALLAS?
CHOOM CHOOM
EVERY LITTLE MISTAKE WE MAKE COULD BE FATAL FOR SOMEONE.
AND THE WHOLE WORLD IS WATCHING!

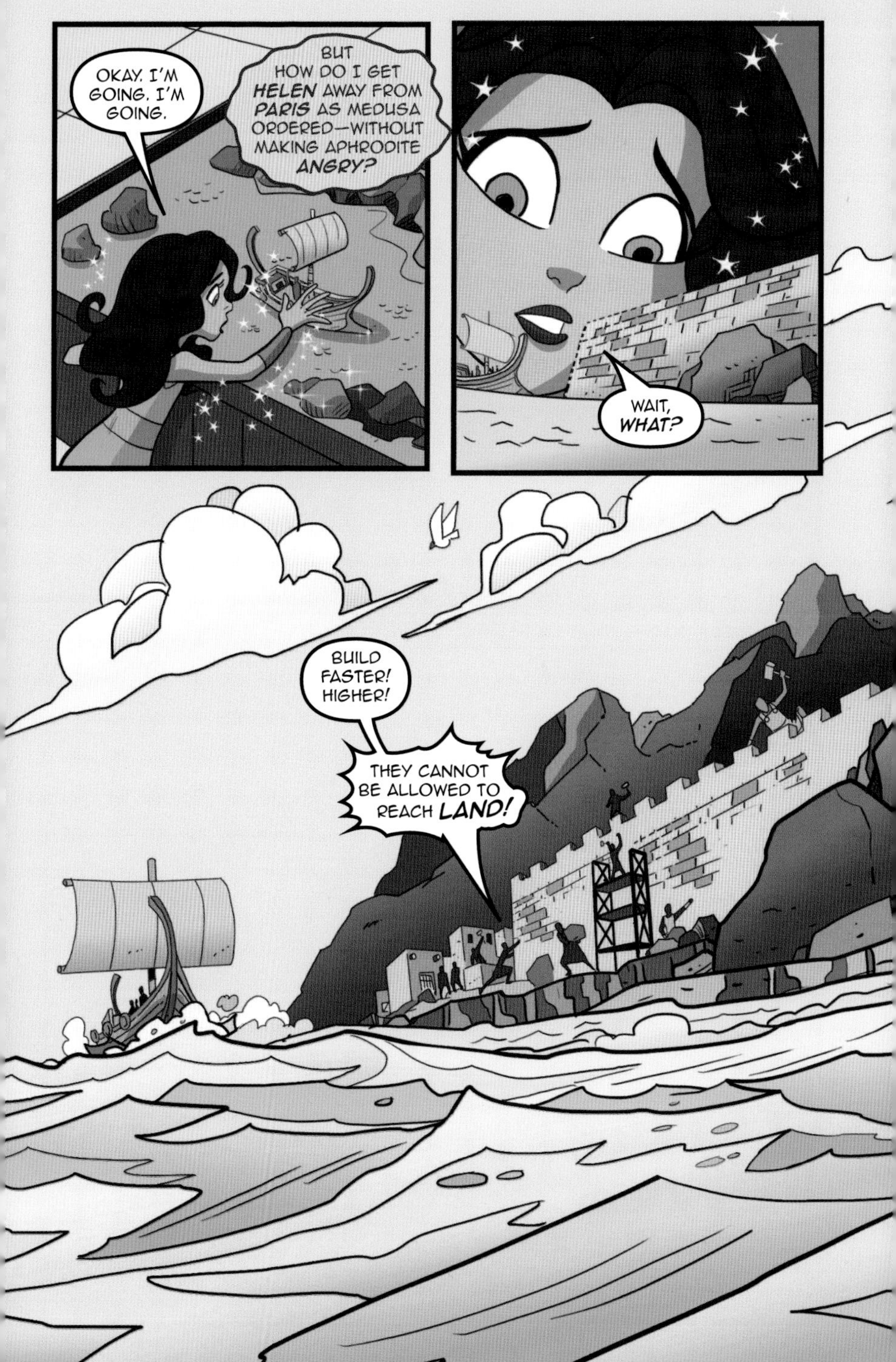

OKAY. I'M GOING. I'M GOING.
BUT HOW DO I GET HELEN AWAY FROM PARIS AS MEDUSA ORDERED—WITHOUT MAKING APHRODITE ANGRY?
WAIT, WHAT?
BUILD FASTER! HIGHER!
THEY CANNOT BE ALLOWED TO REACH LAND!

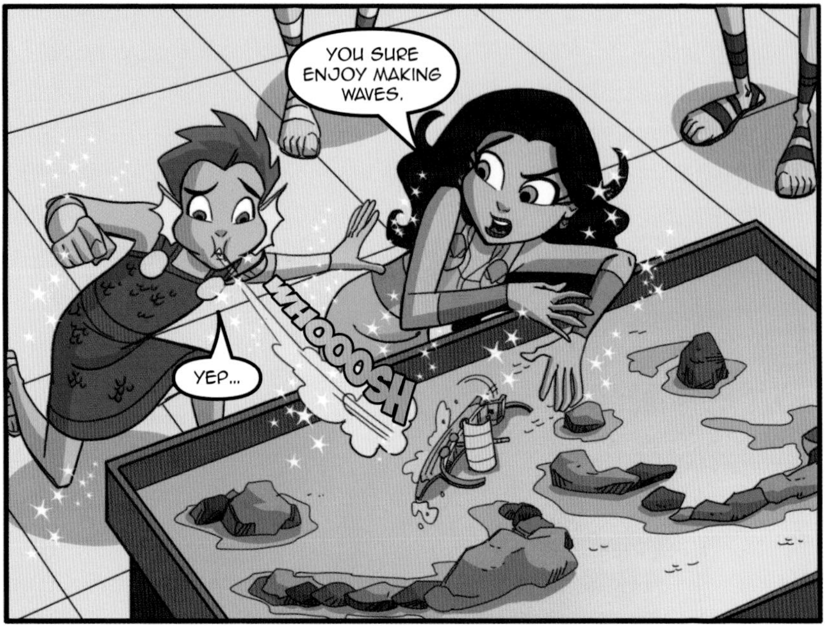
YOU SURE ENJOY MAKING WAVES.
YEP...
WHOOOSH

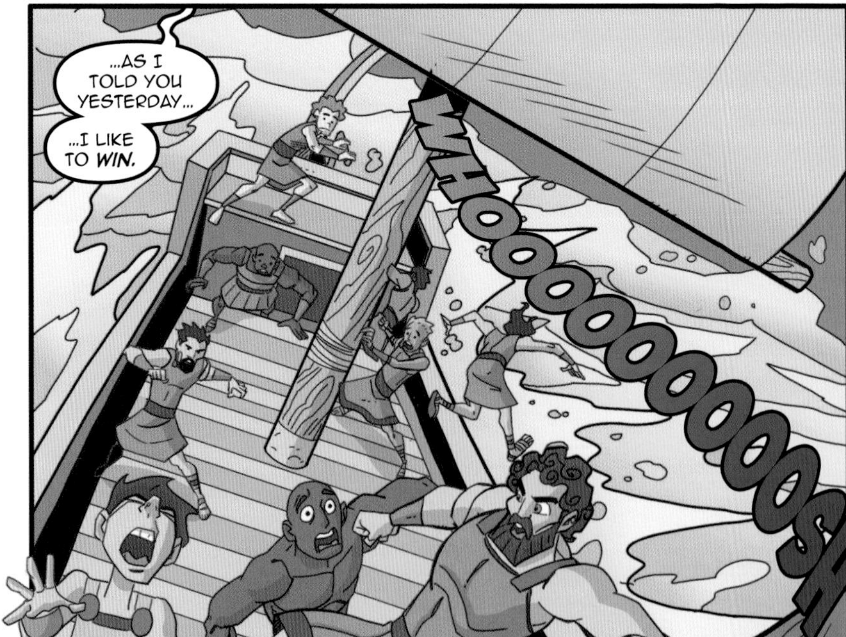
...AS I TOLD YOU YESTERDAY...
...I LIKE TO WIN.
WHOOOOOOOOOOOSH

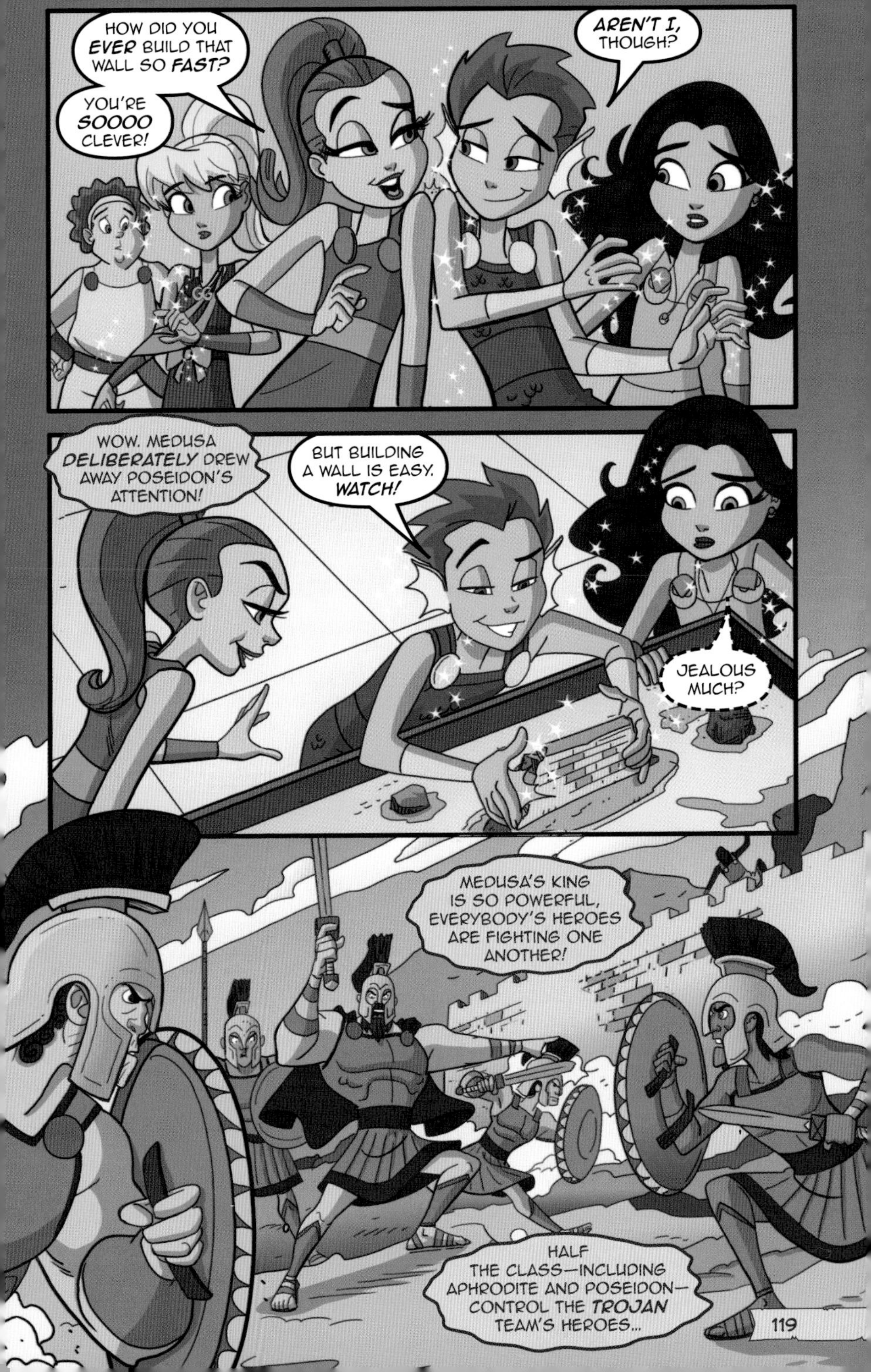
HOW DID YOU EVER BUILD THAT WALL SO FAST?
YOU'RE SOOOO CLEVER!
AREN'T I, THOUGH?
WOW. MEDUSA DELIBERATELY DREW AWAY POSEIDON'S ATTENTION!
BUT BUILDING A WALL IS EASY. WATCH!
JEALOUS MUCH?
MEDUSA'S KING IS SO POWERFUL, EVERYBODY'S HEROES ARE FIGHTING ONE ANOTHER!
HALF THE CLASS—INCLUDING APHRODITE AND POSEIDON—CONTROL THE TROJAN TEAM'S HEROES...

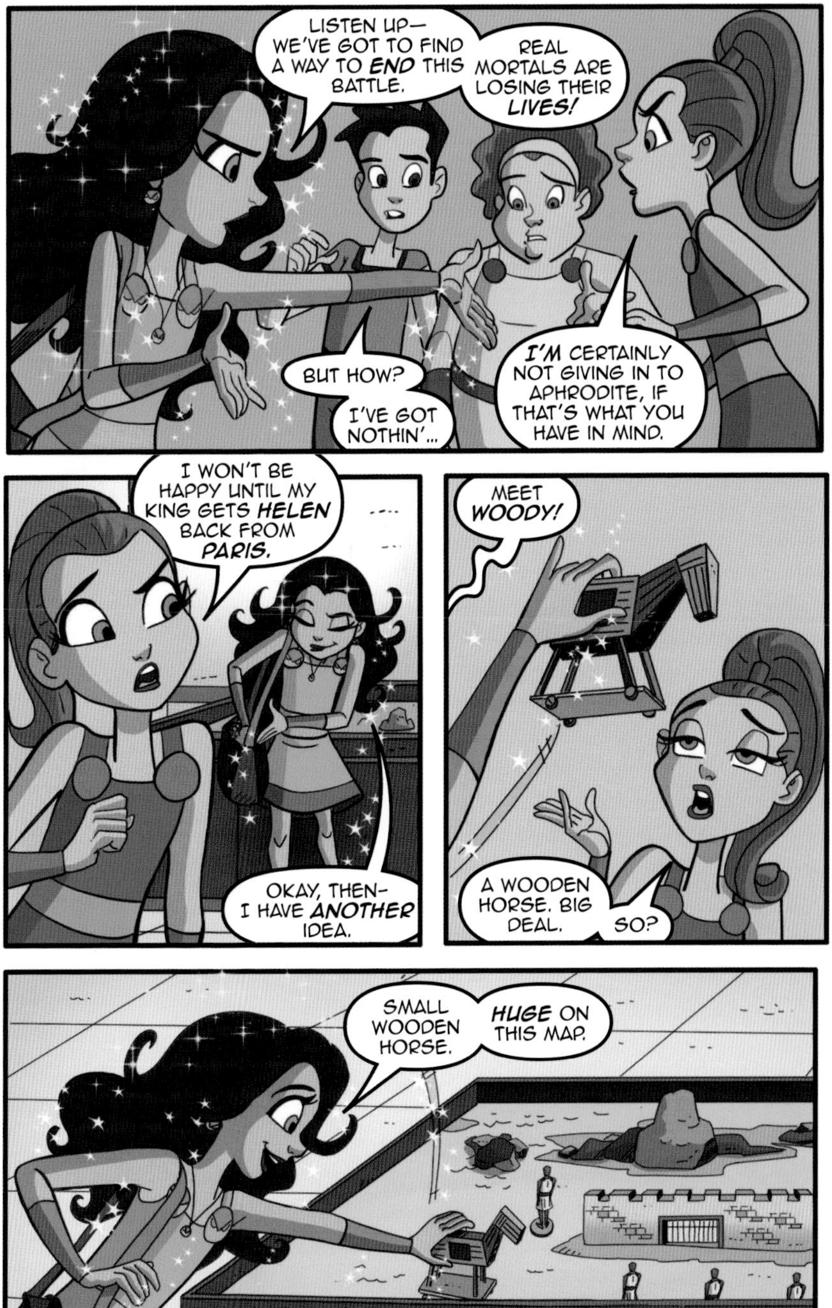
LISTEN UP— WE'VE GOT TO FIND A WAY TO *END* THIS BATTLE.
REAL MORTALS ARE LOSING THEIR *LIVES!*
BUT HOW?
I'VE GOT NOTHIN'...
I'M CERTAINLY NOT GIVING IN TO APHRODITE, IF THAT'S WHAT YOU HAVE IN MIND.
I WON'T BE HAPPY UNTIL MY KING GETS *HELEN* BACK FROM *PARIS.*
OKAY, THEN- I HAVE *ANOTHER* IDEA.
MEET *WOODY!*
A WOODEN HORSE. BIG DEAL.
SO?
SMALL WOODEN HORSE.
HUGE ON THIS MAP.

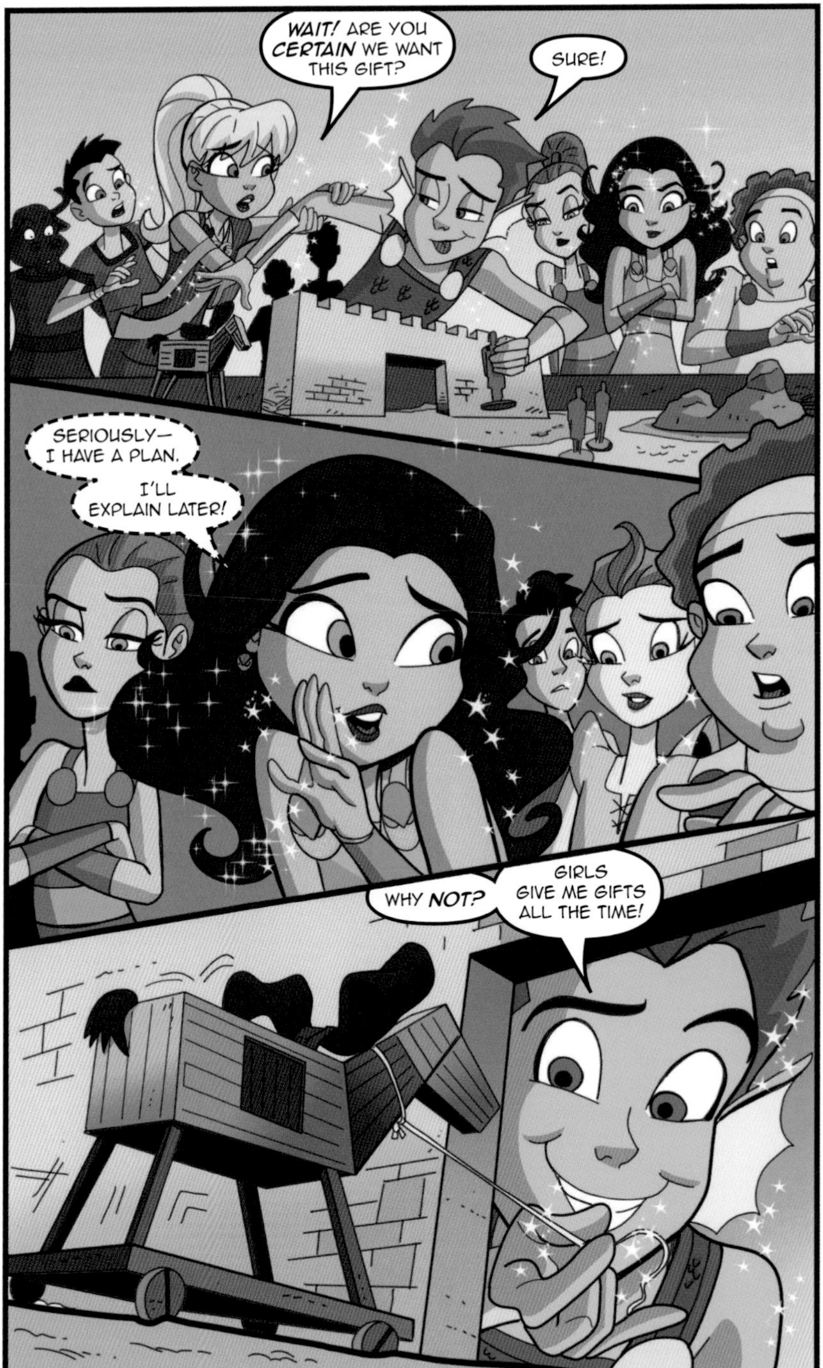
WAIT! ARE YOU CERTAIN WE WANT THIS GIFT?
SURE!
SERIOUSLY— I HAVE A PLAN.
I'LL EXPLAIN LATER!
WHY NOT?
GIRLS GIVE ME GIFTS ALL THE TIME!

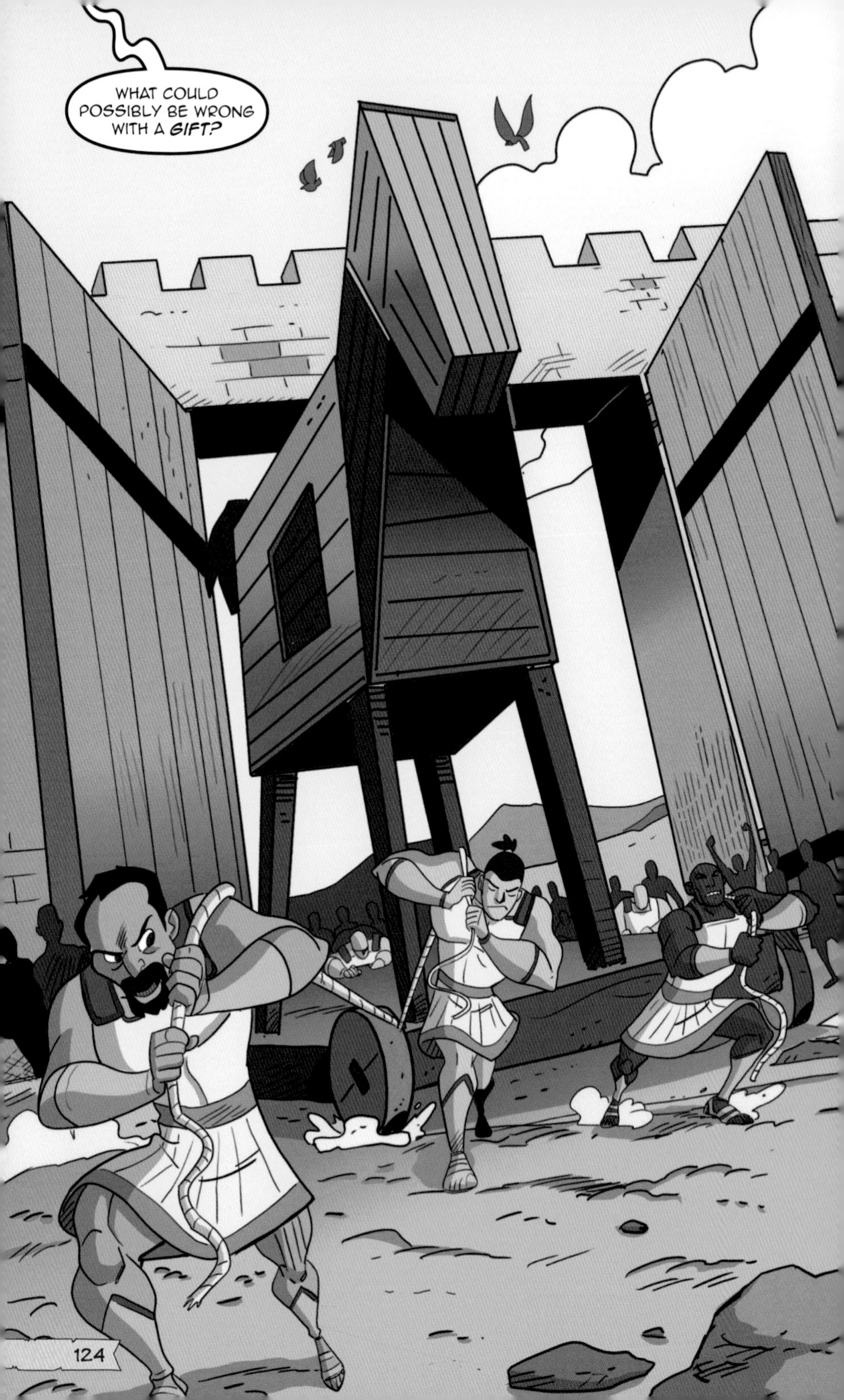
WHAT COULD POSSIBLY BE WRONG WITH A GIFT?

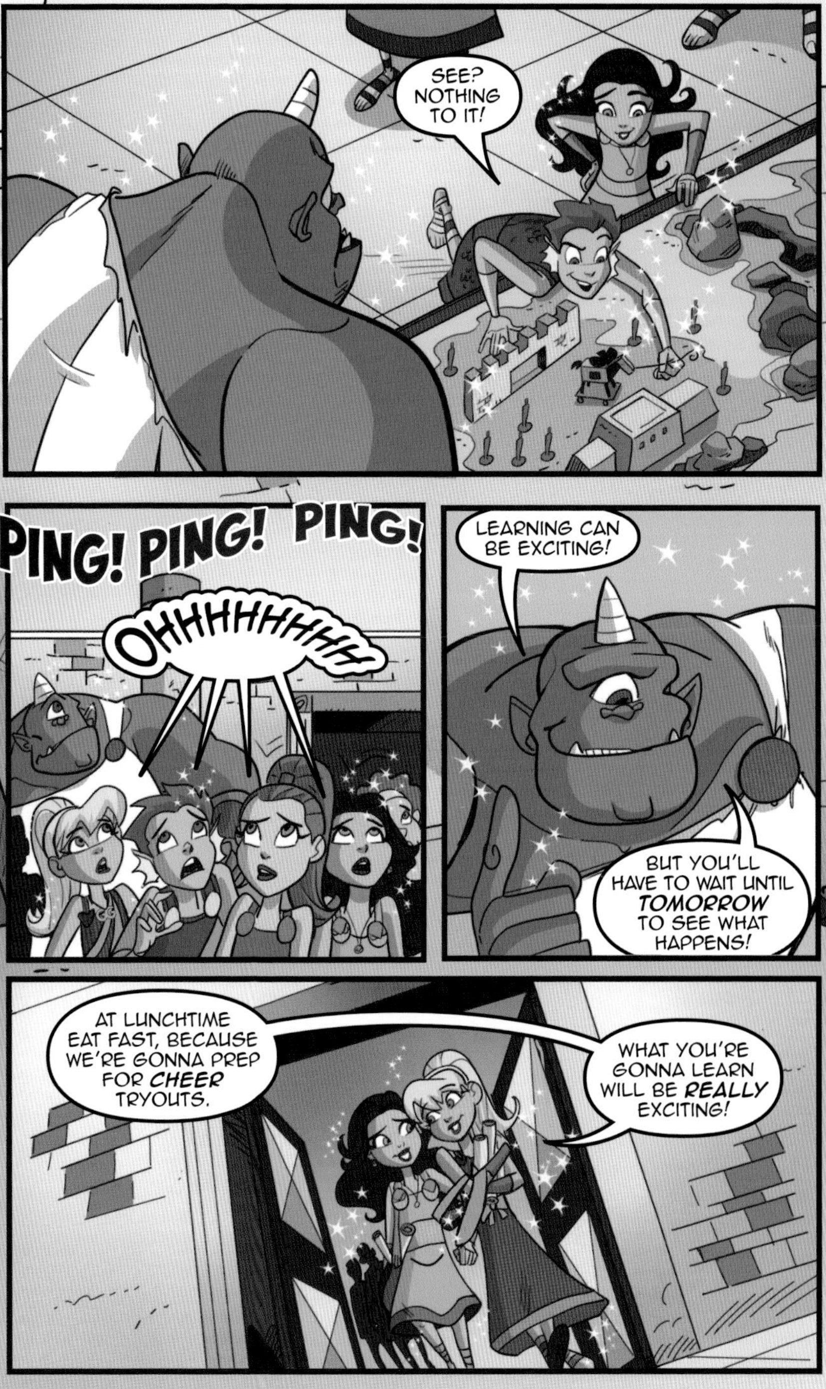
SEE? NOTHING TO IT!
PING! PING! PING!
OHHHHHHHH
LEARNING CAN BE EXCITING!
BUT YOU'LL HAVE TO WAIT UNTIL *TOMORROW* TO SEE WHAT HAPPENS!
AT LUNCHTIME EAT FAST, BECAUSE WE'RE GONNA PREP FOR *CHEER* TRYOUTS.
WHAT YOU'RE GONNA LEARN WILL BE *REALLY* EXCITING!

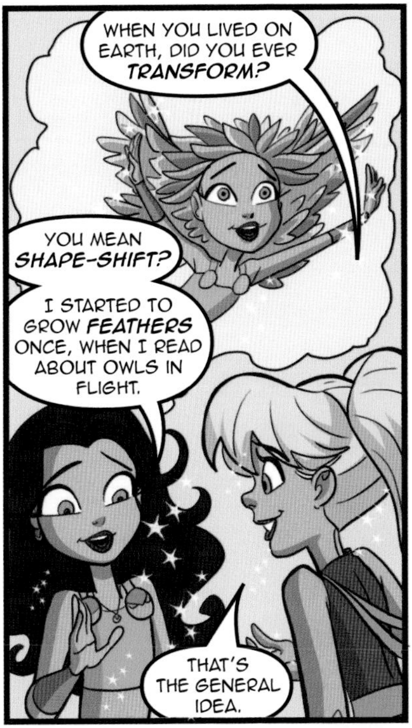
WHEN YOU LIVED ON EARTH, DID YOU EVER TRANSFORM?
YOU MEAN SHAPE-SHIFT?
I STARTED TO GROW FEATHERS ONCE, WHEN I READ ABOUT OWLS IN FLIGHT.
THAT'S THE GENERAL IDEA.

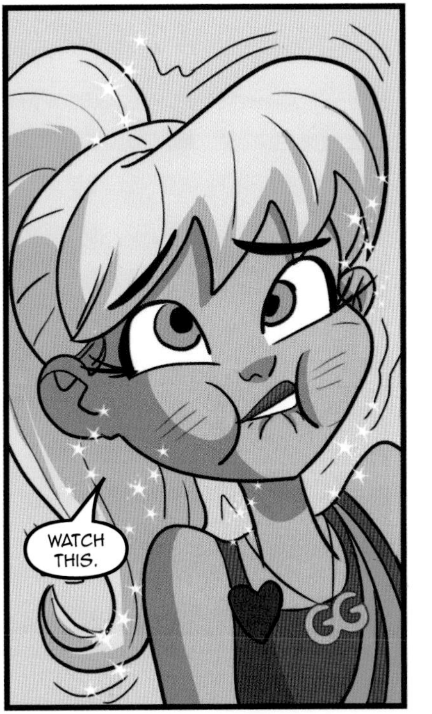
WATCH THIS.
GG

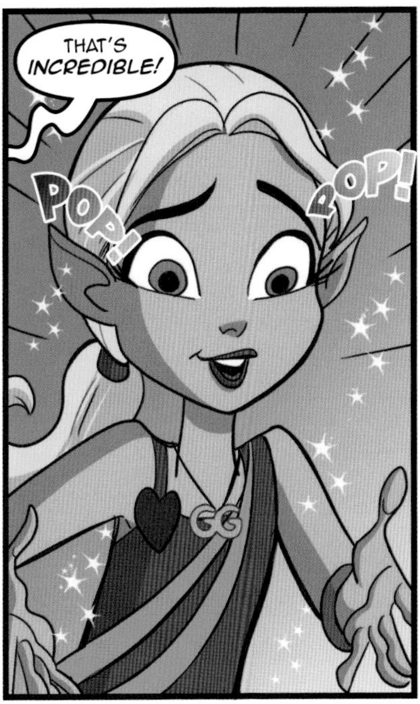
THAT'S INCREDIBLE!
POP!
POP!
GG

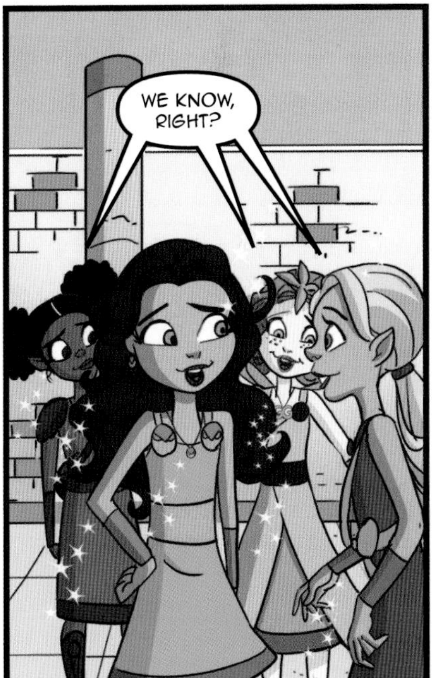
WE KNOW, RIGHT?

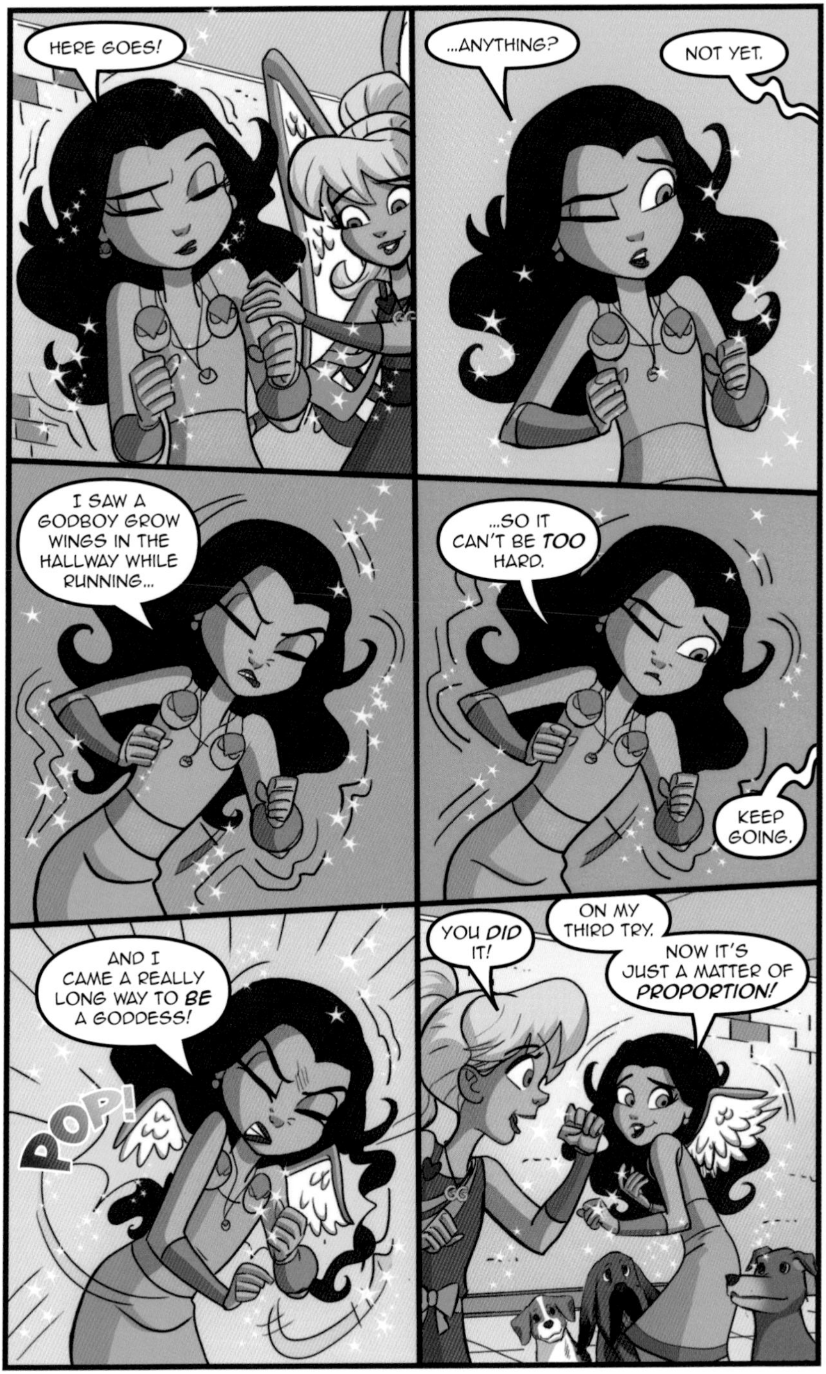
HERE GOES!
...ANYTHING?
NOT YET.
I SAW A GODBOY GROW WINGS IN THE HALLWAY WHILE RUNNING...
...SO IT CAN'T BE *TOO* HARD.
KEEP GOING.
AND I CAME A REALLY LONG WAY TO *BE* A GODDESS!
POP!
YOU *DID* IT!
ON MY THIRD TRY.
NOW IT'S JUST A MATTER OF *PROPORTION!*

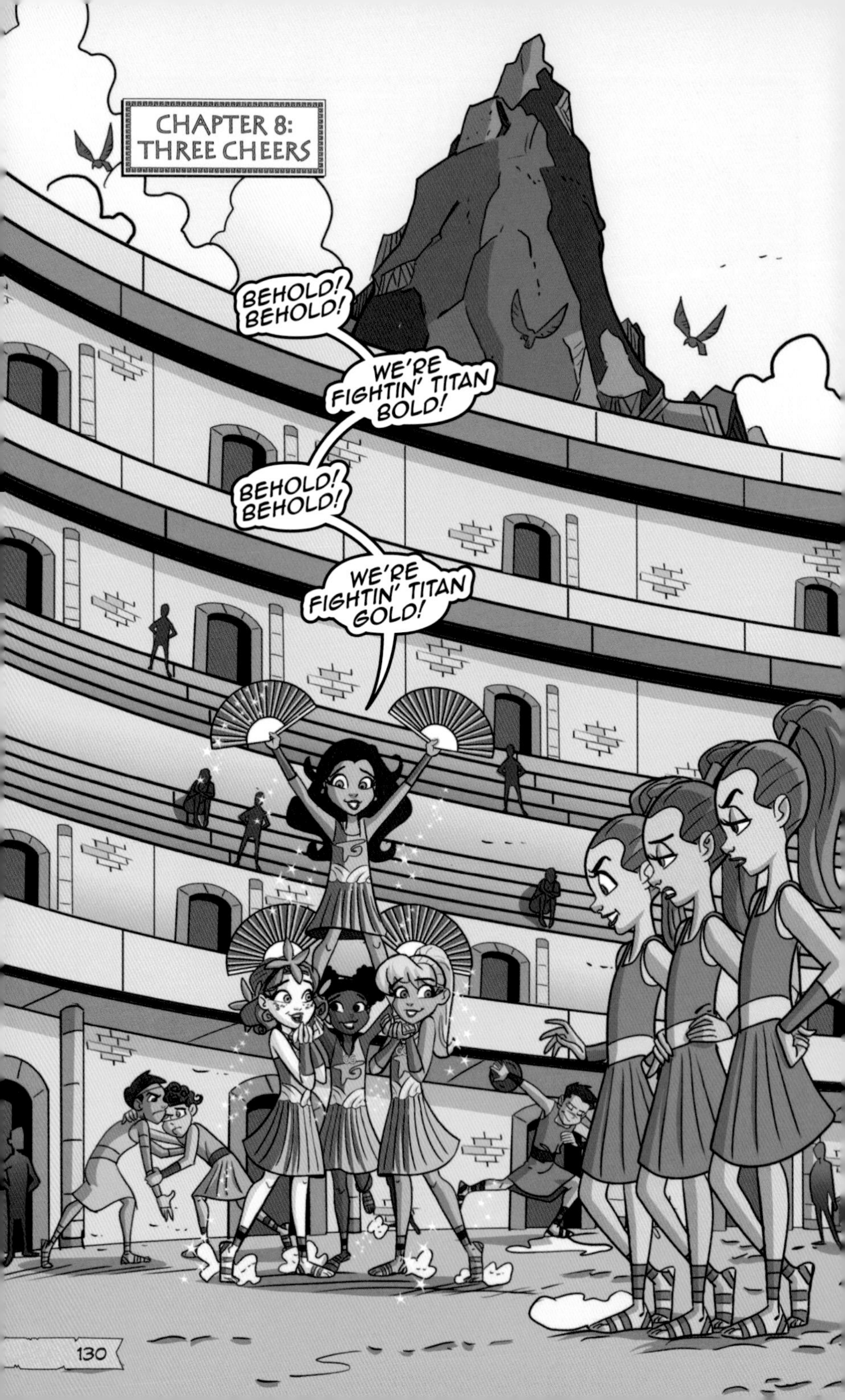
CHAPTER 8: THREE CHEERS
BEHOLD! BEHOLD!
WE'RE FIGHTIN' TITAN BOLD!
BEHOLD! BEHOLD!
WE'RE FIGHTIN' TITAN GOLD!

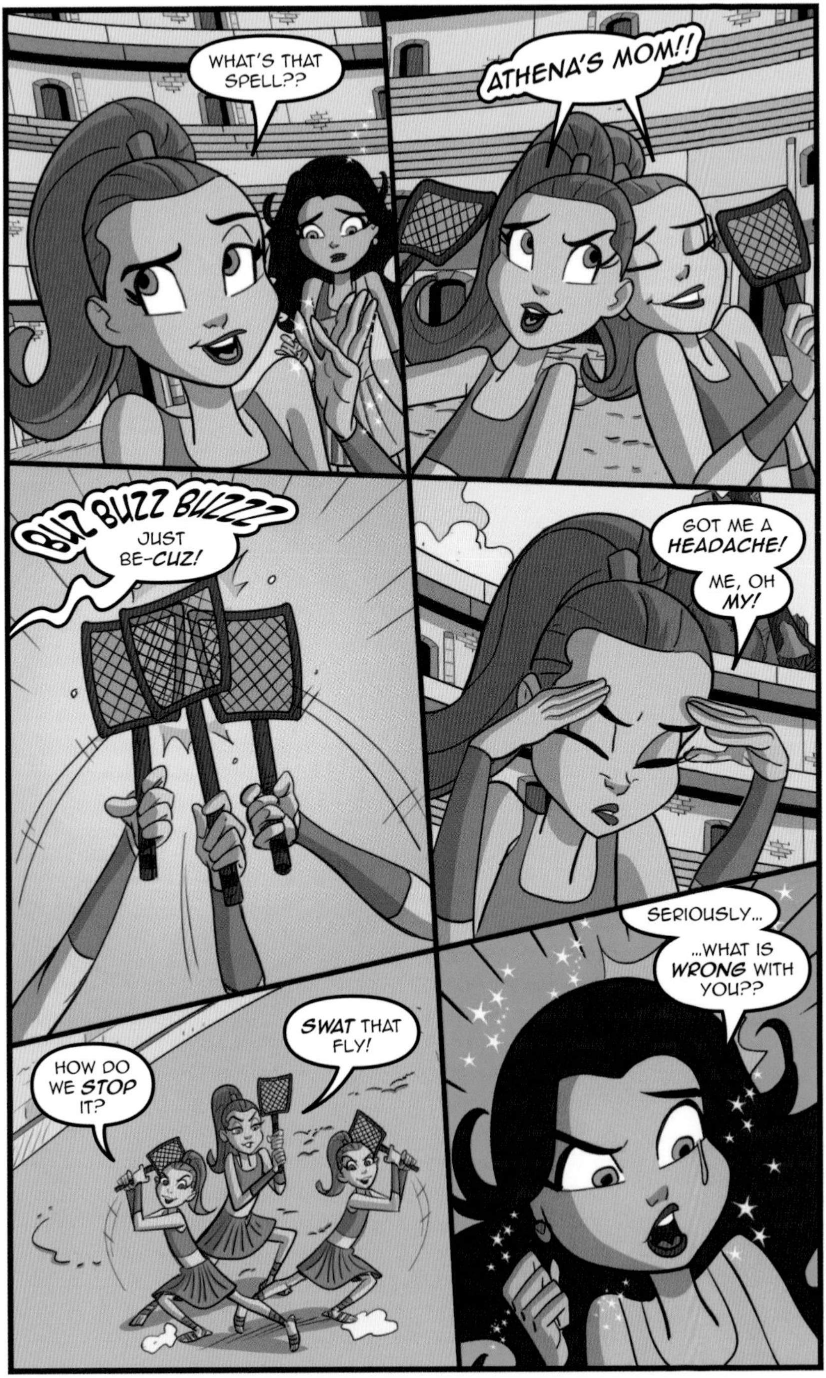
WHAT'S THAT SPELL??
ATHENA'S MOM!!
BUZ BUZZ BUZZZZ
JUST BE-CUZ!
GOT ME A HEADACHE!
ME, OH MY!
HOW DO WE STOP IT?
SWAT THAT FLY!
SERIOUSLY...
...WHAT IS WRONG WITH YOU??

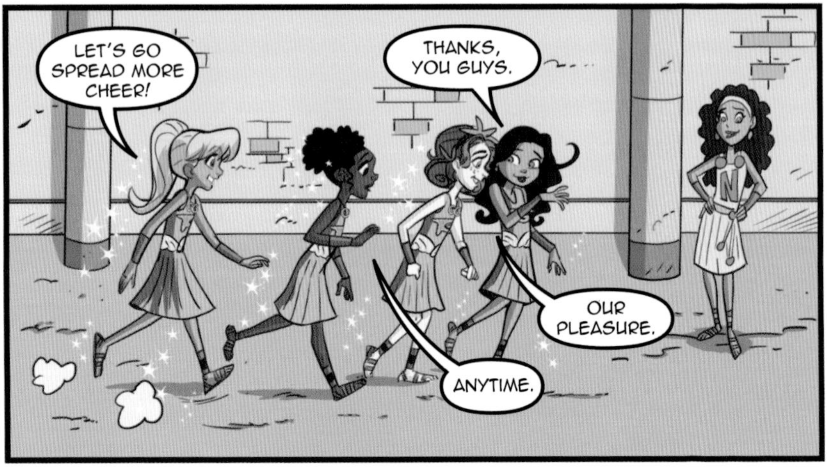
LET'S GO SPREAD MORE CHEER!
THANKS, YOU GUYS.
OUR PLEASURE.
ANYTIME.

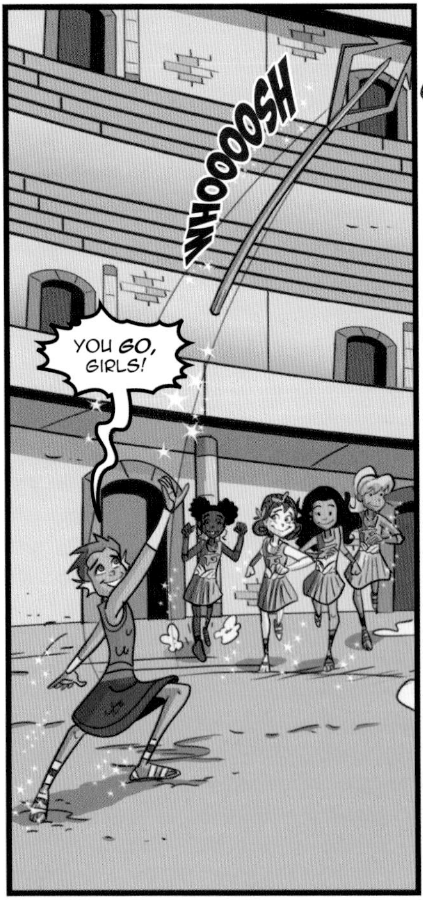
WHOOOOSH
YOU GO, GIRLS!

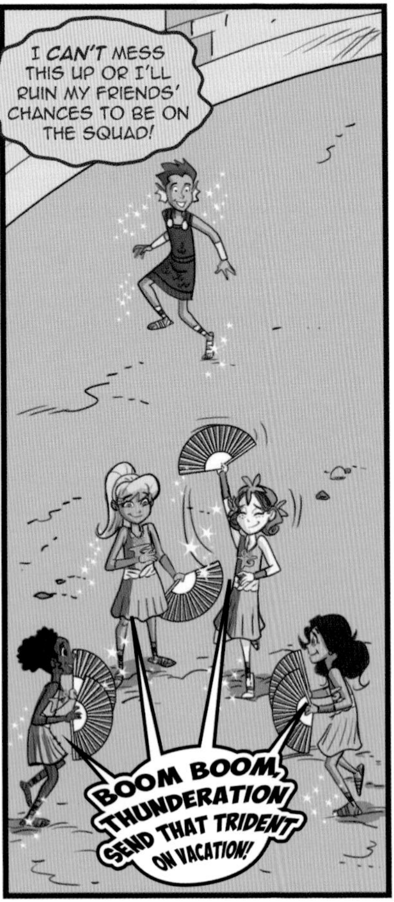
I CAN'T MESS THIS UP OR I'LL RUIN MY FRIENDS' CHANCES TO BE ON THE SQUAD!
BOOM BOOM, THUNDERATION SEND THAT TRIDENT ON VACATION!

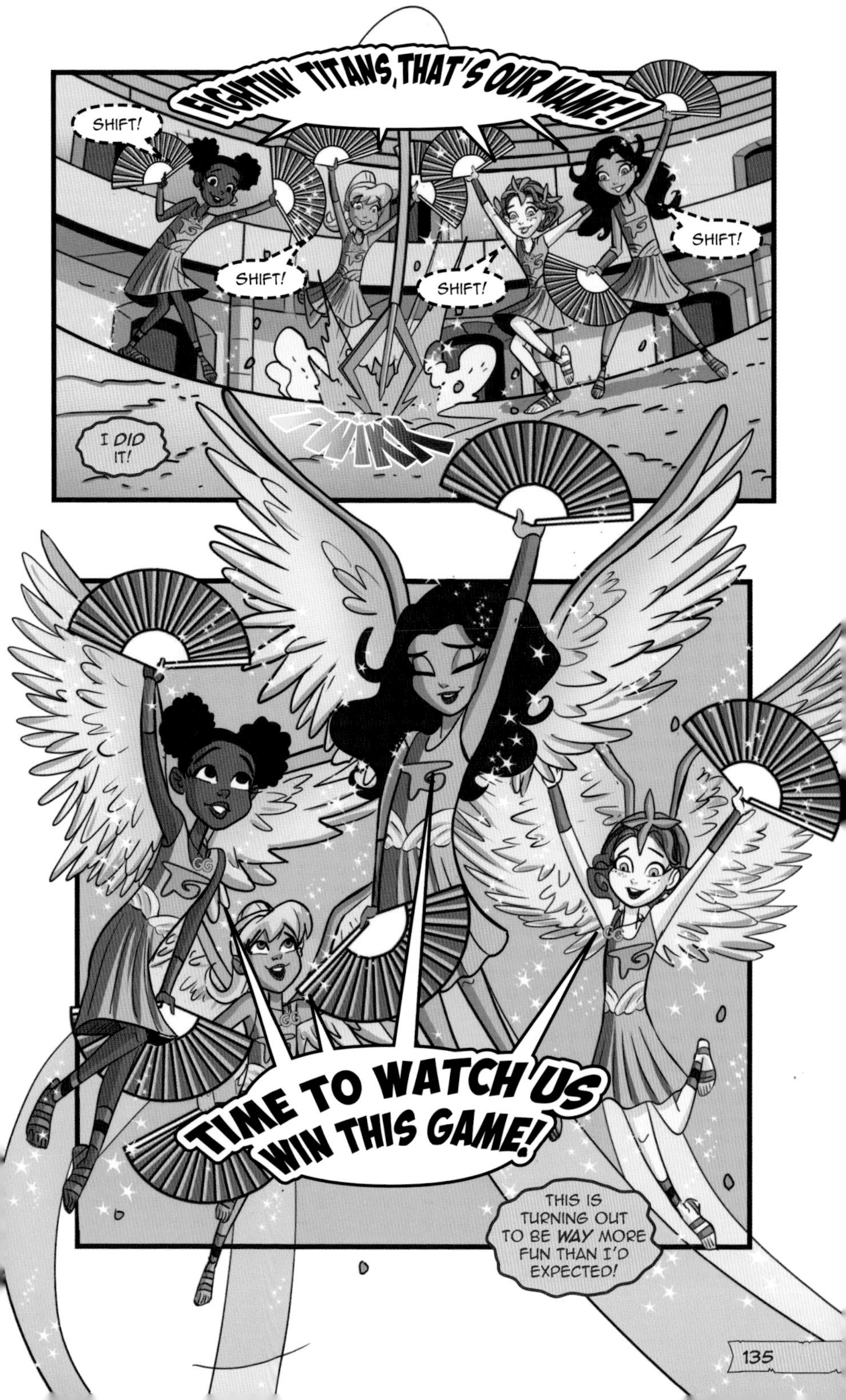
FIGHTIN' TITANS, THAT'S OUR NAME!
SHIFT!
SHIFT!
SHIFT!
SHIFT!
I DID IT!
TIME TO WATCH US WIN THIS GAME!
THIS IS TURNING OUT TO BE *WAY* MORE FUN THAN I'D EXPECTED!

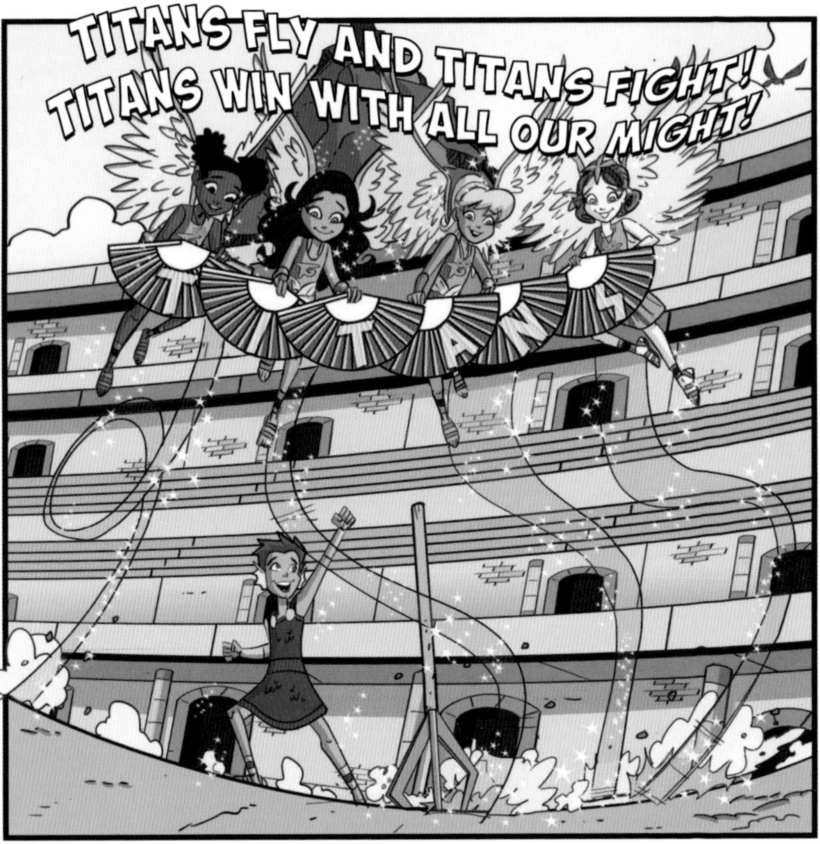
TITANS FLY AND TITANS FIGHT!
TITANS WIN WITH ALL OUR MIGHT!

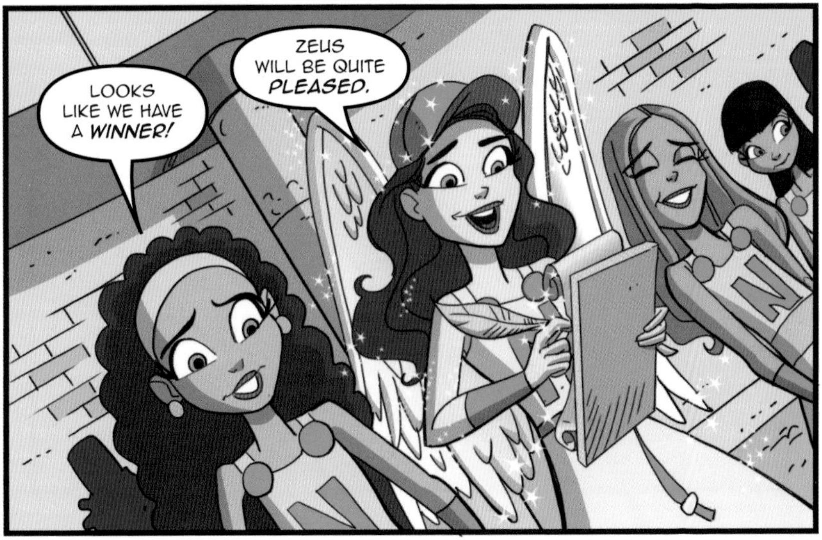
LOOKS LIKE WE HAVE A *WINNER!*
ZEUS WILL BE QUITE *PLEASED.*

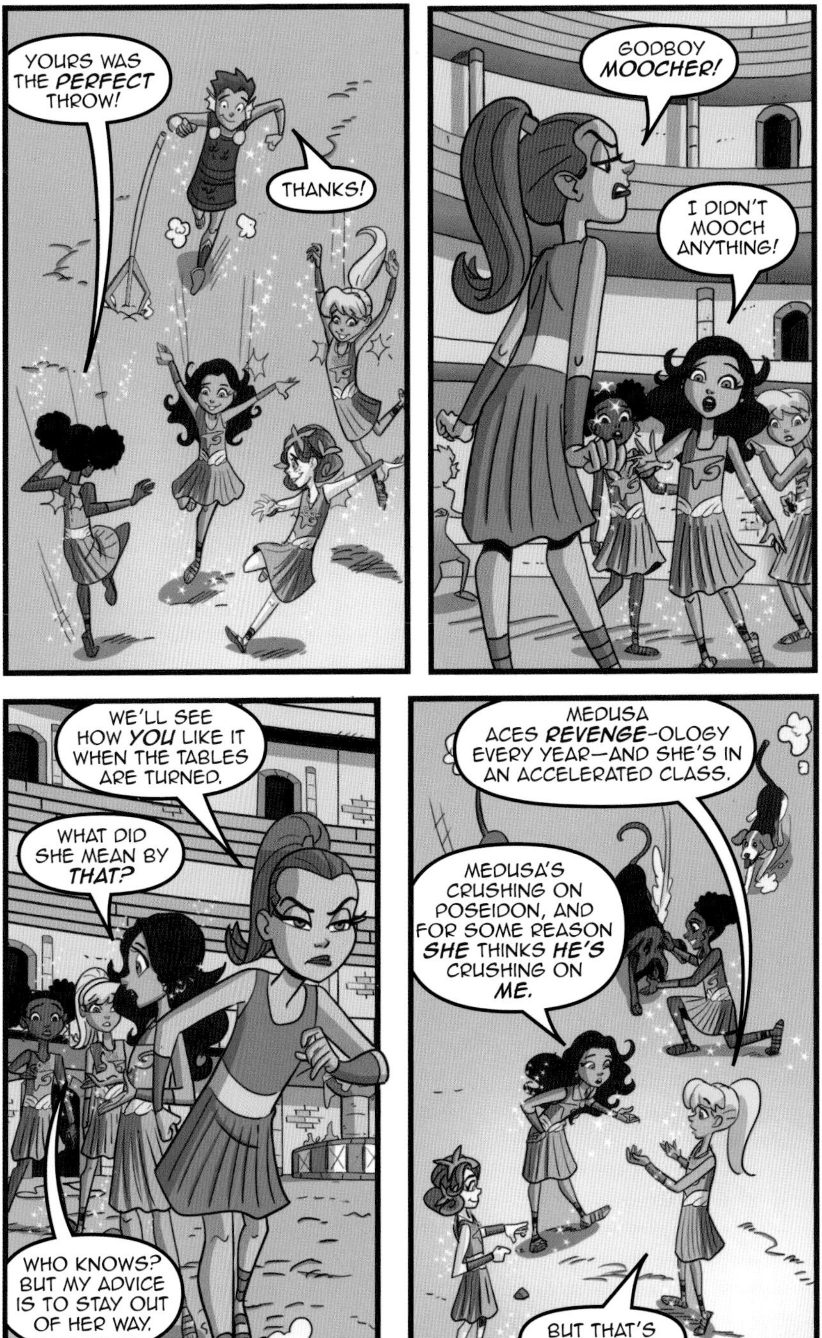
YOURS WAS THE PERFECT THROW!
THANKS!
GODBOY MOOCHER!
I DIDN'T MOOCH ANYTHING!
WE'LL SEE HOW YOU LIKE IT WHEN THE TABLES ARE TURNED.
WHAT DID SHE MEAN BY THAT?
WHO KNOWS? BUT MY ADVICE IS TO STAY OUT OF HER WAY.
MEDUSA ACES REVENGE-OLOGY EVERY YEAR—AND SHE'S IN AN ACCELERATED CLASS.
MEDUSA'S CRUSHING ON POSEIDON, AND FOR SOME REASON SHE THINKS HE'S CRUSHING ON ME.
BUT THAT'S TRUE—HE IS.

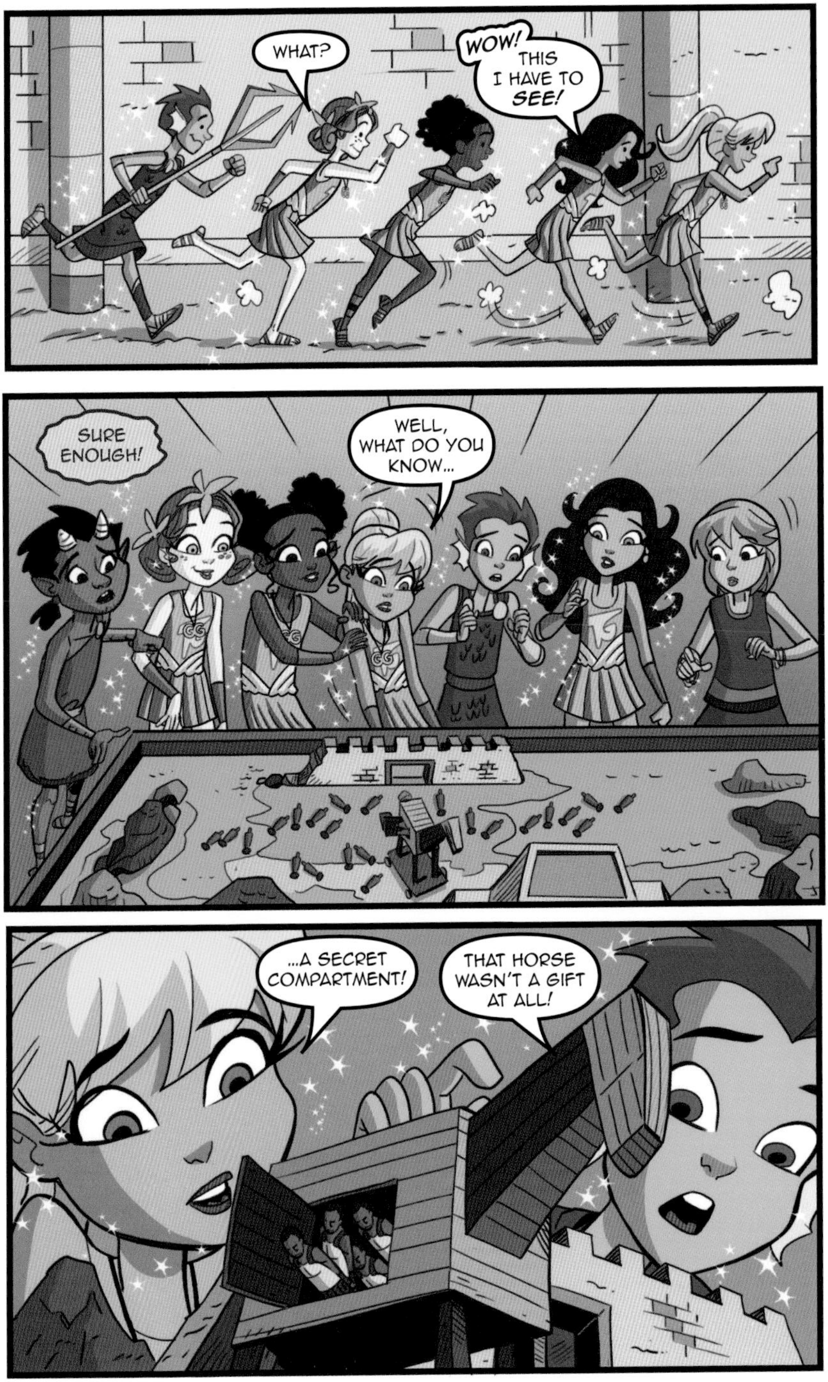
WHAT?
WOW! THIS I HAVE TO SEE!
SURE ENOUGH!
WELL, WHAT DO YOU KNOW...
...A SECRET COMPARTMENT!
THAT HORSE WASN'T A GIFT AT ALL!

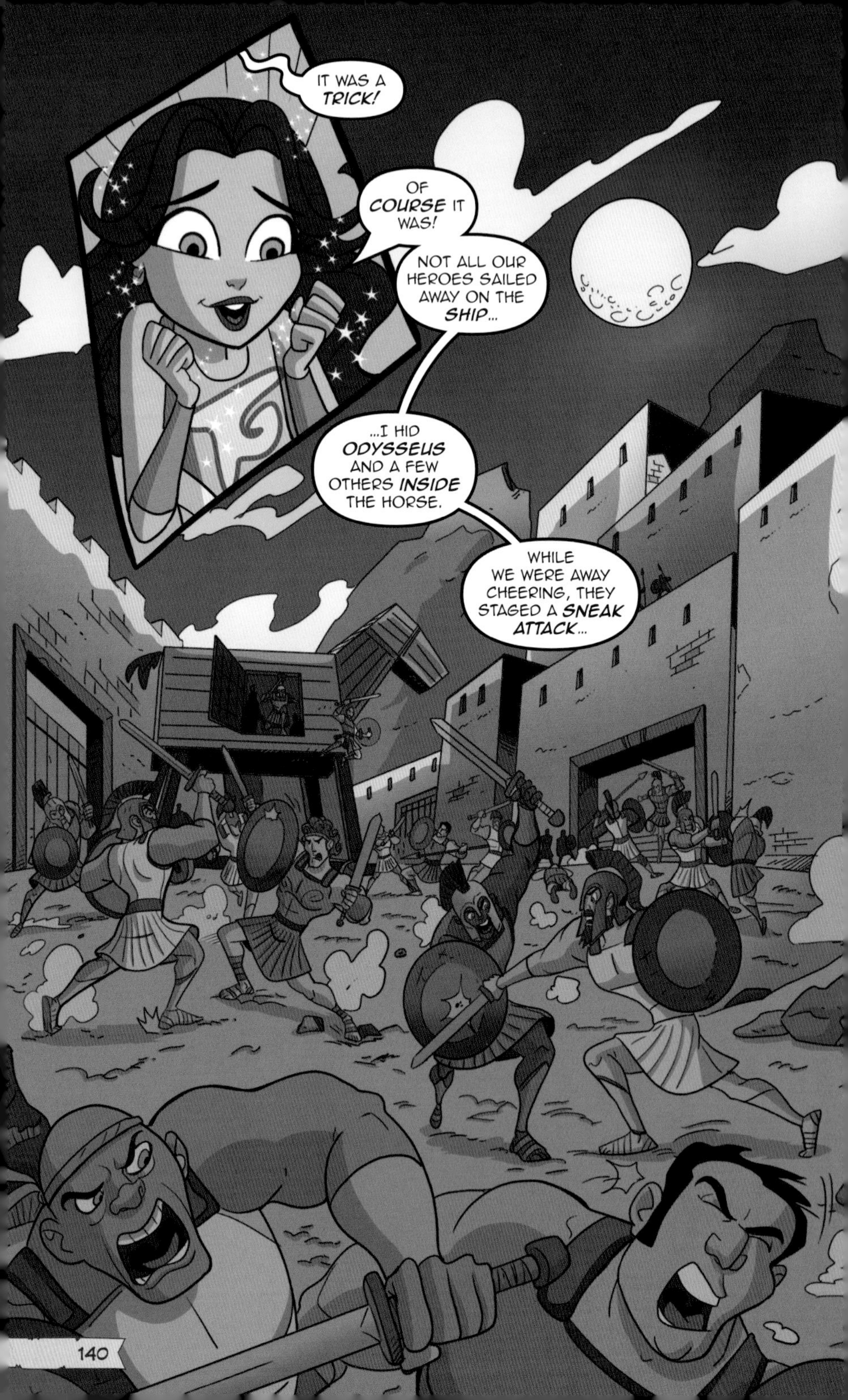
IT WAS A TRICK!
OF COURSE IT WAS!
NOT ALL OUR HEROES SAILED AWAY ON THE SHIP...
...I HID ODYSSEUS AND A FEW OTHERS INSIDE THE HORSE.
WHILE WE WERE AWAY CHEERING, THEY STAGED A SNEAK ATTACK...

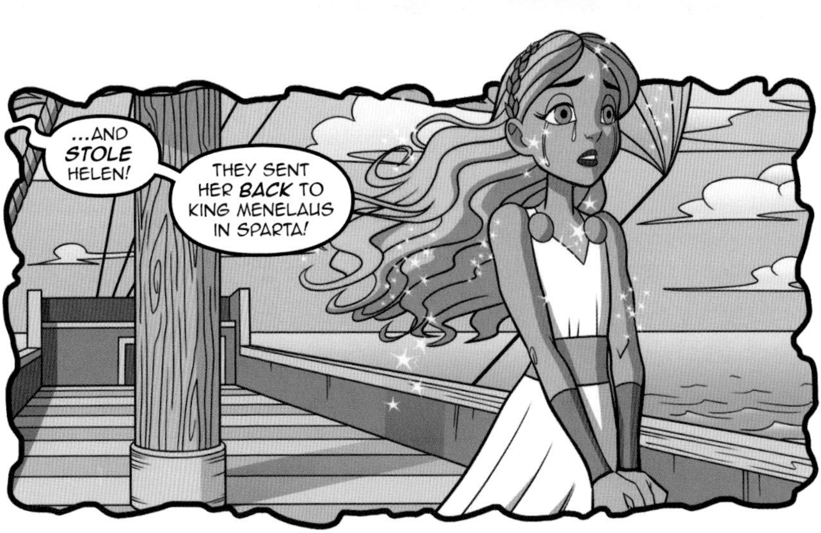
...AND STOLE HELEN!
THEY SENT HER BACK TO KING MENELAUS IN SPARTA!

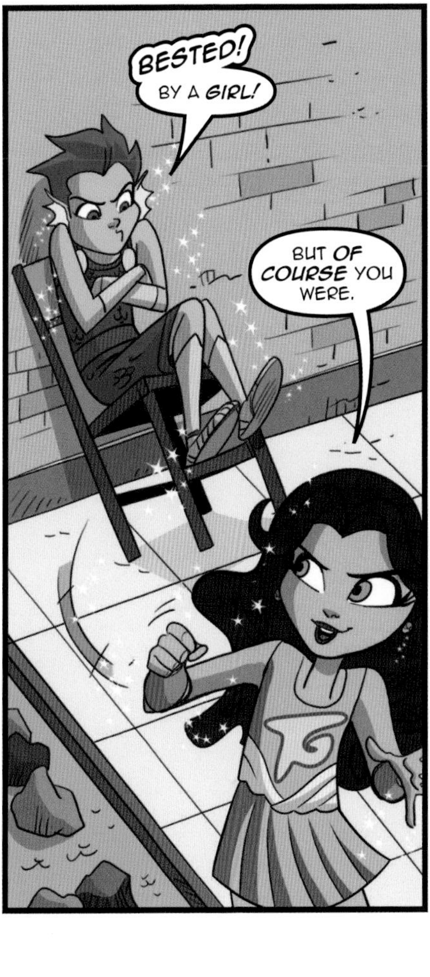
BESTED! BY A GIRL!
BUT OF COURSE YOU WERE.

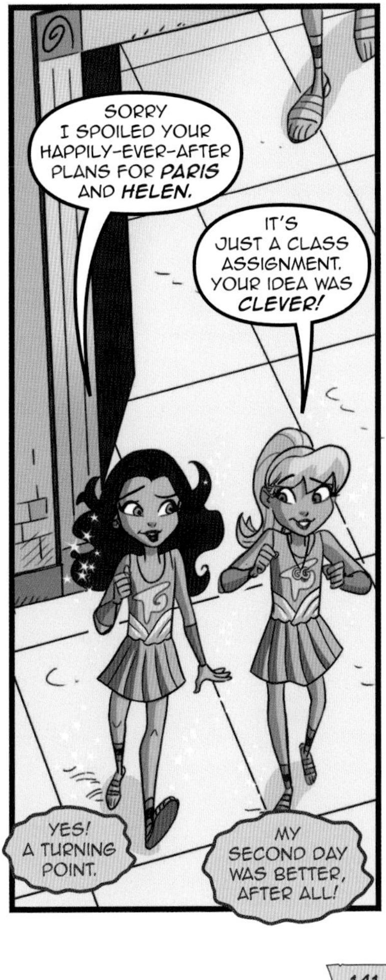
SORRY I SPOILED YOUR HAPPILY-EVER-AFTER PLANS FOR PARIS AND HELEN.
IT'S JUST A CLASS ASSIGNMENT. YOUR IDEA WAS CLEVER!
YES! A TURNING POINT.
MY SECOND DAY WAS BETTER, AFTER ALL!

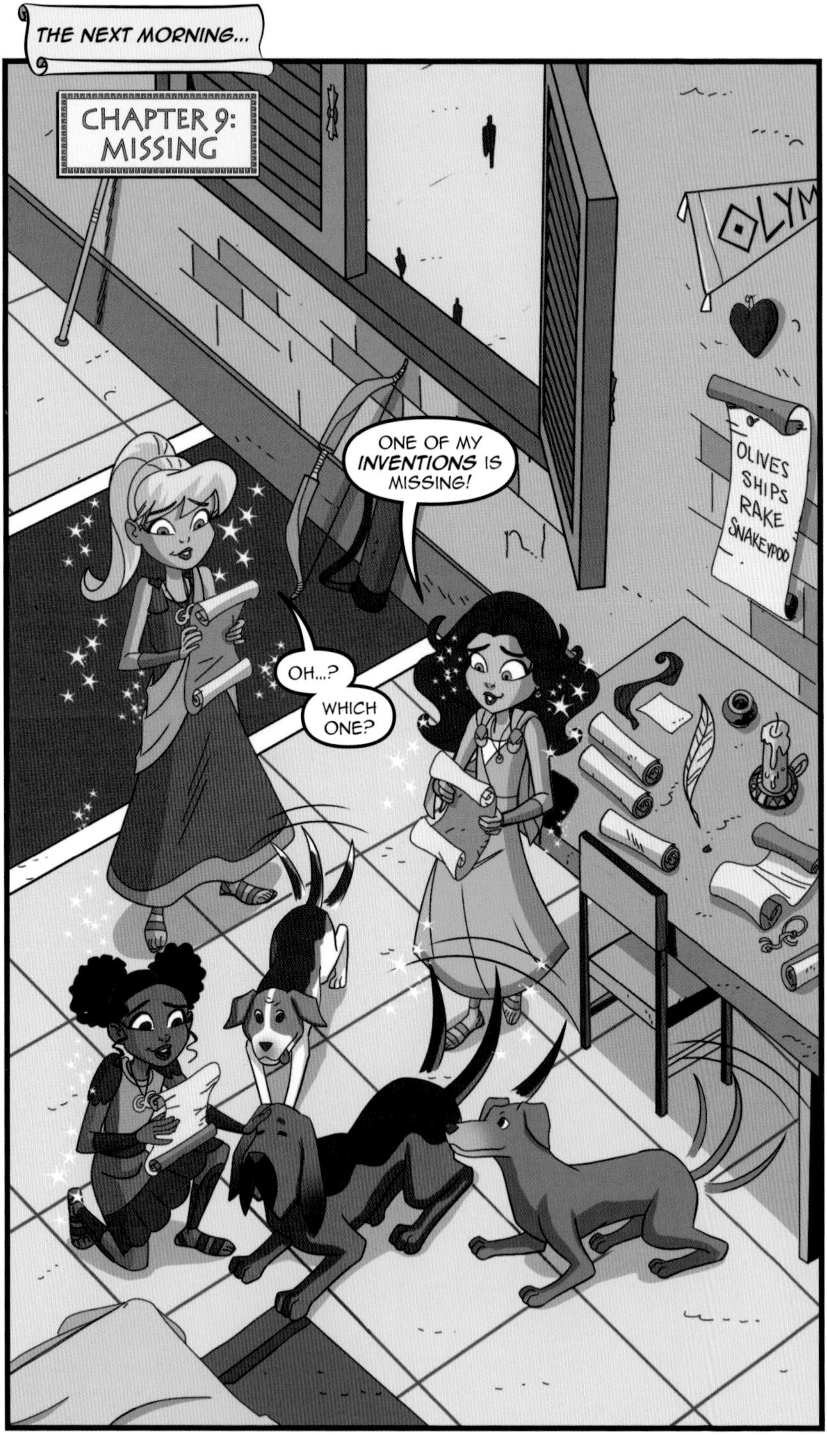
THE NEXT MORNING...
CHAPTER 9: MISSING
OLIVES
SHIPS
RAKE
SNAKEYPOO
ONE OF MY *INVENTIONS* IS MISSING!
OH...?
WHICH ONE?

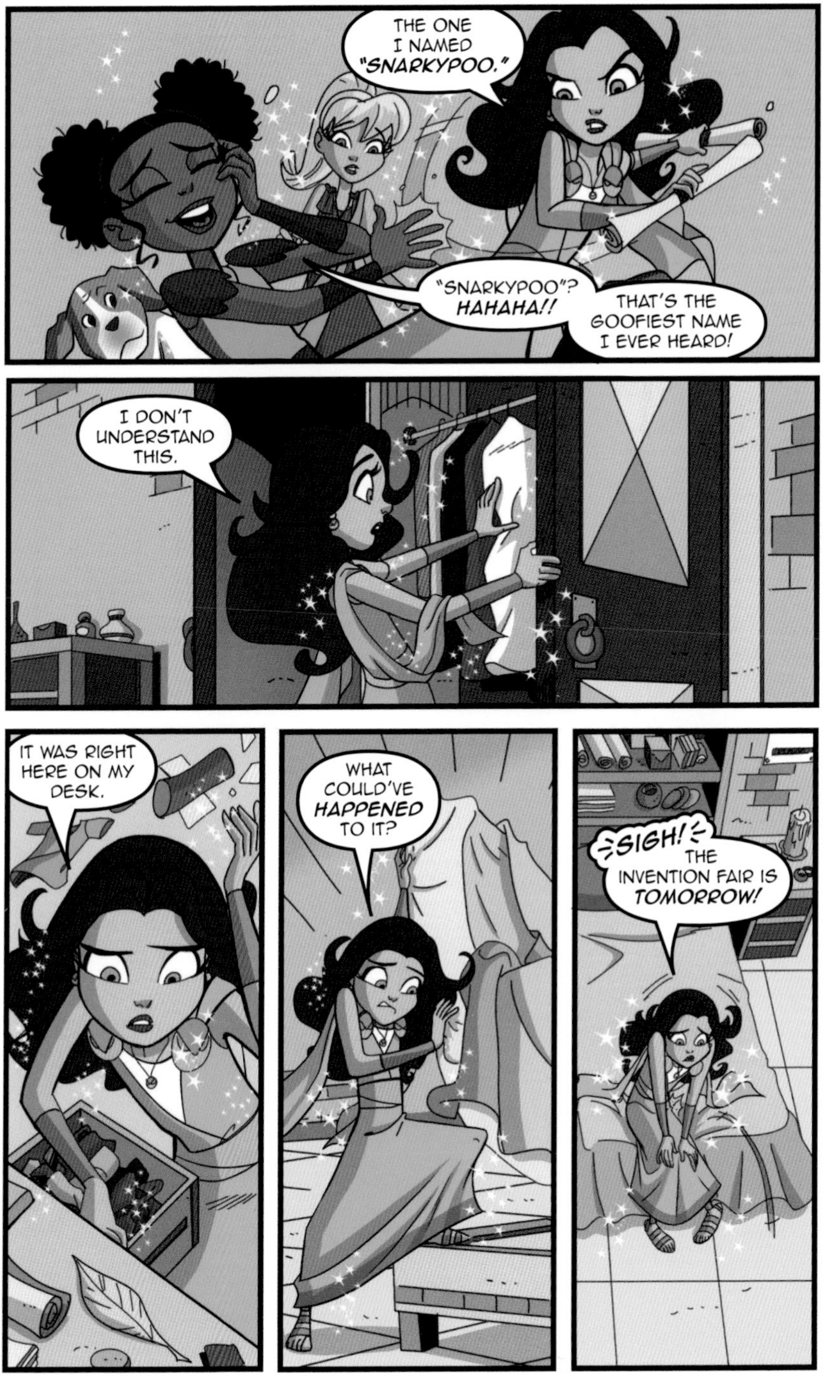
THE ONE I NAMED "SNARKYPOO."
"SNARKYPOO"? HAHAHA!!
THAT'S THE GOOFIEST NAME I EVER HEARD!
I DON'T UNDERSTAND THIS.
IT WAS RIGHT HERE ON MY DESK.
WHAT COULD'VE HAPPENED TO IT?
SIGH!
THE INVENTION FAIR IS TOMORROW!

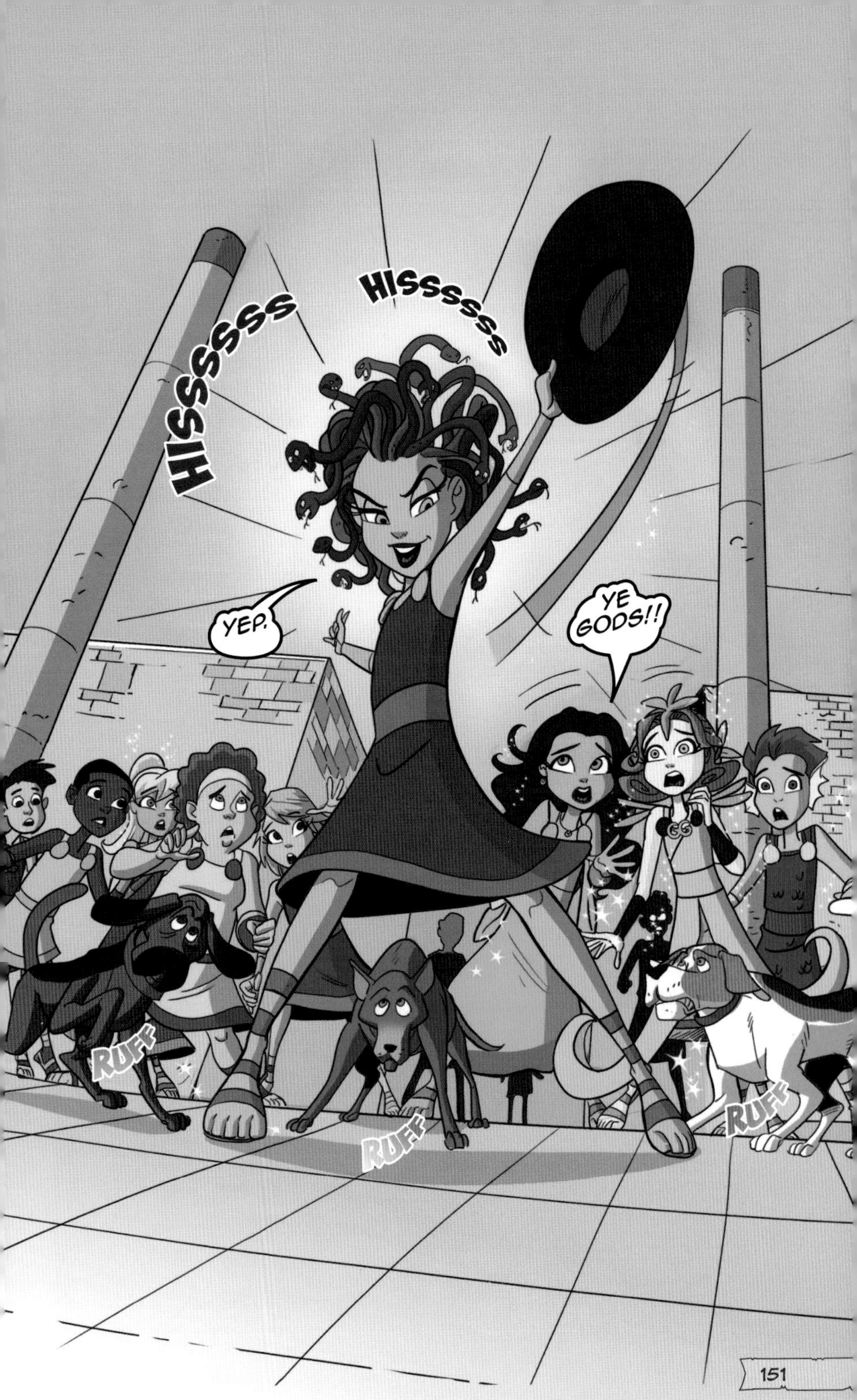
HISSSSSS
HISSSSSS
YEP.
YE GODS!!
RUFF
RUFF
RUFF

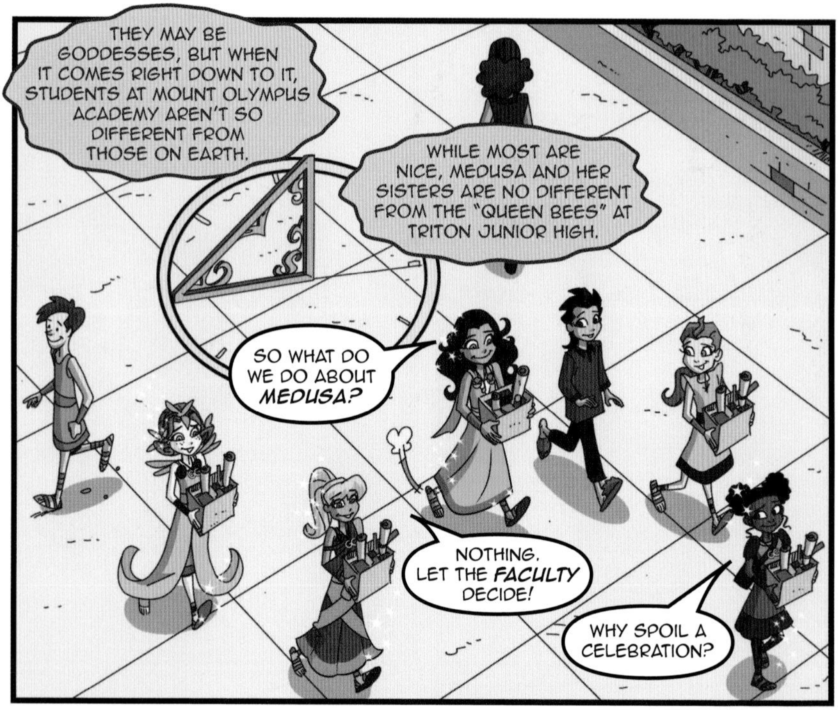
THEY MAY BE GODDESSES, BUT WHEN IT COMES RIGHT DOWN TO IT, STUDENTS AT MOUNT OLYMPUS ACADEMY AREN'T SO DIFFERENT FROM THOSE ON EARTH.
WHILE MOST ARE NICE, MEDUSA AND HER SISTERS ARE NO DIFFERENT FROM THE "QUEEN BEES" AT TRITON JUNIOR HIGH.
SO WHAT DO WE DO ABOUT *MEDUSA?*
NOTHING. LET THE *FACULTY* DECIDE!
WHY SPOIL A CELEBRATION?

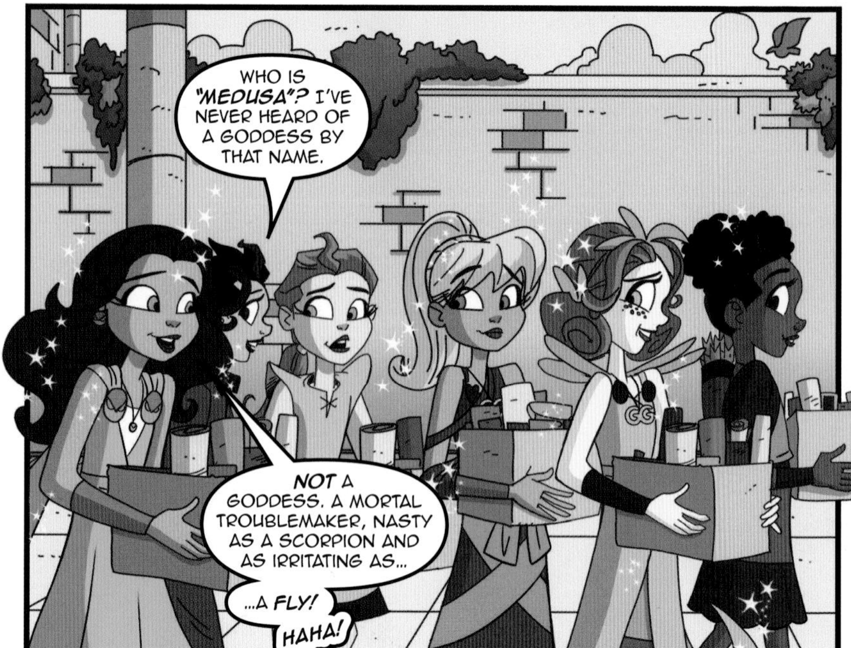
WHO IS *"MEDUSA"?* I'VE NEVER HEARD OF A GODDESS BY THAT NAME.
NOT A GODDESS. A MORTAL TROUBLEMAKER, NASTY AS A SCORPION AND AS IRRITATING AS...
...A *FLY!*
HAHA!

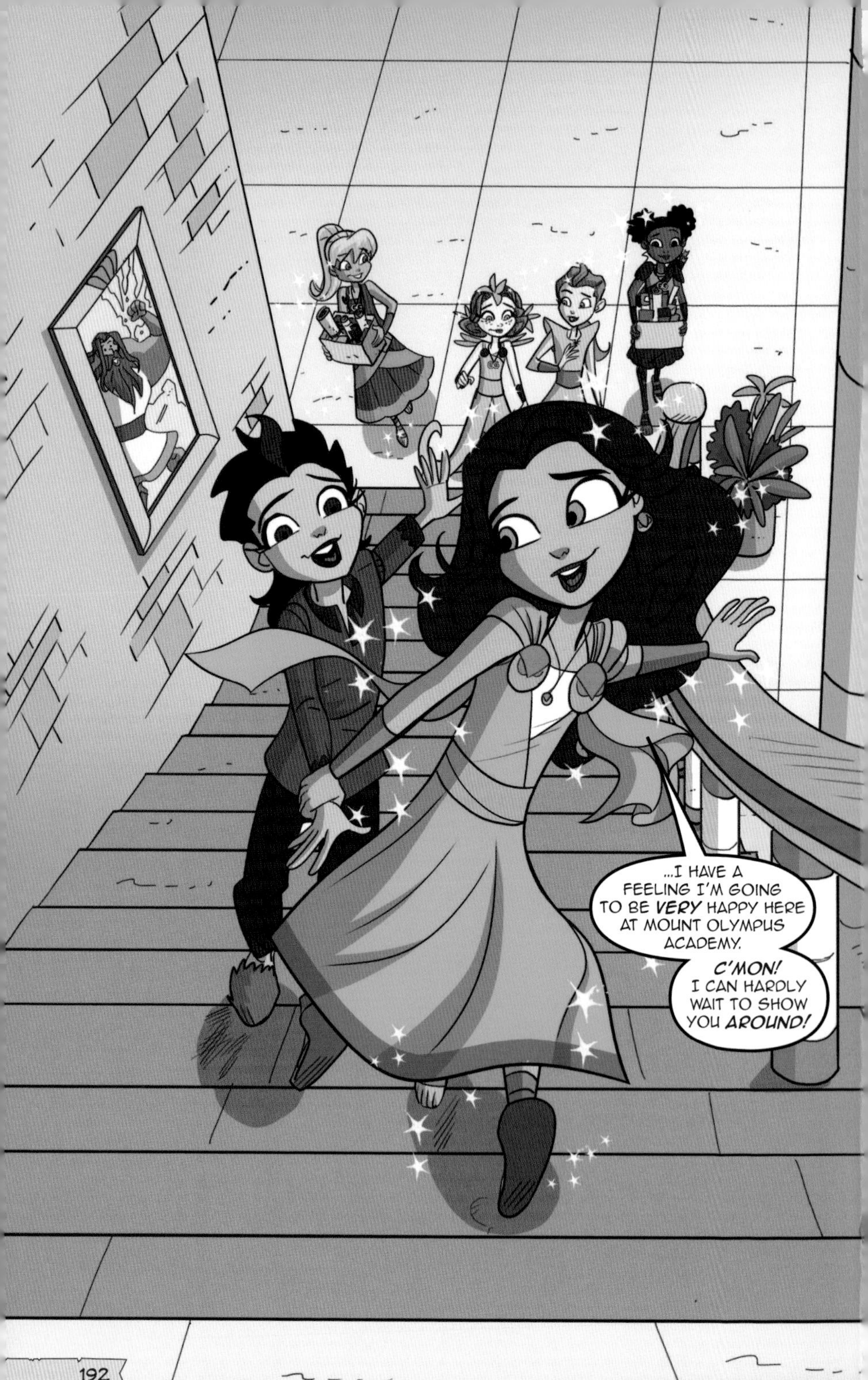
...I HAVE A FEELING I'M GOING TO BE VERY HAPPY HERE AT MOUNT OLYMPUS ACADEMY.
C'MON! I CAN HARDLY WAIT TO SHOW YOU AROUND!